SHIELD OF MERCIA

BOOK 8 THE EAGLE OF MERCIA CHRONICLES

MJ PORTER

Boldwood

First published in Great Britain in 2025 by Boldwood Books Ltd.

Copyright © MJ Porter, 2025

Cover Design by Head Design Ltd.

Cover Images: Shutterstock and iStock

Map designed by Flintlock Covers

The moral right of MJ Porter to be identified as the author of this work has been asserted in accordance with the Copyright, Designs and Patents Act 1988.

Every effort has been made to obtain the necessary permissions with reference to copyright material, both illustrative and quoted. We apologise for any omissions in this respect and will be pleased to make the appropriate acknowledgements in any future edition.

A CIP catalogue record for this book is available from the British Library.

Paperback ISBN 978-1-83617-516-2

Large Print ISBN 978-1-83617-515-5

Hardback ISBN 978-1-83617-514-8

Trade Paperback ISBN 978-1-80656-013-4

Ebook ISBN 978-1-83617-517-9

Kindle ISBN 978-1-83617-518-6

Audio CD ISBN 978-1-83617-509-4

MP3 CD ISBN 978-1-83617-510-0

Digital audio download ISBN 978-1-83617-512-4

This book is printed on certified sustainable paper. Boldwood Books is dedicated to putting sustainability at the heart of our business. For more information please visit https://www.boldwoodbooks.com/about-us/sustainability/

Boldwood Books Ltd, 23 Bowerdean Street, London, SW6 3TN

www.boldwoodbooks.com

For my dad, Michael John Cooke. See you on the beach.

CAST OF CHARACTERS

Bicwide, one of Icel's horses
Brute, Icel's favoured horse
Cenfrith, Icel's uncle, brother of Ceolburh (Icel's mother) and one of the
Mercian king's warriors, who dies in *Son of Mercia*
Edwin, Icel's childhood friend, was in exile with Lord Coenwulf but has
now returned
Icel, warrior of Mercia, his mother was Ceolburh, his father a previous king
of Mercia, although only he and Wynflæd know this
Wine, Cenfrith's horse, now Icel's alongside Brute
Wynflæd, an old herbwoman at the Mercian king's court at Tamworth

The Kings of Mercia
Coenwulf, king of Mercia r.796–821 (died)
His son, Coenhelm, murdered before his father's death
His daughter, Cwenthryth, abbess at Winchcombe Nunnery, now dead
Coelwulf, king of Mercia r.821–825 (deposed), father of Lord Coenwulf, Lady
Ælflæd and Lady Cynewise
Beornwulf, king of Mercia r.825–826 (killed by King Athelstan of the East
Angles)
Lady Cynehild, King Beornwulf's wife before marrying Lord Coenwulf,
now dead

Wiglaf, king of Mercia r.827–829 (deposed) r.830–
Ecgberht, king of Wessex r.802 onwards, r.829 in Mercia
The former queen, Cynethryth, once King Wiglaf's wife
Wigmund, Wiglaf's son, married to Lady Ælflæd, sister of Lord Coenwulf
Wigstan, Wigmund and Lady Ælflæd's young son

The Ealdormen/Bishops of Mercia
Ælfstan, one of King Wiglaf's supporters, an ally to Icel who is a member of his war band
Ælflæd, Lord Coenwulf's sister, married to Lord Wigmund, the king's son
Æthelheard, ealdorman of Mercia
Æthelwulf, ealdorman of Mercia
Beornoth, one of King Wiglaf's ealdormen
Beorhtwulf, a lord of Mercia
Ceolbeorht, bishop of Londonia
Ceolnoth, archbishop of Canterbury
Cuthbert, abbot of Malmesbury
Cynfrith, bishop of Lichfield
Ealhstan, bishop of Sherborne
Edgar, Ealdorman Muca's commander
Heahbeorht, bishop of Worcester
Humberht, ealdorman of Hanbury
Muca, one of King Wiglaf's ealdormen
Sigered, a long-standing ealdorman who's survived the troubled years of the 820s
Tidwulf, an ally of King Wiglaf

Bishops of Other Kingdoms
Beornmod, bishop of Rochester (Wessex)
Cunda, a bishop in the kingdom of the East Angles
Husa, bishop of Elmham (the kingdom of the East Angles)

Rulers of Other Kingdoms
Æthelwulf, Ecgberht of Wessex's son, king of Kent, under his father
Athelstan, king of the East Angles
Ecgberht, king of Wessex

Ealdorman Ælfstan's Warriors
Bada, Wulfheard's horse
Cenred, Mercian warrior
Goðeman, Mercian warrior
Kyre, Mercian warrior
Landwine, Mercian warrior
Maneca, Mercian warrior
Ordlaf, Mercian warrior
Oswy, Mercian warrior, once an ally of the former queen
Uor, Mercian warrior
Waldhere, Mercian warrior
Wulfgar, Mercian warrior
Wulfheard, Mercian warrior, Ealdorman Ælfstan's commander

In Kingsholm
Coenwulf and Coelwulf, the sons of Lord Coenwulf and Lady Cynehild (now dead)
Lady Cynewise, younger sister of Lord Coenwulf and Lady Ælflæd
Eadburg, living in Kingsholm, protector of the children, her mother was their wet nurse, now married to Edwin, Icel's childhood friend
Edwin, Icel's childhood friend, now married to Eadburg
Hatel, stableman
Pega, stableman

In Tamworth
Cuthred, training to be a healer with Wynflæd
Eahric, commander of the king's household warriors

In Londinium
Gaya, a healer
Brother James, monk scribe
Brother Matthew, monk scribe
Brother Michael, monk scribe
Theodore, a healer

In Malmesbury

Abbot Cuthbert
Aldhelm

Places mentioned
Brent Knoll, a hill fort location close to modern-day Burnham-on-Sea, in the kingdom of Wessex
Canterbury, home of the archbishop in the kingdom of Kent, was Mercian but claimed by the king of Wessex in the 820s
Carhampton, in Somerset
Croft, in Mercia (Leicestershire), site of a synod with the archbishop of Canterbury in 836
Ermine Street (not to be confused with Ermin Way), running from London to Lincoln and further north
Ermin Way (not to be confused with Ermine Street), running between Gloucester and Cirencester
Fosse/Foss Way, ancient road running from Exeter to Lincoln
Isle of Sheppey, now part of Kent, where the Viking raiders held Lord Coenwulf captive
Kingdom of Mercia, roughly the area of the modern-day Midlands
Kingdom of Wessex, the area south of the River Thames, including Kent at this time, but not Dumnonia (Cornwall and Devon)
Kingsholm, associated with the ruling family of King Coelwulf, close to Gloucester, home to Lord Coenwulf. Lady Ælflæd, his sister, is now living there
Lichfield, close to Tamworth and one of the holy sites in Mercia
Londonia, combining the ruins of Roman Londinium and Saxon Lundenwic
Peterborough, a monastery
Tamworth, the capital of the Mercian kingdom
Watling Street, ancient road, running from Canterbury to Wroxeter, via Wall (close to Tamworth and Lichfield)
Winchcombe Nunnery, a nunnery in Mercia where the former queen is now imprisoned

CHESTER

GWYNEDD

BARDNEY

LICHFIELD   REPTON

POWYS   THETFORD

TAMWORTH

PETERBOROUGH

EAST

OFFA'S   ELY   ANGLIA

DYKE

WORCESTER   MERCIA

DYFED

HEREFORD   KINGSHOLM

GWENT   GLOUCESTER

LONDON

BRISTOL

KENT

CANTERBURY

WESSEX

WINCHESTER

SOUTHAMPTON

ERMINE ST.

WATLING ST.

MAP OF EARLY ENGLAND

0   50 Miles

THE STORY SO FAR

Icel is a warrior of Mercia, and his endeavours to bring the conspiracy against Mercia's ruling line have finally been resolved, but not without immense peril to his person. The former queen is now imprisoned in Winchcombe Nunnery and King Wiglaf is free to marry again, if he so desires, to protect the Mercian ruling line. His only son, Lord Wigmund, has been wounded after his involvement with his mother's conspiracy. Although he survived, he's not the man he once was, and even then, he was no warrior of Mercia.

It's hoped King Wiglaf will live long enough his grandson can rule after him, sidestepping his weak son, who's not proven to be the most loyal, although he has escaped punishment for his mother's meddling. But Wigstan, the son of Wigmund, is a small child, and with Lord Wigmund and his wife, Lady Ælflæd, living separate lives, it's unlikely he'll have siblings. King Wiglaf must survive for many years yet, and Mercia's numerous enemies are by no means quelled. All recall how easily the Wessex force overwhelmed Mercia only a few years ago. No one wishes to see them succeed again, either with military might, or the deceit of treachery.

To the south of the River Thames border with Wessex, the archbishop of Canterbury has been angered by King Ecgberht of Wessex after he became embroiled in the conspiracy against Mercia through the connivance of King Ecgberht, and his son, King Æthelwulf of Kent, without realising. Archbishop Ceolnoth's determined to forge closer ties with Mercia and the other Saxon kingdoms, including the kingdom of the East Angles, disproving the belief he's too much under the sway of the Wessex king and his son, and in that way, imperilling the future of the island's Christian beliefs.

The Viking raiders have once more been sighted on the Isle of Sheppey, to the west of Canterbury. King Æthelwulf of Kent, however, seems little concerned with them, unlike the archbishop of Canterbury, who believes his king should protect him and Canterbury. King Æthelwulf makes no move to disperse the Viking raiders, despite their lingering presence. He's foolish, or too consumed with thoughts of overwhelming Mercia, not to fear them.

King Athelstan, king-slayer, of the East Angles and Wiglaf of Mercia currently enjoy an uneasy truce. They're more alert to the danger of the Viking raiders having already worked together to prevent them from over-wintering in either of their kingdoms. Lord Coenwulf, returned from his exile in Frankia, also perceives the dangerous threat from the Viking raiders. He's determined to protect his family, and Mercia, from any attack.

THE MERCIAN REGISTER
AD836

In this year, a synod was convened at Croft in the kingdom of Mercia by Archbishop Ceolnoth to make good on the failed meeting in Canterbury the year before, which was forced to disperse when aggression between the Mercians and Wessex warriors erupted.

1

WINTER AD835

Tamworth, the kingdom of Mercia

Wynflæd snaps at my hand, and it's only thanks to my honed warrior's instincts I don't cut through my thumb with the knife I'm using.

'What?' I growl angrily, shaking my thumb all the same. It might not be cut but the blade has pressed hard enough into my cold skin, it feels as though I bleed.

'Not like that,' she admonishes, her voice as sharp as ever, despite the frailty of her body. Huddled within the thickest fur-lined cloak she owns, one the king has personally gifted to her, she resembles a child wearing adult's clothing.

'I think I know how to cut the roots of burdock,' I complain.

'You do, do you?' she counters aggressively, taking the knife from my large hand with her much smaller one. I try not to wince at the whiteness of her knuckles as she grips it tightly. Outside, the wind howls spitefully, bringing with it the promise of more snow and icy weather. Even I'm wearing a thick cloak and two tunics. And all of my socks. I don't know when I could last walk easily without having to be mindful as my toes feel like they might snap off if I unexpectedly kick something.

I share a pained glance with Cuthred, who sits close to the blazing fire, ostensibly stirring some new concoction to alleviate winter coughs and colds, but really to stay as warm as possible within the workshop. I'd like Wynflæd, the wizened and petite healer of Tamworth, to seek shelter within the king's hall, with its roaring hearth fire and thick tapestry wall coverings working to keep the cold from penetrating too deeply within the space. But she refuses. If it gets much colder, I'll carry her within myself. Cuthred and I have already agreed to this by looks as opposed to words. Wynflæd might be small but she's attuned to everything the pair of us think. She knows us better than we know ourselves.

'You know how to cut a man so he bleeds to death, not how to extract the goodness from a root long past its best and yet the only supplies left to us during this terrible winter.'

I uneasily acknowledge that. I'm a warrior of Mercia, a lord of Mercia, where once I believed I was only a healer of Mercia. How times have changed since the death of my father, King Beornwulf, over a decade ago. Not that I knew he was my father at the time. Not that anyone, aside from Wynflæd, now knows he was my father. The secret once angered me. I'm more resolved to it now, but it often hangs between us, unspoken, but there all the same. She wishes I'd claim my birthright. I've no intention of doing so. Not unless something terrible befalls the Mercian king and his blood-line. And, alas, that might happen any day now.

King Wiglaf has rid himself of his pestilent wife, the traitorous and cold-blooded murderess, Cynethryth. Unfortunately, it leaves him with two æthelings who are his relatives. One is his son who's never fully recovered from wounds gained last summer outside Londonia, despite the best efforts of Mercia's finest healers, amongst them Theodore and Gaya. The other is his small grandchild, Wigstan, once deemed weak but growing stronger and sturdier with each passing week. A pity, really, time can't be rushed forward to make him a man full-grown. The kingship is tenuous, especially with so many enemies keen to attack Mercia. There are, however, two other acknowledged æthelings, the grandsons of King Coelwulf, the first of his name. They might share no blood with King Wiglaf, but he's recognised their position, all the same. He sees Mercia must continue, whether his family rules her or not. In that, he shows more wisdom than many others who share his position. He looks to the future, whereas most men think only of their lifetime. Why my father kept my identity a secret I do not know. Perhaps he wished to have a child born while he was a reigning king and, in that way, make that child even more worthy of being his successor.

To the south, Wessex is currently quiet after the failures of last summer, when King Æthelwulf, the son of King Ecgberht of Wessex, tried to meddle in the future of Mercia's ruling line. To the east, Athelstan, king of the East Angles, has been suspiciously serene of late. And to the west? Well, the Welsh can be problematic, although they currently aren't bothering us either. That might all be because there's a new enemy, one I fear coming closer and closer with each passing month. One I've already faced on a number of occasions, but who I suspect is now the main threat to the stability of Mercia.

The Viking raiders whom we defeated in the kingdom of the East Angles a few years ago, and on the Isle of Sheppey two years ago, are proving to be challenging. Even now, news from the Isle of Sheppey is they've spent the winter there. Admittedly on land beholden to King Ecgberht of Wessex, and his son, King Æthelwulf of Kent, but the Isle of Sheppey isn't far from Mercia. Nowhere is very far from Mercia if the wind's kind, the sea calm and sails filled with wind able to take the enemy where they wish to go. It is, unfortunately, a collection of events which too often proves fruitful.

'Then show me how to cut the root,' I suggest, recalled to the here and now, although Wynflæd's already doing so. The pungent aroma of the burdock root floods the space, momentarily reminding me of warmer times, and of excess and profusion. Last year's harvest was poor. The dank and damp summer did little to encourage the crops to ripen with abundance. My belly growls at the thought. We're all lacking the surplus of good food we might expect from living in the same settlement as Mercia's king. But, if we suffer here, then others will be struggling to endure even more. Especially those on unproductive land and lacking the strict restrictions placed over all within Tamworth. I hunger for the better weather, and not just because I'm tired of being cold all the time. Sometimes, it feels as though the fires aren't as warm as in earlier dark times of the year. There are worried rumours the bitter winter of 825, of which I have unfond memories, was nothing compared to this.

'Why are you here?' Wynflæd queries, handing me back the knife, now her hands are shaking with the effort of gripping the sharp blade. I endeavour not to reveal I've noticed the effort it takes her to saw through the root.

'I came to help you. It's too cold to train. Brute won't leave the stable, either, because he's a stubborn git.'

'And you thought to steal the heat from my fire, did you?' Yet the bark of her complaint's fading. Wynflæd, despite all evidence to the contrary, is pleased to see me. Just as I'm overjoyed to see her.

'I did, yes. The king sent me to guarantee all was well at Winchcombe Nunnery, where the former queen's imprisoned. Now I've returned. I visited my holdings at Budworth and ensured all was well there. Wine and Bicwide were pleased to meet one another.'

'Tell me again, young Icel, why you need three horses?' Her tone is rich with disdain.

I bite back my initial reply, and offer a more reasoned one. 'Wine was my uncle's horse. She's seen me through some difficult times, especially after his death. Bicwide was purchased in Southampton, as you know, when I travelled to Wessex, on the orders of King Wiglaf. I like them both, but, as you rightly point out, I only have one backside.'

'Shouldn't you sell them?'

I'm not alone in gasping at this statement, even Cuthred is astounded at Wynflæd's comment.

'No. I can afford to keep them, and have the means to keep them stabled at Budworth. Wine's really too old to ride these days, but she was a faithful servant to my uncle and me. I'll keep her for as many summers as she has left to her. And Bicwide's also a good horse. My steward will ride him and keep him in full fitness in case anything happens to Brute, which I hope it won't. A warrior of Mercia always needs spare horses, just in case something terrible befalls the one he rides.' I am indeed much richer in horses than many of my fellow warriors, if lacking in landholdings compared to other lords of Mercia, of which I'm also one.

'Humm,' she harrumphs, but I believe she's arguing for argument's sake. Perhaps it warms her insides to rankle with me like this. 'How was our former queen?' Wynflæd changes tack quickly, perhaps realising I won't rise to her endeavours to anger me.

I shrug my wide shoulders. 'I didn't speak to her. I saw she was there, and that the abbess had all she needed, as did the king's warriors stationed there, and was on my way. The former queen's adopted the coarse clothing of a penitent, although I don't believe it even for three breaths. But, she sees no one else aside from the nuns and the king's guards and can hardly be devising any more conspiracies against her husband. I left word of how her son fares but nothing else. The king thought it a kindness but I don't believe she deserves as such. She imperilled many and murdered without thought to those left behind to grieve.'

'Perhaps,' Wynflæd suggests. Her expression remains pensive. She told me before of Mercia's past queens who suffer from bad reputations. I doubt they were quite as twisted as the former queen's. She tried to place her son as king instead of her husband. Why she couldn't wait for Wiglaf's death, I've no idea. Now, because of it all, King Wiglaf has been cast low, and his son, Wigmund, has been further weakened. He was never a warrior. Now, he can't become one either. Despite everything, the former queen has had her wish. She's disrupted the ruling line. What will happen when King Wiglaf meets his end, which I hope won't be for many, many years, I truly don't know.

'But there's little she can do from behind the walls at Winchcombe's nunnery, not unless she manages to entice one of the nuns to her cause. I don't believe that will happen. The women of Winchcombe Nunnery have been too often slandered, what with the alleged involvement of King Coenwulf's daughter, Cwenthryth, in the death of her brother, Coenhelm, two decades ago. I think they'd welcome the former queen being kept elsewhere, but the king pays them handsomely for keeping her under guard. And they desire the coin. And the patronage of Mercia's ruling line.'

'Do you think he'll remarry?' Cuthred asks from his place beside the hearth. His cheeks are rosy from the heat. But his skin also looks dry and painful, his nose reddened from a cold only just leaving him. I hope Wynflæd doesn't fall victim to it. It's left Cuthred breathless, and if the well wasn't frozen solid, I'd be transporting water on his behalf. He needs time to heal and regain his willowy strength.

'What, King Wiglaf?' Wynflæd flashes an ire-filled look his way. 'He's too old, and I doubt he wishes to fall prey to another overly ambitious woman.'

'But he'll need another heir, won't he?' This Cuthred says more quietly. Despite the howling wind, it's still treason to speak of the king's death. All of us look towards the doorway, but it stays firmly closed and barred against the wind, with no sound of anyone coming towards it.

'The king's hale. He has his grandson, if no one else.'

'But his grandson is likely to stay an only child as well, isn't he?' This Cuthred directs to me. He knows of my friendship with Lady Ælflæd, the wife of Lord Wigmund, the king's son. He knows, as I know, Lady Ælflæd, the daughter of the former King Coelwulf, and the king's son are estranged.

'That might be true,' Wynflæd muses. I don't miss her appraising glance my way.

I shake my head, purse my lips and return to the task at hand. Wynflæd won't mention the truth of my birth before Cuthred, but she doesn't need to say anything aloud. As with me and Cuthred, we know one another well enough to be able to use our eyes to convey our thoughts. I grow tired of telling her I don't wish the name of my father to be known. If any knew I had a claim to the Mercian kingship, there'd be vast repercussions, which I don't even like to consider. Mercia needs consistency in the kingship, and not the threat of another usurper.

'Who would you suggest he marries?' Wynflæd questions our young friend. I grin. This is hypothetical, but it will pass the time. It might even warm us, if we have strong opinions.

'Someone young and virile,' Cuthred suggests, with the surety of youth. 'Of good birth, and perhaps related to another of Mercia's kings. I take it Lady Ælflæd's sister is too young?'

I shudder at the thought of the girl, not yet a young woman, being wed to a man as old as Wiglaf. Cuthred notices my look.

'Then who? There aren't many women of the right age, and with the correct ancestry. Someone from outside Mercia? Perhaps Lord Coenwulf of Kingsholm could suggest a noble lady from Frankia?' I smile at this answer. It shows Cuthred has been considering it carefully.

'You've lofty ambitions for our king,' Wynflæd announces with an arched eyebrow. 'A bride from Frankia? The daughter of a king of Frankia, no less.'

'Why not? He's proven himself. Now. He'd make a fine match for any woman.' I admire Cuthred for his stout defence of the king. There are many who would say exactly the opposite. King Wiglaf has been weak, and then strong, and then weakened again. He needs to rebuild his reputation before any king from Frankia thinks to part with his precious daughter. Cuthred's gaze is searing as he looks between us. But, he's not finished yet.

'Well, he should do something. That Lord Beorhtwulf managed to escape the court trial with no tarnish to his name, and all know he asserts a claim to the Mercian kingship, even if the king has made it clear he's not to be considered an ætheling.' Cuthred's becoming very alert to the frissons running through the Mercian court. And the potential dangers. I don't like Lord Beorhtwulf. He's too keen to align himself with Ealdorman Sigered's court faction. I don't like either of them. Sigered's too old and weak, and Beorhtwulf too ambitious and young. It's not a good combination.

'Beorhtwulf will never be king,' Wynflæd denounces swiftly, shaking her head as though Cuthred speaks of an elf becoming Mercia's next ruler. I believe Cuthred's correct to be wary. The faction is strong. I'm still to determine where Lord Beorhtwulf's claim comes from. Is he related to King Offa, or perhaps King Æthelbald? Both were rulers nearly a hundred years ago. Lord Beorhtwulf's claim to the kingship is, at best, I would suggest, tenuous.

'What the king needs,' Wynflæd continues, 'is a battle. He should show his strength in a fight, as he did outside Londonia. In that way, he'll win back the respect he's lost amongst the Mercian nobility.'

'The Welsh?' I question, but Wynflæd shakes her head, narrowing her lips.

'No, not the Welsh. The true enemy, the Viking raiders. When he defeated them in the kingdom of the East Angles, his reputation was high. He should do the same again.'

'What? You want the Viking raiders to attack Mercia?' I grumble, unhappy at the thought of even considering such an act would be good. The Isle of Sheppey might be closer to Mercia than I might like, but it is, at least, now part of Wessex.

'Did I say that?' Wynflæd rejects. 'No. The Viking raiders remain on the Isle of Sheppey. He should send warriors to scare them away.' But I'm shaking my head. Wynflæd's not been to Sheppey. She wasn't there when we had to free Lord Coenwulf from his captivity and lost good men – and perhaps some not so good men – in the process. I never wish to return to the Isle of Sheppey. It holds many memories for me, and they're not good.

'No, not that,' I reject. 'It would be better to face enemies who are more alike to us and who fight as we do. The Northumbrians? Even the bloody

Welsh,' I counter. After all, I'm the one who's fought in the shield wall. I should know.

'First,' Wynflæd dismisses with a soft huff, although no longer denying my words, 'we must win the battle against this pestilent winter, and it'll be no easy thing.'

I shudder as yet another cold blast of cool air rushes through the workshop, setting the flames guttering and swirling in the hearth fire and from the few spluttering candles scented with warm herbs.

'There's still months to go until the better weather,' Cuthred complains, and this, I realise, is the problem. The ground's been ice-bound for the last month. It's made everything difficult. Many of the people within Tamworth have taken to sleeping in one venue, all together, making use of the combined body heat of others to stay warm. If this continues for much longer, I fear what will happen. The supplies of prepared wood won't last forever, and I don't envy the poor buggers sent to coppice the trees for more wood to replace that already burnt. And that coppiced wood will be damp and likely to smoke more than flame.

I shudder at the thought of being outside the relative protection of the workshop walls, as poor as they are in contrast to the king's hall.

It is, I fear, only going to get worse before it gets better. Winter has its teeth firmly into the kingdom of Mercia, and no one, not even the king, can be assured of surviving it. I must hope we endure its ravages relatively unscathed, and Wynflæd keeps herself alive with her fiery nature. I don't know what I'd do without her. She's my connection to my past, and while she believes she also links me to my future, I would deny that. For now, I need her for what she has been to me, not what she knows about me. I hope never to have to use that knowledge.

2

We're all within the king's hall at Tamworth, a few days later, when the frozen and almost-rigid messenger is escorted within by one of the poor sods on gate duty. Those guards, and I've taken my turn at it as well, are allowed to wear as many cloaks as they can force over their shoulders and byrnies. Commander Eahric refuses to obey the king's command to stop the watch duties. I think Commander Eahric's correct to do so. It might take a foolhardy individual to be about with the weather so brutally vicious, but all those who intend to cause harm to the king fall into that category. All here know the story of the mighty king, Penda's last battle, centuries ago, as winter covered the land north of here. He died because of the weather conditions. Others might think to emulate the victor of that battle, the bloody Northumbrian king, Oswiu. That can't be allowed to happen. Not in this day and age.

I eye the man from my position close to the hearth. Wynflæd's there, almost sat in the flames, but at least she's warm. Cuthred and I have been forced to be harsh with her. Even the king had to intervene to ensure she did as ordered when she endeavoured to return to her workshop after we managed to get her into the hall and were sleeping. I'm grateful to him for his involvement. Many wouldn't trouble themselves with an aged, stubborn woman who some would think merely a drain on the dwindling resources.

'Come closer to the fire.' I beckon to the guard and the messenger, but neither do so; instead, they seek out the king. King Wiglaf sits to the tip of the fire, with his royal chair brought close to the flames. There's a constant stream of warm drinks being handed out, the only problem being this leads to us all needing to leave the king's hall to piss more often than we'd like. We could have piss buckets within the hall, after all, they might freeze. But the stink's too much to contend with. So, we must all drink enough to stay warm, without immediately needing to get cold to remove the excesses from our body. It's a delicate balancing act.

King Wiglaf, his face pinched despite his thick fur cloak and hat perched on his head, watches the guard and messenger carefully. The fact Commander Eahric's allowed the man within Tamworth means he carries important news. He must have already passed the commander's litany of questions directed towards any visitors to Tamworth, which have even less warmth than the bitter wind blowing outside.

'My lord king.' The gate warden bows low. 'This is Eanstan, a messenger from the archbishop of Canterbury.'

I wince at the knowledge. After the events of last year, when Mercia's bishops ventured to Canterbury, only to be chased away by King Æthelwulf of Kent, Wiglaf has had little good to say about the archbishop. Most openly complain the archbishop is too much under the sway of the Wessex king and his son. All the same, I wait to see what the king does.

'There must be something urgent to have you sent out in weather like this?' he directs towards Eanstan, without malice. Eanstan stands, face pale as the dead, eyeing the fire with eagerness. I see steam rising from his cloak at suddenly being so warm.

'Indeed, my lord king. The archbishop's concerned by your restriction on Mercia's bishops, holy men and women journeying to the most holy site of Canterbury. However, he also understands it, and requests he be allowed to visit Mercia. He's keen to convene a synod to discuss matters with his brethren and sisters, but only with your approval, of course.'

Like me, I suspect King Wiglaf has been anticipating something like this from the archbishop. If there's to be peace between the holy men and women of Mercia and Canterbury, the archbishop must make reparation.

'When would this take place?'

'In the spring, when the weather's better,' Eanstan states quickly, shuddering even while being handed a warm beaker of berry-sweetened water.

There are also warm spicy drinks for those sniffing and coughing, which is quite a lot of those within the hall.'

'Then I'll agree to that, but I fear it wasn't so imperative a matter the archbishop needed to risk sending you in such terrible conditions.'

'Perhaps not, my lord king. The archbishop also wished to appraise you of the situation with the enemy who've claimed the Isle of Sheppey. There are rumours more of the Viking raiders have been invited to join the growing Norse settlement there. The local inhabitants on the mainland have fled their homes. The Viking raiders, it appears, intend to stay. The archbishop's concerned,' the messenger admits.

'I imagine he is. Alas, he should be sharing his worries with King Ecgberht of Wessex and his son, King Æthelwulf of Kent.' I detect the slight sneer as the king mentions his fellow rulers, especially Ecgberht, his reign-long enemy.

'He is, my lord king. The king of Wessex and his son aren't much concerned with such matters. They're licking their wounds within Winchester after their defeat last summer.'

'Surely, the enemy won't attack when the weather's so bad?' the king counters.

'They're from places that are often inhospitable,' Eanstan continues urgently. 'They don't find the weather as disruptive as we do.'

'That's a pity, but provided they remain distant from Mercia, I won't send my warriors to face them. The Isle of Sheppey is far from Mercia. Mercia's shields will protect Mercia. Not Wessex.'

'As you say, my lord king. The archbishop merely wishes to keep you informed.'

'Then express my thanks to him, and if he needs support, he must turn to his king. However, if Canterbury is overwhelmed, like the Isle of Sheppey, he's welcome to come to Mercia. He can take lodgings in Londonia. He'll not be turned away by the bishop there and I'll also ensure he's protected.'

'I'll inform him, my lord king. You're most graceful.' Eanstan bows low at the suggestion from Wiglaf. Whether it surprises him or not, he absorbs it well.

King Wiglaf harrumphs, and dismisses the messenger. Eanstan's allowed closer to the fire, and gratefully extends his hands towards the warmth. I watch Commander Eahric's man do the same. The wind's less fierce than in recent days, but the temperature's not risen despite the watery warmth from the winter sun. It's cold. The earth's too frozen to permit burials of the dead. Indeed, the bodies of the unfortunates have been left beneath the church's floor until such time as they can be interred. It's an unpleasant situation, but the cold ensures the bodies don't corrupt. I don't welcome the task of hewing through the frozen earth to find gaps to lay to rest the old and frail, or the young and weak. The cold weather, and lack of copious good food, is having a devastating effect on all, even within the king's capital at Tamworth.

There are grumblings it's the king's fault, that somehow he's angered our Lord God, but the men and women of Mercia are mostly level-headed enough to appreciate the weather isn't in the king's command. More's the pity.

I eye Eanstan, trying to decide if I recognise him from Canterbury, but as he wears so many layers, it's impossible. I struggle to recognise Wulf-heard when I encounter him outside. Which reminds me. As nice as it is to be warm, I must tend to Brute.

Standing, I walk towards the door, and when enough of us are waiting it's opened wide and we slip outside into a world turned pristine with ice. Everywhere I look, there are icicles and slick patches of roadway. No one strides with confidence. Instead, we all waddle like ducks out of water, desperate to avoid falling and injuring ourselves. There are already three broken arms within Tamworth, and one poor fool who cracked his leg trying to catch a runaway goat. Anyone could have told him the animal would return when it was hungry enough. The wounded are being cared for within the king's hall. I can't say Wynflæd has been particularly sympathetic to them, but Cuthred's ensuring they're as comfortable as possible. The king's keeping them warm, even sharing his blankets and fur cloaks with any who need one.

Carefully, I direct my steps towards the stables. From inside, I hear the familiar shuffle of animals nestling in the hay, and also many people talking in low voices. The king's horses have company during the bitter weather. The horses don't seem to mind. They're doing the best they can to keep warm. There are braziers within the stables now, and a small area has been layered with stones to allow a hearth fire on it. Everyone's under strict instructions to watch the fire and braziers at all times. We can't risk the building burning down with such valuable stock inside.

Within, I greet those I know, including Edwin's mother and her husband, forced to abandon the blacksmith's furnace because the wood and charcoal are needed elsewhere, and there's not enough room in his workshop for people to shelter. I note cold-looking faces, but also appreciate the men and women of Tamworth are making the best of it. I doubt the horses have ever been kept so clean, it's better to warm cold arms and legs by removing any shit from the stalls.

'Hello, boy,' I greet Brute. He offers me an assessing look, but quickly returns to the task of pulling pieces from a hay net. We might lack some foodstuffs, but there's abundant hay for the horses, and for bedding within the stables. Oats are in less plentiful supply, but the horses aren't being skimped. Commander Eahric's keeping a wary look on the granaries. If anyone's found to be stealing, there'll be terrible retribution. So far, no one has become so desperate. The rats, however, are another matter entirely.

I check Brute, ensuring he has everything he needs, including fresh water. It's become easier to take water from the rivers each morning than crack through the well water because the rivers are wider, and deeper, and don't freeze as quickly. It's another way of keeping warm. I also secure the ties on his blanket. How he manages to worry them free, I don't know. He feels hot enough, which is a good sign.

'Ah, Icel, how are you this warm and sunny day?' Wulfheard calls to me. I shake my head. The colder it gets, the more sarcastic Wulfheard becomes. I can't say he's enjoying the bitter weather, but he's determined not to wallow in misery, as some are doing.

'Not bad, and you?' I reply.

'I'll be better if the archbishop wasn't sending tales of woe about the Isle of Sheppey,' he comments. 'That's for bloody King Ecgberht and his bastard son to resolve.'

'It is, yes,' I agree willingly, looking at the man who's taught me so much. He might not be feeling the cold, or rather he might be refusing to acknowledge he's feeling it, but his face is becoming lined with the weight of the years behind him.

'Still, it warms me to consider killing the bastards.'

I shake my head at his assertion. 'Do you never grow weary of it all?' I question him suddenly.

'No. Little point in doing that. It won't make the bastards stop, will it? If I ever grow tired of riding to battle, killing my enemy, and luxuriating in the feel of their shed blood on my face, I'll no longer be a warrior of Mercia, and worthy of carrying an eagle-daubed shield, my young friend.'

I consider that. Wulfheard has been a warrior for as long as I've known him. It might be the position in life he's chosen, but he doesn't seem too concerned by it.

'Perhaps,' I murmur, considering my path to becoming a warrior of Mercia. It wasn't my intention, despite my uncle's hopes.

'Come now, no point dwelling on it. We take the path we're given. It helps if we enjoy it. Commander Eahric has asked if one of my men would replace one of his. The poor bugger has a nose redder than a spanked arse, and his sneezes keep startling the crows.'

I shudder at the thought of being outside, but I'd welcome some respite from the heavy scent within the king's hall. So many people all in one place doesn't smell the freshest. The stables stink less.

'Aye, I'll do it,' I confirm, and with a parting stroke for Brute, who eyes me with what I can only describe as a self-satisfied look because he doesn't need to leave the warmth, I shrug deeper into my cloak and walk towards the gateway.

There's only one open at the moment. The others have all been closed because there are so few people about. My breath pools before me, temporarily warming my face. I keep my eyes on the gateway, watching the few hardy individuals about their duties. They have three braziers, and the men are taking it in turns to extend their hands towards the flames, while others watch the open gate. I arrive and seek out the view before me. We've yet to have much snow, but the ice is so widespread, everything shimmers white.

'Icel, thank you,' Commander Eahric calls to me from his place to the side of the gate.

'Not a problem,' I reply, but already I feel the wintriness biting into the parts of my exposed face between my beard, moustache and the linen cap from my warrior's helm that all have taken to wearing.

'Keep yourself warm, no matter what,' Commandeer Eahric orders me. I know what I need to do. Stamping my feet on the ground, I drive heat into my body, grateful the ground isn't frozen here. It's about the only place within Tamworth, other than inside, where anyone can risk such movements and that's only because the guards and braziers are ensuring the ground doesn't freeze.

I keep my hands beneath my cloak, not far from my blades, should they be needed. But anyone trying to attack Tamworth at the moment would be risking losing fingers and toes to frostbite. It wouldn't be worth it.

'Another quiet day,' one of the men complains, joining me in a cloud of his breath. 'I wish this bloody weather would sod off,' he announces ferociously. 'It's too damn cold.'

It's not something I need to reply to, and so I hold my tongue. I feel as though my eyes are freezing. I keep blinking to hold some moisture in them. Eventually, after not much time has gone by, I retreat to the brazier, allowing the heat to work its way into my hands, and then into my back. It really is bloody cold.

It's a relief when, as the sun starts to set, I'm replaced by another unlucky warrior. All the same, it's pleasant to return to the king's hall and be offered hot pottage, flavoured with beans and vegetables, and only small chunks of salted fish, and warm myself through. I see Wynflæd asleep close to the hearth. She's joined by others who are old and frail. No one begrudges them the heat, even if we'd like to be warmer as well.

I seek out the rest of my friends when I've eaten, and find them playing a desultory game of chance involving one of the king's coins being flipped in the air to see which way up it lands. The men are laughing, and none of them are drinking. It's better this way. The king has ordered only small quantities of ale and mead are served, because he doesn't wish to risk fights breaking out with the attendant chance of injury. He's a wise man.

'Enjoy your guard duty?' Oswy asks me slyly.

'Not really, no. It's perishing out there.' I narrow my eyes. 'Were you supposed to do it?'

'Nope.' But his reply is too quick, and he looks guilty.

'Oh well, better one of the young and fit men took on the task,' I tease him, even though being outside does reawaken some of my old hurts gained two summers ago at the hands of Mercia's enemies. Immediately, Oswy looks aggrieved.

'Now, now, that's not it at all.'

'Isn't it? A fit, young man wouldn't object to standing his turn.'

His lips twist and I find myself grinning at his angry expression. 'Bastard,' he huffs, reaching towards me to slap my cheeks, which are flushed from coming inside. I try to evade his strike but one lands with a sharpness that slices. 'Some say it'll snow tonight,' Oswy continues.

'Isn't it too cold to snow?' I question, rubbing my left cheek. His eyebrows furrow.

'Can it be too bloody cold to snow?'

'I think so,' I murmur, but I'm not sure.

'If it did snow, it might actually warm up,' Wulfheard comments, joining us in a blast of cool air. 'It's this bitter cold making it so awful. A bit of snow would heat everyone up.'

'Seems strange,' Oswy continues, far from convinced by the argument.

'Not as strange as you,' Wulfheard taunts, grinning broadly.

I shake my head, and my eyes rest on the messenger from the archbishop. He holds my gaze, and then stands and walks towards me. I watch him. He comes to a halt before me.

'Are you Icel?' he questions, his words thrumming with his Canterbury accent.

'I am, yes, why?' I demand, a shiver of unease rippling my spine despite the heat in the room.

'A word, if you would,' he continues. I sense Wulfheard beside me, but join Eanstan all the same. He takes me to the far corner of the king's hall, where no one else sits or rests, because it's too far from the hearth fire, and the wall hangings don't extend that far either.

'I have a message for you.' His tone has dropped colder than the rising wind outside.

'Yes,' I mutter when he doesn't speak.

'Be wary of everyone. The archbishop has heard rumours there are those seeking vengeance against you, and they're some very well-connected individuals.' For a brief moment, my heart beats too fast, but I school my expression to one of indifference, and offer a wry smirk.

'King Æthelwulf won't waste his time on me,' I comment.

Eanstan winces, as though wishing I hadn't said the name aloud. 'Perhaps, but he and his father have men who'll do anything to win their regard.'

I nod, still trying to maintain my façade of unconcern. 'Thank the archbishop for his warning. I'll be wise to it.'

Eanstan nods, and then offers me a bleak smile. 'It's surprising men such as them, with all they have, have taken so much against a minor lord of Mercia.'

I grin, but it lacks mirth. 'I'm not just a minor lord, but a shield of Mercia.'

'Perhaps,' Eanstan muses, and then from nearby I hear the voice of the scop beginning a tale. Everyone quiets at the noise, and I walk back to my fellow warriors, my mind a whirl of thought. Of course, Wulfheard is alert to my conversation with the man from Canterbury.

'What was all that about?' he questions me.

'A warning.'

'A warning?' Wulfheard sounds confused, and only just remembers to drop his voice as the scop begins another tale to pass another dreary night.

'It seems I might have made some enemies in high places.'

'What, the archbishop?' His whispered voice lifts to a shriek in surprise.

I find myself shaking my head, and a tight smile touches my lips. 'Oh no, not him. The other arseholes from Wessex.'

'Well now, my young friend,' Wulfheard says with an assessing look. 'You really do know how to get yourself in trouble, don't you?'

'It seems that way,' I mutter, determined to dispel the frisson of fear in my belly.

'We'll just have to keep a close eye on you, and then all will be well,' he murmurs, but even I sense he's trying too hard to sound casual. After all, if King Æthelwulf and the former queen of Mercia could manage to abduct children and kill their enemies deep within the heart of Mercia then there's absolutely no guarantee they can't get to me.

In the background, the scop finishes with a story of the coming summer, and that, more than anything, warms me so I sleep confident the cold weather will come to an end. Eventually. Even if the prospect of King

Ecgberht and his son wanting vengeance against me for my part in unravelling their plots to take control of Mercia does unsettle me. Perhaps, then, I won't welcome the warmer weather, when it's easier to travel and plot my downfall at their hands. The thought is as far from comforting as an icy shard down my neck.

3

We wake to a world coated in snow, and somehow it does feel warmer.

I leave the king's hall, with a lingering glance to where the messenger from Canterbury still sleeps, and immediately grimace as a snowball hits my back. I turn and catch sight of Oswy, grinning like a child from where he's hiding to the side of Wynflæd's workshop.

'A pity your aim isn't as good with a spear,' I shout, but not before scooping and collecting my own snowball to throw towards him. He scampers from sight, and more and more people join the fun in the snow. There's little wind, although the pink-tinged clouds promise more snow throughout the day. Still, with the snow covering my ankles, it's actually easier to walk around than it has been recently. Quickly, I stride towards the stables and saddle Brute. He needs some exercise, and I wish to shake the unease from my body. With the snow lying so thickly, I don't risk him slipping on icy ground. Not that I mount him. Instead, I walk him out the gateway, calling to the men on guard duty, and down to the training field. More and more of the horses and warriors join us there.

'I never thought I'd welcome snow,' Wulfheard snorts from beside me. I eye his horse. Bada seems well enough, as does Brute. All of the horses huff warm air before them. They're as pleased to be released from the stables as we are from the confines of Tamworth. This is the second terrible winter I've experienced in my life. The first, I recall my uncle looking after me. For this second one, I'm in a less cosseted position but still feel largely useless. The weather has its claws into us.

'Let's hope it drives the ice and cool wind away,' I murmur, thinking the same. We walk together, side by side, the horses occasionally lowering their muzzles onto the snow and then shaking their heads in disgust.

'Stop doing that,' I eventually urge Brute, tired of having my arm yanked around by his bridle. He eyes me with disdain. I chuckle as Bada again plunges his head into the snow only to jerk away from it. 'It's nice on your hooves but not on your face,' I tell them both.

Wulfheard and I lapse into silence. I know he's spoken to Ealdorman Ælfstan about Eanstan's words. I know because I caught them both whispering and looking guilty. Now the menace of the threat hangs between us, and I'm unwilling to put words to it.

'It's nearly Christ's Mass,' Wulfheard eventually comments. 'We'll be summoned to the church, and I hope this new bishop is less wordy than the previous one.' Thoughts of Bishop Æthelweald remind me of Brihthild, and I do spare a thought for the Wessex woman. She was a despicable person, but in the end I found I almost liked her. I wish her no ill. She killed her brother, yes, but whether he was ever likely to recover from his illness, I can't honestly say. Perhaps, then, she did him a favour by ending his life so painlessly. To die choking on his blood, as his illness would have eventually caused, would have been terrible.

'Let's hope it stays warmer,' I murmur, reminded of all the times I stood and shivered within Tamworth's church. I'll never understand why the holy men and women build the monstrosities to our Lord God to be so damn cold, even in summer. Although it does, I've been told, ensure those people buried beneath the church's floor don't flood the place with their corrupt smell before becoming little more than bones. I shudder at the thought of decomposing bodies, reminded of the dead who do still need burying. One day of snowfall won't make that come any quicker.

'Aye,' Wulfheard agrees, and then turns to face me. 'The king's asked Ealdorman Ælfstan to escort Archbishop Ceolnoth to this meeting, when it's arranged. We'll have the honour of seeing him again, and also attending. We're to stand a guard against any enemy who might think to come in the archbishop's party, and also any Viking raiders who decide to try their luck.

It'll allow us to keep an eye on anyone who shows too much interest in you,' he concludes.

'Wonderful,' I murmur, a spark of fear making my voice crack, and earning me a sharp look from Wulfheard.

'Ealdorman Muca continues to hold Londonia for the king. He and his men will be reinforced by Ealdorman Tidwulf's before, during and after the meeting. They'll be watching for any renewed attack from Wessex.'

'Surely, they won't persist in their attempts to take Mercia? King Ecgberht's failed three times now. Will he not give up?' I perhaps speak with more hope than belief.

Here Wulfheard turns to meet my gaze, his eyes hard. 'Some men never know when they're beaten, alas. King Ecgberht and his son are men like that. In some, it's seen as fiery determination and lauded, in others, it's desperation.'

'Speaking of which. Has anything been heard from Lord Beorhtwulf since the summer?' I'm keen to move the conversation away from King Ecgberht and his son.

'He's keeping a low profile, not that the weather hasn't forced everyone to keep to their properties.'

'I don't trust him,' I glower, reminded of another of the traitors against Mercia. 'Or Ealdorman Sigered.'

Wulfheard sighs softly. 'The sooner that man is dead, the better for everyone. Why is it the twisted arseholes live such long lives and the good men all perish too soon?'

'I wish I knew,' I mutter. 'King Wiglaf should get rid of him.'

'Yes, he should, but as is so often the case, Sigered came out of this well. His nephew took the brunt of the king's rage, and was also the one found to be actively involved. Sigered's worn himself out assuring the king he knew nothing of it. The king doesn't trust him, but needs his support to keep the kingship secure until his grandson is grown to adulthood. And, Ealdorman Ælfstan assures me, it's better to keep Sigered close, where we can keep our eye on him.'

'So, the holy men and women?' I'm reminded of how our conversation started. 'They'll be Mercian only, aside from the archbishop of Canterbury, Ceolnoth?'

'I don't believe so, no. I think the archbishop will summon all his holy

men and women from Mercia, Wessex and the other kingdoms. King
Wiglaf intends to make much of his part in providing a safe place for the
holy men and women to meet. It's another weapon in the war against King
Ecgberht. King Ecgberht won't take kindly to the archbishop coming to
Mercia.'

'Will it never end?' I sigh unhappily. 'I feel as though my entire life has
been spent with kings vying for power.'

Wulfheard surprises me by laughing. 'Ah, young Icel, you've hardly lived
a long life. It'll only get worse. Men who believe they should be king, and
women who believe they should be queen, will always bicker and argue.
They intend to prevail, just as King Ecgberht does. I'd get used to it, if I were
you. One day, when you're old and wizened, you'll look back on these years
as some sort of Golden Age, when King Wiglaf held Mercia safe from her
enemies – well, just about safe. No, I'll rephrase, when he was powerful
enough to counter all threats, both from within and without Mercia. It'll
not always be that way. Weak men will become king. They'll be "persuaded"
by others to do things that benefit them and no one else. I've seen it before,
my young friend, and I'll no doubt see it again in my lifetime.'

His words are as comforting as a wet sack over my cold body. But Wulfheard merely chuckles some more.

'Come, Icel, this is why Mercia needs warriors and their shields and
weapons to protect her. For us, there's an enemy, and an ally, we need not
look between those two strands. We kill the enemy, we protect the allies.
And I wouldn't want it any other way. I'm not a meddler, as you well know.' I
nod, reminded of his brother, Wulfnoth, who was a pestilent arse and
caused no end of problems, including being behind the kidnapping of Lord
Coenwulf's children.

'I'll try to think as you do,' I confirm. But Wulfheard's shaking his head.

'Now, I didn't tell you to do that, did I? You, my friend, need not think as
I do. You can be a more reasoned man than me, and I know you are. I rely
on you to offer me a little more than enemy and ally, even if, when it comes
down to the pointy ends of our seaxes, I'll always kill the enemy.'

I nod, finding it comforting to know he doesn't deride me for considering all the different viewpoints making the men and women of Mercia
who they are.

'I hope, when we get to this meeting, we need not spend all our time bloody praying.' Wulfheard laughs now, loud and long.

'I'm sure we'll both find something better to do with our time,' I reassure, but I share his hope. There really is only so much praying a man can do.

* * *

The new bishop of Lichfield, Cynfrith, arrives at Tamworth a few days later. The snow persists, but it's no longer bitter and bitingly cold. Gradually, people have begun to remove themselves back to their homes from the king's hall. We all hope the weather stays more seasonally snowy as opposed to bitterly frigid. We've even allowed Wynflæd back to her workshop. It was either that, or endure more of her complaining.

Bishop Cynfrith comes with little fanfare from Lichfield. I decide I like him on sight. Perhaps, I admit, I'm just pleased he's not the traitorous Bishop Æthelweald.

'My lord king,' he greets King Wiglaf in the courtyard. 'It's good to see you, and I look forward to celebrating Christ's Mass with you.'

King Wiglaf welcomes Bishop Cynfrith warmly, and the two move inside the king's hall, while my eyes remain on the men and women who escort him. It's not a long journey from Lichfield, where Cynfrith has made his home. All the same, he comes with a large following of monks, nuns and priests. There are really far too many when Tamworth is filled with those who usually live here.

'Where will they all sleep?' I ask Oswy. He grins broadly.

'Not in my bed.' We too have returned to the communal sleeping hall. It's been pleasant to sleep on a bed as opposed to the floor, although it's cooler with fewer people crammed together, almost lying one on top of the other, as we were in the king's hall.

'I'm sure the king has somewhere for them.' Wulfheard joins us, and then we fall silent as an unwelcome figure rides into Tamworth.

'I didn't know he was coming,' I grumble, eyeing Ealdorman Sigered unhappily, where he sits atop a horse that's far too tall for him. It's strange to see him without his nephew at his side, but we'll never see Sigegar again.

Not now he's been banished, along with others involved in the conspiracy against Mercia's ruling line.

'I'm surprised he waited as long as he has,' Oswy agrees. 'He's desperate to win back the king's regard.'

'What of Lord Wigmund?'

'He remains at Londonia, for the time being. Well, in Lundenwic's fort, to be more precise. The king doesn't want him moved for fear of injuring him again.'

Mention of Lord Wigmund sits uneasily with me. I genuinely thought I'd saved the fool from being killed by the enemy, but a single blow against him has threatened his life ever since. Once more, I'm reminded King Wiglaf must live long enough for his grandson to become Mercia's king. If not, well, I won't claim my birthright, not unless Lord Beorhtwulf tries to stick his nose in. And even then, provided it's a Mercian and not one of the Wessex bastards, I'd happily allow another to rule.

'Well, this is going to be a delightful Christ's Mass,' I complain. My fellow warriors grunt their agreement. It should be a time of celebration and excess food. It's going to be neither of those things.

'All we need is for the former queen to bloody appear,' Oswy mutters bitterly. But that, of course, isn't going to happen. She'll never again step foot in Tamworth, and at least with Eanstan returned to Canterbury now the weather's more seasonal, I need not consider his warning for the fore-seeable future. I hope the winter puts off any who might think to seek vengeance against me, but I know Ealdorman Ælfstan has spoken to Commander Eahric. All those entering Tamworth must be vouched for. Mercia has had enough of devious enemies.

4

The Christ's Mass church service is long and tedious, but the scop enthrals his audience when he spins stories of times long past, as we all share a feast of less than ostentatious proportions, but which still feels extravagant considering the severe limits previously placed on consuming salted fish and meat. I hope the king doesn't regret his largesse if the weather should turn deadly again.

Admittedly, now there's snow on the ground, and not an icy layer almost impossible to risk travelling over, settlements owing him their excess are able to send it to Tamworth.

I listen to the song of the scop, allowing his words to take me to long-ago battles that raged, and to past winters as bitter as this one, and all the time I drink sparingly, and eat well. Ealdorman Ælfstan sits beside the king, Ealdorman Sigered demoted to far down the royal dais, as Bishop Cynfrith is also positioned beside the king. Everyone's dressed in their finery – well, as fine as you can be while still keeping warm. The scop promises us much when he lifts his voice to proclaim:

'The world grows rigid, aside from the flames, devouring wood,
Bridges of ice crest land never joined before
Water is encased, as a warrior before a battle

The shoots in the earth, are locked up tighter than a moneyer's
    chest
But they promise good weather will come again
That it must come again.'

And we all cheer his final statement, warmed from the good ale, and also the promise of summer. I'm not alone in hoping the coming summer will be better than the one we've just endured, which remained dank and largely cold, the fields flooded so the crops were stunted or failed altogether.

'My lord king.' The man bows low towards King Wiglaf, and then he smiles. 'A song to inspire every man, boy and child within this room to fight at your side.' And he launches into an oft-repeated tale, heard before, but that never makes it grow tired.

'Destroyer of the chariot of the sea, the steerer of the seahorse.
You made ready your armoured ships and you mustered the red
    shield at sea.
The wind filled the canvas and you turned all your prows west-
    ward out to sea.
You carried the shield of war and so dealt death mightily,
giving swollen flesh to the raven and marking men with the print
    of the sword's edge.
There was food for the ravens from the spears as you fought.
Red spears soared as you fought on.
Eagles flew over the rows of corpses left in your wake, beaks of the
    ravens dripped red while the wolves tore at wounds.
You offered Mercian corpses to the wolf by the sea.
Dwellings and houses of men burned,
Many times you caused the people to give warning of deadly
    attack
While your men reddened the land of the Mercians.
You broke the raven's sleep, waker of battle,
Blunting swords upon weapons they could not defend their strong-
    holds when you attacked.

The she-wolf got much wolf's food,
The raven did not go hungry as the stud horses waded in blood.'

Once more, we all cheer, but I can't help the judder running down my spine.

Wulfheard was right to caution me.

There will always be battles and wars to be won and, of course, vengeance to take against men who mean us harm. I'll need to be wary of King Ecgberht, and his son. I really will.

* * *

I take my leave of a crotchety and sneezing Wynflæd at the beginning of a warm spring day. The weather has changed for the better. The snow, when it came, was welcome and stopped the terrible biting cold of *Winterfylleð*, *Blotmonað* and *Geola*. Now men and women move amongst the settlement of Tamworth with far more eagerness than throughout the earlier months of winter. There are tasks to be undertaken, repairing holes in roofs from the fierce winds, and other problems, including clearing a number of fallen trees from the watercourse close to the mill. The dead have also been buried, thankfully. For the warriors of Ealdorman Ælfstan, we must travel to Londonia and greet the archbishop of Canterbury as well as others from the kingdom of Wessex who'll journey to Croft, which is where it's been decided the meeting will take place. The thought of travelling to Londonia unsettles me, and I know Wulfheard shares my worries. It's too close to those who mean me ill.

The king will leave in a few days' time, but has less distance to travel than we do. I've also heard he intends to wait for Lady Ælflæd, his son's estranged wife, and young grandson, Lord Wigstan, to journey to Tamworth. They'll present a united front before the holy men and women of the southern parts of this island. Admittedly, Lord Wigmund won't be attending. News reaches the king often of how his son fares. He's better much of the time, but not always. Theodore and Gaya are using all of the knowledge they have, as well as all that gathered by Ealdorman Tidwulf and his book of healing, to ensure Lord Wigmund lives.

'Look after her,' I cautioned Cuthred last night, when speaking of Wynflæd. I'm astounded she survived the winter. She looks even more shrunken than before, and her temper remains fiery, and her cold terrible, making her weak and even more ill-tempered, if that were possible.

'I will,' he offered, but Cuthred's growing up. His youthful exuberance is giving way to the reasoned mind of a healer who knows when someone's beginning the slow decline towards their death. Wynflæd's so very old, and she simply can't keep going forever. It's a sober realisation. 'Well,' he quickly retracted, 'I'll try,' and we both laughed at that. Wynflæd always says warriors make terrible patients. She should try bloody tending to herself to find out how truly difficult it can be to aid those who think there's nothing wrong with them. All the same, I hope Wynflæd persists with her stubborn refusal to acknowledge her many winters are slowing her down. If she ever admits it, her death will quickly follow. I've seen it happen with old horses. And, when that occurs, I'll have to finally address the fact she's the only person who can attest to the truth of my birth.

'Come on, you lazy bastards,' Wulfheard calls from where we're preparing beside the stables. 'We need to make some headway today,' he grumbles. Ealdorman Ælfstan's not yet ready, taking his leave of the king and being given last-moment instructions. As such, none of us are really hurrying. I sense Wulfheard growing frustrated, but then he's been desperate to leave Tamworth for the last few weeks. As soon as the weather became bright enough, and warm enough, for us to sleep outdoors, Wulfheard wished to be on his way.

'We're coming,' Cenred mutters, as I pull myself into Brute's saddle. I've had to tighten his saddle. My horse has lost some weight during the winter. Not that he's been poorly fed. Far from it. But a horse lacking exercise will eat less, or so Wulfheard's assured me. I've felt the same. My trews are a little loose around my belly. I can't say the same for all of Ealdorman Ælfstan's men. Some of them could have done with drinking and eating more sparsely when the supplies were delivered from those owing dues to the king.

'I'm ready,' I chirp, and now more of the men growl, while Wulfheard shakes his head at my attempt to encourage the others.

Eventually, all are prepared, but just before we leave there's a flurry of activity at the gates, and I turn to meet the assessing eyes of Lady Ælflæd, mounted on her horse, Sewenna, although the children are within a roofed cart following on behind. Ealdorman Ælfstan falters in striding to his horse. The king, who had come to bid us farewell, smiles brightly.

'Ah, daughter,' he calls. 'You've made good time.'

'I have, my lord king. It's good to see you.'

I can't deny I feel a stirring of desire for Lady Ælflæd, as I hungrily drink in the sight of her, pink-cheeked and bright-eyed from the cold. It's unfortunate we're leaving. She could certainly have brightened some of the tedious winter days had she arrived earlier. From within the covered cart, I hear the giggles of the children, and find myself smiling with delight.

'And you, now come within, while Ealdorman Ælfstan makes his departure.'

At that, I meet Lady Ælflæd's cool gaze. If she has any feelings for me, they don't show, but I offer her a smile and then incline my head all the same.

'Good luck, my loyal warriors,' King Wiglaf calls, as Ealdorman Ælfstan leads us out of Tamworth. I cast a lingering look over my shoulder but, of course, Lady Ælflæd pays me no mind as the horses' hooves ring loudly on the wooden bridge over the ditch surrounding Tamworth. It's currently filled with the detritus of the winter, which must be cleared away to ensure it remains an effective deterrent to any who think to attack.

Quickly, we turn towards Watling Street. Wulfheard sets a decent pace, with Ealdorman Ælfstan at his side, but the intention isn't to push the horses too fast. Not yet. They need time to regain their stamina of previous summers. Perhaps the warriors do as well.

'Eyes forward,' Oswy mutters to me, his tone taunting. I growl and concentrate on where I'm going and not where I've been.

My wounds have fully healed throughout the winter although I wear a new scar on my cheek thanks to the former queen. There are an increasing number of marks on my body showing I'm a warrior of Mercia. These add to the cock depicted on my belly which refuses to fade away with time, much to Oswy's delight, which resulted from the attack on me by those who stole the children away. And the imprinted mark of an eagle on my hand, only visible in the right light, which I gained holding my uncle's blade with my naked hand, having heated it to seal a cut. None of these wounds show I'm anything different to the other shields of Mercia. We all have scars on our bodies because we're warriors of Mercia, even Ealdorman Ælfstan.

Oswy rides at my side. Cenred's to my other side. We don't talk. Instead, the sound of hooves over the road, some of it stone, and some of it being reclaimed by the plants to either side, fills our hearing.

The wind's gentle, the smells and sights a welcome balm after a long and difficult winter. It's a pity we ride to find the archbishop of Canterbury and the promise of a tedious religious convocation. If not, it would be enjoyable to be out and about. It's a pity I might be riding towards personal danger, and not away from it.

That night, we find lodgings in a roadside alehouse, and the following day Londonia comes into view. I eye it with trepidation. I've not been here since late last summer. It holds many memories for me. Not all of them are good. It also brings the threat from Wessex closer. The River Thames, the grey ribbon shimmering in the distance, recalls me to the practicalities of keeping Wessex from interfering in Mercia. It's too close. I'm grateful there's no bridge to allow easy access, and that, at this time of year, the river will be less navigable than during the winter, although the few fording points might be more accessible. I'm sure Ealdormen Tidwulf and Muca are only too conscious of this and have guards at the fording points, and men at the quayside.

Quickly, we reach the gateway inside Londinium, and it's to the fort we go, greeted warmly by Ealdorman Tidwulf, although I'm more pleased to see Theodore and Gaya, who wait to welcome me in the main hall, once Brute has been placed in the stables.

'Ah, Icel, it's good to see you.' Theodore nods towards me, but Gaya comes forward to embrace me. She remains as slight as ever, but there's iron in her body. She's small and strong. I'm beginning to think all healers are like this.

'And it's good to see you, as well. I'm pleased to see you've survived the terrible winter.'

At this, Gaya wrinkles her nose. 'It was too cold, far too cold. I felt as though my bones would never warm. I'll never grow to love a Mercian winter.' Even now, I see she's huddled within a thick cloak, and the hearth fire's roaring behind her. I'm too hot, but her hands are cold.

'We'll have to arrange some warming spices for you.' Theodore chuckles. 'I can't endure another winter of such complaints.'

'Now, tell me,' Gaya shoots Theodore a censorious look, 'how's Wynflæd?'

'Well, but a little frailer than when you last saw her. Cuthred has his instructions.'

At this Gaya nods sagely and with understanding. There's no need to voice my concerns. I can already tell she's considering what salve she can send to Wynflæd to reinvigorate her.

'How's Lord Wigmund?' I ask the question that's been plaguing me more and more the closer I've ridden to Londonia.

'He's stronger but also weaker. He grows frustrated and feeble, but generally, he's not too bad. He will, as you know, never be as hale as he once was. But, as you know, he was never really that hale.' It's surprising Lord Wigmund hasn't demanded some sort of vengeance from me, but perhaps he shows wisdom in not doing so. After all, I was trying to protect him from the terrible allies he'd made amongst the men from Wessex.

I absorb this, and force a smile to my lips. 'So tell me, how's the book of healing coming along?'

At this, both Theodore and Gaya relax, as though discussing Lord Wigmund is awkward, and quickly inform me what's been accomplished so far. As we talk, the rest of Ealdorman Ælfstan's men make themselves comfortable. I see Ealdormen Ælfstan and Tidwulf speaking urgently with one another.

'Come,' Theodore then surprises me by saying. 'You should see the work. It's here.'

'Is it?' I gasp, reminded of the many law books the bishop made use of last summer to ensure the correct procedure was followed at the trial of Brihthild and the former queen. I swallow as the memory recalls me to Eanstan's warning. Unconsciously, I peer into the dark corners of the main hall, keen to reassure myself I've met everyone here before.

Together, we leave the main hall. I'm led to a smaller room, one I've never realised was anything other than a storeroom, and in which there are three monks. One of them bends low over a piece of stretched vellum, quill in hand, and ink nearby, while one of the others reads something to him.

I stay entirely quiet, not wanting to disturb the two monks, and while the third looks up and I think he'll ban me from the room, he smiles on seeing Theodore and Gaya and beckons us closer. I see he's busy with a collection of random items, and pots.

He notices my interest.

'Icel, it's good to meet you,' he comments softly. 'I'm Brother Michael. Today, I'm making ink for the book of healing. Sometimes I write, and sometimes I read. All three of us work together to bring about this great feat of healing to share with all.'

'It looks complicated,' I comment, wrinkling my nose at the sour smell in the room I suspect comes from one of the pots which contain anything from walnuts to berries to madder root. It's not much different to Wynflæd's workshop.

'Not really, no. As long as you know what you're doing.' He laughs very softly, and I consider where his thoughts have taken him. 'You can look at the words when my two fellow scribes have concluded their work for the morning. It's tedious and one has to be careful or else your hand cramps and the vellum is ruined with ink splatters.'

'So, it's like training with a seax then? Or cutting herbs with a knife?'

'Very much so.' Brother Michael beams at me. I find I like him already.

'Do you copy everything from other books?' I ask, because that seems to be what the two monks are doing, the one reading to the other.

'Not at all. Theodore and Gaya have told us much that's not book lore, and some of it must also be translated from Latin into our tongue. If not, it'll be little help to anyone. Not all can read and understand Latin.'

'But there's a small problem, which we have, alas, only just realised,' Theodore interjects.

'What's that?'

'Ah.' And now Brother Michael looks uneasy. I look between the monk and the tall former slave and consider what it is that unnerves them so much. It must be something very serious.

'Measurements,' they both say at the same time.

'Measurements?' I query, truly perplexed by their concerns.

'We've realised everyone uses different measurements in their books of healing, and some use none at all. How then are we to ensure people use the correct amount of each herb or ingredient?'

'Ah.' Sudden comprehension has me nodding along with them, and I appreciate why they're so troubled.

'We risk people poisoning one another, or thinking the remedies are useless if we can't provide the correct quantity of each ingredient to use.'

'What will you do?'

Here Theodore shrugs, and the monk shakes his head. 'It's unlikely we'll encounter every illness we mean to provide a remedy for, but when we do, we intend to annotate the recipes. And, we're now attempting to provide some measurements as we move forward.'

I shake my head, forehead furrowing in thought. 'It's a true problem, and not one I've considered. Wynflæd has her own small containers for weighing and measuring. Don't all healers use the same?'

'No, there's no consistency. Theodore and Gaya use different measurements to Wynflæd, and indeed, to our own brethren in the religious houses. But, we will endeavour to find a solution now we've discovered the problem.'

I become aware the other monk's stopped reading aloud, and turn to find the scribe bending backwards to alleviate the tension in his back. He's also opening and closing his quill hand, while the other monk carefully covers the vellum with something, no doubt to prevent the ink from running or something happening to the priceless words they've spent the morning picking out on the vellum sheets.

'Well, the work on *Hundes heafod* is now complete,' the one monk calls to Brother Michael. 'We can move on to another of the many herbs,' he announces decisively. I look to Theodore, confused once more.

'In this we mean to list the uses each herb can be put to. We thought it the best way to proceed. If not, how would anyone ever find anything?'

I nod, appreciating how much prior thought has gone into the task. It's not about throwing words onto the vellum.

'Of course, we'll have missed something,' the one who's been writing adds with a grimace. 'We always do, but we're then able to insert a sheet of vellum, and we can continue to do so until it's finally bound together. You must be Icel,' he offers, and comes forward to greet me. 'I'm Brother Matthew.' He extends his hand, which I realise is splattered with a variety of inks. He notices the staining and shrugs ruefully. 'It's impossible to keep my hands clean,' he comments. 'The ink has a mind of its own, and not all of it's the same consistency. We must remember which ink runs freely, and which doesn't.'

'Brother Matthew is our illustrator. He has the most skill with inks and depicting animals. He uses the most variety of ink. We two, Brother James and I,' and Brother Michael points to the so far unnamed monk who must be Brother James, 'can only be trusted with the most basic of shades, but we can write a little more quickly than our more talented friend.' I appreciate the three monks are unlike all other monks I've ever met. They share an easy camaraderie with one another, and don't appear to be wearing their knees out with praying. I'd ask them about that, but first I'm encouraged to gaze at the work undertaken that morning.

The page is revealed for me, and I gasp in delight at the vibrant shades and beautiful decoration flowing from the first letter on the page, a huge letter 'H'.

'This is for *Hundes heafod*, some might call it snapdragon. It's only a very short entry, but worthwhile including.'

Slowly, I trace the words with my finger above the page:

For soreness and swelling of the eyes take the roots of the plant that is called Canis caput *and in our language snapdragon; simmer in water, and after this bathe the eyes with this water. It will quickly relieve the pain.*

'Does this work?' I question. I've not heard of *Hundes heafod* before, or indeed *Canis caput*, and they seem to mean the same thing as snapdragon, which also perplexes me. How can one herb have three different names?

'It does, yes. It's a remedy I've used many times,' Gaya informs me, her eyes lighting with some memory or other.

'Then it's good we have it here, written down for all to see,' I confirm, relishing in the challenge they've set themselves, and in how much good it can achieve. Admittedly, there are no measurements, but I don't point that out. For someone who knows *Hundes heafod*, I assume they can determine how much of the root would be too much, and how much not enough. I feel it's a problem for another day, and I don't have time to ask the question either, for Wulfheard pokes his head into the room.

'Come on, Icel. The archbishop's arrived.'

With an incline of my head, and a smile for Theodore and Gaya, I take my leave. As intriguing as it's been to see the book of healing and to speak with the three monks, it's no longer my task. No. I must serve my king as a warrior of Mercia, and be alert to any who show too much interest in me. I might be trying to dismiss the warning from Eanstan, but I'm not a fool. The king of Wessex and his son are arrogant arseholes. I'll never allow them to prevail over me. It would be embarrassing if they were to be successful in obtaining their vengeance.

5

Archbishop Ceolnoth arrives with much fanfare, escorted from the river by Ealdorman Muca. The men and women in his entourage carry a whiff of water about them. I realise they've used ships to cross the River Thames. The nearby shallows must be too deep, or they merely wished to make the journey as quickly as possible, directly across the River Thames rather than travelling west for some time to reach Laleham Gulls.

I join Ealdorman Ælfstan's warriors, lining the roadway inside Londinium's fort, and eye the archbishop. Not that this is the first time I've met him. His eyes are bright. He shows no fear at being within Mercia. But then, King Wiglaf has no argument with the archbishop. It's King Ecgberht and King Æthelwulf who trouble Mercia's king, not the archbishop of Canterbury. Although, Wulfheard has spent some time telling me that's not always been the case, especially when Mercia had control over Kent. Before the events after my father's unfortunate reign. I consider if the archbishop knows who I am or if I'm just a name to him. His eyes sweep me, but I don't know if it's because he recognises me, or whether he's merely mildly interested in the men sent to guard him.

'Well met, my lord bishop, and welcome to Mercia.' Ealdorman Ælfstan and Tidwulf both greet the archbishop as soon as he's dismounted from his placid horse. It must have been sent for him by the ealdormen. I can't see a horse forced to cross the River Thames on a ship being so calm. Certainly,

Brute wouldn't be. I have my blades to hand on my weapons belt, but they're merely a show of Mercian strength. I wouldn't attack the archbishop – well, provided he doesn't prove too traitorous, I won't. If the warning Eanstan delivered came from him, then he's a peaceful man of God seeking reconciliation not violence.

'Good day, Ealdormen Ælfstan and Tidwulf. Thank you for greeting me. And to Ealdorman Muca for getting me this far.' The archbishop's timbre is rich. I can tell he's used to delivering sermons.

I see Ealdorman Muca to the rear of the archbishop's party. His face is pensive, but whether it's worry about the archbishop or a desire to ensure his duty is performed well, I don't know.

'You're most welcome, my lord bishop. Come within. Lord Wigmund will formally receive you, on behalf of his father, the king. Then we'll share food and drink.'

While the senior men make their way into the fort building, the rest of us wait and watch. We've been tasked with assessing those within the archbishop's entourage to determine if any of them are more loyal to Wessex than they are to the archbishop. I'm sure there are some amongst the grouping who would rather incite discord between the two rival kingdoms than heal past hurts. Admittedly, my experience with holy men and women hasn't always been a pleasant one. I might see them as meddling fools. And, of course, I have a personal reason for wanting to know whether the men and women mean me ill or not. With my involvement in the conspiracy against Mercia, I'm aware, if there is a traitor, they'll be working hard to mask their identity.

'How many of them are there?' Oswy huffs, as we're still standing, sometime later, with more men and women entering Londonia, mostly on foot. I can see it'll be a slow journey to Croft from here. Unless we can encourage them to mount up and ride. Not that I imagine there are enough spare horses to accommodate them all. I've not yet seen anyone I suspect, but with so many, they could be hiding in plain sight and I wouldn't know. It would be easy to don the garb of a monk and hide weapons beneath the rough robe.

'Too many,' Wulfheard grunts from beside Oswy. The men and women – there are certainly more men than women, I realise – eye Londinium's fort with unease and trepidation. That doesn't surprise me. It's a formidable building, even now. I'm sure they've heard of what happened within its walls. I consider if they fear being locked up in one of the windowless cells in the cellar. I shudder at the thought. I certainly wouldn't like it. Cut off from the sun and unable to see any natural light, and with the scent of damp, piss and shit pervading everything.

Just as the line of men and women runs out, another collection of rattling carts and pack ponies begins to traipse inside. I've not seen Eanstan, the messenger, which surprises me.

'Have they brought the bloody furniture with them?' Oswy growls. Wulfheard looks far from happy. Again, that's unsurprising. Some of the wooden chests are so huge, they could certainly hide a man within and many, many sharp blades. I reach to grip my seax, mindful Wulfheard notes the action. He doesn't say anything.

'Have these been searched, Edgar?' Wulfheard strides to Ealdorman Muca's commander, who'd been overseeing the unloading of the ships.

He shakes his head. 'Not yet, no. Ealdorman Muca was most eager to get them off the ship and inside Londinium. After all, if there's something amiss, it'll be easier to contain within these walls than where they came ashore between the two settlements, and to this side of the River Fleet. They purposefully didn't use the quayside, although I suspect that's because the ships didn't want to risk running aground on the old wooden struts sinking beneath the water.'

Wulfheard nods, but he's deeply unhappy. I don't miss some of the cart drivers cast suspicious looks at the far from quiet conversation taking place between Wulfheard and Edgar. These must be men from Wessex. I consider where the Mercians are, unless, of course, the wagons have been travelling for longer and have made use of the shallows at Laleham Gulls to get here after all.

'Then we'll check them,' Wulfheard announces, occasioning a groan from Cenred, although I don't share the same complaint. Wulfheard flashes him an ire-filled look, and as the gates of Londinium close behind the huge party of holy men and women, we follow the carts to where the oxen and horses are being relieved of their burdens.

There's a scribe there, wearing his monk's robes, who seems to be assessing everything. Wulfheard stamps towards him, while the rest of us try not to get in the way of servants running hither and thither with water and oats for the horses and oxen. With Cenred to one side of me, and Oswy to the other, we cast an eye over all the activity, trying to ignore the fierce argument taking place between Wulfheard and the monk.

I narrow my eyes. It seems to be too confusing, almost as though the men and women here have determined to make it impossible to get a true accounting of what's here. Immediately, I realise there are no weapons, aside from eating knives, on display at their waists, but perhaps they're hidden within one of the many wooden chests. I swallow, once more, keen to dispel my unease.

I see Wulfheard stamp his way to one of the carts, the clerk-monk at his side, hands gesticulating angrily, as Wulfheard orders the chest opened. A flash of colours over Wulfheard's face and I realise the chest contains clothing, priceless clothing, repeatedly dyed to make it so vibrant, and with chalk perhaps added to the mix to ensure it's the brightest shade of it. It is, I suspect, the archbishop's holiest robes, brought to Mercia to be worn when the king's present.

Not that Wulfheard seems content with that. He plunges his hands into the mass of coloured robes, all while the monk at his side continues to shriek.

'Bloody hell,' Oswy huffs, and strides to stop the clerk-monk from clawing Wulfheard's body with his desperate entreaties to get him to stop. 'Come now, good man. Let the man work.' And Oswy effortlessly holds the clerk-monk's hands in his, so Wulfheard can continue his perusal.

'That's the archbishop's,' the man squeaks with outrage, his bald pate shimmering beneath the bright sunlight.

'And I'm sure he won't object to a bit of judicial scrutiny,' Oswy continues conversationally. I keep my eyes on the others, as do Cenred and the rest of Ealdorman Ælfstan's men. But, in all honesty, the carters and holy men and women merely look scared not angry. I don't sense any particular scrutiny on me.

'What is this?' a deep voice booms. All eyes turn to rest on a man I don't know. It's evident, however, he's one of the southern bishops who's escorted Archbishop Ceolnoth to Mercia.

'My lord bishop.' Wulfheard offers an incline of his head. 'As the king demanded, we're ensuring no traitors endeavour to sneak their way into Mercia.'

'Do you know who I am?' the man demands, puffing up his non-existent chest. He's a skinny one. His head is narrow, his ears almost joining together without the aid of his face.

'I did say "my lord bishop", my lord bishop,' Wulfheard continues, his tone obnoxious, closing the wooden chest carefully, although the clothing within has been severely disturbed, I notice with a wince.

'I'm Bishop Beornmod of Rochester,' the man continues. I grimace at his pompous tone.

'My lord bishop.' Wulfheard inclines his head once more. 'I think you can agree, there's a great deal of luggage here for a brief journey to Mercia.'

'It's all needed, and required. And you cast aspersions on the archbishop with your handling of his personal possessions.'

'I do not,' Wulfheard announces firmly, reminding me why he's Ealdorman Ælfstan's commander. 'I obey my king's orders, just as you do your archbishop's. Now, it would be much quicker and easier if the chests were all open, and the sacks as well. I must ensure Mercia isn't threatened. If you're unhappy, my lord bishop, I suggest you speak with Ealdorman Ælfstan, my oath-sworn lord.' And with that, Wulfheard strides to the next chest, which is immediately opened by a worried-looking nun, her hair covered with a pale grey headdress so only her eyes peer at Wulfheard. Immediately, every other chest or sack is also opened. Wulfheard's thorough in his assessment of everything brought to Mercia, even rifling through sacks clearly containing clothing or oats for the horses.

I stand with my fellow warriors, allowing the sun to warm my face, but alert to anything that might happen. I notice Bishop Beornmod stalk away, his nose in the air, and wish I'd not noticed his appraising eyes rest on me. However, the anticipated arrival of Archbishop Ceolnoth doesn't materialise. Neither does Bishop Ceolbeorht of Londonia appear to berate Wulfheard for being too efficient, or, indeed, Ealdorman Ælfstan.

Finally content, Wulfheard bows towards the men and women in thanks, and with a flick of his wrist, orders us to follow him back towards the fort building.

'Bloody fools,' he huffs, as we stand in a loose circle around him, with Londinium's gate at his back. 'That could have gone much more easily if they'd argued less.'

None of us comments. Wulfheard eventually grins.

'Arseholes, all of them. I've never seen so much fine cloth in my entire life. No wonder it's all guarded so closely. Why they bedeck themselves as they do, I'll never know.' So spoken, he indicates we can re-enter the fort building, and we do so, quietly, because the archbishop, his bishops, Mercia's three ealdormen and the king's son are busy undertaking an official welcoming ceremony. The tediousness of it is evident in the fact it's still underway, despite Wulfheard's rankling with the baggage train which has taken a great deal of time.

'Bloody hell,' I hear Oswy huff from beside me, as we take our places to the rear of the main hall, but my focus is entirely on Lord Wigmund. He sits, pale of face, and evidently in some pain, at the front of the hall. I take no pleasure in seeing him. Not for the first time, I consider whether I did the correct thing in trying to save him in the way I did last summer. And not for the first time, I'm entirely conflicted.

The king's son lives, but whether he'll ever thrive again isn't for me to say. He looks ill, and he was never a particularly forbidding character anyway, as Gaya reminded me. Yet I don't miss that, no matter his ill health, there are many in the room who've aligned themselves with Lord Wigmund. Some of his allies have been missing from Tamworth, but they've evidently made their way to Londinium. However it might look to my eyes, Lord Wigmund's supporters are determined that, in time, he'll succeed his father as Mercia's king.

It won't end well for him, I'm sure of it. I have to hope it ends better for Mercia, and for me. I've learned something valuable however, as once more I sense the scrutiny of the bishop of Rochester. He knows who I am. I need to determine if this is because he's to bring about King Æthelwulf's alleged vengeance. Or not.

6

We don't leave Londinium the next day, or even the one after that. Instead, the archbishop seems determined to delay moving away from the River Thames for as long as possible. Perhaps he fears leaving Kent, after all. Maybe he'll simply request to be taken back across the river. It could be accomplished easily. The ships await his return from Croft anyway. And I'd appreciate not fearing someone means me ill with every step I take. I'm determined to stay out of the way of Beornmod, the bishop of Rochester, but I suspect he merely doesn't like me, and it's from others any move against me will come.

'It's not even that far to bloody Croft,' Oswy grumbles when we share guard duty that evening. Fires have been lit within Lundenwic and Londinium, but even I can sense it's taking longer each night for darkness to fall. We're truly moving towards the better weather. I'm grateful for it as I pull my cloak tight, and refasten the two silver pins securing it in place.

'Well, it's five days' travel, isn't it?' I question. 'With all these carts and people walking, that is. I know we could get there on horseback much quicker. So, what is preventing him from leaving?'

'Some argument about which road they'll follow. The archbishop wishes to travel along Ermine Street, but of course, that'll bring him close to the kingdom of the East Angles. The ealdormen aren't keen to risk war with the king-slayer, King Athelstan, if he misinterprets our intentions. After all, there are a lot of warriors as well as holy men and women.' I wince at King Athelstan's title. I might never become used to it, especially as one of those kings who was slain was my father. But King Athelstan is now an ally of Mercia. Or so I think. Perhaps, then, there's more to the determination not to go that way.

'So, take Watling Street as planned,' I state, shrugging. It seems easy to resolve.

'But the archbishop wishes to speak with the bishops of the kingdom of the East Angles.'

'I thought all this had been sorted,' Cenred grumbles to my other side.

'So did the ealdormen, but the archbishop isn't happy, not yet. And if the archbishop isn't happy, we can't leave Londinium.'

'Arse,' Cenred grouses. I focus on the far distance, looking over the River Thames. Bishop Beornmod of Rochester hasn't made a friend of himself to the Mercians. Indeed, his complaints about Mercian transgressions through his bishopric have caused some problems since his arrival. If I didn't already have my eye on him, I'd certainly do so now. Bishop Beornmod's bishopric is opposite Londonia, and I realise we must have ridden through it. More than once. Lord Wigmund has been attempting to soothe him, but has proven to be largely unsuccessful. Archbishop Ceolnoth has also made some endeavours, but I feel Bishop Beornmod is more an ally of the Wessex king than his archbishop. I suspect, if Bishop Beornmod isn't careful, he'll be sent back to Rochester by the archbishop because he's so bloody disagreeable. It can't come soon enough as far as I'm concerned.

'You don't think this is all a ruse from the Wessex king, do you?' Oswy suddenly questions.

'What, annoy the Mercian ealdormen so they'll what? Attack the bishop of Rochester? I don't think we're going to do that, are we?' I reply, aware I don't quite achieve the dismissive tone I'd like. My eyes turn to the east, where I know the Viking raiders have overwintered on the Isle of Sheppey. It's impossible to see so far to Sheppey, yet I imagine I can see it all the same. They decimated the religious community when they first took Sheppey. They slaughtered the animals. I can't imagine there's anything there to make it agreeable to them, aside from angering the Wessex king, that is, which does beg the question, why are they still there?

The archbishop has also shared his concerns with the ealdormen about the proximity of the Viking raiders to Canterbury, but the Mercians aren't minded to rush to the aid of the West Saxons. Not again. I don't blame them. It should be King Ecgberht's primary concern. There shouldn't be any need for the archbishop to mention it to the Mercians again. Kent's no longer Mercian. I find it strange he now seeks their aid considering, as Wulfheard told me, when Mercia did control Canterbury, the archbishops of the time didn't much like being beholden to a Mercian king.

'Perhaps not,' Oswy accedes. 'I'd relish a bloody good fight, though.'

Oswy took little part in last summer's attack on Londonia. He was unwell, and forced to return to the fort rather than aid us in ejecting King Æthelwulf from Lundenwic. I think he feels shorted by that. I'm not convinced I would.

'I'm sure there'll be a fight soon,' Cenred soothes. 'The Wessex bastard won't be able to help himself.' It's far from a comforting thought. While none of my allies died last summer, we still had to risk our lives. I don't relish that as much as Oswy does.

Neither do I appreciate his sentiment as dawn eventually crests the horizon in a welter of pale pinks and purples.

'Do you see that?' Cenred startles, pointing towards the east.

'What?' I glower, grumpy and tired. I don't like night-watch duties. They leave me feeling unrested for days afterwards, and Oswy and Cenred are even more unsettled with them.

'That,' Cenred repeats unhelpfully. I blink grit from my eyes, and look where he indicates.

'Bollocks,' Oswy expels, already turning to shout down to our fellow warriors. 'Ships. They're not bloody friendly, either,' he announces, as though the bellow of his voice isn't enough to assure everyone knows that.

'What is it?' Wulfheard's answering boom comes from below.

'Ships. They have shields.'

'Bollocks,' Wulfheard roars, and while I stand there, instantly awake and unsure whether I should rush to the river gate by the quayside or not, a cacophony of sound thrums through the fort. 'Get your arses down here,' Wulfheard roars.

Sharing a quick assessing look at my companions, I hurry to do as I'm told. Down the stone steps, the courtyard's rapidly filling with men who are less than half dressed. The clatter of shields and spears hitting the stone ground is jarring.

'Right.' Wulfheard's taken command. 'Icel, Oswy, Cenred, Kyre, Land-wine and Ure, get your arses down to the riverside gate and reinforce the warriors on guard duty there.' Without pausing for more instruction, I hurry towards the small tunnel leading out of the fort into Londinium itself, only to collide with a furious-looking Bishop Beornmod, shrugging into his clothing.

'What's the meaning of this?' he demands, blocking the tunnel so no one can come in or out of the fort building.

'Ships,' Oswy shouts loudly, startling the bishop, although Beornmod's eyes stay on my face.

'Enemy ships?'

'We could bloody find out if you'd get your arse out of the way,' Oswy informs him, none too quietly, and when the bishop still doesn't move, he barges past him.

I hurry to follow, not enjoying the sensation of Beornmod's scrutiny. Neither do I like his voice, which I hear all the way through the tunnel complaining and casting down God and all his holy saints on us. I do hear him cry, 'We were promised protection.'

'Come on, to the horses.' Oswy hurries to a run, and I follow behind. My tiredness has gone. I don't know who the enemy are. Is this a ruse by the king of Wessex to attack Mercia? It wouldn't surprise me. Whether the arch-bishop is aware of it, I'm unsure. I hope Wulfheard's thought to leave some people within the fort to protect Lord Wigmund, just in case.

Brute's contentedly chewing from his hay net when I hurry within the stables. I fling his saddle in place, and hurry to mount and direct him towards the quayside. The main gate into Londinium's closed. I see it as I turn my back to it. Ealdorman Tidwulf's warriors are standing there, ready to protect it. I consider what's happening within Lundenwic. The ditches have been repaired since last summer but they're not quite the impediment the ancient walls of Londinium are.

Quickly, I'm dismounting at the quayside, ensuring Brute won't trip on his reins, pleased to see the warriors on guard duty have the gate tightly closed, multiple wooden bars in place to ensure it can't be forced open. But, here, the walls aren't the most secure. Last summer, the queen escaped through one, and while it's since been reinforced to prevent the same, it doesn't mean there aren't other places where the enemy could gain entry.

'Who are they?' I direct towards the first man, who I realise is Edgar, Ealdorman Muca's commander.

'Bastards, all of them,' he growls, face etched with determination.

'Yes, but from Wessex or Viking raiders?'

At the question, Edgar stills, and his eyes narrow. 'Ah,' he mumbles. 'I assumed from Wessex. Bloody hell. I forgot about the Viking raiders at Sheppey. You,' he indicates a young man, probably my age, who's exceptionally tall, 'tell me, who are the enemy?'

I watch the youngster stretch as high as possible on tiptoes, and then when that fails, he clambers along the wooden bars as though it's a ladder. He peers over the top, only to hastily duck down and, in the process, lose his balance. He drops down, as a war axe thuds into the ground just below my feet. I feel a scowl form on my lips.

'Bastard Viking raiders,' I mutter, looking at all the confirmation we need as to who our enemy are.

'They won't let a gate or a wall put them off,' Oswy informs Edgar hurriedly, who's already nodding, as he assesses his force, and those streaming towards us.

'You take the gate,' Edgar directs to us, and none of us argue. This is where we're most noticeably at risk. I assume this is the place the enemy will try and break through. It's the most obvious location through which to gain entry to Londinium.

'We need to know how many bloody ships,' I mutter as a collection of metallic bangs sound against the wooden gate. I turn my eyes upwards, but keep my head lowered.

'Too bloody many,' Cenred glowers. I look amongst my fellow warriors. There are six of us, but no one has taken command.

'You take a look,' Oswy urges me, and I'd argue with him, but it sounds as though there are a hundred warriors on the far side of the gate. If there are, we need reinforcements. Quickly. They've chosen the time of their attack well. Those on night watch are sleepy. Those on day watch are just waking. None of us is as awake as we should be, and the grey light isn't aiding us.

'Bloody hell,' I huff, and wishing I could climb the wooden bars with my shield in hand, I scamper up them, with less grace than the gangly man. The higher I climb, the more I feel the gate vibrate and hear the shrieks of those determined to break through.

'Hurry up,' Oswy demands. From nearby, Ealdorman Muca commands his warriors, and somehow, I detect the querulous tone of Bishop Beornmod, who should have stayed within the fort building, but evidently hasn't. Bloody fool. Does he want to die with a Viking raider blade in his belly?

'You bloody do it,' I mutter angrily, and with my feet resting on the highest wooden bar, and my feet turned outwards along them, I grip the top of the stone archway, and tentatively lift myself higher.

I need only poke my head above the gateway to see how many enemy there are in the half-light. But the bastards have other ideas. Just as I'm as upright as I can get, a spear clatters over the stone. I'm forced to duck low, as the weapon pings on the stone walkway below me.

'Thanks for the bloody warning,' Uor complains. I bite my tongue to stop my fury pouring from my lips. I don't want to give away my position by speaking. I'm sure the spear throw was a lucky one, not because they know I'm here. Or at least, that's how I convince myself, as I prepare to glance over the wall once more.

This time, I get my helm above the parapet before a ping resounds. I blink, but it's with surprise, and not because I need to clear the sleep from my eyes. Or the accumulation of grit. But the weapon doesn't fall. I brace for another attack. My heart's thundering in my chest. The gate's shaking. I know I need to get on with it or I'll have the answer when it's already self-evident.

Without pausing to consider the merits of whether I should or not, I surge upwards, but I'm bending low too quickly to do more than see there are a lot of bastard Viking raiders. Edgar and his warriors have taken their positions protecting the wall, and I realise Ealdorman Ælfstan's also arrived because I hear him asking Oswy what the hell I'm doing.

Once more, I push upwards. This time, I'm confident enough to take my time. The enemy are entirely consumed with trying to get inside the gate. I scour the mostly abandoned quayside, and see three Viking raider ships bobbing on the surface of the dark water, with most warriors rushing towards the stone wall.

I can't peer all the way over the top of the wall to see if the enemy are

only focused on the gateway entrance, or if they're endeavouring to find
weaknesses, but I decide I've seen enough, and slowly lower myself, as the
banging on the wooden door grows ever louder, and more violent. I wish I
spoke Norse because someone's shouting themselves hoarse trying to direct
the bastards.

'Three ships,' I huff, deeply bending my knees to absorb the impact of
jumping down.

'Bollocks,' Oswy grunts. I peer around me. Wulfheard's arrived, as have
the rest of Ealdorman Ælfstan's warriors, as the daylight grows.

'Why here?' I pant. 'It would be easier to attack Lundenwic.'

'They don't know that though, do they?' Ealdorman Ælfstan surprises
me by stating. He's wearing his byrnie and has his shield and weapons to
hand.

'Is the main gate being guarded?' I question, just to be sure. I hope
Ealdorman Tidwulf hasn't pulled his men away to protect the quayside.
There could be more ships on the foreshore between Lundenwic and
Londinium, where the ships that brought the archbishop from the far side
of the River Thames deposited their cargoes.

'Yes, Icel.' The ealdorman offers me a wry smirk from all that's visible of
his face below his helm. 'We've bloody done this before, you know.'

I nod, but it's not as reassuring as I'd like it to be. 'I still think we need to
know why they've come here?' I mutter beneath my breath.

'No, we must merely repel them, and only then think of that,'
Ealdorman Ælfstan cautions me, hearing me despite the soft tone I
employed. I shake my head, uneasy, my thoughts tumbling to the archbishop of Canterbury and his collection of monks and nuns. And to Bishop
Beornmod of Rochester. I suspect the involvement of someone in this. I
can't see how the Viking raiders would know to attack here when the archbishop was in residence. After all, there's a wide expanse of riverbank
before they reach Londinium if they've come here from Sheppey, over
which I've spent too much time scouting and protecting, and there are
settlements there. But then there's no more time for thought.

The gate seems to bow before my eyes. I step backwards, reaching for
my shield, and quickly, with Ealdorman Ælfstan and my other warrior
allies, we're standing ready to defend against any incursion.

'Come on, men,' Ealdorman Ælfstan roars. 'We'll gut the bastards and feed them to the fish.' I like the idea, but still, I swallow heavily as the gate thunders once more.

'What do they have out there?' Oswy complains. 'A bloody ox?'

'More likely a thick-headed, ale-sodden arsehole,' Cenred adds. I'm stood between the two of them. Of late, this seems to be our preferred positions. Uor's to the side of Cenred, Wulfheard to the side of Oswy, and on it goes. Ealdorman Ælfstan, I realise, is beside Wulfheard. I'm surprised Wulfheard's not told him to leave the fighting to us, but then, we need every body in the shield wall we have. Mercia must be protected. We can't allow the enemy within Londinium, not with the king's son unable to protect himself.

A movement to my right catches my eye.

'We're breached,' I call, but before any other can see what I have, a huge axe head plunges its way through the reinforced Mercian oak, and the gate crashes inwards, despite the lines of reinforcing bars, and our presence.

'Advance,' Ealdorman Ælfstan bellows. I think him half mad, but shuffle my feet to do just that. The gateway's wide enough for a horse and cart to manoeuvre through, but the stone floor and the warped wooden gate mean it only goes so far. No matter the efforts of the enemy, the door only opens wide enough to allow two men through at a time.

Stealing myself to brace against the enemy, I take steps forward, aware it'll be my shield first coming into contact with the foemen. I lick my dry lips, narrow my gaze so it rests on the blackened helm of the men and hold my seax loosely, but tight enough I won't lose it when I lash out with it.

I hear Oswy's harsh breath beside me, and Cenred's repeated words, perhaps a prayer, but more likely a foul-mouthed complaint against the enemy. Then we crash into them.

I feel a vibration in my shield, and the resultant shudder of stress along my shield arm as I hold firm.

'Stay where you bloody are,' I glower angrily. The sweat of these men is as noxious as the stink of the River Thames. At least, I console myself, it's not low tide. Then it would be almost impossible to take a deep breath. It would, however, mean the Viking raiders couldn't have attacked us as they do now.

A blade impacts my helm, jarring me, but my focus remains on holding firm, right foot bracing my body. I'll not give way.

I'm aware of movement behind me, but it's what's happening ahead that has my attention.

Another blow, and then another. I see shimmering war-axe heads, and hear the angry cries of those stuck behind the two foemen at the front, but there's nothing they can do. The gateway's well and truly blocked. It can't be widened, and not just because I know there's a huge piece of fallen masonry wedged in place there. Those on guard duty often sit on it, or stand on it, or just mess about with it. The traders curse it, but for now I'm pleased it's fallen where it has.

'Hold,' Ealdorman Ælfstan bellows. I realise I'm the stopper in the bottle. Over my head, spears are being thrust towards the enemy by someone, perhaps Edgar and his warriors. I hear pings against the helms of our foe and more and more angry growls. I sense a scrapping over the top of my shield, and duck aside from the shimmering blade. I lift my seax hand to pull the blade away, but my elbow hits the man behind me, and instead I almost fumble my blade. And still the enemy weapon comes closer and closer.

'Ware,' I bellow, hoping Oswy will see the danger. He does but all he can do is veer aside as well. 'Give me some more bloody room,' I roar, and sense a lessening in the pressure behind me. Now I do manage to get my elbow up. I stab forwards, hoping the enemy's so focused on trying to score first blood, he's unaware of my counter.

With a sudden thrust, I feel the blade encountering something warm and experience the blood of my enemy on my face, or rather, on my helm, temporarily obscuring my view as a scream of pain ripples the air.

'Keep at it,' Oswy roars.

'I'm doing my bloody best,' I grunt, still being jostled by those in front and those behind.

'Ware,' I hear from someone else. I lift my eyes, sensing a shadow over me, and grimace. One of the crazy fools has decided to use the shields of their allies to gain entry.

'Up,' I roar. The spear behind me changes position. I attempt to twist my grip on the seax as well, but it's impossible. Not that I need do everything myself. A sudden dripping over my helm and down my nose guard assures me the enemy is bleeding. Another stab from the spear blade, and a heavy weight lands on my head. 'Get him bloody off me,' I urge. Hands reach upwards, and move the dead man. He lands on the ground with as much grace as a jangle of iron tools thrown into the air and dropped on a stone floor. At least the bastard's dead.

'Ware,' comes again. Once more, I sense shadow, and now I'm stabbing upwards, through the gaps in my shield and the one protecting my head. I'll kill all of these damn arseholes. I hope they're having no success elsewhere either.

A shriek, followed by a low moan, and another dead weight thunders to the ground. People jostle me, perhaps keen to move the dead body, or because they don't realise how precarious my position is, but suddenly I sense myself falling forward, my shield dragging me down, and I swear I hear someone whisper, 'From the king of Wessex,' but I have no time to truly grasp what's happening to me.

Some sort of incomprehensible sound erupts from my mouth, as I flail to stay upright, but it's impossible. I crash against the enemy shields, trying to avoid the shield bosses, and suddenly they're tumbling as well, backwards. I hear shouts and shrieks, cries of terror and anger. My knees hit the heavy ground, and then my entire body, one hand still gripping my shield, the other wrapped around my seax hilt, which I manage to loosen just as all my weight goes onto my hands. My left wrist screams in agony. I'm lying all to cock, as I try to release the tension in my shield hand or risk breaking it, but my fellow warriors aren't aware of my difficulties.

I feel a boot on my arse, and then another, as my allies swarm over me. I huff air into the legs of one of the enemy, desperately trying to keep my head clear, but it's almost impossible.

'Help,' I cry, but the word cuts off halfway through as another boot lands on my arse, pushing me further into the ground, and the wriggling legs of the enemy warrior. 'Help,' I shriek again, but no one hears, or if they do, they can't get to me because more and more of my fellow Mercians surge over me. My fall has undone the enemy. The twisting legs beneath me abruptly still and I know the man's dead. 'Bloody hell,' I growl, finally getting my left hand free from the shield and using it to push myself upright, against the angry Mercians seeking vengeance against our enemy.

I feel the whoosh of air over me, and smell the sharp stink of voided bowels, and then there's a hand on my shoulder, in fact two of them.

'Icel, Icel.' The cry is frantic. 'Icel. Help me. Get out of the way, you damn fools.' And like that, Wulfheard powers to my side, and pushes everyone else clear so I can breathe, which I badly need to do.

With the aid of Ealdorman Ælfstan, Wulfheard drags me away from the dead enemy – well, enemies: there are at least two of them. I rip my helm free from my head, desperate to get some cool air on my face, and into my body. Wide-eyed, unsure how I've survived, I look around. I furrow my brow. Did I really hear what I did before I fell? Or was it just a trick of my mind.

'Bloody arseholes,' Wulfheard's raging, marching to and from the gate, now devoid of the enemy, because it's flooded with Mercians, while Ealdorman Ælfstan bends low on his haunches to look at me.

'Are you well?' he demands. 'Icel, are you well?'

'Yes, yes,' I gasp, although I'm not entirely sure I am. My chest hurts, my back too. 'Are they gone?' I demand, my voice whistly through thickening lips.

'They're going,' Ealdorman Ælfstan confirms. I see he's bleeding, the madder fluid dripping down his nose to coat his lips, but he doesn't notice. 'What happened?' he questions me, as I decide I'd rather stand than sit slumped on my arse.

'I fell, or was pushed, I don't know.'

He nods, but his eyes look puzzled. 'It's not like you,' he confirms, and I know what he means. I peer all around me, considering who stood at my back, and might have been responsible for my fall. Was it malicious? I don't know, but I'm alive, and while I don't vow to discover the truth, I do determine to be much more cautious in future. I was warned about the possibility of recriminations from the Wessex king. I didn't take it seriously. Perhaps I should have done, especially with so many people from Kent in the archbishop's entourage.

In no time at all, the attack's over. The Viking raiders who still live scurry back to their ships like the opposite of rats abandoning a sinking ship, and we're all left wondering what they hoped to achieve. Or, at least, that's what most of the Mercians think as the guard's doubled on the gate. Another huge stone is brought to protect it from being forced wide open again, and the sound of hammering floods the air. The gate has a number of holes that need filling. Better if no one uses the gate at all, or so the ealdormen decide. But my thoughts are different. I want to know why I fell.

I want to know if someone meant me ill, and more importantly, I want to know who that might have been. I can't stop myself from gazing at Bishop Beornmod, who shows no signs of being involved in the fight, as he prays over the dead enemy, but who I'm aware glances at me from time to time with evident dislike.

* * *

The following day, very bruised and feeling decidedly sorry for myself, we finally begin our journey north. The archbishop has had his way after messengers were sent to King Athelstan of the East Angles to inform him of our route.

'I can imagine that bastard taking great delight in the request,' Wulfheard grumbles.

'Our two kingdoms are supposed to be allies,' I comment blandly, trying not to cough, ensuring there's no heat to my words. After all, as I now know, King Athelstan of the East Angles was responsible for my father's death. If not for him, it's possible my father might have claimed me as his son. Although whether I'd have really wanted that remains a question I can't answer honestly.

'Are they?' Wulfheard rounds on me. We've been given the tedious task of bringing up the rear of the long train of carts and pedestrians. It's hardly a great prize for keeping Londinium safe from the enemy. Brute's already fed up with the slow pace, sidestepping with wild abandon, and with every failure to make much progress, Wulfheard's growing more and more frustrated. It's going to be a far from pleasant task, despite the warm conditions and welcome heat from the sun. And despite my aching back, chest and left wrist, which still hurts a great deal.

I don't respond to Wulfheard. I've been forced to ride at his side because the others have conspired to ensure the task fell to me. I'll thank them for it later. I can hear them ahead, laughing and joking with one another, no thoughts for why the Viking raiders attacked when they did. I doubt Wulfheard's face will crack into a smile at any point today. He, after all, has given the matter a great deal of thought. As much as Ealdorman Ælfstan. I appreciate not being the only one to have suspicions. At Londinium, Ealdorman Muca has doubled the guard in our absence, calling on all of his reserves.

The Viking raiders left many dead men. The rest escaped. It's to be hoped they don't try the same trick again.

'King Athelstan's a cocky bastard. He enjoys killing Mercians too much for this to be a good idea.'

Once more, I don't respond, mainly because I can't argue with him.

'What's the matter with you?' Wulfheard demands to know. 'It's not like you to keep your opinions to yourself.'

'What do you want me to bloody say? I can't say you're wrong. King Athelstan has had too much influence in Mercian politics throughout the last eleven years. Even with King Wiglaf in such a dominant position within Mercia, he could still cause problems.' I cough again, wishing it didn't hurt so much to speak.

'Wonderful,' Wulfheard growls. 'Even you bloody agree with me. That means I'm entirely justified in hating this so much.'

'Indeed,' I confirm, focusing on the way ahead. The road's covered in dust from the passage of so many horses, carts, oxen and people. At the back of the slow-moving snake, I can still see Londonia if I look behind me, and we've been mounted for half the day already. I'm uneasy at leaving Londinium, although the ealdormen believe it's unlikely the Viking raiders will attack again when they were so firmly rebuffed and left a third of their number dead on the quayside when they escaped.

'This is going to take more than five days,' I complain. I don't welcome being forced to ride when I ache so much.

'It can't. The king will be expecting us at Croft.'

'What would you have us do? Whip the pedestrians?'

A wicked gleam enters Wulfheard's eye. I think he really would have us do that.

'If they're too slow, we'll have to get them on the carts or borrow horses along the way.'

'Isn't there some rule about holy men and women riding horses?'

'If there is, I don't see the archbishop and his two pet bishops doing so. Bishop Ceolbeorht of Londonia's mounted.'

'Hum,' I subside. I remain unsettled. I keep looking behind me, but I can't tell if anything untoward has befallen Londonia since we left. Ealdorman Muca has remained at Londonia to ensure all is well and the king's son is protected. He'll travel swiftly to Croft in a few days' time, and return just as quickly. Theodore and Gaya both advised Lord Wigmund against making the trip to Croft when he demanded to go, even though Wiglaf had already said he wouldn't be needed. Perhaps it was more worry that he'd be unable to defend himself if attacked. But I think it's a wise caution, even if Lord Wigmund tried to argue against the necessity of it. I confess, I've never liked Lord Wigmund. Perhaps now, as he battles his wounds, he proves himself the best warrior of all – a man determined not to be dismissed because of them. Or perhaps he's just an arrogant arse, as always, refusing to accept he's weak and ineffectual. Or maybe, like Ealdorman Sigered, he'll do anything to escape a fight.

But my thoughts return to Wessex and Londonia. King Ecgberht's as stubborn as Lord Wigmund is being these days. He's gained Londonia and lost it again in my lifetime. Will he accept that, or will he try once more? And his bloody son, King Æthelwulf, shares his father's ambitions. Will he move against Mercia or will he concentrate, as his role of king of Kent should make him do, on freeing the Isle of Sheppey from the Viking raiders? And what, if anything, are their intentions towards me? I'm deeply suspicious of everyone, and yet can't shake the feeling if I was pushed, it must have been by a Mercian. I can't believe Bishop Beornmod stood in the shield wall.

Later in the day, we're ordered to rest. I can't say Wulfheard's mood has improved. I can't honestly say we've made much progress either, along Ermine Street, the road running from Londonia northwards, out of Mercia, to Lincoln and, eventually, to Eoforwic, in the kingdom of the Northumbrians. Instead, we're brought to a halt, and ahead there's a flurry of activity as the ealdormen and bishops seek shelter in a roadside tavern and the rest of us are forced to either throw up canvas structures or camp under the stars. It's really still too cold to sleep outdoors, and this makes my fellow warriors grumble even more. The weather's warm enough during the day, but not at night, as our many guard duties have shown us.

Cenred quickly lights a fire, using branches fallen in a recent storm. We hunker around it, waiting for the pottage to cook. Well, that is until Ealdorman Ælfstan seeks us out.

'Ah, good to see you're feeding yourselves. There's no room for anyone within the tavern aside from the bishops and archbishops, and one of those bishops is still bloody moaning about the lack of "facilities", bloody arse,'

Ealdorman Ælfstan huffs, joining us perching on the ground, with our cloaks under our arses. 'It'll be a cool night out here,' he further grumbles. I'm not surprised he's so out of sorts. Our journey from Tamworth to Londonia involved arranging staging posts for the archbishop, but now we're travelling along Ermine Street, we won't be making use of them. There'll be some angry tavern keepers on Ermine Street and Watling Street in the coming days.

'We'll do our best to keep warm,' Wulfheard confirms, a warning glance assessing the rest of us, for the moaning from my fellow warriors has been the warmest thing we've encountered so far on our travels.

Ealdorman Ælfstan winces. 'Perhaps not, alas, you've been tasked with guard duty.'

A heartfelt groan issues from all our mouths. Bad enough to be sleeping outside, even worse to not be sleeping outside.

'What are we guarding from?'

'Who knows?' Ealdorman Ælfstan sighs, gratefully taking a bowl of pottage and spooning it into his mouth when it's far too hot, so Wulfheard hands him his water to soothe his mouth. 'But the bishops have prevailed upon the archbishop. And the king told us to perform whatever it took to ensure the archbishop felt safer within Mercia than he does Kent. So, we must keep guard, as directed.'

'It surely won't take all of us?' Oswy questions hopefully, and I grin at his innocent-looking face. But Ealdorman Ælfstan knows Oswy far too well.

'No, it won't, but you can certainly take the middle watch,' he suggests, an arched eyebrow as he breathes on his too-hot spoon before eating the food carefully so as not to burn his mouth again.

'Wonderful,' Oswy huffs. 'I'll have young Icel with me,' he then compounds his transgression by stating. While I shoot him a hate-filled look, Wulfheard turns to the rest of the men. I've already endured Wulfheard's ill humour all day. Now I must endure the same with Oswy. And in the middle of the bloody night. When I'm already wounded. Most of the others have little more than a bruise or cut on their faces to tell of our victory against the enemy outside Londinium.

'Cenred, you can join them. The three of you cause me enough problems when you've had a good night's sleep. A broken night will at least keep you quiet tomorrow.'

Amongst much groaning, the night-guard duties are divided between us all, and despite the hum of praying greeting the setting of the sun from the many religious we're escorting, we all settle to sleep on the hard, and slightly damp, ground. Even me, and even though it's impossible to find a position where something doesn't dig into my bruised flesh. Aside from the three on first guard duty: Uor, Waldhere and Kyre. They stride to their positions, and the rest of us grumble ourselves comfortable.

It feels as though I've only just closed my eyes when Waldhere wakes me with a yawn of meaty pottage into my face.

'Come on, youngster. It's your turn. You have the position to the east, looking for any bastard warriors from the kingdom of the East Angles.'

I rise from the damp ground as though a man twice my age, astounded by how much I ache. 'My thanks,' I murmur, and hobble through the campsite. There's a sliver of moon with which to see, and a handful of sentry fires have been lit, but mostly it's the few lights from inside the tavern and surrounding buildings providing illumination. Not that I can hear people moving around, not at the dead time of the night.

I catch sight of Oswy and Cenred by the light of the campfires, and raise my arm in greeting, walking towards the horses to ensure Brute's well. I run my hand along his nose. He whiffles the smell of hay towards me, which is much more pleasant than Waldhere's stale breath. Then I find somewhere comfortable to stand, trying not to yawn and blinking my eyes. I shiver into my cloak, grimacing at the reawakened hurts, cursing Oswy and his bloody mouth, but slowly the beauty and mysticism of being awake when everyone else is asleep overwhelms me. I don't even consider previous sentry duties, when we've been set upon by our enemies. I'm a stronger man than I've ever been before. I'm confident I could just about contend with any enemy sent against me, provided he wasn't a giant or some other mythical creature, and even with all my bruises.

Stamping some heat into my feet, I walk in a tight circle, my gaze assessing the small settlement we're sheltered outside off, and then looking up at the moon and stars overhead. There are many thoughts about how far away the stars are, and what they portend, but I merely admire their brightness. It comes as a surprise when I hear the voices of Oswy and Cenred rousing their replacements. I stride to Wulfgar and wake him with the touch of my hand. He scampers upright quickly, far more quickly than I managed earlier, and with a wink leaves me to sleep.

Once more, I'm woken when I'm sure I've only just closed my eyes, but dawn's shading the sky in the gentle colours of the changing season, pinks and mauves, and not at all the fiery reds and yellows of the summer. I attempt to stand quickly, but everything hurts once more. My clothing's damp with dew. I feel properly miserable, my head pounding and my tongue thick in my mouth. I wish I'd had the ale to go with the feeling of having drunk too much of it.

'Ah, Icel, a good night's sleep?' Wulfheard calls to me jauntily.

I'm saved from having to answer him by Oswy's aggrieved reply of, 'No, we bloody didn't.'

That makes me chuckle, as I relieve myself and then take myself to Brute. At least he's slept well. As we ride out, again consigned to the rear of the slow-moving cavalcade, I can rely on Brute to keep to the path, while my eyes close with exhaustion.

7

The next two days are slow, laboured and tedious, although it gives my bruises time to heal, even as we're wary of how close we are to the kingdom of the East Angles. Not even Oswy and his joy of playing games has managed to keep us all amused, and our ill humour only continues when we receive a messenger from King Wiglaf. He's been alerted to our change of itinerary, and has determined to make good on it. We're to collect King Athelstan of the East Angles from Peterborough.

'Why?' Wulfheard speaks for us all when Ealdorman Ælfstan relays the news.

'The king's orders are ours to follow,' he murmurs, but then relents. 'This is a coup for King Wiglaf. He'll have every bishop, and a king of another kingdom within Mercia. It speaks of his resurgence as a great king.' That might be true, I consider, but I still don't like it.

'Do you recall the fight outside Peterborough?' Uor questions me, as we resume our journey the next day, my eyes looking at his exposed left hand, and the missing finger there, because he's removed his glove to pick his nose. I grimace as he flicks whatever he's found away. I hope he's not about to launch into his rendition of the scop song he coined that day praising me. But he's swept up in the moment and the words trip easily from his tongue. 'Young Icel killed the bloody bastard jarl, the steerer of the seahorses. He offered Viking corpses to the wolf by the sea,' Uor states, a grin on his face, as he pushes his hand back into his glove. 'Just as he did a few days ago outside Londinium.'

'I could hardly forget,' I murmur, trying not to grimace at hearing my name amongst those words the scop regaled us with at Peterborough and which Uor bastardised. The king rewarded me that day, but we lost good friends, or, at least, acquaintances. The death of young Garwulf isn't a memory I prefer to linger on, even if he was a terrible warrior. And, I'm honest enough to admit, my endeavours at Londinium weren't the best. Falling and, in that way, overpowering the enemy is hardly the thing scop songs are made of. Even if I was pushed. I remain very wary when anyone I don't know comes too close to me. I know Wulfheard's also alert to the possibility of trouble.

'The Viking raiders were crafty outside Peterborough,' Oswy comments. 'But,' and now his forehead furrows, 'what did you do with the armrings the king gifted you?'

'I gave them to Wynflæd. She needed them for herbs.'

'So, the proceeds of a bloody death allowed others to be healed and live? Icel, you do make the most remarkable of contradictions seem acceptable.' He shakes his head, but it's not really a complaint. Perhaps, he even admires me? But Wulfheard's having none of it.

'Well, there are no bloody Viking raiders this time, only the archbishop and his monks and nuns. And soon King Athelstan of the East Angles and however many bishops he has.'

'They're just as troublesome,' Uor proposes. 'The religious ones are often very tricky, as we well know.' When no one argues with him, I appreciate it's not only the treasonous former bishop of Lichfield who causes problems for Mercia's warriors and her king. Or the archbishop of Canterbury.

'They have too much influence, and too few people to hold it over,' Wulfheard confirms, half an eye to where Bishop Beornmod rides on ahead, his back rigid. 'They meddle and cause problems where they shouldn't.' We all offer our agreement. 'But the king has allowed the archbishop of Canterbury to visit Mercia, and so we must go along with this, whatever "this" is.'

'We'll arrive at Peterborough tomorrow, I'm sure of it,' Wulfheard decides. We make camp with the stream to keep us and the horses in water, and with a copse of trees to protect us from the strengthening wind. 'Tomorrow we'll be in Fen country, with the stink of stagnant water and those pestilent bugs biting our skin,' Wulfheard complains as he settles for sleep.

* * *

Peterborough Monastery hasn't changed since our last visit. Not that I expected it to have done so. We're welcomed within in some fanfare because the archbishop is with us. I eye the surroundings, the vivid memory of Garwulf's death almost too much for me to bear, but I'm curious to see King Athelstan, the king-slayer, in the flesh.

I find I'm not disappointed, as I and the rest of the warriors are given food and water by the monastery's servants. The archbishop and the two ealdormen are led forwards to meet King Athelstan. Even from the way King Athelstan sits, I can tell he's a tall man. He has a potency about him other kings lack. By that, I mean King Ecgberht and his son. King Athelstan is the authority here, although Peterborough is Mercian. He exudes confidence and resolve, from his thick black beard to his sharp blue eyes, to the shimmering seax he wears on his weapons belt, sheathed, but the hilt clearly visible.

'My lord king.' Ealdorman Ælfstan knows how to conduct himself when representing his king.

'My lord king,' the archbishop further intones, his eyes taking in all.

'At King Wiglaf's command, we've come to escort you to Croft, a journey of two days, if we make good speed.'

'Well met.' King Athelstan's voice is booming. I wince to hear it, as do others within the room. His words could perhaps be heard on the other side of the river. 'I thank your king for allowing me and my bishops to attend upon the archbishop of Canterbury, and to the archbishop for visiting me in person. It's a privilege, and one we certainly couldn't prevail upon King Ecgberht of Wessex and his son to allow.' A slight grimace reveals whatever we once thought of King Athelstan and a possible alliance with the Wessex king, any friendship that might have existed has long since dissipated. 'These men are bishops Husa and Cunda.' King Athelstan introduces the bishops who escort him.

The men are opposites of one another. The one squat and rotund, the other tall and stringy. I can't shake the image they're like wheat after either a wet summer, or a dry one. I duck my head so none can see the amusement playing on my lips.

Both men have tonsured scalps. The squat man's pate shimmers with sweat, even though it's far from warm within the hall. The other man's head is paler than dead flesh. I'm not sure I'm going to like either man, although, of course, I only have to escort them to Croft, and no doubt back to Peterborough again. Whether I like them or not is irrelevant.

'We're here at the orders of our king, and will provide you with the protection you need, as we already do the archbishop and bishops from Wessex.' Ealdorman Ælfstan speaks clearly.

At this, King Athelstan's eyes narrow a little and he suppresses a small smile. The little snipe hasn't gone unnoticed, by anyone.

'We'll set off tomorrow, if that pleases you, my lord king.'

'Very well. Tomorrow, early. The bishops are passable riders, if I do say so myself. Now, eat well, and rest.'

'You're most gracious,' the archbishop intones, 'although I understand this place is beholden to Mercia, and so I'll join my brothers and sisters within their fine church and pray for the continuing peace.' I startle at the archbishop's far from gentle admonition and note the surprised look on King Athelstan's face. It seems the archbishop is nobody's fool.

Despite my unease at returning to Peterborough and the memories surfacing as I listen to the glug of the rising and falling water outside the walls, I rest better than I have since before the attack on Londinium, and we're ready to leave before the sun rises. I wait, mounted, for the archbishop and his entourage, King Athelstan, his two bishops and his small warrior band to join us, my eyes assessing the river where I once fought the Viking raiders alongside my fellow warriors. I realise now that was the day I understood how far I'd come as a warrior. That was the day I appreciated I'd never be a healer, but always a warrior, using my shield to protect Mercia. I'm reconciled to it, and yet, sometimes, I do think of what my life would have been like had I remained the boy I was when my uncle lived.

'Come on, stop daydreaming,' Oswy calls to me. I'm conscious everyone's preparing to ride out, apart from those still travelling by foot. 'We have the advance,' Oswy informs me. I narrow my eyes at Wulfheard, but he nods slightly. I grin, and look down to hide it. King Athelstan bragged about his fleet horses last night. Wulfheard means me to test them, even though we'll leave many of those who walked this far in our wake.

'As you wish,' I murmur, and direct Brute through the mass of horse-flesh. King Athelstan's allowed to bring twelve warriors with him, but I notice the bishops each have two priests attending upon them. At least this addition to our party is small compared to that the archbishop's brought with him. 'You ready for this?' I ask Oswy.

He turns to me, the gentle breeze blowing through his mop of hair. 'Always.' He offers an arched eyebrow and, together, we encourage the horses on.

I don't imagine we'll find any enemy warriors this far into the heartland of Mercia, almost within the kingdom of the East Angles, and so, as Wulf-heard commanded, I allow Brute to stretch his long legs, and bend low over his neck. Our passage is swift, although it doesn't last for long.

'Rein in, Icel,' Oswy calls to me. I look behind, and can't see the collection of warriors, bishops and kings.

'That went well.' I laugh.

'Arrogant sod,' Oswy grumbles. 'But we better wait for them to catch us, and then try a slower pace.'

We wait impatiently. Brute's restless beneath me. Oswy's horse is little better. Finally, Wulfheard rides into view, a brief grimace on his face, the king of the East Angles behind him, his expression far too easy to decipher.

'That's a very fast horse,' King Athelstan compliments me, perhaps a little unwillingly.

'My thanks, my lord king. He can be a little difficult to manage,' I attempt to mitigate, but all here know I'm trying to placate the ruffled feathers of the king of the East Angles. His pride has been dented.

More slowly, we resume our journey westwards, and at night find shelter near a tavern, although some of those walking are far distant. Then the following day, with dusk a hint on the horizon, we arrive at Croft, or at least those with horses do. I'm grateful we've not been forced to take the rear again. With relief, we allow Commander Eahric to take over our duties of escorting the king of the East Angles and the archbishop and his mass of followers, and while they're taken to properties given over to their use in the nearby monastery, we join the rest of the Mercian warriors, beneath canvas.

'Why was this location chosen?' I mutter, seeing little that's appealing. Indeed, it's on top of about the only hill to be seen for a good distance and that means, up here, it's going to be windier, and colder, than it is down there.

'Who knows?' Wulfheard grumbles. He's in need of a shave, his grey-flecked beard and moustache grown ragged during the journey. Usually, such things wouldn't concern any of us, but as the king's here, and we're supposed to be representing Mercia and her king, we all know we need to find hot water and the means to tidy our hair and faces.

'An assembly was held here by King Æthelbald, near enough a century ago. For that reason, it has some significance,' Ealdorman Ælfstan comments. I'd not realised he'd joined us. 'King Wiglaf's keen to make much of the continuity. I'm sure you can imagine why.'

'Perhaps,' I grumble, dismounting and stretching my back, while Ealdorman Ælfstan walks to speak with Wulfheard more quietly. I watch the pair of them, considering what terrible duty we'll be given next. For all the times we've fought for King Wiglaf and protected Mercia, it only ever seems to result in us being given even more onerous duties, not lesser ones, but for now it seems the two talk of something that doesn't immediately affect us.

Surveying the landscape, I appreciate that perhaps this location does have something to offer. At least it can be seen from a good distance. Maybe the intention is as many as possible will witness this gathering and perceive it for what it is. I know the king intends to use it as an excuse to proclaim a number of charters. What the archbishop of Canterbury intends is unknown at this time. And King Athelstan of the East Angles.

The real work of the synod will begin the next day. I hope we're not forced to listen to the tedious words of the archbishop of Canterbury, the bishops and the two kings. But, of course, I'm not to get my wish.

8

The two kings wear all their finery. They're only outshone by the brightness and golden thread depicting religious imagery on the archbishop of Canterbury's robes. The three men convene in the main hall of the monastery. I've had a quick look around. It's no different to any other monastery I've ever been to, and in that I include Winchcombe, Peterborough, Canterbury and Bardney. There are many religious buildings, not all of them for monks. I see the king's summoned some of Mercia's abbesses, and I do note the abbess of Winchcombe is attending. In her absence, I hope someone's keeping a very close eye on the former queen of Mercia. She's not exactly chained at Winchcombe. Perhaps she should be. I also realise Lady Ælflæd's here, although the children aren't within the hall. She sits close to the king, perhaps in place of his discarded wife. I consider where the children are. Maybe they've been left at Tamworth. It must be better to keep Mercia's king and his æthelings apart, just in case something should befall one of them.

We've already attended a dawn religious ceremony in the monastery's church, and now it seems there's to be some formal discussion between the kings and holy men and women.

I listen to Archbishop Ceolnoth. With the two kings here, he's either decided to take charge or has been asked to do so. I'm not sure which.

'My lord kings, my lord bishops, abbesses, and abbots, and all who

attend. You're welcomed to this synod, held close to Croft, with the agreement of King Wiglaf, the first of his name, within the ancient kingdom
Mercia. We thank you, my lord king, for providing such a safe environment
for us to meet and discuss matters of the church. Alas, with the Viking
raiders close to Londinium and the Isle of Sheppey, the risk couldn't have
been taken to summon you to my home at Canterbury.'

I note the archbishop doesn't mention the problems of last year, when
King Æthelwulf of Kent and his conniving father endeavoured to tumble
Mercia's ruling line, even using the archbishop's name in their attempts.
Perhaps it's politic not to, but there are none here who don't know about it.
This, I suspect, is how it'll be noted in any accounting of King Wiglaf's
reign. Few will mention it. Maybe it's better if future generations don't truly
comprehend the ambitions of the bastard Wessex ruling house.

'Now, we've much to discuss about the state of the church within
Mercia, and the kingdom of the East Angles, and there are also some new
teachings I must inform you about.' As the archbishop of Canterbury
continues to drone, I find my thoughts distracted. None of what he says is
actually of interest to me. I've no concerns with how long religious services
should be, or how frequently they should take place, or even what should
happen to those who fornicate outside the restrictions of a church-sanc-
tioned union. Admittedly, that one takes me a little while to unpick. Why
these religious men and women must use such words to discuss marriage,
sex, adultery and everything in between is beyond me. It appears there's an
issue with the sanctity of marriages, as far as I can tell. Or so I suspect.

Thankfully, while I've no interest in what the archbishop has to say, I
can distract myself by assessing the men and women brought together for
the synod. I'm becoming quite fascinated by King Athelstan. He's arrogant
but also comfortable with his surroundings. He doesn't fidget or look
aggrieved by the long and tedious speech the archbishop's making.
Neither does he eye everything with acquisitive eyes, as I've seen King
Ecgberht of Wessex do. He's a confident man even in such a place. He, I
suspect, is content with his kingship of the East Angles. That was probably
all it ever was, I can acknowledge, a man desperate to have his kingdom
under the command of one of their own. After all, isn't that why we've
been fighting King Ecgberht of Wessex for all these years? We merely want
the same. He might have brought about the death of my father, but did

King Beornwulf truly have any right to rule in the kingdom of the East Angles? I doubt it.

All of the bishops listen carefully to everything the archbishop says to them, some nodding along. I notice there are a handful of scribes recording the transactions of the synod. These holy men and women do like to write everything down. I remain suspicious of Bishop Beornmod of Rochester. He has constantly shifting eyes. It could be he knows everything the archbishop says already, but I'm unconvinced.

It's a relief when the archbishop stops talking and others join the discussion, although their concerns aren't mine. The Mercian bishops seek clarity on the archbishop's loyalties, and the bishops from the kingdom of the East Angles nod along. They evidently share the same worries. King Ecgberht of Wessex's ambitions cause problems for many.

'King Ecgberht doesn't exercise any influence over me,' Archbishop Ceolnoth announces archly, and with a thread of aggravation warming his voice. 'He's the king of Wessex. I'm the archbishop, appointed by the pope. Canterbury is mine, not his.'

I glower at Bishop Beornmod of Rochester, curious to see if his expression will bely that statement. But it doesn't. He believes it just as much as the archbishop.

Aside from the holy men and women, the two kings and the radiant Lady Ælflæd, the main hall is crammed with others. There are lords I've never met before, including the local lord, a man known as Humberht. He's never fought in any of the king's battles with Wessex or the East Angles, as far as I know. That might be explained by the fact he's almost as old as Ealdorman Sigered.

There are also new ealdormen of Mercia, King Wiglaf evidently deciding to ensure his control after the events of last summer by appointing men loyal to him. Amongst them is Ealdorman Æthelwulf, not to be confused with King Æthelwulf of Kent, and Cyneberht and Ealhelm. I don't miss that Lord Beorhtwulf hasn't been made an ealdorman. That'll annoy him.

Indeed, King Wiglaf has surrounded himself with those he deems loyal, including Lady Ælflæd, the mother of his grandson. There are twenty-two ealdormen and high-ranking lords, as well as the archbishop and almost all the main bishops from Mercia, including the new bishop of Lichfield, the two from Wessex and the two from the kingdom of the East Angles. If King Ecgberht knows of this synod, he'll be angry. It's a statement of King Wiglaf's influence he's been able to host the archbishop of Canterbury deep within Mercian-held territory. Momentarily, my thoughts turn to Londonia, but Ealdorman Muca has arrived and assured the king there's no threat from Wessex, and the Viking raiders haven't attempted to renew their attack. I hope that continues, and not just for the next few days but for weeks, months and, perhaps, even years.

The heat in the hall continues to grow with so many within, including as many of the monks as can be squeezed inside. With my stiff embroidered tunic, I feel increasingly uncomfortable. It's a relief when the day's proceedings are brought to an end. I can't say anything of substance appears to have been agreed upon. But what do I know?

My thoughts turn to the feast being prepared in honour of the two kings and the archbishop. Already delightful smells infuse the air. My belly's been grumbling for much of the afternoon. I'm not alone in that. We'll also be entertained by the king's scop. I hope the king has carefully considered what scop song will be suitable before his audience. After all, he can't proclaim Mercian dominance while the king of the East Angles is here. Neither, I suspect, should there be too much bloody battle violence, or it will upset the holy men and women. Nor can the scop merely recount tales of the holy martyrs of Mercia. It would be too tedious for the warriors here, even if the monks and holy men and women would appreciate it.

My fellow Mercian warriors and I are seated to the rear of the hall when the feast begins. On the raised dais are the two kings, the archbishop, the local abbot, Humberht and as many of the bishops as can be squeezed into one place, including Beornmod of Rochester, and Lady Ælflæd. I do find it easy to pick her out on the dais. She emanates beauty.

There's no room for the other Mercian ealdormen, but the men have all been given positions of honour as close to the king as possible, the lesser noblemen and warriors taking the seats further away. We're the furthest away. I suspect that's so we can protect the doorway, should we need to do so. Not that any seems concerned we're likely to be attacked. Commander Eahric has the king's household warriors keeping watch from some distance away, using the peak of the hill at Croft itself to ensure no long-distance riders slip through. Others watch the roads giving access to Croft.

Despite a lack of protective exterior walls or ditches behind which we could shelter should there be an attack, I feel as though everything that needs to be done has been done to ensure no one faces assault from an unknown enemy. Or a known one. It's a pity I can't shake my unease then.

King Athelstan's warriors have also been invited to the feast. They have the table two rows in front of us. They're effectively trapped within the hall. I'm not sure the fools even realise. They, like me, are only concerned with feeding their hungry bellies. I catch sight of Commander Eahric on door duty. He inclines his head towards me respectfully. Despite all evidence to the contrary, he's alert to the potential for problems.

That said, all goes well as we're fed a pottage flavoured with onions and parsnips, and then a meat course of roasted boar and venison. What follows are sweet treats of last year's apples, baked and sweetened with honey. I don't know how the monks managed to store them through the long, bleak winter and not consume them. Perhaps they forgot about them. Maybe they decided to keep them in order to honour the archbishop. There's also ample ale, but I find myself reaching for water, not ale. I don't wish to become addled. Throughout the feast, my eyes are drawn time and time again to Lady Ælflæd, her softer tones easier to detect than the rougher ones of the many men in attendance. I'd like to find time to speak with her.

And then the scop appears. We all know the wizened man by sight. I consider what he's been tasked with performing here, today. It can't be a tale of the ancient and mighty King Penda, for Penda killed a king of the East Angles, long ago. His name was Onna or Anna, or something like that. It's a relief when the scop opens his mouth and begins to perform his song of beating back the Viking raiders. There, at least, we all share an enemy. It's good to have a common enemy when we could so easily fight amongst ourselves.

And from there the scop continues to regale all with songs that don't reference the animosity between the two kingdoms, even as those in atten- dance grow ever merrier on the ale on offer. At this, I cast a glance towards Commander Eahric and realise he too senses it. The scop has performed admirably, but King Athelstan's warriors are becoming very loud, calling for certain songs they enjoy. I fear the scop will be forced to acquiesce and then there might be a real problem. For now, he's busy reciting the tale of the mythical warriors of the Goddodin, the kingdom itself lost to the mists of myth. Their names, however, live on. Again, this shouldn't cause problems, the events recounted took place far to the north of here, between enemies none of us have heard of, even the names strange to our ears.

'Keep your wits about you,' Wulfheard orders, his gaze as assessing as Commander Eahric's. He especially holds the eyes of Oswy and Cenred while giving the caution. I consider whether they're the most likely to start a fight. Perhaps not them. Maybe Kyre or Maneca, but in the end it's not one of the Mercian warriors at all, but instead one of the priests escorting Bishop Beornmod. I knew he'd cause problems. Bishop Beornmod, that is, not his monk. I consider if he's even instigated it.

The monk stands, face red and flushed, his robe stained with spilt ale, as he jabs a furious finger towards the scop and then towards King Wiglaf. Commander Eahric's already noticed. He strides through the mass of rolling men and women, only to be stopped in his tracks by King Athelstan's warriors, who don't even seem to notice they block the Mercian commander and leader of King Wiglaf's household troop when they stand and seek out the source of the interruption.

The scop, trying to appease all, has begun a tale of Mercia's domination over Wessex during the reign of King Offa. He has, perhaps, forgotten about those from Wessex in the party. King Wiglaf's not thought to stop him, engrossed in conversation with King Athelstan, the two men doing their best to put aside all past animosity.

But now, the priest scuttles forwards, towards King Wiglaf, somehow managing to weave a path through everyone until Ealdorman Ælfstan finally succeeds in getting in his way. Ealdorman Ælfstan moves to block his progress, only for Bishop Beornmod to grow angry. I watch it all unfolding before me, grateful no one's armed with anything above an eating knife within the hall, although, of course, they're still bloody sharp to cut through the meat.

As Bishop Beornmod berates Ealdorman Ælfstan, the priest somehow stumbles through and up towards the two kings and Lady Ælflæd, arms waving, a goblet and a jug in either hand. King Athelstan's warriors are abruptly alert. There's a great deal of shoving and screaming as people try to get out of the way of the surging warriors, with stools and boards over-turning and crashing to the ground. The king's hounds, tricky buggers that they are, make their way through more quickly than anyone else can.

'Bloody hell,' Oswy huffs, Wulfheard at his side. I entirely agree with him, as I see Lady Ælflæd's face whiten with fear, and my hand reaches for my seax, although it's not on my weapons belt. I know there's only one way to prevent accidental damage to the two kings, Lady Ælflæd and the arch-bishop. I'm grateful I've only drunk water and no ale at all.

Quickly, I jump onto the bench I've been resting my arse on, and then onto the table, knocking plates and beakers flying with my boots. Then I turn to face the front of the hall. Shaking my head, while the roar of coming violence intensifies, I jump forward, clouting one of the men sitting at the board around the head with my boot. I utter an apology lost in the swelling hubbub while I fight for balance. I take another step, and then another, my gaze directly on Lady Ælflæd, seeking protection behind King Wiglaf, arms windmilling to aid me in keeping my balance.

There are, I know because I counted, ten such boards within the hall, not including the one behind which the kings, Lady Ælflæd and the arch-bishop sat.

I stand on the third one, abandoned by all of the warriors owing alle-giance to King Athelstan, and then the fourth, weaving a path through furious and very ale-sodden men and women. The abbesses, I note, shriek and stand to the side of the hall, clutching their robes and wooden crosses, as though it'll help them against men who've drunk too much and are spoiling for a fist fight. Servants stand, mouths agape, unsure what to do. King Æthelstan's warriors surge forward to protect their king from the perceived attack and Commander Eahric can't get close to King Wiglaf.

'Bloody hell,' I growl, my boot slipping on spilt ale, so my balance is all wrong. I only just reach the next table without falling to the floor. I move quickly, keen to avoid the fists, cups and beakers being flung around the place by men roaring with anger and fury.

I'm astounded such a peaceful meal has become such chaos, and so quickly.

The next board's fallen to the ground. I jump down, my knees absorbing the impact, and avoid a flying fist, as I find myself between two men, busy trying to beat the crap out of one another. I shake my head, sliding between them. The damn fools are both Mercians.

'Duck,' Oswy bellows from behind. I do so, even though I'm unsure who he directs it towards. I sense something flying over my head, and turn to offer him a smirk of thanks. Abruptly, he disappears from view, a crash of wood assuring me the board he was standing on is no longer upright.

There should now be a clear path towards the raised dais, but the broken-down and overturned boards and benches block my path, as do the brawls breaking out between Mercians and anyone else who fancies exchanging fists. I skip over the long benches, and even more men taking the opportunity to have a bloody big fight.

I punch one man, his nose bleeding fiercely, a knife dripping blood in his right hand. He shudders to the ground, his senses all gone. The man he fought, one of the local lord's men, nods his thanks, and starts forward as well. He gets no further than the next flying fist, which I duck below, but which knocks him to the ground. Almost on my hands and knees now, I scurry forwards, alert to fists, feet and the odd jug and beaker crashing down around my head.

'Cease,' I hear Commander Eahric bellow, but it's not going to stop the fools from fighting. Too much ale. Too little sense. Too much unease. Damn arses. I hear a scream of fear above the noise, and look to see Lady Ælflæd cowering.

I risk standing upright, a pool of ale ahead which I don't wish to stain my knees with. I swerve away from a flying piece of debris, shaking my head. I don't know what that was. I think it might have been a bone from the roasted boar. A big bloody bone. A shriek, and I realise someone else was less lucky with it than me.

I can't see King Wiglaf and Lady Ælflæd ahead any more. All is chaos. I see a great deal of fists and bleeding noses, and swaying men endeavouring to punch and kick one another.

'Arseholes,' I grumble to myself, glancing sideways, pleased to see Cenred and Maneca have had the same idea as me. Not that I know where the rest of the ealdorman's warriors are. I can't even see Wulfheard or Ealdorman Ælfstan. And I don't know what's happened to Commander Eahric, although I still hear him shouting for everyone to stop, King Wiglaf also bellowing.

The wizened scop crawls past me in the opposite direction, his lyre held close to his chest. I'd like to offer him a safer passage out of the fighting, but I can't determine on one. I must reach the king and Lady Ælflæd before this really gets out of hand, and then who knows what the consequences might be? I don't believe this has been orchestrated by King Athelstan, or Bishop Beornmod, but I'm not prepared to take any risks.

Two fighting warriors trade punches, leering drunkenly at one another as they do so. I veer around them, offering my foot behind the ankle to the one, who goes down with a bellow of outrage, only matched by the other man, who overbalances on his punch when his opponent's not there and follows him down. Better to have them down on the ground than fighting. I recognise the two of them. I'm sure they're allies of Ealdorman Sigered.

The thought of him has me assessing the heaving crowd, wondering where that old bastard has got to. It would be good if he took a blow to the head, or something similar. It would remove him from the king's closest circle. That would benefit everyone. But no, I catch sight of him, sheltering, of all things, behind the two kings, trying to push Lady Ælflæd out of the way. What a noble and honourable warrior the whoreson is.

'My lord king,' I bellow towards King Wiglaf when the space between us abruptly opens up. He eyes me, far from aghast. If anything, he seems quite calm, as Ealdorman Ælfstan manages to join me as well, Cenred and Maneca crowding into the space opening up between us.

I rush to reach King Wiglaf and Lady Ælflæd.

'Get behind the king,' I order her, and she nods, her chest heaving with fear. My eyes scour the area ahead of us, as I turn my back on the kings and Lady Ælflæd.

'My thanks,' I hear Lady Ælflæd gasp, whereas Ealdorman Sigered complains at being squashed.

While Ealdorman Ælfstan's warriors rushed towards their king, almost everyone else has been trying to escape through the door. I wince on seeing something else heavy flying through the air, and smacking into the back of someone's head outside the double doors. They fall immediately. The space between the kings, Lady Ælflæd and the archbishop, and the fighting warriors and holy men, I notice with a shake of my head, grows ever bigger.

But this time, there's a different reason for it.

'Bloody bollocks,' I exclaim, the scent of smoke having me observing the hearth fire. In my headlong dash towards the kings and archbishop I've not realised what's happened.

'Get that out of the hearth,' I call, but of course, no one's listening to me, aside from those this side of the crackling flames. 'My lord king,' I murmur to King Wiglaf, so only he can hear. 'Perhaps less ale next time.' He grimaces, his hand also on his eating knife, as mine is, but really, he's not threatened. Neither's King Athelstan, Lady Ælflæd or the archbishop by warriors, but the fire will be a problem.

'Arseholes,' King Athelstan mutters. I realise he's talking about his warriors. Aside from one of the men, who's joined us on the dais, the others are nursing bleeding noses, or are lying, senseless, on the ground.

'Get them out of here,' I roar, and now everyone perceives the problem, stunned faces looking from the fire to the unconscious men. 'If you'd be so kind as to leave,' I instruct the kings, archbishop and Lady Ælflæd, with a slight bow, pulling Cenred with me towards the growing fire. 'There's too much wood,' I grumble to myself, kicking senseless men as I go. 'Wake up and get out of here,' I shout, listening to heavy feet over floorboards. I hope it means King Wiglaf and his guests are beating a hasty retreat from the growing flames. I wouldn't want Lady Ælflæd to suffer either.

I stop as close to the stones surrounding the hearth fire as I can. It's not nearly close enough. Frantically, I pull the feet of the man there whose clothing's already smoking. He's entirely out of it. I realise why as soon as I've stamped on his feet and stopped the flames from spreading. He's senseless, blood bubbling from his nose with each exhalation.

'Get him out of here,' I roar, hoping someone will do so. 'And get some bloody water.'

I'm aware of Cenred at my side, and Ealdorman Ælfstan, but the room has certainly emptied quickly. I glimpse Lady Ælflæd's skirts disappearing into the darkness beyond. There are precious few rushing to aid us in extinguishing the flames. Already, a number of discarded cloaks flare in the glowing flames. The smoke's growing thicker.

'Icel, we can't stop it spreading,' Cenred calls to me, but I shake my head.

'We can. We just need some bloody water.' Abruptly, a sizzling sound reaches my ears. Someone's finally started a water chain. Buckets pass from one to another through the open doorway and outside, where the occasional heavy thud assures me some of the arseholes are still fighting, despite the threat from the fire.

I stamp to the far side of the hearth, and strain to pull clear the wooden boards that have fallen into the flames. They're heavy, and half of them already smoulder.

'Leave it, Icel,' Ealdorman Ælfstan commands. His voice thrums with fear. I'm unsurprised. The fire's spreading quickly, despite the water. I'd expect there to be much more water available. After all, the king has been to see the watermill the monastery's so proud of having. Surely then, there should be a great deal of water.

'Is there no sand or soil?' I call next, when the quantity of water remains low.

'We need to get out of here,' Ealdorman Ælfstan coughs. I turn to view him. It's already difficult to see in the swirling smoke. The flames are making very short work of the wooden boards and other abandoned items of clothing as well as wooden beakers.

'Bollocks,' I complain, abandoning the boards. 'This place is going to burn,' I unwillingly acknowledge, rushing to collect the ealdorman. 'Get everyone out of here,' I call, aware of other figures moving in the smoky gloom. We'll be lucky if no one's left behind.

'Retreat,' I hear Commander Eahric below from the doorway. I cough, and then snatch up a piece of cloth and hold it against my mouth. I don't want to inhale too much smoke.

Quickly, with Ealdorman Ælfstan to one side, and Cenred to the other, we stagger outside, the last to leave the rolling inferno working its way through the building.

'The abbot's going to be pissed,' Cenred coughs, down on his hands and knees, but way back from the doors.

The man who started it all, the holy man beholden to the bishop of Rochester, lies insensible on the ground, not far from us, his robe absorbing all the spilt ale. He has no wounds I can see in the flickering flame light.

'Well, that went bloody well,' King Wiglaf comments sourly, striding through his protective guard to join us. I'm pleased to see he's unhurt. I check for Lady Ælflæd and see her standing behind the guards. I'd like to think she looks at me, but I suspect her gaze is focused on the blazing building.

'My lord king.' Of course, it's the outraged cry of Beornmod of Rochester calling for our attention. Oswy's busy bending and checking on the wounded. So far, he's shown no concern, and neither have I. 'What an outrage, to imperil the life of the archbishop like this. We'd have been safer staying within Wessex,' the bishop coughs. 'You let the Viking raiders attack him at Londinium, and now, well this,' and he indicates the inferno.

I shake my head, eyeing the aggrieved and bright red face of the holy man in the dancing flames.

'I believe, my lord bishop, it was one of your men who started the fight,' the archbishop swiftly intervenes. 'Perhaps the monk is unused to such strong Mercian ale. And as to the fire? Well, who knew that would happen?'

'My lord bishop, I'm astounded you'd blame one of your monks, for this, this horror that's erupted here.'

'Oh no, my lord bishop, you misunderstand me. I blame one of your monks, not one of mine,' the archbishop cautions. Oswy tries not to chuckle, bending low, pretending to aid one of the wounded.

'I...' the bishop begins. 'I...' he persists, even while wood cracks and buckles, and we all move further and further away from the inferno. I shake my head, amazed by how much damage has been done in such a short time. The fighting between the drunken fools has begun to lessen, but not enough for King Wiglaf.

'Desist,' he roars, using his battlefield voice.

Finally, it works. The Mercians are so accustomed to obeying their king, they all stop, many of them mid-strike, and step away from their opponents, only then realising how terrible the fire is.

'This is a disgrace,' King Wiglaf continues. 'Now, Mercians, clear up the mess, and extinguish the flames before they spread to the other monastery buildings. Get digging some fire breaks,' he roars before turning to King Athelstan, Lady Ælflæd and the archbishop. 'My lords, lady, I think it best we remove ourselves to my accommodation. We can conclude our evening there. Icel, Oswy, Cenred and Ealdorman Ælfstan, you'll protect us,' King Wiglaf announces. I follow where he points, Commander Eahric rushing to walk ahead of the king and ensure his accommodation is free from interference.

As we stride through the mass of men, abruptly drained of their desire to fight, mostly because it's unbearably hot as the flames lick their way higher, I note those who'll have black eyes come the morning, and those whose heads will pound. I find I have absolutely no sympathy for them. Damn arses.

'At least we won't have to clean up,' Oswy mutters to me, Wulfheard hurrying to join us, wiping his face clear of the blood showing on his cheek.

'Aye, a small blessing,' I mutter, wrinkling my nose at the aroma of shed blood and ale, the swirling smoke and scent of sweating men. It's not very pleasant.

'But we'll have to remain awake all night,' Ealdorman Ælfstan confirms. 'Those daft sods won't be up to protecting the king, and the flames could act as a beacon to any enemy.' I suppress a groan as we duck inside the king's accommodation. It's usually the abbot's home within the monastery, but now the king has command of it. It's built half of stone and half of wood, and inside it has the advantage of not stinking of ale.

Indeed, the king's servants, not expecting his early return, seem to be taking their ease. At our arrival they abruptly stand and jump to fulfil his requests for ale, wine and water to be made available, for the fire to be built up high and for chairs to be brought close to its light. I suspect they've had too much ale to drink as well because they seem unaware of the fire outside.

'Icel, Oswy, you have door duty,' Wulfheard offers us, while he follows the king closer to the hearth fire. Ealdorman Ælfstan's speaking to the archbishop, their voices low. 'And Cenred. Go and find the bloody scop. Ensure he's well, and bring him here as well,' Wulfheard continues, again running his hand over his bleeding cheek. Ealdorman Ælfstan sweeps an assessing gaze over him, but says nothing else. I imagine, though, come the morning Ealdorman Ælfstan might have a few words to say to his commander, who has evidently been fighting someone. I hope he won.

'One of the East Angles,' Oswy bends low to whisper into my ear.

'Or that damn fool monk from Rochester,' I counter, and we shake hands on it.

There's always time for a wager. Outside, a fierce crack rings through the night and I know, come the morning, there'll be nothing but a smoking ruin where the monks' hall once stood. How the king will make amends, I don't know, but he'll have to do so.

9

The night's long and tedious, the two kings deciding it's better to talk than leave the building for sleep. The archbishop does eventually take his leave, but only to conduct the prayers in the monastery church. Lady Ælflæd quickly retires to her room as well, and I don't manage to more than bow my head towards her as she passes me in the company of Wulfheard. Eventually, the two kings slump to sleep in their chairs, while Oswy and I suppress yawns. Ealdorman Ælfstan departs, escorting the found scop, filled with apologies, to his own lodgings.

'Lucky sod,' Oswy complains. Wulfheard has been suspiciously absent since taking Lady Ælflæd away.

'I'm sure we'll get some sleep, eventually.' I sniff deeply and then regret it. No matter how much I tried to avoid it, I do seem to be sodden with ale. My trews feel sticky at my knees. I'd welcome a bloody bath.

'Perhaps. I won't make it through another day of them talking about bugger all.' He yawns widely, stretching his arms to either side of him so he fills the doorway.

In the growing light of a new day, I'm aware there are still people hurrying to fulfil the king's orders.

'There are going to be a lot of tired people today,' I murmur, inclining my heads towards them.

'But they bloody deserve it,' Oswy comments with no sympathy, yawning so widely his jaw audibly cracks. 'Bloody hell,' he complains, jumping up and down in an effort to wake up.

'I could punch you,' I offer.

'You couldn't,' he counters quickly, his eyes flashing with indignation.

'I bloody could.'

And so we bicker. Better to bicker than fall asleep on duty. With King Wiglaf already embarrassed I dread to think what our punishment might be.

Eventually, Commander Eahric comes himself to relieve us. His eyes are bloodshot.

'Have you had any sleep?' I question him.

'Some, not much. Arseholes,' he glowers. 'But you get some. The king will want his warriors to be very visible later in the day, and most of the bastards have ripped tunics or bleeding faces. You'll have to do the job of looking smart and alert.'

With leaden legs, Oswy and I quickly return to our lodgings, in a smoky dawn, which we find almost empty, although the residual heat in the canvas has me suspecting the others have had some sleep, perhaps like Commander Eahric, only the length of a usual third watch. I pity them.

Eagerly, I curl to sleep and when I'm woken, by an aggrieved Wulfheard's insistent foot, I don't welcome it.

'What?' I huff.

'It's time to get up and perform. The kings and archbishop will reconvene shortly. You need to be there and on your best behaviour.'

From outside, I hear men and women moving around. I've no idea what they're doing, or even how I've managed to sleep through it. Wulfheard stamps to Oswy, who proves to be much harder to wake. He's grouchy and even rolls over and refuses to rise.

'Arsehole,' Wulfheard glowers. Standing, I eye him, grinning.

'Who did that to you?' I ask, indicating his cut cheek while I quickly change my trews. I should have done so before sleeping.

'I don't bloody know. It was a melee in there.'

'Was it?' I question him, eyebrows high. 'Or did you get a little piece of revenge against someone, perhaps one of the warriors from the kingdom of the East Angles? Or one of the bastard West Saxon monks?'

'It was most certainly a melee,' he replies too quickly. My grin broadens.

'Come on, Oswy, you lazy sod. Up and about.' I offer him a kick for his backside, and when that does nothing, I rip his blanket from him before he can grip it tightly and hold it in place.

Outside, I finally understand what's happening. Extra boards have been found, as well as benches, and they're being vigorously washed and cleaned. There are any number of green faces fighting nausea from too much ale, and more black eyes than I've ever seen before, even after a battle.

I smile again, a spring in my step at seeing how buggered they all are.

'Are they attending upon the kings and archbishop?' I ask Wulfheard, nudging him with my elbow, so he winces. 'What else have you done to yourself?'

'It's nothing,' he mutters darkly.

'Well, make sure it doesn't get the wound rot,' I admonish him, striding towards where I see King Wiglaf talking with some of his ealdormen. I note Ealdorman Sigered with a downturned smile. He looks none the worse for last night's little fracas. Ealdorman Ælfstan's also in attendance, and the local lord, Humberht, who looks furious. Lady Ælflæd's also with the king. She looks serene and as though she's slept well. I've still not managed to speak to her.

I listen carefully to what they're saying as we get closer.

'There was no harm done,' King Wiglaf's trying to placate. 'King Athelstan and the archbishop have taken no offence. It was little more than a tavern brawl. I'm sure everyone's experienced one of them before. The loss of the monks' hall, is of course, a problem for the monastery.'

'But my lord king,' Ealdorman Humberht persists. 'News of this will reach Wessex.'

'And? It was one of the Wessex monks who started it.'

'But it was Mercian warriors who finished it.'

'Not really, my good man.' Despite it all, King Wiglaf appears very jolly. 'It was Mercians who stopped it. Now, stop complaining. It's forgotten about, apart from by those with headaches and pulsing black eyes. Although we haven't forgotten about the lack of somewhere to feast this night. We'll resume the discussions of the day.'

'And will that include the land grants, as previously discussed?' Ealdorman Humberht is a bit of an arsehole, I've decided.

'It will, yes,' King Wiglaf murmurs, although, knowing him better, I can tell he's far from happy at being repeatedly questioned.

'Then, perhaps that will be acceptable,' the man mutters, 'but there'll also need to be restitution for the monks.' And he bows towards the king with a curt incline of his head.

Over the top of his deference, I catch King Wiglaf's aggrieved expression and offer him a smile. He shakes his head, but by the time Ealdorman Humberht has stood upright, the king has replaced his expression with one of his more usual unconcerned ones. I imagine this won't be the end of it. No doubt the king will think of a way to resolve the problems.

'With me,' the king commands us all, and now we stride, not towards the hall, but instead to the church. It's the biggest building still standing. In the smoky gloom, it almost looks inviting, until, that is, the abbot stops before the king. His eyes are wild, his clothing dishevelled. Here then is a man who's not had much sleep during the night.

'My lord king,' he expels, 'what's to be done?'

'Fear not,' the king offers with a smile. 'We'll have the hall rebuilt, and of course, compensation for the monastery as well.'

'What sort of compensation?' I shake my head, lips downcast. How quickly these bloody holy men go from wailing and moaning to financial gain for themselves and their communities.

'A freeing of some burdens, I assume that would be acceptable?' the king suggests. The abbot's eyes alight. I'm not alone in growling at the blatant ambition there, as Oswy joins me.

'Perhaps, my lord king.' He half bows. 'I'll consult the archbishop and bishop.'

'There'll be no need to do that,' King Wiglaf counters. 'I well know what will be acceptable. Now, if you'll excuse me, I've other more pressing matters than the events of last night to discuss.'

'Of course, my lord king, of course.' The abbot bows more deeply. We follow King Wiglaf into the church, ablaze with so many candles, it's as if the fire has spread here.

'Arsehole,' I hear King Wiglaf mutter. Oswy grimaces at me. Wiglaf isn't in the best of moods, despite his efforts to look placid, but that doesn't stop the debating. Although there's a great deal of yawning, the two kings and archbishop spend another day discussing no end of matters while Lady

Ælflæd watches on. When it comes to the problem of King Ecgberht in Wessex, the archbishop's conciliatory.

'I'll send a good man to Mercia, and another to the kingdom of the East Angles. They'll speak with my voice, and should anything occur within Canterbury, they'll be able to provide you and your bishops with everything you require.' It's much more than any of us expected, but it makes a frisson of worry worm its way through my body. If even the archbishop is conscious of impending difficulties, Mercia should be as well. And I hope this 'good man' isn't Bishop Beornmod of Rochester. He doesn't seem to be keen to ensure peace prevails between Mercia and Wessex. Once more, I'm sure he assesses me, and not even the delightful presence of Lady Ælflæd dispels my growing unease.

This night there's no feast, but instead the two kings, Lady Ælflæd and the archbishop enjoy a more intimate meal within the abbot's home. Luckily, we're excused from attending it. I take to my bed once more, exhaustion weighing me down. Tomorrow will be the final day of the synod. Then, I suspect, we'll be tasked with escorting King Athelstan back to his kingdom, and then we might be able to return to Tamworth. Hopefully, Ealdorman Muca will be required to escort the archbishop and his bishops back to Londonia and then to Wessex. I don't want to spend any more time in the vicinity of the tricky bishop of Rochester.

There's much splendour, and far less yawning, during the final day of the proceedings. Perhaps inspired by the archbishop's gesture towards Mercia and the kingdom of the East Angles, King Wiglaf's overly generous to the monks. They're gifted a great deal of land including salt pits, lead furnaces and villages in the surrounding area. It's more than adequate recompense for the loss of their main hall, destroyed in the fire. Not only that, but true to his intentions, King Wiglaf also frees the gifted locations from entertaining himself and his ealdormen. And from building royal residences and from the burden of providing accommodation to the king's servants as they travel the kingdom on the king's business. It's generous. Perhaps too generous.

What others don't realise is the king's forced to compensate two of his ealdormen for such largesse towards the monastery because the gift includes land that was theirs. It pleases me Ealdorman Sigered is one of those ealdormen, but not so much Ealdorman Muca. He's done nothing to upset the king, but then, while Sigered grumbles and growls, Ealdorman Muca seems unconcerned. I hear him discussing it with Ealdorman Ælfstan.

'They're welcome to it. The villages aren't the most cooperative and the salt pit's more trouble than it's worth.' Perhaps then, the gift isn't quite as substantial as the abbot seems to think it is. It's possible the king, while appearing to be lavish towards the abbot and monks, is merely placating them and will be pleased to leave the location. I know I will be.

That night, another great feast's planned, and luckily the weather holds fine, and it takes place outside, to the side of the ruined hall. The blackened remnants of the wreck still smoke occasionally. For that reason, no one has yet begun the task of clearing away the broken wooden struts, but it'll need to be accomplished. King Wiglaf has arranged for some of his entourage to remain behind to perform the function. I don't miss that these are many of the men sporting black eyes which are slowing turning green. They'll have to atone for their actions.

At the feast, the scop's once more allowed to perform, songs that don't offend anyone, and there's much less ale on hand for the warriors. The mood's decidedly muted. If not for Lady Ælflæd's presence there, I'd have thought it a waste of good food.

'Serves 'em bloody right,' Oswy mutters, helping himself to one of the ale jugs intended for the king's board. I shake my head, and cover my beaker to prevent him from pouring more into it. I'm not on guard duty, but neither do I wish to have a pounding head the following day when we provide escort duty to King Athelstan on his return to Peterborough.

'You'll regret that,' I murmur to him.

'Maybe, or maybe not,' Oswy offers with a grin, as Maneca and Cenred both lift their beakers to be filled.

The smell of the ale almost turns my stomach. The events of two nights ago saw too much of the stuff on the ground, and my trews still reek of it even though I've had them washed two times since then. I might have to admit defeat and get some new ones.

'Anyway, we weren't involved in the fight, so we needn't be punished,' Oswy continues, drinking deeply of his ale, and belching so loudly the passage of air expelled from within him moves Cenred's hair where he sits opposite him. Cenred wafts his hand beneath his nose, wincing away from

the smell. 'They can enjoy the food,' Oswy continues. I think he's determined to upset others not allowed ale. I don't miss the furious gazes being
sent his way by those with nothing but water to drink. 'Pretty bunch.' Oswy
raises his beaker towards them. The three men turn back to their food,
shoulders hunched with fury.

'If you're not careful, they'll be fighting you without the benefit of being
drink-addled,' Wulfheard growls at Oswy. His wound has healed, and still
Oswy and I don't know how he gained it. We'll find out, eventually. But
perhaps not at Croft. For now, our wager has yet to be settled.

'Then that'll be their fault as well,' Oswy chuckles. 'And I'll put them on
their arses all the same.'

I shake my head at Oswy's swagger, but he's probably correct to be so
confident. If any of the others had been able to fight a damn, the hall might
not have caught fire, and they might not be in disgrace with the king.

10

King Athelstan and King Wiglaf take their leave from one another quietly the following morning, Lady Ælflæd at King Wiglaf's side. The official conclusion of the synod occurred yesterday, in front of everyone, with the archbishop blessing those within the church and asking God to ensure peace prevailed between us all. I doubt he'll get that wish, but I suppose it's worth a try.

While I watch the two exchange handshakes of friendship, I consider why my father, and King Ludica, who came after him, couldn't have done the same with the king-slayer.

'Come on. Hurry up,' Oswy calls to me grouchily, from where he's already mounted. As I suspected would happen, he has a raging headache and has been foul for even the short time he's been awake. I've already seen Wulfheard berate him, and Ealdorman Ælfstan, watching the two kings make their goodbyes, has scowled at him as well. I'd like to feel superior about the whole thing, but while I didn't drink last night, my belly has been grumbling. I suspect some of the meat we were served was either off, or not cooked properly. Covered in herbs and spices, it tasted fine last night, but I and the latrine think differently now. Momentarily, and minded of the many men and women from Wessex at Croft, I was worried someone might have put something in my food, but I'm sure it's just a rolling gut and nothing else. I've taken the herbs Wynflæd prepares for me, in such an eventuality, but so far, they're not helping.

It's going to be as difficult for me today as it is for Oswy. I consider if those preparing the food decided to take some revenge against the warriors for burning down their hall. If they did, they've done well. I know I'm far from alone. Luckily, the two kings and the bishops haven't been afflicted. Lucky bastards.

I move to mount up, only for my belly to roll once more.

'I'll be back.' I hurry to the latrine ditch and, crouching, empty all I can from my aching belly. I know I just need to get everything out, and then I might start to feel better. Returning to Brute, I realise everyone has already left to journey east apart from Cenred. I see the back of Lady Ælflæd entering the abbot's lodgings and appreciate I've still not spoken to her. Nor can I do so now. Not without worrying I might fart or worse.

'Come on. We need to catch them,' Cenred informs me, and, crossing everything, I swing myself into Brute's saddle, hoping it doesn't cause any further discomfort for my arse. Just as I'm about to leave, I sense eyes on me, and turn, somehow unsurprised to find Bishop Beornmod of Rochester watching me from where he's mounted and ready to return to Londonia. As soon as he senses my interest he looks away, but I growl, and not just because my belly clenches painfully. I'll feel much better when he's back in Rochester.

Cenred encourages his horse to a quick canter. I knee Brute onwards, wincing painfully, and worrying I might be sick as well. That would make the day much better.

Much later, after a day of clenching my arse tightly, I'm pleased to dismount without having soiled myself, and tend to Brute.

'How you feeling?' Cenred asks.

'No idea. Not as bad, but bloody hungry. I'm not going to eat though, not today.'

'Probably wise. Look at Oswy. I doubt he's ever going to drink again.'

And Oswy does look terrible. His face is bleached and he's even more thirsty than I am. To avoid Wulfheard's fury, Oswy rode with me and Cenred, to the back of the escort. There, we've all tried to keep away from Wulfheard and the appraising gaze of King Athelstan. I've noticed his warriors aren't suffering with a bad gut, and indeed, neither are the rest of Ealdorman Ælfstan's warriors.

'Get some bloody rest,' Wulfheard growls roughly to me, as he moves amongst the men and horses, ensuring everyone is well. 'Oswy.' He lifts his voice to the other man. 'You have the middle watch tonight.' I wince to hear the order. It's a terrible punishment, but Oswy nods, his face green, showing he accepts it for what it is. 'And next time,' Wulfheard continues, 'do yourself a favour and drink a little less, you bloody fool.'

We once more arrive at Peterborough Monastery before dusk. It's been a long day of travelling, but while I'm hungry, my gut's being much kinder to me. Even Oswy's perked up.

King Athelstan of the East Angles is welcomed within by the abbot, and I breathe a sigh of relief. Come the morning, he won't be our responsibility any more.

'Icel, you can have first watch tonight, with Maneca and Kyre,' Wulfheard orders us. I don't have a problem with the duty. As I listen to the other assignments, I appreciate Wulfheard's not going to punish Oswy any more after last night's watch duty. He gets to spend the night sleeping within the monks' main hall.

'Are we going back to Tamworth?' I ask Wulfheard.

He shakes his head, eyes flashing. 'No, we're bound for Londonia after this. We need to provide some relief for Ealdorman Muca's men after the attack by the Viking raiders. Only then do we return to Tamworth.'

I nod. 'At least we don't need to escort the archbishop and bishops back to Wessex.'

'Indeed,' Wulfheard agrees. The fervent activity of the escort eventually calms, the horses stabled for the night, and King Athelstan welcomed within by the abbot and monks. For this reason, the abbot didn't attend at Croft. Now I'm sure the pair are busy talking about events there. As the night draws in, and I eat some bread, but not much else, I take myself to guard the main gateway. Maneca and Kyre are slower to arrive. Before the gates are closed, I eye the river where I fought the Viking raiders. It's so peaceful now. There's no hint of what happened here those few summers ago. There's nothing to show of the men who lost their lives. Instead, there's the hum of the monks at their prayers, and the shush of the water in the river.

Come the morning, King Athelstan will ride over the bridge and be back in the kingdom of the East Angles. I consider if I'll ever see him again. I hope not, but that will depend on whether he continues to be an ally of Mercia or not. That remains to be seen. But he's of a similar age to King Wiglaf. Neither man will live forever. At some point in the future, there'll be change. I only hope it also includes King Ecgberht. If I understand it correctly, he's older than both Wiglaf and Athelstan. Admittedly, his son will be problematic when he's king of Wessex. I don't wish to hurry that eventuality.

Perhaps, then, it would be good for Wessex to have a different foe to face. At some point, they'll have to counter the threat from the Viking raiders at Sheppey. If not, the enemy will grow more and more ambitious, just as Wessex has towards Mercia.

There's much for me to digest as the gates close on that scene, and Kyre and Maneca join me. But it's a peaceful night, and with the dawn, King Athelstan bids farewell to us with little fanfare. We do the same to him, and then we journey south. Of course, only after we've ensured King Athelstan is firmly on the other side of the river. There might be an accord with the kingdom of the East Angles, but there's still a lack of trust, especially from Wulfheard, who commands us. The two bishops are kinder with their farewells. All the same, I'm pleased the tasks are concluded. The religious synod of Croft will perhaps be swiftly forgotten about, especially once the monks' main hall is rebuilt after the fire damage. There are other worries to consume me.

* * *

We find Londonia peaceful. The archbishop and his bishops have thankfully already left because Wulfheard didn't force us to rush to Londonia from Peterborough. Ealdorman Muca meets us as we dismount within Londinium, a rueful smile on his face. I note Lord Wigmund isn't there. He rarely leaves his bedchamber.

'Well met.' Ealdorman Muca walks towards Wulfheard and they grasp forearms. Ealdorman Muca's a staunch warrior of Mercia, but his days of fighting are behind him. However, he has a firm grip on events within

Londonia now the threat of the conspiracy has receded, and Mercia must guard against attack from the Viking raiders.

'My warriors are looking forward to a few days away from here,' Muca confirms congenially. He shakes his head, his eyes sparkling. 'Sometimes, warriors are contrary bastards. They both do and don't want the enemy to be attacking.'

'Not so much that,' Oswy interjects. 'A little threat without the actual attack and then I'm happy.' As we remove the horses to the stable and generally make ourselves comfortable within the fort's main building, I'm aware it does seem very quiet. There's no wind to trouble us, and the sun's warming on our backs. The men and women we encounter are relaxed and even desultory in their duties. Maybe we all deserve some peace and quiet.

But of course, we're not to get it.

* * *

Four days after arriving at Londonia, already finding the task tedious, even though I do get to spend time with Theodore and Gaya, a messenger arrives from the west. He's escorted to Wulfheard although he asks for Lord Wigmund.

'My lord?' the man questions, his face dusty aside from where sweat has streaked through it.

'Not quite. Just Wulfheard.'

'I was bid to seek out Lord Wigmund.'

'And yet you find yourself talking to me. I'm the commander of Ealdorman Ælfstan's warriors. Now, get on with it. Anything so urgent should be shared as opposed to bickered about. But first, what's your name?'

'I'm Æthelred. I'm known to Edwin and others of Lord Coenwulf's warriors. And, of course, my... Wulfheard.' Æthelred inclines his head, and then shares his message. 'Lord Coenwulf of Kingsholm has sent me. Another messenger has gone to Tamworth.' Immediately I'm on my guard, thinking all sorts of terrible things, but before the words can escape my mouth, Æthelred gets to the point. 'The kingdom of Wessex is under attack from Viking raiders.'

'Excellent.' Wulfheard's face splits into a wide grin, but the messenger hasn't finished. Instead, he looks pained.

'If they weren't so close to Mercia, it would be good news. But they're at Carhampton, which some would say is far from Mercia, but with their ships, and a favourable wind, the distance could be covered quickly. It's too close to Mercia for Lord Coenwulf's liking. He requests the king or his son send reinforcements to protect the border with Wessex, and the River Severn, in case of such an eventuality.'

At this, Wulfheard flicks a glance towards me, but it's Goðemon who answers.

'Carhampton's deep within Wessex territory, surely?'

'It is, and it isn't. The worry is there are reports of over twenty shiploads of Viking raiders, and they're not far from reaching the River Severn, as I said, with a good wind and a will to battle the rigours of the currents.'

I feel my forehead furrow at this. My appreciation of Wessex is woeful and yet I must have travelled that way with the traders to reach Southampton. Now Wulfheard looks to me, but the location means little to me. I shrug my shoulders. I recall Bristol, after that it appeared to be a collection of small ports and quays indistinguishable one from another.

'It's on the dragon's leg, admittedly, but Lord Coenwulf thinks no chances should be taken. King Ecgberht has been forced to muster every warrior he has to counter the threat, according to the reports he's heard.'

Wulfheard nods, his expression pensive. I'm surprised he doesn't know where Carhampton is. After all, he's taught me much about Wessex and Mercia. 'The king's also being informed?' Wulfheard questions, to be sure.

'He is, Wulfheard, yes.'

Wulfheard shakes his head from side to side. 'We're in a difficult predicament. We're tasked with protecting Londonia while Ealdorman Muca and his warriors get some rest. There are few of us here. Ealdorman Ælfstan has returned to his holdings, so I can't seek advice from him either. We can't leave the king's son and Londonia unprotected, not after the last attack from the Viking raiders.'

Æthelred nods, biting his lip, perhaps to stop from saying something he might regret.

'But Lord Coenwulf isn't a man to panic. He's shown himself to be staunch. I'll have to send word to the king myself, and ask for his advice. It's to be hoped a plan is already in place.'

'Perhaps, Wulfheard,' the man concedes. I find it amusing he must keep biting back his 'my lord' response. I imagine Wulfheard wouldn't take kindly to it when the man's been told not to address him as such.

'How many warriors are in twenty shiploads?' Wulfheard questions.

'Depends on the size of the bloody ship,' Oswy mutters, but if he intended his comment not to be heard, he fails. We all turn to look at him, Wulfheard shaking his head.

'A lot more than went to the Isle of Sheppey,' Godemon comments, and this is sobering. We all remember fighting on the Isle of Sheppey, as well as outside the walls of Londinium a few weeks ago.

'And a lot more than in the kingdom of the East Angles, as well,' Oswy suggests, trying to redeem himself from his earlier comment.

'So, there are many Viking raiders attacking King Ecgberht of Wessex south of here, and somehow,' Wulfheard pauses, 'this isn't the bloody good news for Mercia it should be.'

I'm not alone in holding my tongue. Indeed, silence falls amongst us. No doubt, I'm not alone in considering the warriors we've already lost fighting the Viking raiders.

'Bollocks,' Wulfheard eventually expels. 'I can spare five of you to ride with Æthelred and assess what's happening. As we don't know if these are different to the men who attacked Londinium recently, we must maintain our defence here. For the rest of us, we'll have to wait for Ealdorman Muca to return or Ælfstan, or for new orders from the king. Oswy, Icel, Cenred, Maneca and Kyre, you'll go to Kingsholm and seek our Lord Coenwulf. If needed, you can cross into Wessex and discover what's happening. But, don't get caught up in anything. This is Wessex's fight, not ours.' His caution is firm and he particularly holds my gaze, which I find a little insulting. But I don't argue with him.

I'd complain about being forced on the road once more, but I welcome it. I'd like to see Lord Coenwulf's children, as well as Lady Ælflæd's son, because they weren't at Croft. Neither have I actually managed to speak with Lady Ælflæd. I'd also like to spend time with Edwin and Eadburg and discover how married life suits them. Indeed, if it weren't for the Viking raiders, it would be a most enjoyable encounter. But of course, if it's not

Wessex warriors, or Welsh ones, or those from the kingdom of the East Angles, then there's always the bloody Viking raiders to prevent peace upon this island.

'You leave in the morning, at first light,' Wulfheard commands. 'Ensure you have everything you need.' Æthelred inclines his head towards Wulfheard, but the show of obeisance is lost on my commander. Instead, Wulfheard strides from the main hall, no doubt to seek an audience with Lord Wigmund, who demands to be kept informed of even the most tedious of details from his bedchamber. Admittedly, this isn't a tedious detail, but in the last few days Wulfheard has grown increasingly frustrated by the stipulations of the king's son. The burden of keeping Londonia safe from Wessex or Viking raider attack has been replaced by something much worse: the understanding that he, and the rest of us, simply don't know what will happen between the Wessex and Viking raider force.

'I can't see King Ecgberht will have the force to overwhelm them. If they didn't stir themselves to get rid of the bastards on the Isle of Sheppey who have three ships, or at least did when they attacked Londinium, what are they going to do with so many more of them at Carhampton?' Oswy's words are far from reassuring, but they're not wrong, either. King Ecgberht and his son have done nothing to protect the Isle of Sheppey from the enemy. Why then would they bestir themselves to stop an attack on Carhampton? And if they don't, then the seaway to Mercia does indeed lie open to the enemy. I recall only too well how quick a ship can move.

I growl under my breath, taking myself to Brute to ensure his equipment is clean and ready for our journey west. We don't know what we'll find when we get there. We've faced the Viking raiders once this summer. It appears it might only be the first such encounter.

11

We leave before it's light. I don't think any of us has slept. Neither has Wulfheard. I've heard him stamping about on the battlements for much of the night. He's as restful as a sick belly.

'I don't like this,' he complains, while bidding us farewell. 'Don't do anything bloody stupid. I won't have Ealdorman Ælfstan berating me for losing nearly half of his warrior band.'

I grimace, and then grimace again as he stamps his way towards me. His face is filled with unease.

'Icel, I charge you with being the most careful of all. Be wary of being alone with any of the Wessex bastards. This could be the very opportunity they're looking for, and Ealdorman Ælfstan, not to mention King Wiglaf, will be furious with me should anything untoward befall you.'

I swallow back the apprehension I was already feeling, and offer Wulfheard what I hope is a jaunty retort. 'The bastards won't get me. I assure you of that.'

He grips my shoulder and grunts. I don't think he's at all convinced. Admittedly, neither am I.

Behind us, Wulfgar, Godeman, Landwine, Ordlaf, Uor and Waldhere also wait to say farewell. They're alert – well, three of them are. Wulfgar, Landwine and Uor have managed to sleep. Godeman and Waldhere have been on guard duty with Wulfheard, the three of them forced to remain awake all night. Lord Wigmund's personal escort will have to be pressed into service in the coming days. I can see Wulfheard will have difficulties in doing that. The twelve men, who have a collection of allegiances to Lord Wigmund, King Wiglaf, Ealdorman Sigered and Ealdorman Muca, aren't an easy lot. I doubt more than two of them respect one another, and none of them are much in awe of Wulfheard. They don't like Lord Wigmund much either. It'll be better once Ealdorman Muca and his men return, although that's still ten days in the future. Ealdorman Muca has an uneasy accord with Lord Wigmund, and his warriors are respectful towards the king's son.

'We won't,' Oswy assures Wulfheard, but it's Wulfheard's gaze on me that has me offering assurances I'm not sure I feel compelled to keep. If Kingsholm's threatened, and with it the children I've already nearly died to protect, more than once, I'll probably take action Wulfheard wouldn't agree with. That doesn't even factor in what I would do to protect Lady Ælflæd, Edwin and Eadburg. Equally, if we can cause King Ecgberht and his bloody son any difficulties, then we should do so. I'd be more than happy to play my part in that, especially with the memory of the threat from Eanstan, and the unease about what happened when fighting the Viking raiders, never far from my mind.

'Make sure you don't,' Wulfheard huffs. With a smack for Brute's backside, we erupt into the grey dawn, the messenger leading the way, although we all know it well enough. We've undertaken the journey on many occasions in the past. Indeed, Brute might know the way without me even having to direct him. We've travelled along the River Thames repeatedly. We've ridden towards the mouth of the River Thames seeking out the enemy from Wessex and from the Isle of Sheppey. We've ridden far inland, to where the River Thames is little more than a gurgling stream, and the division between Mercia and Wessex becomes hazy at best, and perhaps more down to personal preference than Wiglaf or Ecgberht might like.

We pass Laleham Gulls the following morning, all of us pleased to see the river's running high for the time of year, which means the Wessex bastards won't be crossing there, but making it easier for Viking raiders in their pestilent ships to travel deep within the physical boundary between Mercia and Wessex. It's as though conditions can never be entirely right to keep Mercia safe from attack.

Two days later, we arrive at Kingsholm, the horses having travelled well, although not at their greatest speed. It wouldn't do to exhaust them before we reach our destination and have to, perhaps, venture inside Wessex. We've been kind to them, and to ourselves. In recent weeks, we've travelled a long way, to Londonia, to Peterborough, to Croft, and then repeated many of those journeys in reverse. The horses have at least had some time to recover within Londinium. But Brute's never happy when stabled. He much prefers to be racing through the landscape. I admit, I enjoy it as well.

As we ride closer, I notice Kingsholm's great wooden gate is barred and shut even though it's the middle of the day. It reminds me of my journey here with my uncle, when Wessex overwhelmed Mercia, which feels like lifetimes ago. However, there are people outside Kingsholm, tending to the burgeoning crops. I feel my forehead furrow when I see so many horses paddocked between some of the highest hedgerows, just starting to turn green once more. That's a new one. It seems Lord Coenwulf has either increased the size of his warrior band, or he's begun breeding horses. That perhaps shouldn't surprise me. His time in Frankia opened his eyes to many new possibilities.

'Hail,' Æthelred calls as we ride towards the gates and come to a stop. Quickly, the men on guard duty, one of whom I'm sure is Edwin, recognise the man who leads us, and allow one of the gates to be opened. Before the door shuts on us, I look towards Gloucester. It's not a huge settlement, mostly centred around the church there, but it's close to the River Severn. Even closer than Kingsholm. I wish they had walls as tall and well built as those which shelter Kingsholm itself. However, everyone in that settlement can rely on Lord Coenwulf to protect them. For now, then, Kingsholm takes precautions during the daytime, but still has people tending crops and horses, and the people of Gloucester also go about their daily business. I consider if the gates are shut because it frees up the guards to perform other tasks. It wouldn't surprise me.

I dismount quickly, and feel warm hands on me. I turn to embrace Edwin, who greets me with a beaming grin on his familiar face, although it remains thickly bearded.

'You look well,' he comments, standing back to appraise me, as though I'm a small child about to be measured against a horse's leg.

'You don't look bad yourself, either. Tell me, how's married life?' Here I detect a slight wince on Edwin's face and immediately worry all isn't well between him and Eadburg. That would be a terrible shame. She waited for him while he was in exile with Lord Coenwulf. He waited for her. But perhaps her injuries cause her difficulties that only became relevant once she was married.

'No, no, nothing bad. She isn't here, and neither are the children, Lady Ælflæd or young Cynewise. Lord Coenwulf's taken extreme precautions and sent them to the king's side for protection within Tamworth.' I don't deny the news dismays me, but only because I wished to see Lady Ælflæd, and the children. I've been in the same place as her twice this year and not managed to speak to her. Now I'm at her home, and still I won't be speaking to her any time soon. It would also have been good to discover how Lady Cynewise's progressing with her studies in healing.

'Then that's good,' I state around the pang of my disappointment.

'Perhaps,' Edwin mutters. 'Eadburg's with child. It'll be a hard journey for her.'

'Then you have my heartfelt congratulations. Your mother will help her within Tamworth and with the children, I'm sure.' At this, Edwin's worries are banished from his face.

'She will, yes, and that's good. The boys are getting rowdy. They might benefit from Commander Eahric's eagle eye over them, as well. Maybe discourage some of the cheek and make them more obedient.'

'They're only small, surely they don't need that yet? Would you truly wish that on them, after he made our lives hell?'

'I would, yes. Look at us now. Fine warriors and men of Mercia.' He stands proudly, chest jutted out. I note the thickness of his beard, and the muscles along his arms.

I laugh, not prepared to remind Edwin of how Commander Eahric used to make his life hell. The advantage of distance through time is how we forget such things, even the pangs of grief growing lesser.

'Now, come and get Brute settled. Lord Coenwulf will wish to speak to you. Why are there only five of you?' Edwin thinks to ask. 'And why were you in Londonia? The messenger was to speak to Lord Wigmund.'

'We were sent to relieve the force there. After all, they've been in place since before last summer. The ealdorman thought everyone deserved some time away. So, Wulfheard and the rest of us have been there. He's spared five of us, but hopes news will come from the king soon.'

'It needs to,' Edwin mutters. 'But we'll talk shortly. I'm on guard duty. I mustn't derelict my duty.'

'Get to it, then,' I command him, and lead Brute towards the familiar stable building, where Hatel and Pega both greet me warmly.

'Icel, stop growing,' Pega complains, moving aside to allow Brute within.

Hatel looks up from cleaning a horse's hoof with brush and hoof pick.

'And tell that horse to stop growing as well,' he adds. 'And, ensure he knows he's not to kick any more stable doors down.' I wince, reminded Brute spent much time here last summer. My purse still feels the loss of those coins paid in recompense.

'Tell me, why are there so many horses?'

'Two reasons,' Pega offers. 'Lord Coenwulf's growing his warrior band, and he also intends to trade good horses. After he returned from Frankia, we received five new mares, good ones as well, a little taller than the usual we have around here. Lord Coenwulf will breed from them and make a good profit, if I know horses.'

I run my eyes along those animals inside the stables, looking for Lady Ælflæd's horse, Sewenna, but of course, she's not here because her rider has gone to Tamworth.

Kingsholm isn't my home, and yet it feels like coming home, more than at Budworth. Much here is familiar to me, as it is within Tamworth. There's also sorrow, however. As I leave the stable, and Brute, chewing contentedly on a hay net, unbidden, I glance towards the church. I know King Coelwulf, the first of his name, lies interred there. If he'd lived. If he's not been overthrown by my father. Well, how different all this might have been.

I catch sight of some of the monks, noting Brother Fassel. I'm surprised to find him bent double. The passage of time seems to be increasing with the more summers I have to my name.

We make our way to the main hall, and not a moment too soon, for Lord Coenwulf emerges from his hall, walking stick to hand, and comes up short on seeing us, a smile breaking out on his careworn face. He's not ageing well either.

'Ah, Icel and Oswy.' His eyes narrow in thought, and then he beams. 'And Cenred, Kyre and Maneca. It's good to see you. I wish it were under better circumstances.' Of course, Lord Coenwulf knows us all from our time rescuing him from the Isle of Sheppey. 'Come within. I've had food and ale prepared.' His welcome is warm, despite his obvious agitation. 'Some might say I'm jumping at shadows, but the news from Wessex is dire. If the Viking raiders are there, and so many of them, Mercia must prepare, although I hear you had your own problems before Croft.' Now I consider it, I realise Coenwulf wasn't at Croft, although his sister was. He was wise to avoid it. It was tedious.

I nod, my eyes raking in the familiar line of shields on display within the main hall, all of them, I notice, clear of dust and perhaps even with new lines of paint on them. Lord Coenwulf might well be a different man since his return from exile in Frankia.

'Come, sit.' He takes us towards the hearth fire, embers turning over although there are no huge logs upon it. It's not a bitter day outside, the warmth needed simply to reach the darker, shadowed corners of the room.

Oswy appraises the food with a broad grin, but I'm more hesitant. Like Lord Coenwulf, I share his concerns about this huge force of Viking raiders in Wessex.

'Tell us all you know,' I ask when none of the others take the lead. Perhaps they expect me, the youngest of them all, but of course, a lord in my own right, to conduct the conversation. Luckily, my curiosity doesn't make it a hardship.

'We've had reports from multiple people, traders mostly, but also from those across the River Severn, that the fleet is huge and causes the Wessex people no end of trouble. There are fears the Cornish will aid the Viking raiders. There's little love between them and the Wessex king. It's the number of enemy that worries me the most. They say there have been isolated attacks along the coastal area, from where the River Severn feeds into the sea. Believe it or not,' and here Lord Coenwulf pauses and meets my gaze, 'there's little distance, truly, between the people of the Welsh kingdoms and those within Cornwall. On a clear day, you can see almost the entire distance.'

'Share all you've heard,' I suggest.

He nods, offering a brief smile as an apology for his muddled explosion of news. 'In my agitation, I jumble it all. Now, where to begin. Well, the first word came from traders at Gloucester. They spoke of evading four Viking raider ships before managing to make a run towards the River Severn. Next, there were reports of burning visible from the high peaks of the escarpment, in a southerly direction.'

He points towards the escarpment we've used in the past but not on this journey. I nod. I know of the viewpoint. Indeed, the other men groan with memories of the place. It wasn't kind on beast or man. It did allow for a stunning view of the surrounding landscape, however.

'Next, those who trade in Gloucester from the other side of the River Severn came with tales of ships stopping in isolated locations, and the theft of sheep. To begin with, we thought little of it. Sheep are always being stolen. Fires are a regular occurrence but then one trader ship limped into Gloucester, missing half its oars and three of the crew. They told of an attack out at sea, and being boarded by an enemy they weren't expecting to see. The ship originated in Frankia and while the Viking raiders aren't unknown to them, here, in the sea between Cornwall and the Welsh kingdoms, they didn't expect to encounter them. Since then, there have been more and more reports, and even some people escaping into Mercia across the land boundary separating the two kingdoms.'

My forehead furrows at this. 'That's a long way from Carhampton.'

'It is, yes, Icel. But these people are terrified. I sent Cuthwalh and Edwin to speak with them. It was more whispers and rumour than anything, with little hard evidence for the Viking raiders, but fear's running through them, otherwise they wouldn't risk coming to Mercia. They know we're hardly friends. I would expect them to go to Malmesbury, where the abbey would take them in. But no, they're gambling on coming to Mercia.'

'And you've also sent word to the king?'

'Yes, and my sisters and sons and my nephew are also on their way to Tamworth. I won't risk them. Kingsholm's too close to the River Severn. Tamworth, while on two rivers, is at least trickier to reach. The Viking raiders would need to follow the River Trent from the north and come south that way. Here, we're much easier to visit because we're so much closer to the sea. I don't believe there have been reports of attack from the north, have there? I don't suppose the king has heard from Northumbria.' Lord Coenwulf once more sounds anxious, perhaps realising he should have considered an attack from the north as well.

'Not as far as we know,' I confirm quickly, keen to offer reassurance. My mind's busy. I'm unsure what we can do. Oswy has other plans.

'Tomorrow,' he announces, 'we'll seek out the truth of the rumours. We'll journey south, following the coastline.'

'Wouldn't it be better to wait for more Mercians?' Lord Coenwulf fusses.

'Perhaps, but a small force will move more quickly, and hopefully, evade detection.'

'Do you think that's for the best?' Lord Coenwulf reiterates. I don't think he's a weak man, but with his limp, and terrible experiences at the hands of the Viking raiders, he only has a light touch on his terror. I pity him for such fear even while understanding it only too well. If I didn't know I could kill my enemy with a well-placed stab, or even a crafty punch to the throat, I'd be anxious as well. There was a time when I wished to be a healer, when even watching my uncle training filled me with fear. Those days are long gone, and yet a niggle at the back of my mind reminds me I still don't know if I was intentionally pushed into the enemy at Londinium, or if I imagined it all. Even strong men should be wary, I remind myself. Arrogance will only bring my death much closer.

'It would be better than waiting here and feeding off the terror of the Wessex refugees and traders. The king will want facts. He'll want to know if we need to move to protect the coast and riverways, or if the Viking raiders are content with facing the Wessex warriors, which of course, we hope.'

'Of course, of course,' Lord Coenwulf acquiesces. 'And yes, there are reports of some going straight to Malmesbury Abbey, as I said,' he confirms. I'm listening with half an ear to the discussion. I'm not looking forward to what Oswy proposes. I've spent far too much time in Wessex in recent years. I wish to be in Mercia, with Mercians, not to the south, where even the way I speak marks me as different.

'Come, lads.' Oswy tries to cheer our glum faces. 'It'll be better than playing escort duty to the archbishop of Canterbury and King Athelstan of the East Angles. We might even get to blood our seaxes and I'd welcome doing so. All this conspiracy and politicking makes a man hunger for a simple test of strength against an adversary. I hardly got to test my blade's sharpness at Londinium.'

I shake my head at the broad grin on Oswy's face.

I suppose he makes a good argument. I too would welcome no politics but whether I like the prospect of exchanging it for a fight with such a vast force of Viking raiders as would fill twenty ships, I'm far from convinced.

12

Once more, we leave at dawn, first directing our horses towards the settlement of Gloucester, to assess what's happening there, and then when we learn nothing further than what Lord Coenwulf has told us, following the River Severn to where it eventually meets the sea.

First, however, I'm distracted by odd shapes in the landscape, not far south from Gloucester. Well, not far really. It's taken over half a day to reach it, at a steady trot. We're not pushing the horses. Our intention is to discover what we can, and do it quickly. As such, we carry only the smallest amount of food for the horses, and for ourselves, and will rely mostly on streams to provide us with water. We don't wish to weigh the beasts down. But, if we were going to travel as far as Carhampton, we'd probably need more supplies than we currently have.

'What is this place?' I call to my fellow warriors, eyes round with surprise at what I've discovered. I bring Brute to a stop, too fascinated to ride past without paying more attention. Inland from the River Severn, I detect shapes jutting out of the grassy ground, and if I squint, and tilt my head from side to side, I'm convinced I can detect the shadow of a shape running through the grass. It looks far too straight to be naturally occurring. Brute walks towards a small stream, and I dismount so he can drink deeply. The water looks clear and inviting. In fact, the whole place appears welcoming, with a gentle breeze drying the sweat from my face, and endeavouring to dry that which snakes down my back from beneath my byrnie. It's not even that warm, but riding isn't just a task for my horse to complete.

'A ruined settlement, nothing more,' Cenred dismisses, his eyes never leaving the expanse of the River Severn, unlike mine, although he's also dismounted and allows his horse to drink.

Intrigued, I allow Brute to walk forwards when he's finished, keen to see what this ruin might be.

'Icel, we don't have time for this,' Oswy calls, annoyed, but Maneca stays with me. He's as curious as I am. Cenred might dismiss the place as a ruin, but I sense something else here.

'It was a settlement, many hundreds of years ago,' Maneca decides, leading his horse through what I decide is the remnant of a turf embankment, and ditch, long since filled in, or rather filled with the accumulation of windblown soil and other items. 'I've seen places like this before.'

'Was it built by the Romans?' I question. 'They seemed to get everywhere, although, there's no road here, is there?' I furrow my brow, trying to decide if I can detect a road, like Watling Street. But I can't. There are animal tracks and sheep trails, but nothing as substantial as the roads we often travel, able to move quickly over their surfaces.

'Who knows? Maybe. Although...' Maneca's eyes narrow. He too tilts his head from side to side. 'I believe that mound over there isn't a natural hill.'

I look where he points, and feel a shudder work its way along my body at the sight of the tall grass embankment, rising to about twice my height. It's unusual. There are hills in the distance, stretching away, but this is quite incongruous. I almost cross myself, as the holy bishops do, but stop myself, gripping Brute's reins more tightly. I won't be scared by something that looks so innocuous.

'You feel it as well?' Maneca comments, nodding. 'It can be like that. In Londinium, where it's little more than stone and statues that survive, it feels more normal. Here, in the countryside, with the wind rustling your hair, it's hard not to jump at shadows. There are any number of hummocks like this one, and arrangements of standing stones as well, not at all like the crosses the old priests had built and from which they preached, back in the days when Christianity was newly come to this island.'

I nod, not willing to trust my voice because it would betray my fear.

'Come on, before Oswy gets even angrier than he already is.' And Maneca rides away, leaving me alone to eye the grassy rise. I'd like to explore the place further. Behind me, it's now easy to see where grass and weeds have reclaimed old stone walls, hidden now, but which could perhaps be released with some effort. Only the smallest glimpses of the stone walls are visible. I can also tell where fields used to be enclosed, with remnants of hedgerows marching close to the turfed embankment hinting at when they were more complete. I consider why the place was abandoned and who once lived here. Who died here? I shiver again, and as Brute paws the ground, a shrill nicker erupts from his lips.

I turn him, aware the others are almost out of sight. I swallow, and mount up, and encourage Brute to greater speed. I only slow him when I'm back with my four fellow warriors.

'Scare yourself?' Cenred taunts, but he's grinning.

'No.' But my response is too hastily given.

'We've all done it. You should see these places with weird stones, some together, some apart, all bloody huge. It's enough to scare yourself half to death, and believe in all that crap about mystical creatures inhabiting the shadows between this life and the next. Not that you believe in all that rubbish, not with your healer skills.'

'Well...' I pause, aware Wynflæd and the Wolf Lady aren't above asking for some aid from these spirits with their charms and talismans. Not, of course, I need say that. Anyway, my unease with the place wasn't to do with the presence of such things, but rather with the ghosts of those who once lived there. Sometimes, I realise, it's difficult to truly comprehend people lived so long ago no one even remembers the settlements they dwelt within any more. Not even their memorial to the dead, or the ditch they enclosed their home with, leaves much mark on the landscape. Faced with an enemy, now, deep within Wessex, it's somehow reassuring to appreciate that, no matter what, people will prevail. Mercia will always be Mercia.

With that thought, I turn my attention back to what I should be doing. Hunting the enemy, and ensuring they're not hiding within Mercia.

The River Severn grows ever wider and then before me is the swell of the sea. There's little wind on land, but the waves are heaving, white-peaked and vicious-looking. I look at my fellow warriors.

'It's better on land than at sea,' I mutter darkly, reminded of my journey with the traders last year. It took me some time to get accustomed to the swell of the sea beneath my feet, when there was little but wood between me and the watery depths.

'I imagine it is,' Oswy suggests. He, like me, much prefers being on dry land than on board a boat. We know we make poor fishermen. I'm also not a good trader. The only item I purchased on that trip, Bicwide, caused me many difficulties. Admittedly, in the end, he also solved many. Now he's at Budworth, being cared for alongside Wine. I consider if Lord Coenwulf might like to add him to his breeding stock. He's a fine, tall horse, and lacks the contrariness of Brute. I wouldn't wish anyone to breed my disagreeable horse.

'I don't see anything from here,' Cenred comments, his hand above his eyes to shield them from the sun.

'It's a bloody long way,' I comment. 'It took us over seven days to travel to Southampton on board ship. And that was with a good wind.'

'Hum,' Cenred muses. I leave him to it. I also peer towards the south. What do I hope to see? A burning settlement, grey smoke rising into the air to show us the direction to take, or a host of Viking raiders, attacking the Wessex warriors?

'We carry on,' Oswy asserts.

'We're almost in Wessex,' I caution.

'And that's where the enemy are, if there are any enemy,' Oswy reminds me, his grin broadening.

'Truly, you mean to ride into Wessex and risk a fight with them as well as the Viking raiders?'

'Why, young Icel, you're not frightened, are you?'

'No,' I comment angrily. 'But I am bloody sensible.'

'Perhaps you are, although I think we might argue with you about that,' he suggests. 'Would you rather stay here, then?'

'No.' But really, I would, and Oswy knows it. I suspect the others would rather linger as well. But Oswy, having been too sick to take part in much of the fighting last summer at Londonia, is keen for another good battle. The brawl at Croft hasn't satisfied him. Far from it. Neither, if he's to be believed, did he kill enough Viking raiders at Londinium.

'We carry on. I doubt we'll encounter anyone who wants to fight us. After all, we're not Viking raiders.'

All the same, I remain unhappy about it. While the River Thames is a physical boundary between Mercia and Wessex, where it doesn't flow, the borderland is more fluid. No doubt, King Ecgberht will have an ealdorman in command here who doesn't much like Mercians. I hope we don't encounter him, or his warriors.

'We should seek out their defences, the dyke, or whatever it is,' Oswy decides. 'From there, we might be able to see more.'

'Then lead on, Oswy,' Cenred calls. I detect unease amongst us all, but we were sent to discover what's happening within Wessex and with the Viking raiders, and that we must do.

Not that we make it much further that day, although we're certainly in Wessex and not Mercia any more. We don't encourage the horses to great speed, instead picking a path following the coastline as closely as possible. It might make us visible to the enemy, but so far, we've come upon few people, and many of them were fisher people, and all those we have seen have merely stayed away from us. Mounted warriors are to be feared, whether they're Mercians or Wessex warriors.

For most of the day, the kingdoms of the Welsh opposite us over the expanse of water are visible. I realised when I travelled with the traders just how close the two places were to one another, but now it seems as though they're far apart. On board a ship it would be easy to turn with the direction of the wind and go between Mercia or Wessex and the Welsh kingdoms. With the aid of a horse, it's much slower and would take a lot more effort, as the River Severn would need crossing. That, then, is where the Viking raiders have an advantage.

We stop for the night in an abandoned animal barn, within sight of the sea. The sound of the waves is a counterpart to the snoring of my allies when they sleep as I keep guard for the final part of the night. I can't decide whether it's soothing or terrifying. How easy would it be for the Viking raiders to come ashore under cover of darkness and attack?

The next day, we continue, evading the settlements close to the wide river, but making use of a wooden bridge to cross. I don't know its name. I feel we're going too deeply within Wessex and there are more and more people who see us, but none of them ask us what we're doing, cowed by the visible presence of shields, swords and seaxes on our weapons belts.

'Shouldn't we make more effort to move under cover of darkness?'

Maneca questions Oswy, and I'm pleased he does so. I've been thinking the same.

'Why? No one here seems to care who we are. They merely fear our blades.'

'But that won't always be the case. There must be an ealdorman who rules here? One of his people will tell him, won't they?'

Oswy shrugs, looking far from concerned.

'If that happens, we'll find the Fosse Way and run north. We can easily make it to Malmesbury Abbey from here. They'll intervene in any fight the Wessex warriors want to start. But I suspect everyone's more concerned with what's happening to the south.'

'All the same. We're not here to start a fight with Wessex.'

'You're right,' Oswy admits grudgingly. 'We'll make our way with more caution tomorrow. In all honesty, we've travelled for two days and seen nothing. We could return to Gloucester and let Lord Coenwulf know there's nothing to fear.'

As much as I'd like to do that, I find myself speaking. 'Two days on horse can be covered in less than a day by ship,' I mutter, unwillingly. 'Especially with a favourable wind.'

'So, you wish to carry on?'

'I think we should at least try and catch sight of one of the ships, or someone who will tell us what's happening.'

Here Oswy pauses, assessing me.

'We could return to the river settlement, and ask for news there.'

'Will the traders not share their news when they reach Mercia anyway?'

'Hum, probably, yes. Then what?'

'Travel inland along the Fosse Way?'

'But the enemy have ships, not horses.'

'Then we should return to Mercia,' Cenred argues. 'There's nothing to see. The Wessex forces aren't massing here. While some people might be heading to Mercia, as Lord Coenwulf told us, not everyone is.'

Cenred's correct. We've seen few people moving north, but equally, we've not been using a well-travelled roadway.

'They must be using the Fosse Way. They won't want to be close to the coast,' I reason.

Kyre interjects. 'If we find the Fosse Way we can speak to those who've seen the enemy.'

'Hum,' Oswy continues to muse, his eyes gazing into the distance, as though willing sight of the enemy. I'd sooner know where they are as well. This not knowing is making me as uneasy as the abandoned settlement not far from Gloucester. It makes me judder with trepidation. 'We've seen what we can, or rather, can't,' Oswy concludes. 'We'll turn and head back towards Gloucester. It'll take us two days to reach there, and by then, the king should have sent word to Lord Coenwulf, and Wulfheard might have arrived. I'd sooner he made these decisions than us. But,' he continues, 'we travel inland. We'll go up, use the viewpoint from the hills as opposed to the coastal path. Maybe find our way to Malmesbury Abbey. We might be able to see further, and will be away from any possible attack.'

'Not so eager to face the enemy now, are we?' Maneca teases, but I suspect we all feel much more settled as we turn our horses inland. There are trackways, probably used by the sheep, that we follow until coming upon a likely-looking woodland we take shelter in within that night.

As darkness falls, and it is bloody dark, the hooting of owls and scurrying of other animals disturbs my sleep. I'm restless and still tired when I wake in the morning, despite not taking one of the night watches.

Brute's also uneasy, and as we emerge from the woodlands, and the ground begins to rise, I keep turning to look at what's behind me. I'd welcome a view of our surroundings. I'd like to know if we're being followed, but throughout the day, as we climb higher, we see no telltale signs of an attack. There are more and more people. They watch us warily as we ride past their farming land or dwellings, but no one calls to us. I suspect they know we're Mercians, but we offer no threat to them. I hope they offer no threat to me, either. We're five mounted warriors, alone. And some of these people are perhaps Mercians. They may have married West Saxons. They may have moved over the border, tempted by more prosperity, but mostly, they simply don't want to engage in a fight they wouldn't be able to win.

'How do you know the way?' I eventually question Oswy.

'This landscape has long been argued over by the Mercians and the West Saxons. This isn't the first time I've been here. I doubt it is for the others either. Remember, young Icel, we're older than you. We lived when

Mercia's kings held more control than they do now. I suspect, if you asked some of Mercia's older lords, they once owned land here, gifted to them by the king, and lost when King Ecgberht decided to counter Mercia's influence. I mentioned Malmesbury Abbey yesterday. They say one of their greatest abbots was a member of the Mercian nobility, admittedly, over a hundred years ago, but all the same. Mercia has influence here.'

'So, what, this was once Mercian?'

'It was, yes. If you went that way,' and he points inland, 'you'd encounter the Wansdyke.'

'Like the dyke between Mercia and the Welsh kingdoms?'

'Indeed, my young friend. But come on. Let's hurry along. I'd also welcome being back on land that is without question Mercian.'

The following day, I sense we're closer to home and almost allow the tension of being in Wessex in my shoulders to drain away. But we're still elevated, and when I turn back to look the way we've come, my eyes are drawn to the distant coastline, and the billowing cloud of smoke, seeming to pulse as though with a heartbeat.

'Look at that,' I point, and my fellow warriors do. Oswy squints.

'Where is that?' he questions, but I shrug. I can't truly tell. Everything looks different from inland looking towards the sea than from when I was on board a ship looking inland.

'It's further south than we went,' Cenred confirms. 'A lot further south.'

'What's burning then, to be visible from here?'

Cenred shrugs as I look at him. 'I'd say everything. Crops, dwellings, anything flammable.'

None of us moves as we consider this. We've travelled two days away from Mercia, and now we're nearly back within our kingdom. We've seen no one but the people of Wessex. Yet, from here, we can see what I assume is the work of our common enemy, the Viking raiders. I swallow my disquiet.

I've been thinking about how quickly they can move with their ships. And now, before me, I see only too well how much damage they can do, and how prepared they are to do that damage. I shudder once more. I hate the bastard West Saxons, but there will be people there who've lost everything.

With a grimace, Oswy speaks.

'Come on. We need to report this to Lord Coenwulf and King Wiglaf.

The enemy are very much nearby. We'll have to prepare, even if it comes to nothing.'

Unsettled once more, I encourage Brute to Mercia, but time and time again, I turn to face the rising smoke. Not once does the smoke seem to grow any less dense. Not once do I feel as though our enemy are contained within Wessex. It's not a happy thought. We don't direct the horses towards Malmesbury Abbey, although Oswy does point it out to me, nestled on a peak dipping sharply away to flatter land leading towards the far distant coast.

And then, when I feel as though I almost recognise where we are, our path is blocked.

'Who the hell are you?' an angry voice calls, accent rolling as I know the Wessex tongue does.

'Get out of the way,' Oswy growls at them. 'We mean you no harm.'

'Bloody Mercians,' another of the ten men shouts, and I breathe deeply. This isn't going to end well. At least, I don't think they know our exact identity. They've not, then, come to exact revenge against me on behalf of the Wessex king and his son.

'We mean you no harm,' Oswy repeats, but his words fall without being heard. The ten warriors have already pulled forth their seaxes. If they have horses, they've left them hidden, for they stand, belligerent, before us.

'Always trying to steal what's not theirs,' the first man growls, his shield before him now as well as his seax. 'Bastards,' he roars. 'This is Wessex, not Mercia.'

Oswy astounds me by lifting his hands to either side, no weapon in either, and attempting to placate them.

'I assure you, we mean no harm. We're nearly back in Mercia now. Let us go, and we'll speak no more of this.'

'Hah.' The second of the men barks a laugh. 'He thinks to come here. Steal our,' and here he falters because we have no obvious stolen goods with us, 'possessions, and escape into Mercia and all under our noses. I don't bloody think so,' he roars.

'Dismount, men,' Oswy orders. I don't argue with him. This is only going to be resolved with a bloody good fight. I know it. Oswy knows it. Cenred, Maneca and Kyre think the same.

Quickly, not taking my eyes from the ten men who are evidently preparing themselves to fight us by growling, grumbling and generally shouting at one another, what some of it means, I don't bloody know, are still not yet ready to attack.

They're well provided with equipment. Perhaps they're the local ealdorman's warriors. Whatever they are, the damn fools don't seem to know Wessex faces attack from the Viking raiders. No, this fight is about an older threat than that, perhaps even decades, if not centuries of unease between Mercia and Wessex who've both claimed this area in the past. I don't miss that we're outnumbered two to one. I consider if they can beat us, but I'm far from worried. These might be the local ealdorman's warriors, but we've been fighting for Mercia for a long time now. We can beat the Wessex warriors just as we did the Viking raiders outside Londinium.

I tie Brute's reins high and slap his arse so he and the other horses move to the side of the road, already cropping the grass with their huge teeth. It's good to know they don't fear the enemy. I do, but only in so much as they're slowing us down and we really do have places to be.

'On me,' Oswy calls. I stand at his right, with Cenred, while Maneca and Kyre take up position to his left. We have our shields overlapped, and now the Wessex warriors notice our stances. The lead warrior startles, just a little, but he doesn't have the stones to renege on his desire to fight us, even if he already regrets the decision.

'Come on then, you sacks of shit,' Cenred bellows so loudly I wince as my ear vibrates with his voice. I turn to glower at him. He shrugs his huge shoulders in a clatter of iron and leather. The Wessex warriors also judder at the menace in his words. And the promise.

'You can still let us pass,' Oswy suggests, his voice much quieter, but the Wessex warriors are having none of it.

'Come on, we outnumber them. And those horses will make a fine addition to the stables.' This is shouted by another of the enemy, one of the men who stands to the rear and, indeed, seems entirely unconcerned by what's about to unfold here. He's either an arrogant arsehole, or genuinely so vicious he has nothing to fear. I swallow my unease at the lack of emotion in his voice. Warriors who fight, driven by rage, are easier to defeat. Men such as him, not so much.

'Attack,' the first warrior roars, starting to move forward, two men to either side of him, and the other five behind him. These men are desperate to attack, something.

'Come on, you arseholes,' Maneca menaces. I shake my head. I feel my eyes roll behind my helm, crammed onto my head and, perhaps, not quite tight enough because I've loosened it a little to allow some cool air in, and now realise I've not retightened it.

Now the Mercians move together. The Wessex warriors hold their shields in front of their faces, protecting their bodies, but revealing their legs and booted feet. We, I suspect, hold our shields a little lower. I want to be free to drive my seax blade against the enemy, as opposed to cowering behind my shield. These bags of wind are precisely that, but the single warrior at the back, the man who spoke almost with disdain, does concern me.

The Wessex warriors continue to encourage one another.

'For my mother,' one of the fools bellows, his voice cracking with grief. I'd shake my head again, but we're close enough for our shields to touch, if we want them to do so. But I don't, not yet. There's less than a large man's foot between us, about the length of a seax, but still the Wessex warriors hold off from actually starting the bout.

'We can still walk away from this,' Oswy calls, but of course, that was never going to happen when arsehole Wessex warriors encountered some Mercians just going about their business.

13

We come together in the sharp crack of iron and wood meeting. The sound, I confess, rings delightfully in my head – well, it does to my right. To the left I can still hear absolutely nothing after Cenred's bellowing shout.

'Hold,' Oswy instructs, the noise very faint in my ears. The enemy press against our shields. It takes me but a moment, and I have my rear foot planted to withstand the assault. These men might have the intellectual capacity of a snail, yet they're strong. But then, warriors have to be strong, even just to walk around in byrnie with shield before them, and seax and perhaps sword on their weapons belt. At least, I think, they don't have spears. Spears are the dirty weapons of the shield wall. I like a spear, but not when the fight's so small, and at least in their eyes, so weighted in their favour, as they outnumber us.

A clang echoes on my helm. The ringing now reaches my other ear. All sound's muted, aside from a faint chiming. I'll thank Cenred for that when this is done. The damn fool who hit me with his blade will also feel my wrath.

I grimace, sweat beading my face, and realise Oswy's attacking with his seax over the top of his metalled shield rim. Cenred's doing the same. I must have missed the command because of the blow to my head and Cenred's bloody loud bellow.

Hastily, with my left hand and shoulder holding my shield firmly against the enemy, I lift my seax, and endeavour to repay the favour. There are blades and hands, and sweating, straining men, in a very small space. It's impossible to determine whose weapon is whose. So, instead of countering any attack – after all, I already can't bloody hear anything – I aim for the glinting metal on my counterpart's helm. I land a heavy blow with my seax's hilt. I can't see the man's face. I sense his blade falter from where it endeavours to hit me again. Grunting, I snatch back my weapon, reset my hand, and stab out.

The blade comes away bloody, but whether I've killed him or not is impossible to determine. Certainly, there's no lessening in the pressure against my shield.

I spit aside the taste of blood hanging suspended in the air, and jab once more. This time, there's more resistance, but not from iron or padded byrnie. No. It's from flesh being forced to part in the wake of my strike. I hammer the blade further and further in, being careful not to lose my balance as the other Mercians jostle to land their blows. The shield wall, as small as it is, is a living, breathing beast, one section of it affecting the other.

I retract my blade, blood shimmering again, only then I feel a jolt on my back. I swivel, and face the grinning face of one of the Wessex warriors.

'Ware,' I bellow, turning my body so I still hold my shield against those attacking from the front, but my seax, dripping with the gore of the man I've skewered, is aimed towards the other foeman. I think the fool's half cracked, his eyes glinting in the light from the sun, but then he comes towards me, sword extended, and it's as though he dances with the bloody thing.

It's all I can do to counter his blows with my seax. I really need my sword.

The only advantage is he appears to be the only Wessex warrior who's thought to attack from the rear while the rest face us from ahead. For a moment, I consider if he knows who I am after all. Is he specifically attacking me?

The thud of his blade meeting my seax threatens to yank me forwards, releasing my grip on the shield. I can't let it go, not when my fellow Mercians are so fiercely battling the enemy, who attack in a more conventional way.

But he's a skilled warrior. His strikes land well against my seax blade, which tries to counter them. Any moment now, he'll cut me, and I'll be bloody furious.

'Ware,' I bellow once more, as he skips aside from me and threatens Maneca's back. 'Maneca,' I urge, but my fellow warrior is too engrossed in the fight ahead. If he responds, I can't hear him. Oswy, however, is more alert.

'Go,' he orders loudly enough I can hear. When I hesitate he repeats himself. 'Kill the mad bastard, and ensure he doesn't injure you or Wulf-heard will never let me hear the bloody end of it,' he urges. At his insis-tence, I release my hold on the shield, wedged as it is between Cenred and Oswy. Freed from the impediment, I follow the Wessex warrior, feeling no solace that Oswy also thinks the man might be singling me out.

Maneca shouts with pain. I jab forwards with my seax, releasing my sword from my weapons belt at the same time. My foeman has a blade in either hand. I need two blades as well. Neither of us has a shield. Mine remains in the shield wall. I don't know where his is.

I slide between Maneca's back and the enemy warrior's attack, mindful of Maneca's extended leg bracing him. My seax whirls while my sword, in my shield hand, is held before me. I'll use it as my shield, instead of my bloody arm, that is.

The Wessex warrior rumbles loudly, but not with anger. I'd almost think the damn fool was enjoying this.

'One of you, at least, has some bloody warrior skill,' he mutters loud enough that I can hear. I know he plans to anger me. I can't say I don't feel a frisson of fury coursing through my body. I shake it off. He means to drive me to rage. I understand what anger does to warriors. I won't make this easy for him.

I stab towards him with my seax, keen to get more room between me and the back of my fellow warriors, or risk tangling my legs with theirs. Or worse, knocking into them with my elbow or back, and in that way allowing my enemy to overwhelm me. Chance and luck have a way of playing their part in every bloody fight.

The Wessex warrior counters my move with his sword. It means his blade is closer to my body than I am to his. I move forward, deploying my sword to block his. Only my sword's in my shield hand. I can brawl that way, if needed, but my left arm's more used to holding firm in a fight than moving a blade.

I sense he believes this could be an easy victory for him. I skip aside, out of the reach of him and both blades. Briefly, he steps back, as though to reassess everything. In that moment, I catch sight of the cloud of black smoke in the far, far distance, malignant against the summer-blue sky, and also my damn horse. Brute eyes me, mouth filled with long grasses and a questioning expression, as though asking if I'll be much longer at this task.

I shake my head, dislodge my helm a little, and then hammer it back into place with my seax hilt. My face is slick with sweat, my back sodden. I grimace at the sensation and then advance on my enemy, winning free from the rear of my allies fighting in the shield wall.

His seax blade goes wide, as though to encourage me to advance on that side of his body, opening up his shoulder for me. I watch his sword. That's where the true menace is. He's a good warrior, I don't doubt it, but his skill is also with his right hand.

He grimaces behind his helm as my eyes flicker from his sword hand to his face. He shrugs, accepting the bluff hasn't worked. Then he pivots into me, showing me his back, his seax blade obscuring it, while his sword covers the front of his body. For a brief moment, I'm confused. I've not seen this before but I refocus on his sword, and move to meet his weapons.

His blade shimmers. I know it's a good one, but the heft of a sword makes it a killing blade. His actions have me suspecting it's perhaps more lightweight. How else would he be able to dance with it as he does?

I jab my seax towards his upper chest, where his sword doesn't protect him. In the time it takes to change the grip on his blade, I've perforated his byrnie, a shimmer of the wool lining erupting into the air, reminiscent of ash from a hearth fire, but there's no blood. He doesn't like that, a flurry of emotions swimming in his eyes. I close on him, coming even closer until his sword erupts between us. I veer abruptly backwards before the blade can slice across my face. It comes so near, I close my eyes without intending to do so.

'Come on,' I huff, ducking away from his blade and getting nearer to him. Only now, with his sword almost behind me, his seax starts to do some work. It pokes against the side of my helm, the thud of it dimming my ringing hearing once more. Now I blink even more, wishing the buzzing in my ears from my hearing attempting to return wasn't so bloody distracting.

My foeman's sword is behind me, his seax to the side of me. I appreciate, he might fight in an unorthodox way, but it is refreshing. And effective.

Well, it is until, frustrated, and with my head already pounding, I veer into him, my helmed forehead smacking into his with such fierceness I swear I hear thunder and see lightning even though my eyes are closed.

I sense him sag before me, and take a step back, mindful of his legs kicking out below him. I don't hear his body land on the hard ground, with my hearing compromised, but I see it.

'Bastard,' I mutter, swallowing the nausea of too many knocks on the head in too close a space of time. I bend towards him, my seax ready to take the final, cutting blow across his neck.

From far away, I hear sound, but can't decipher it, and then there's a hand on my arm, pulling me upright. I turn, seax blade lifted menacingly, but it's Oswy. He has a bloodied face, and a rip in his byrnie. His mouth's opening and closing, but I can't hear what he's saying.

The fight's over, I realise, flicking a look over his shoulders. The Wessex warriors aren't dead, mind. Instead, they all, sporting cuts along some of their exposed faces, peer behind me. I appreciate they've realised Wessex is under attack. While battling this single man, I've missed the fight, and whatever's brought it to an end.

Still, Oswy's mouth opens and closes and I can't hear the words.

'What?' I bellow. 'I can't hear you.' I point to my ears. He veers back from me, with shock. I sense even Brute looking towards me, and belatedly realise he actually rears in shock.

Oswy's mouth moves again. I shake my head, even pulling my helm free to point at my ears and shake my head. I sense him sharing a look with the others. Then he smiles, and shrugs, indicating the slumped man isn't to be killed. I'd like to kill him, but evidently that's not how this fight will end.

I turn, surveying the Wessex warriors. All of them, apart from the sense-less man at my feet, stare into the distance, mouths agape, or frantically talking one to another. It seems the damn fools have realised what's happening in their own kingdom. Oswy's evidently brokered some sort of peaceful resolution to our attack, perhaps being reminded that while the West Saxons are our enemy, the Viking raiders imperil all of us. Or perhaps the enemy have also seen the smoke, and have demanded peace. Whatever's happened, there's to be no more fighting. A pity really because I was winning.

Instead, the man below me stirs, blinking upwards into the bright sky, before leaping upright, recovering his weapons, and advancing on me once more.

Two of his warriors rush to intercept him.

'Aldhelm, no,' the one must shout, because I hear it.

When this Aldhelm still tries to come at me, they physically turn him, and make him listen to their words. I determine when he sees what they're telling him. His entire body slumps, blades hanging forgotten and loose in his hands.

I turn to Oswy, but he thumps me on the back and points towards Brute, evidently still wild with shock from my shouting.

'I'll go to him,' I must bellow once more, while Oswy holds a finger to his lips. He wants me to be quiet. I consider how loudly I'm shouting, as I stride towards Brute, a slight limp for my right ankle, which hurts a little, but nothing compared to the banging in my head. It's not like last year when I intervened to save Brihthild from the queen's blade, I don't believe, but it's so strange to move without hearing anything other than a high-pitched ringing. I don't like it, I really don't. As I reach for Brute, eyes wild and still bucking, I open my mouth to speak, and then snap it shut again. With my hands reached out to run them along his black and white nose, I appreciate that if I try and soothe my horse, I'll merely shout even louder, being that much closer to him. Wisely, I hold my tongue, and eventually I mount up alongside the rest of my warriors, and turn Brute to the north.

That's when I realise Oswy and the Wessex warriors have arranged more than a truce, for they've brought forth their horses and ride with us, towards Mercia.

I don't bloody like that either, but I can't open my mouth to argue. Not without sending Brute off on one of his out-of-control gallops. I don't want that. Not in front of the Wessex warriors.

I sense there's a hubbub of conversation between Oswy and the Wessex warriors. I can't hear it. It's a relief when Kingsholm coalesces before us quickly. I reflect on why, as I ride closer, unable to ask my fellow warriors if they see the same. Kingsholm's surrounded by a collection of canvases, horses and warriors. Indeed, there are so many horses now paddocked outside the wooden walls of the main settlement, I consider how Lord Coenwulf could have bred so many, so quickly. But then I understand. As the smoke of a hundred cook fires floods the air, the raucous cries of men shouting one to another permeating even my compromised hearing, I realise King Wiglaf has arrived. And he's not come alone. I don't believe I've seen so many Mercian warriors in one place for a long time. Not since the attack on Londinium when we ejected King Ecgberht and sent him back to Wessex.

I sense growing unease from the Wessex warriors who escort us, but I can't offer any reassurances, and neither can Oswy, as far as I can tell.

Wulfheard greets us as we bring the horses to a halt, even while men under Commander Eahric's instructions shout their greetings to us from where they train in a defined area, cleared of crops and horse shit. I can only tell because they stand and lift their arms. I also see their mouths opening and closing and assume it's in welcome. Many of them know Oswy well. Admittedly, by now, they know all of us. Wulfheard takes one look at Oswy's face, and then the Wessex warriors besides us, and I suspect he grunts.

'I take it the news isn't good, although at least you're still in one piece,' he growls as he directs it towards me, or at least I think that's what he says. It's been half a day since the fight. I'm starting to be able to hear more but not everything. I watch him carefully. 'It never bloody is,' I believe he further mutters. 'I see you found some friends,' he continues. 'They won't be alone, I assure you.' Again, I suspect that's what he says, as we dismount inside Kingsholm proper, grooms rushing to tend to the sweating horses, while Pega looks on from the open stable doorway, shaking his head as though he can't believe what's happening to his normally quiet home. I don't see Edwin, but assume he's busy on guard duty.

I'm aware of Wulfheard giving me a funny look, but Oswy must inform him of what's happened. I sense no real fear about having the Wessex warriors here. That astounds me. Wessex warriors aren't welcome within Kingsholm. Or, at least, they shouldn't be.

I find I agree with Pega's disbelief at what's happening to Kingsholm, but quickly we make our way inside the hall, escorted by the Wessex warriors as well, dodging servants with platters, jugs and beakers to keep the warriors of Mercia fed and watered, to where Lord Coenwulf, King Wiglaf, Ealdormen Ælfstan and Muca await us. They're a little piece of calm in the maelstrom of such chaos. And with them is someone else I'd hoped never to see again.

That bastard, King Æthelwulf of Kent. And he looks far too pleased with himself, although it quickly turns to surprise as he notes the Wessex warriors who walk at our side. Indeed, all ten of those men take to their knees in obeisance. I stand aside, startled by such a show of subservience from those I know to be quite decent warriors.

I growl at finding King Æthelwulf in one of the few places I consider my home. Oswy, standing close to me, holds my bunched fist at my side. I welcome his intervention. I'm not sure what I might have done had he not held me tight. I shake my head, trying to dispel the buzzing noise, and when that fails, settle to stand and watch, endeavouring to decipher as much as I can from gestures and who speaks.

I didn't much like allowing the Wessex warriors into Mercia, but I couldn't argue about it without shouting and scaring my horse. I really don't like seeing King Æthelwulf here. Not at all, but know not to argue now. Not when it would also be shouted. I console myself by glaring at King Æthelwulf, and he surprises me by meeting my gaze. What I see in his eyes has me clenching my fists once more, but wisely I stay my hand. For now. Yet, undoubtedly, King Æthelwulf knows my identity, just as much as I know his. It was bad enough risking a trip into Wessex with unknown enemy potentially dogging my steps. It's much worse to find my enemy once more in my kingdom. I will need to be very wary of King Æthelwulf and his most loyal warriors who've escorted him here.

14

I swallow down my immediate unease at finding King Æthelwulf within Kingsholm, trying to work the tension from my fist. It must work, because Oswy releases his grip on me. Now the Mercians bow low to King Wiglaf. When I'm upright once more I look from Ealdorman Ælfstan to Muca to Tidwulf, hoping, somehow, they might be able to convey some idea of what's happening here. It's been less than a year since we banished the bastard from Londonia. I don't welcome seeing King Æthelwulf of Kent, son of King Ecgberht of Wessex, again, especially not when Eanstan's warning hangs over me. However, I do note any smugness has drained from his face at our arrival. Is it because it's me, or because we're escorted by some Wessex warriors? I wish I knew.

'Ah, good men.' King Wiglaf beckons us forwards. His voice comes from far away, but I can faintly make out his words. The Wessex warriors escort us, although they're less eager than we are, which surprises me. Oswy nods smartly when I look towards him. The ringing in my ears has subsided to a duller throb. I can hear voices but they're muffled.

'My lord king.' Oswy inclines his head rigidly. His eyes never leave King Æthelwulf. He might have cautioned me not to punch the bastard in the face, but he's not far from wanting to do the same. I stumble to follow on.

Of all the things I might have expected to see at Kingsholm, bloody King Æthelwulf wasn't one of them, even when we've brought the Wessex warriors here. I might have hoped for every armed man of Mercia, which it's possible has happened for there are many warriors outside. Perhaps I might also have expected to see the beginning of the raising of the local fyrd, although that would take more time than we've been away. But the king of Kent, the son of King Ecgberht of Wessex? No. I didn't in a hundred summers anticipate seeing him here, sitting beside the man whose children he tried to have murdered.

Indeed, now I look with less heat and more ice in my veins, I notice Lord Coenwulf sits as far from King Æthelwulf as possible. He casts a disbelieving look towards the Wessex warriors. Ealdormen Ælfstan, Muca and Tidwulf are between the two men, with King Wiglaf facing us. I realise why Wulfheard had to greet us to gain entry to Kingsholm, and why I didn't see Edwin and his allies on guard duty. No doubt, everyone's being careful with whom they allow close to King Æthelwulf. I imagine the arrival of more Wessex warriors, for now I realise King Æthelwulf has an escort in the hall, bedecked in tunics showing the black and white wyvern of Wessex, and it has perhaps not caused as much consternation as I feel.

There are ten Wessex warriors already present, watching their king fiercely, as well as the ten new warriors we've brought. King Æthelwulf has twenty men to protect him. All the same, I find it strange King Æthelwulf knew of the attack on Wessex, but the men we encountered were ignorant. I don't recognise any of those with King Æthelwulf. Hopefully, we killed all those truly loyal to the king when last we met.

'Come, tell us of what you've discovered.' King Wiglaf beckons us to hurry, his voice still coming from far away.

'My lord king?' Oswy questions uncertainly, his words sounding as though they're shouted from the top of the battlements at Londinium, while I stand below.

'Yes, come, come. King Æthelwulf's aware of where you've been. Now, we must know what the Wessex warriors face. Alas, it appears the Viking raiders have finally managed to coordinate a devastating attack on our neighbour.' I notice the hesitation over the word 'neighbour' and muse on what else King Wiglaf might have wanted to say. My king looks hale, perhaps too hale. I consider if the prospect of fighting the Viking raiders has imbibed him with some youthful vigour, but dismiss that. I suspect it's more to do with King Æthelwulf being forced to come to Mercia, not as a conqueror as he endeavoured to do last summer, but to demand aid against the enemy. Indeed, as we now know, he's sought out Mercian help before calling on all his warriors. That's telling. There's no other reason for King Æthelwulf to be here, or to even have been permitted to step foot within Mercia unless it was to conduct some negotiations with King Wiglaf.

How the mighty have fallen. Nine summers ago, King Ecgberht claimed to rule Mercia, as well as Wessex, and also staked a claim to Northumbria and the Welsh kingdoms. The year after, he was ejected from his final holding of Londonia by King Wiglaf and his warriors, me amongst them. Last summer King Ecgberht once more tried to interfere in the ruling line of Mercia, and might also have allied with some Viking raiders to have them attack Mercia using the waterways through the kingdom of the East Angles. Now, he sends his son, set as king over Kent, which was Mercian until nine years ago, and asks for the aid of the Mercians. I consider how King Æthelwulf doesn't choke over the request. It must be bad at Carhampton if King Æthelwulf has come in person and not sent one of the meddling bishops to intervene on his behalf. Not that I'd welcome seeing Bishop Beornmod again. I don't trust him.

I wish King Wiglaf would refuse to aid the Wessex kings, but it seems doubtful, as King Æthelwulf sits within Kingsholm, which is very definitely situated inside Mercian territory. Evidently, King Wiglaf means to consider the request carefully. I deliberate on why Lord Coenwulf allows it, but, of course, his time within Frankia taught him much about politics. And about the Viking raiders. Perhaps he suspects only the Mercians can counter the enemy. Or, he believes, despite everything, the Viking raider scrouge can only be defeated with a combined force. Or he just wants the enemy gone and will countenance whatever tactic must be employed.

'Then, my lord king, I'll tell you we rode two days south of here, using the coastal paths, and then came back using the advantage of the high escarpment. We saw little on the way south, but when journeying north, we noticed a huge fire to the south. We suspect the enemy burns the crops as well as the settlements.' Oswy delivers the details with cool detachment that has King Æthelwulf wincing. I suspect we're all grimacing at the thought of problems during the coming winter when people will struggle to feed themselves and their animals if the crop has been incinerated. We endured the dearth after last summer's damp growing season. There could be more hardship on the way.

In Wessex, there will certainly be problems. The fire we saw wasn't small.

'We encountered these men half a day from here. They determined to confront us, but then also realised Wessex was under attack.' Oswy's developing quite a skill with his words. He's as devastating with them as he is with seax and shield to hand. I wish I could speak so coolly when King Æthelwulf's in the room.

'Hum,' King Wiglaf mutters. The men cluster close to the hearth. We've not been bid to sit, but we've been brought water or ale, whichever we want. I've taken water. Oswy has ale, and over the lip of the beaker, I sense him glaring at King Æthelwulf. I hope someone's sent reinforcements to Winchcombe Nunnery. After all, this could be a means of the West Saxons springing the former queen free from her exile, and continuing to cause King Wiglaf problems. I'd like to know how this was brought about. Who did King Æthelwulf approach? Was it bloody Lord Wigmund at Londonia? Was it King Wiglaf directly? Why didn't the Wessex warriors we encountered and fought know about the Viking raider attack taking place at Carhampton?

'We've news of a terrible slaughter,' King Æthelwulf speaks into the heavy silence. 'Two ealdormen, and two bishops of Winchester are known to have died in a fierce battle at Carhampton. It pains me to say our force was compelled to retreat, the losses so great, the number of enemies they faced so overwhelming, they couldn't hold against them but withdrew in order to regroup. It was a bloody and terrible thing by all accounts. We know the enemy remain on Wessex-held land. We've had conflicting reports but between twenty-five and thirty-five enemy ships beached at Carhampton, far from here, admittedly, to the south and west. The numbers who were slaughtered is horrifying.'

At the news, the ringing silence deepens. My hearing remains hazy. While no one speaks, I hear the muted throbbing of my heartbeat. It makes King Æthelwulf sound strange. However, I grimace to consider the terrible atrocity, and not just on the Wessex warriors but on those unwittingly caught up in the fighting. When we went to the Isle of Sheppey there were, at most, three Viking ships, and they obliterated the religious community there and threatened those who lived opposite. Outside Londinium, we were lucky enough to have the victory, but every person who fought was a warrior, trained and well provisioned. The same won't apply to the men and women of Carhampton.

'My father, King Ecgberht, is gathering together a great host at the peak of Brent Knoll to march on Carhampton and defeat the enemy and beat them back to their ships with a resounding victory that will ensure they never step foot within Wessex again.' Here King Æthelwulf pauses. It doesn't take much wit to determine what his next words will be. 'You men there, your lord should have been summoned. As such, I'm unsure why you're unaware, but that's by the by. King Ecgberht of Wessex requests Mercia is on guard against the enemy moving northwards.' Again, he pauses, as though the next words won't leave his throat. 'And he beseeches Mercia's king to send aid. Many horses were killed in the attack. My father's hurrying to replace the lost horseflesh, but it's as difficult to source as many new horses as it is new warriors. In fact, it's more difficult. I see you have many mounts here,' King Æthelwulf suggests, but no one offers them to him. With a slight turn of his lips, he continues to speak. 'Progress towards Carhampton will be slow but, be assured, the mustering point will allow our forces to keep a firm eye on any intentions the enemy have to move towards Mercia. But my father will not rush to engage without the correct supplies to counter the threat. In the meantime, and until all can muster at Brent Knoll, there are concerns the Viking raiders may move along the ancient roadways and infiltrate deep into Wessex, and of course, Mercia, using the Fosse Way. Only together can we defeat the enemy.' So spoken, King Æthelwulf sits proudly, shoulders rigid, jaw tense, his breathing erratic. It's pained him to be so open. If, of course, he speaks the truth.

What sort of nerve does King Æthelwulf and his father possess to demand this? Last year they tried to take control of Mercia. Now they're too weak to even defend it against an enemy? How much has changed. But then, my own interactions with the Viking raiders assure me they're all bastards. All of them.

'We'll take your request under advisement,' King Wiglaf concedes. His lips are tight with fury between his greying beard and moustache. Once more I look from Ealdorman Ælfstan to Tidwulf to Muca. Surely, some of the other ealdormen could have been prevailed upon to come to Kingsholm and bring their warriors with them. I'm unsurprised Ealdorman Sigered is absent but hope he's not at Winchcombe Nunnery instead. Or indeed, on his way to Londonia. As much as I detest his cravenness, I don't want him anywhere he can cause more difficulties for Mercia by ineffectually defending her. And it would be ineffectual. Ealdorman Sigered's like a sword depicted in sand or mud, quick to disintegrate in the rain.

Maybe the other ealdormen already journey this way. Perhaps this is all just being arranged. I consider what King Wiglaf's intentions were before King Æthelwulf arrived. With so many men garrisoned outside Kingsholm, did he intend to protect the River Severn and the border with Wessex? Perhaps some of the other ealdormen are taking up position on the northern bank of the River Thames. Maybe word has been sent to King Athelstan of the East Angles, now an ally of Mercia.

'As you will, but there's urgency to the matter,' King Æthelwulf remonstrates, his voice high. 'The enemy are mighty and powerful, and already, Wessex warriors lie cold and dead on the slaughter field, ravens circling overhead, the enemy stealing their lives and possessions. We'd not wish it to happen to Mercia.' While speaking, he looks at his warriors, as though to ensure they're filled with the desire for vengeance he hopes to create in the Mercians.

I grimace at his martyred tone, and bite back the complaint I'd prefer to level against him, as well as the question I'd like to ask. Does he mean me harm?

'We understand that,' King Wiglaf concedes. 'My son did the correct thing in bidding you seek me out. This is no decision he could make. It's for the king of Mercia, and her ealdormen, to debate. For now, Mercia's free from attack, but we are, of course, aware of the enemy. The Viking raiders aren't strangers to my fine warriors. We countered their attack against Londinium not many weeks ago,' King Wiglaf adds, another jibe to level against King Æthelwulf. 'Tell us again, what does King Ecgberht plan to do?'

'He's already moving towards the ancient, defended hill fort of Brent Knoll. He takes with him his ealdormen and their warriors, as well as calling for the local fyrd to be raised. He intends to have a force to rival that of the enemy. He's dispatched requests to all who owe him their oath to send horses and supplies to ensure the warriors are well provisioned and can stay in position until the enemy have been evicted from Wessex. These men here will be joining me when I move south.' If the Wessex warriors are unhappy about this, they don't reveal it.

'And what of the people of Cornwall?'

'Cornwall?'

'Are they also being prevailed upon to aid King Ecgberht?'

'My lord king?' King Æthelwulf stutters. Frantically, I'm trying to put the pieces together. Cornwall, I believe, but wish Wulfheard could tell me, is to the west of Wessex, I'm sure. I'm convinced it's the dragon's tail of land we took ship around and where we were less than warmly welcomed, even when they believed us traders. I thought it was part of Wessex, but perhaps not. After all, it's a long way from the heartland of Wessex. A very long way. 'They've been appraised of the situation. Alas, the people of that realm are, shall we say, a stubborn lot. That'll change should the enemy move towards them.'

'So, they're not with your father, but are they working with the enemy?'

At this, a swift look of fury touches King Æthelwulf's lips. I consider whether he knows the answer or not. A heavy silence falls. I open and shut my mouth, as though it might stop the strange thudding in my ears. It doesn't. The silence thrums only with the very distant sound of people busy with their tasks outside. Then, Ealdorman Ælfstan speaks.

'So, your father has, what, over a thousand trained warriors, who can fight with spear, shield, seax and sword?' Ealdorman Ælfstan questions. I don't know how he's calculated that number, but perhaps the Mercians know the strength of the individual Wessex ealdormen and their king, and his son.

'He'll have near enough two thousand,' King Æthelwulf counters aggressively. I consider how he knows this. Has he counted the men we encountered in that number? If he has, how many more Wessex warriors are ignorant of their king's orders? I'm suspicious. Has King Ecgberht truly summoned all these warriors of Wessex, or is he hoping the Mercians will perform the task for him? I wish I knew. Would he truly stake the future of his kingship on Mercian warriors? I know he's a devious bastard, but this would astound me. Astound me, and yet, I still believe it possible.

'Then?'

'He intends to kill them and certainly to prevent them from ever returning again. We've all heard the tales from Frankia. These warriors are fierce and if they even scent victory, they determine to remain in the area and take all the wealth. We'll not allow good citizens of Wessex to lose their lives, or worse, be taken as slaves.' King Æthelwulf is impassioned, and yet I'm not caught up in his fervour. I'd think more of him if he'd sent someone else to treat on his behalf and was joining his father to face the enemy. Or, if the ten men we encountered had known of the attack and had been going towards it, as opposed to away from it. Or, if he'd done anything to evict the Viking raiders from the Isle of Sheppey where they've been sheltering for many months now.

King Ecgberht might think he heaps great honour on the king of Mercia by sending King Æthelwulf, but I suspect it's being done to keep his precious son safe while he fights the enemy. In that way, should anything befall King Ecgberht, his precarious dynasty will continue.

'Of course.' Ealdorman Ælfstan inclines his head respectfully, but I sense Oswy's unhappiness beside me. Indeed, all eyes within the hall are on the discussion. Most no doubt heard how King Æthelwulf spoke. I can't imagine many here have any sympathy for him. Not after everything he tried to accomplish to the detriment of Mercia.

'I'd request an answer by the end of the day, and then tomorrow at dawn, whatever your intentions, an escort to the border. I must reach my father and protect his wealth, and people at Brent Knoll.'

With that, King Æthelwulf marches from our presence, his warriors joining him with a clatter of metal and leather. I watch him go, wishing I could see inside him to know what his true thoughts and intentions are. I don't like him. I never will. I can't trust him. I never will. I eye the ten warriors he brought with him. I need to be alert to where they are. I can't allow them to get too close to me. One of them might mean me ill. Undoubtedly, King Æthelwulf does, if Eanstan's caution is to be believed. And I sense it is.

'Wulfheard,' Ealdorman Ælfstan instructs, 'ensure King Æthelwulf's watched. We can't have him wandering around alone.'

'My lord.' Wulfheard bows, and follows, but doesn't order us five to escort him. No doubt the king and the ealdormen have more questions for us.

'Sit,' Ealdorman Ælfstan instructs, and we do so. I've been riding for the majority of the last four days. It's still pleasant to sit, and know the surface below me won't move or need a heavy hand to have it go where I want it to. Brute is a joy and a trial to endure when riding.

'What do you think?' Ealdorman Muca is the first to question the king.

'I hardly know what to think. I came here to protect Mercia from the enemy Viking raiders. I brought my warriors from Tamworth, and have summoned the other ealdormen from the northern regions to join us. I intended to have the border protected, and patrols arranged and to make sure Mercia wasn't breached by the enemy. I've sent word to King Athelstan of the East Angles as well, to protect his coasts and rivers. Admittedly, I've also dispatched warriors to Peterborough under Ealdorman Humberht to ensure he doesn't take advantage of our preoccupation with the south-west of this island. What I didn't expect was to find King Æthelwulf awaiting me at Kingsholm.' My eyes narrow at the king's words. 'I've only arrived this afternoon,' he explains to the five of us who've been to Wessex and back. 'Reinforcements are on their way to Londonia. Never did I expect King Æthelwulf and his treasonous father to ask for our assistance. Never.' King Wiglaf muses over this.

'It's clear our priority should be the borderland with Wessex, the River Thames, and of course, the River Severn,' Lord Coenwulf comments, bending to rub his wounded leg. I consider if it pains him, or if the memory of his imprisonment at the hands of the Viking raiders has him rubbing it. I know mention of Wulfheard's brother's allies can make me worry at my belly wound.

'It is, yes, you're correct,' King Wiglaf muses. 'And yet, if we can move within Wessex, with the agreement of King Ecgberht, more could be accomplished. It would mean we could prevent the enemy from drawing closer to Mercia.'

'But they have ships, and we don't,' Ealdorman Ælfstan cautions.

'A good argument to make. It's our coast and river lines that might suffer. We don't have ships to counter them.'

'So, we should remain within Mercia,' Lord Coenwulf comments quickly.

'It would appear that way, but still, this is an opportunity for Mercia.'

I narrow my eyes, considering where King Wiglaf's thoughts have taken him.

'It isn't the time to take back land King Ecgberht stole from Mercia, either south or here or in Kent, and to undo the harm done at the battle of Ellendun,' Ealdorman Muca cautions. 'It really isn't. We don't want frightened people who wouldn't know to whom they owed their allegiance. That way lies even more peril.' For a moment, I think King Wiglaf will berate his ealdorman for speaking so freely, but he shakes his head, and offers a smile instead.

'You're wise, Ealdorman Muca, my thanks. It would be a welcome balm to have back our stolen land, but of course, that would open Mercia up to attack from the Viking raiders. Tell me, why do you believe they've gone to Carhampton? What's there? To me, it seems a strange location. The Isle of Sheppey, the kingdom of the East Angles, yes, those places are merely across the sea from their homeland. Even the attack on Londinium makes more sense, but Carhampton? It's a much longer journey. It involves them following the coastline for many more days and not stopping at a host of locations that they could overwhelm.'

'Unless they didn't come from the Isle of Sheppey or from the Frankish lands to the east?' Ealdorman Ælfstan suggests.

'What?' the king demands.

'The Viking raiders are known to have visited locations to the west of here, towards Ireland, and also the northern islands. There are rumours they've travelled beyond all that's been known before as well, to the far north, to a land few even knew of before now, risking their lives over the waves for many long days to make the journey. If we were better allies with the Welsh, perhaps we might know if they'd attacked them. The Isle of Manx, I believe, often plays host to the enemy. Not that host is perhaps the correct word to use, in that regard.'

'It's not an isolated act from them, is it?' King Wiglaf muses. 'The Viking raiders, I mean. Do they even have a king who commands them?' Silence greets his words. There's much about our enemy we simply don't know.

'My lord king, is it wise to expend Mercian warriors against the enemy of Wessex?'

'I understand your sentiments,' King Wiglaf responds to Lord Coenwulf. 'Yet, as Ealdorman Ælfstan states, they can be everywhere, and quickly.'

'So you believe we should fight for Wessex?' Lord Coenwulf's words are hot with fury. He's maintained an uneasy calm until now. He's done better in that than I have. I'd welcome the opportunity to punch King Æthelwulf, or worse.

'It might be better to show some willing, but not too much,' Ealdorman Muca counters. 'The defeat and loss of two ealdormen and two bishops is a difficult blow for Wessex. It suggests the enemy are much more skilled than the Wessex warriors. We might do better to show some eagerness, and then, should the enemy turn to us, Wessex would be compelled to also aid us. Admittedly, for now this arrangement would be very vague, but it could be developed. After all, you have an alliance with King Athelstan of the East Angles, and not that long ago, he was happily killing our kings.'

'That's a polite means of saying we should assess Wessex and then make a decision,' King Wiglaf surmises, but there's no anger in his words, and neither does he show concern at the mention of the former kings Beornwulf or Ludica, killed by King Athelstan. I keep my expression as neutral as possible. It's difficult though. King Æthelwulf is here, and he's certainly an enemy of Mercia. He did far more harm than King Athelstan ever did. Didn't he?

King Wiglaf looks to Ealdorman Ælfstan, who nods slowly, consideringly, and I hear Oswy's muted beast-like rumble.

'Escort King Æthelwulf tomorrow. See him over the border and then continue with him towards this hill fort, Brent Knoll. As you draw closer, assess the situation. I'll not risk many of my warriors. Commander Eahric will hold the border at Lechlade. Ealdorman Muca, you'll hold the River Thames border between Lechlade and Londonia, perhaps as far as Laleham Gulls. That way you and Ealdorman Cyneberht will have clearly defined areas to patrol. Commander Eahric will also deploy warriors across the more indistinct land boundary between Mercia and Wessex, north of Malmesbury, but not by much. We'll inform the abbot of what we're doing. We don't need to cause any unease for the good monks and people of Malmesbury.

'We'll not allow Wessex, or the Viking raiders, to attack Mercia when we're looking the other way. Ealdorman Ælfstan, your men have the most experience within Wessex. Take them, and Ealdorman Tidwulf's warriors. Ealdorman Tidwulf, you will remain here, with me and Lord Coenwulf, but our men will be ready to deploy along the River Severn if we have reports of enemy infiltrations. On this occasion, we'll send word the length of the River Severn, even to our neighbours to the west. There might be no love lost between us and the Welsh kings and their pestilent cattle stealers, but it's better they at least work with us, as against us.

'My orders towards you and your warriors are simple, Ealdorman Ælfstan. Aid Wessex, if it's possible and necessary. If not, stand aside and witness what the Viking raiders can do. Walk the line between Wessex and Mercian interests. It might be perilous. It will certainly aggravate King Æthelwulf and his father. But I care not. That's all I will commit, for now. Mercian warriors will protect Mercia with their shields and their lives. I'll send messengers to you, daily if possible. Keep me appraised of everything, and remember in all your interactions with King Æthelwulf, you're there to do him a favour, and you're not the enemy. Not at the moment, anyway.'

So spoken, the king dismisses us. We stand and make our obeisance before walking away. I can't say I'm happy about any of this, but I'm honest enough to accept I wouldn't be happy sitting on my arse doing nothing either. I'm glad I could hear enough to listen to the king speak so openly with us.

If the Viking raider force is truly so huge, I'd like to see it. From a distance.

I confess, a small part of me would also like to witness King Ecgberht and his son cast low. But only them, not the people of Wessex. I find I have little to argue with them about, even after Brihthild's treason. Indeed, I quite like some of the people of Wessex. Just not their bloody king and his son. Arrogant bastards, the both of them. And it appears they're about to be shown that, by the Viking raiders. Should they fall beneath the blades of the Viking raiders, it will release me from the certain threat of their thirst for vengeance. I would certainly welcome that. It really couldn't happen to nicer people.

15

None of Ealdorman Ælfstan's warriors are happy with our new assignment. And that unease only grows when Ealdorman Ælfstan seeks us out.

'I will accompany you, as the king ordered,' he states, eyeing Wulfheard as though he knows the first argument will come from him.

'I can't allow that, my lord.' Wulfheard inclines his head respectfully, voice firm, eyes flashing with ire.

'I'm your oath-sworn lord. You do as I say,' Ealdorman Ælfstan counters just as calmly. This debate is like watching two very polite people argue about who'll have the last piece of bread at the end of a meal. Both mean to win, and they don't intend to share it. Wulfheard, lips twisted in fury, concedes by bowing again, but we all know he's not convinced by such a weak argument. I imagine, if it were possible, Wulfheard would order us to leave that night, leaving Ealdorman Ælfstan to sleep in his bed. The ealdorman's fury would be intense, but of course, what could he do when it was accomplished? But we have to escort King Æthelwulf and his enlarged group of warriors towards the distant Brent Knoll. That means there must be pomp and ceremony, leaving no opportunity to sneak our way to Wessex.

While the men grumble, I take myself to see my old friend Edwin, my weapons in place. I won't risk being caught out by one of the Wessex bastards winning free from their escort to enact their revenge against me.

As a few days ago, I find Edwin on guard duty above Kingsholm's gate. From here, it's possible to see the River Severn, and Gloucester, as well as to get a good view over the sea of tents covering the land close to Kingsholm. The sound and smells of so many warriors and horses in close proximity is overpowering, even on Kingsholm's wooden walkway, which does benefit from a gentle breeze.

'Icel,' he greets, not looking away from his surveillance of the area, and perhaps recognising the sound of my boots over the wooden walkway. Or maybe he knows me well enough he detects my softly muttered sigh as I near him. It wouldn't surprise me. I'd recognise the sound of him running his hand through his rough beard anywhere. 'I hear your stay here will be brief.'

'It will, yes,' I reply, the words snapped but not angry. My hearing's almost back to normal.

'I don't like it, my friend. King Æthelwulf and his father are arseholes, but I also heard worrying rumours of the Viking raiders while in Frankia. They aren't to be underestimated. I know you thought they were terrible on the Isle of Sheppey, but I've been told things a hundred times worse.'

'How did the Frankish kings defeat them?' I question, curious and keen to be distracted.

'They didn't always. Sometimes they paid them to leave, a foolish endeavour that will surely only encourage the bastards to return and ask for more treasure and coin.'

'What do they want?' I muse, realising Edwin's an unlikely source of news of events far from Mercia.

Edwin turns and fixes me with a grin while his shoulders shrug beneath his byrnie. 'What do the enemy always want? Silver, treasure, to kill the enemy, to make a name for themselves and win the accolades of their allies. To have their name forever shouted in a scop song, or whatever the bastards do.'

'And that's worth the risk of getting killed? Or being killed? Reputation?'

'It would appear so,' Edwin agrees without much thought.

'Don't they have wives and children to care for?'

'My understanding is, they bring their wives and children with them, sometimes. For them, it's about more than merely fighting. It's about travelling as well, and ensuring they protect their families while growing rich and earning a reputation. It's similar to us, but not in the fact they defend their kingdom, only their families and jarls. Their homelands, it's said, aren't like ours. It's also said, it's bloody cold which is why they look half-animal when they venture south. They must live in furs or risk freezing.'

I feel unsettled by his words. Out there, far to the south of Kingsholm, a ravaging pack of warriors defeats a Wessex force, and I know the Wessex force is a strong one. They overwhelmed King Wiglaf nine summers ago. It took many lives to drive them from Mercia, including my uncle's. And even more to ensure they stayed away after that. When that didn't work, the Wessex ruling family tried conspiracy instead. But if the enemy can over-throw Wessex, then surely Mercia can also be subjected to their deprava-tions? Only now do I fully understand why King Wiglaf has mobilised so many of his warriors and ealdormen to protect the border with Wessex, and the riverways which allow far too easy access into the heart of my kingdom.

'Icel, my friend. You've spent much more of your life fighting than I have. It's ironic. You wished to be a healer, not a warrior, but now I say this to you. There's no point worrying about the enemy. They'll come, or they won't. It's for the king and his ealdormen to decide how to counter them. You're one man. Only one man. The kingdom doesn't survive or die because of what you do. It doesn't even rest on the shoulders of King Wiglaf. Not on this occasion. The Viking raiders are a reckoning, but not one coming from our Lord God. No, ambition drives them, and perhaps, or so it's said, an entirely different regard for their lives on this earth. After all, they don't worship our Lord God, as we do. They're something altogether different, but they're still made of flesh and blood. They're still like to fall under the blows of fierce warriors. And that's what you can do with greater skill than the vast majority of us poor imitations of Ealdorman Ælfstan's warriors. Cast down as many of them as possible, and if it's not possible, return to Mercia and protect the Mercians. That's your task and your role. That's what your uncle did, and what you will do, as well.'

I nod at Edwin's words, but I don't find them comforting, despite how reasonable they are and reassuring of this not being my fault. Despite everything I've so far done in the name of Mercia, I couldn't have done anything to prevent the Viking raider attacks on Wessex. I should, no doubt, be pleased they attack Wessex and not Mercia.

I'm only one man, as Edwin states, but I could be much more than that.

If I ever wanted to be. Which I don't. I know I bloody don't. But Mercia thrums in my blood. I can't allow others to needlessly imperil her. I really can't. And I fear, in this, King Wiglaf is too concerned with belittling the Wessex king and his son, and too little concerned with protecting Mercia, and everything I've spent my warrior-life endeavouring to do. Mercia must remain free. From Wessex, and from the Viking raiders. I'm not entirely sure I know who's the greatest enemy. I suspect, while everyone worries about Viking raiders, it's Wessex who's the real threat. Wessex wants more than gold, silver, treasures, slaves and reputation. Wessex wants Mercia. It won't have it. I swear it here, looking out over the view afforded me from my vantage point. Mercia will always remain Mercian. I'll die to ensure that happens. And worse, I'll declare myself as Mercia's king if I ever need to do so. Provided none of the Wessex arseholes get to me first. It's imperative I stay alive, and not just because I would much prefer it to being dead.

* * *

The next morning, we ride out early. Not even the cock has crowed, and most of us are sleepy. King Æthelwulf and his twenty warriors allowed within Kingsholm leave at the head of our line of mounted warriors. I've spent some time assessing them, and ensuring I know who they all are. I don't intend to find myself alone with any of them.

It'll not take us long to reach Wessex from here. I note we don't follow the coastal route of a few days ago, passing the abandoned settlement that so intrigued me. Instead, we move first towards Cirencester on Ermin Way and then to Malmesbury using the Fosse Way. I'm grateful we have Ealdorman Tidwulf's warriors as well as our own. More of King Æthel-wulf's warriors awaited our arrival at the Wessex and Mercian border. They would have easily outnumbered us had we not also been reinforced by Tidwulf's men. I'd not have appreciated so many Wessex warriors riding fully armoured so close to me. Would King Æthelwulf risk starting a fight now when he's journeyed to Mercia to ask for help? I might only be one man, but I've certainly angered him and his father enough to make me think they might have done so.

Ealdorman Ælfstan stays close to King Æthelwulf. He rides confidently, assessing everything as we travel. Just like Oswy and the others, I consider if

Ealdorman Ælfstan's no stranger to this part of Wessex, and if he keeps so close to King Æthelwulf to ensure the king of Kent can't strike against me.

At Malmesbury, which offers a surprisingly elevated view of the surroundings, and is also almost entirely surrounded by the River Avon so we make use of a fording point below the waters to reach it, we're greeted by Abbot Cuthbert and his monks, and spend the night beneath a good roof. Abbot Cuthbert shares his concerns with Ealdorman Ælfstan and King Æthelwulf. If he's astounded to find Mercian warriors with Wessex ones, he makes a good effort at not showing it.

He welcomes the Wessex warriors warmly, hailing Aldhelm by name, and something passes between the two I don't quite understand. Abbot Cuthbert's perplexed as we are as to why he's not been informed of the attacks on Wessex, directing this to King Æthelwulf, who merely murmurs something about the messenger getting waylaid somehow and then endeavours not to spend much time with the abbot.

Once more I muse on why King Æthelwulf came to treat with King Wiglaf, but appears to have forgotten to inform the people of Wessex. Not, of course, that the others share my concern. Oswy tells me to shush when I question him about it before sleeping that night and Wulfheard isn't much better. I can't get close enough to Ealdorman Ælfstan to advise him something feels wrong without drawing attention to myself. However, Abbot Cuthbert gives King Æthelwulf cursory glances from time to time which only adds to my unease. In my lifetime, Malmesbury was Mercian, so I've been informed. It no longer is. Perhaps Abbot Cuthbert wishes it were.

We're fed well, and prayers are said for our success against the enemy, in a blessedly short ceremony. The next day, we continue to travel onwards. As we leave the vantage point of Malmesbury, I look north, towards Mercia, but there's nothing to see that way, other than a last glance at my home for some time. To the south, a bulbous cloud of smoke hovers in the air. Wessex burns.

The Wessex warriors we fought remain with us. It pains me to admit, I find I quite like a few of them, including Aldhelm, who tried to kill me with his unusual tactics. They're gruff men who patrol the borderland with Mercia and receive little thanks for it, from the Mercians, and from those who are now subject to the Wessex kings. For all that, they take no offence, and even share their jokes with us.

Further and further south we go, following the Fosse Way for some distance before turning towards the coast, visible until now from our height of elevation, but which swiftly becomes little more than a cloudy hint on the horizon as we descend.

I realise the roadway's growing busier and busier. While King Æthelwulf's warriors order the people to move aside in gruff voices brokering no argument, I sense too much fear amongst the people. Some have carts laden with belongings, others have little more than the clothes they wear. They all walk as quickly as possible, the scent of fear palpable. They remind me of those we met fleeing from the kingdom of the East Angles when we patrolled the borderlands there. While we ride towards the fight, they must escape it. I wish them luck. I hope the abbot of Malmesbury will aid them, and Lord Coenwulf won't think too harshly on people fleeing the Viking raiders should they go all the way to Mercia. Ahead, King Æthelwulf's warriors grow heavy-handed. I turn to Ealdorman Ælfstan, pointing angrily.

'I know, I know.' He shakes his head and moves off to confront the warriors. I find myself looking into bleak eyes. I can't stop myself from handing out what food I have to children who look half-starved. Abbot Cuthbert fed us last night, we didn't make use of our own rations, so it's no hardship to share. I wish I had more to give them. Eventually, we're forced to a halt. There are too many coming towards us to move through them safely. Ealdorman Ælfstan, after much wrangling with King Æthelwulf, who lacks all compassion, as far as I can tell, has forced him to see sense.

Moving to the side of the road, I dismount and lead Brute to water. I'm grateful I don't have to wrestle with him any more through the crowds of people. I feared he'd hurt someone with his hazy ability to obey my instructions while still ensuring every step he makes is his own decision. He's not comfortable around so many, and finds the slow progress particularly frustrating.

'This is unacceptable,' I hear King Æthelwulf complaining to his warriors. At the nearby stream, I find a young woman and her two small children, bending to fill water bottles and scoop water over their dusty faces. She looks at me fearfully, as she hears me encouraging Brute to drink deeply, while I stand to the side of him. His coat is already matted with sweat and dust. I'll need to brush him when we finally stop for the night.

'No need to worry,' I advise her, as she moves to make away. 'We're with King Æthelwulf. My horse is very thirsty.' I direct to the small children. Their terrified and tired faces remind me too vividly of the sons of Lord Coenwulf.

'But you're Mercians,' she states, confusion on her worry-strewn face.

'We are, yes. Are you going to seek sanctuary within Mercia?'

'Yes, my husband's gone with the fyrd. He bid me take the children away, for safety.'

'What have you heard about the fighting?' I'm curious to know what she believes she's running away from.

'It's terrible. Awful. Many Wessex men have died, and the Viking raiders and their ships simply move from place to place, attacking and thieving from the coastal locations. They take some of the women as well. That's why my husband bid me leave. He fears what they'd do to me and my children if we're unprotected.'

'A wise man,' I offer, but my gaze is drawn to the children with her. Her daughter, little more than five summers to her name, seems to stare without seeing, her hands limp at her side, sweat beading on her forehead. 'Is she well?'

'No, a fever, but we had to move and I can't wait for her to recover.' Her tone's defensive.

'Is there no one who will aid you with their cart?' I look behind me, as though one will appear, and some friendly individual will encourage the woman and small children to ride onwards with them. She has sacks at her feet and I realise she can have no animal to assist her escape.

'Those fleeing won't aid us, no. They don't wish to be ill as well as feel threatened from the enemy.'

'And you have no horse?'

'Not even a donkey, my lord.'

I bite my lip. I feel helpless, but I can't give them Brute, and we ride swiftly, without the aid of baggage carts, so I can't even suggest one of the pack animals is repurposed to help her. 'I suspect you might be safe here, if you wished to stay a while. If not, and your daughter remains unwell, ask for assistance at Malmesbury Abbey. It's closer than the Mercian border and the brothers will have a healer amongst them. I was there only last night. Abbot Cuthbert seems to be a good man. In the meantime, I can offer you a healing potion. I was raised by a healer woman. She always ensures I ride with the means to tend wounds, as well as a bad stomach.'

'My lord.' She bobs, as I hand her a small package from Brute's saddlebags.

'Add this to water, and have her drink it. It should help with the fever.'

I pretend not to see the worry on her face that a Mercian might aid her. After all, she'll need to make her peace with that if she intends to seek sanctuary within my home kingdom.

'It might not be enough, but it'll help, I promise you.'

I lead Brute away, unease warring inside me. I sense the woman watching me as I rejoin Ealdorman Ælfstan, Wulfheard and the others.

'What is it?' Oswy questions, forehead wrinkled from where he's removed his helm to wipe sweat from his brow. His cheeks are almost grey with dust from the road.

'The child's sick. She should be resting.'

'There's no time for that,' is his less than helpful reply.

'No, there's not,' Wulfheard agrees. 'And there'll be more like it. Few will want to remain if the enemy are known to be moving closer.' I take the admonishment but all the same, as we continue onwards, I turn and feel the eyes of many on my back. We have horses. We move with speed. We could help these people who have so little. But that isn't our task. Instead we must hurry, riding towards the danger, and not away from it. And I personally feel the danger is ever-present. I hope King Æthelwulf doesn't take advantage of our presence here to achieve his vengeance against me.

16

Tonight, we sleep beneath the stars, the breeze bringing with it the scent of burning from the distant south. Ealdorman Ælfstan stays close to King Æthelwulf, but their voices carry clearly.

'Are we close to joining forces with King Ecgberht?' Ælfstan questions.

'Tomorrow, we'll find them,' King Æthelwulf asserts. While my fellow warriors are content to eat, drink, allow the horses to graze and generally play games of chance with one another, I feel unease ricocheting along my back. I really don't like this.

I take the middle watch, prevailing upon Wulfheard to allow me to have it, even though he grunts and complains because he's as wary as I am with the Wessex warriors so close. He's not forgotten the threat against me, just as I haven't. I notice there's always a Mercian on sentry duty, no matter how King Æthelwulf and his initial ten warriors try to prevail upon Ealdorman Ælfstan to allow the West Saxons to take the onerous duty. Perhaps, then, Ealdorman Ælfstan is as wary as I am.

Throughout the dark time of the night, I peer into the almost impenetrable blackness, lit only by a scattering of far-distant stars and a sliver of moon, the scent of smoke never dissipating. I can see little, and that makes my apprehension intensify. I stay away from the Wessex guard also given the task of watch duty. I don't want to get close enough to him he might take a chance on attacking me. When Oswy replaces me, grunting at the lack of sleep, I roll in my cloak but don't get much more rest. When I'm roused, it feels as though I have grit in my eyes, as well as dust on my face.

'You look like crap,' Wulfheard calls to me, when the horses have been fed and we're mounted once more. I take Brute towards him.

'I didn't sleep well. I don't like this,' I add in a softer voice. Wulfheard nods, and then offers me a smile.

'Ealdorman Ælfstan doesn't either. Be on your guard for more than just personal reasons. He suspects there'll be Viking raiders soon. He believes the Wessex king's son is too confident. As ever. The smoke from the fires you first saw is drawing closer.'

'That wasn't...' I try, but he moves on, dismissing me, or not hearing me. I try and reconcile myself to whether that's the worry driving me. Is it that the Viking raiders are nearby, or is it something else? Aside from my fears one of the Wessex warriors might attack me, is there also something else niggling in the back of my mind?

'My friend, ride with me,' Aldhelm, the Wessex warrior we fought, calls, and I take Brute to his side. His horse is an older stallion, a little bow-backed, but eager despite that. He's brown with some white markings, and his eyes are intelligent but not arrogant, unlike Brute's. 'I've never been here before,' Aldhelm mutters, as though sharing a confidence.

'Me neither,' I offer with raised eyebrows. He grins and nods.

'You fight pretty well,' he comments a little later, when silence has fallen between us, although it's far from uncomfortable as we trot onwards.

'As do you. Do you never use a shield?'

'Well, if I must, but to be honest, a seax and a sword usually has men running from me.'

I consider this, twisting my lips. 'Did you fight in the Wessex war against Mercia?'

'Not at Ellendun, no. My lord was once beholden to Mercia. It sat ill will him. He made all the right sounds to King Ecgberht, but stayed very firmly to the south of the new Wessex-Mercia divide.'

'What about the rest of them?'

Here Aldhelm shrugs. 'No, none of us fought the Mercians. In fact, that one there, the bald one, he was born in Gloucester. And him there,' and now he points to a black-haired man with a round face and small nose, 'was born at Kingsholm.'

'Ah,' I mutter, understanding more and more. These men have allegiances that have been forced to change. They're not, by birth, staunch Wessex warriors who hate all Mercians. Still, they did fight us when they discovered we were Mercians. Admittedly, the fight didn't last very long.

'My lord was an ally of King Coelwulf, the first of his name. That King Beornwulf. What an arsehole he was.' And just like that, I find myself tensing, unsure what to make of Aldhelm, after all. 'I take it you're too young to have met the man who stole the Mercian warrior helm and managed to be spectacularly defeated by all of Mercia's age-old enemies?'

'Well,' I stutter, but my need to respond is cut off by the shouts of Wessex warriors, greeting King Æthelwulf.

Ahead, the roadway we've been following, drawing closer and closer to the haze of smoke hanging in the air, opens up to reveal a tall hillside and at its peak the visible signs of men making their camp. It's almost so steep I fear we'll need to dismount to get to the peak, but of course, Brute's a stubborn git and willingly leads the way.

Looking at my few fellow Mercians as we near the top, I appreciate how exposed we are. We're deep within Wessex, in a landscape we little know, far from home and with Wessex warriors for company.

I glance at the hill fort, noting the encircling ditch and the mass of canvases scattered here and there. From my brief appraisal, it looks to contain a significant number of warriors and horses. But I don't believe significant equates to large.

King Æthelwulf turns to us, a satisfied smile on his face. 'If you'll excuse me, I'll seek out my father and inform him Ealdorman Ælfstan has arrived. I'm sure he'll welcome you and come and speak to you shortly. Then you can inform your king of what Wessex faces.' So spoken, he moves easily through the encircling ditch around the campsite on the pinnacle of the hill, the guards allowing him within. We're left outside, looking in, stood on the side of the steep hill, with warm air buffeting us. Brute moves forwards and backwards uneasily. I reach down and pat his black and white shoulder as his breathing stills. We have the ten Wessex warriors we fought to keep us company, amongst them Aldhelm, as well as more of King Æthelwulf's warriors. I notice the ten who went to Kingsholm escort King Æthelwulf to his father. Greetings are shouted between warriors, but here, outside the circle of protection, silence rings, and we're under the scrutiny of six men who guard the easy access inside the hill fort itself.

Squinting, I endeavour to determine how large the Wessex force is. The men seem reasonably well equipped. There are horses to the left of us, picketed in a large field. There are also orderly rows of tents leading towards a taller, more elaborate one at the centre. There are guards on duty at the edges of the ditch, no more than half a man deep, and with an attendant rampart of dirt the same size. But there aren't as many warriors as I believed there'd be based on King Æthelwulf's arrogant assessment of his father's number. Not if my reckoning of those I can see training is correct.

I turn to look at Wulfheard. He and Ealdorman Ælfstan are engaged in a conversation. It falls to Aldhelm to say aloud what I'm thinking, and evidently, what others have also observed.

'Well, where by the grace of God are the rest of the bastards?'

* * *

Eventually, we dismount and allow the horses to graze on the nearby grasses dotting the hillside. King Æthelwulf implied we'd be seen by King Ecgberht shortly, but that's not the case. I'm not alone in constantly looking back the way we've come. The road we've followed has tiny people moving north on it to escape the threat from the enemy.

While Brute drinks from the nearby stream, and then returns to grazing, allowing me to brush the dust from his coat, coughing as I do so, I muse on all I know about King Ecgberht.

I don't like him, I comprehend that much. I consider whether that's a reasoned reaction to all I understand about him, or if it's because of his actions. I decide, quite rightly, he's a bloody bastard and that's why I don't like him. I'm also recalled to Wynflæd's words on the battlements of Londinium last summer. She had some interesting things to say about a man who professes to be a Christian king and yet who has an affinity for other beliefs, more pagan than Christian.

I also think about the occasions I've encountered him, and try to remember if I've ever seen him fighting as opposed to running away from Mercians. I'll need to give that more consideration. I've seen more of his arse than his face, I'm sure of it.

I also realise he must be an old man by now, surely. He's been king of Wessex for thirty-four summers. His survival should be a testament to the type of king he is, but I suspect it has more to do with his ability to take advantage of Mercia's self-destructive trend in recent years. While Wessex has enjoyed one king for thirty-four summers, Mercia hasn't had the same luck. As I reckon it, Kings Coenwulf, Coelwulf, Beornwulf, Ludica and Wiglaf have ruled in the same period. Five kings, to their one.

Only as the sun begins to set on the horizon, shrouded strangely because of the smoke fogging the air ahead of us, does King Æthelwulf finally reappear.

'Apologies for keeping you waiting,' he calls, although he clearly doesn't mean it, his voice lacking all sense of an apology, as we begin to lead our horses towards the temporary camp. 'King Ecgberht was scouting, to the south of here.' The words sound reasoned enough, but I suspect them. I can't say I've seen any riders returning to the encampment, aside from the foraging party that swept through not long after we arrived. Admittedly, there might be another entrance I can't see. The flat hill top is huge.

I turn to Ealdorman Ælfstan. In the greying light, he inclines his head towards King Æthelwulf, but I can't see his features. I suspect he's less than happy at being kept waiting.

'There was such urgency to reach here,' Ealdorman Ælfstan comments lightly. 'But of course, scouting is an important task.' The implication is clear, but King Æthelwulf pays no attention to it. Instead, he beckons for us to come within, as though we're being invited to a feast, while we lead our horses. Only then he pauses, and turns to look towards the animal paddock.

'Perhaps they should be left here. There's little room within the encampment for so many horses. The hay and barley are stored close to the animals.' I don't like this either, but after an assessing glance, Ealdorman Ælfstan nods to show he agrees. Now we turn our horses to the paddock. We could have done that as soon as we arrived. Arseholes. Once at the paddock, we lift clear saddles and stirrups, although we leave the reins on the animals.

'This way,' one of the grooms advises us. We take our horses' equipment towards yet another canvas, in which much riding gear has been left, and even more grooms scrub at mud-encrusted stirrups. I release my grip on Brute's saddle uneasily. I can't shake my deep unhappiness at being here.

But none of the others seem to notice it. Indeed, they joke as they jostle one another. Oswy informs one of the young grooms he'll pay him handsomely, with good Mercian coins, of course, if he manages to remove the deeply ingrained mud from his saddle. I doubt the groom cares which king's head is on the coins, as he agrees eagerly. Kings might fight about their heads on coins, but a coin is a coin to everyone else.

Only then do we actually enter the Wessex camp.

It's set up like other military encampments I've experienced. There are tents and cook fires, and men stand or sit around, drinking or eating. They watch us warily as we follow Ealdorman Ælfstan towards the central tent, where I assume King Ecgberht waits to greet us.

There are guards on duty. They stand aside and bow to King Æthelwulf, who enters the canvas, calling for his father. I suddenly realise how many Wessex warriors there are. All of them could mean me harm. Oswy remains so close to me, he almost steps on my ankles. I'd curse him for it, but it's welcome. Between us, Oswy and I could kill a fair few of the bastards before they got close enough to end my life.

Ealdorman Ælfstan pauses before entering, and meets Wulfheard's gaze. Whatever unspoken command passes between them, Wulfheard stops, and turns to us.

'We'll wait here,' he calls, the order ensuring we don't argue with him. I watch Ealdorman Ælfstan duck inside the tent, and hear voices murmuring court niceties. I eye the Wessex warriors standing on duty. They wear the king's colours of black and white. Some have depictions of the Wessex wyvern on their tunics and cloaks, but most don't. They eye us with insolence. I return the favour. Aldhelm sidles up to me. I don't miss he's remained with the Mercians and doesn't move freely amongst the Wessex warriors. We all find something to do, whether it's surveying the encampment in the reducing light of dusk, enjoying the view towards the sea – well, what of it can be seen – or kicking aside bits of mud or torn grasses. As darkness falls more fully, sentry lights spring up at the perimeter of the camp.

'Well, this is all a lot of hurry up and do bugger all,' Aldhelm complains. I nod in agreement.

'We've wasted much time waiting for King Ecgberht to be available.'

'Perhaps King Æthelwulf should have sent a messenger to inform him we were on our way,' Aldhelm mutters.

I hear Oswy talking, too loudly, and with absolutely no reticence about all the Wessex bastards he's killed in his time. I'm astounded not only does Wulfheard not berate him, he's joining in.

'I see your friends are determined to make some new enemies.'

'I think old enemies, and just to reinforce it,' I offer, trying to inject some levity into my tone, but it falls flat. Aldhelm nods, his expression pensive.

Sooner than expected, Ealdorman Ælfstan emerges from the king's tent. I can't see his expression, but his stance is far from reassuring.

'Come, men,' he calls to us. 'We'll camp tonight with our horses.'

That, I find, is the most encouraging thing he could have said. Together, we stride outside the ditch and enclosure, without any complaints from the sentries, and only when we're all together does Ealdorman Ælfstan turn to look at us, his face lit with shadows from the campfire the grooms have constructed to cook on.

'That went as well as you can imagine,' he offers with a grimace. 'King Ecgberht expects much and doesn't condescend to listen to the terms King Wiglaf determined upon before we left Kingsholm. I've asked for details on the size of his force, and where the enemy are, aside from obviously towards the south where the smoke comes from. I received little but evasions. Tomorrow, we'll return north. King Wiglaf won't wish to ally with King Ecgberht.' Here he speaks more quietly. 'Not when there's nothing to gain, and King Ecgberht asks not as a wounded man, but rather as one who thinks he still rules Mercia as well as Wessex. No. King Wiglaf won't desire to aid a man such as him. Now, tonight, we'll have two on watch duty, no matter the Wessex warriors conducting the same. I don't trust that bastard.' Ealdorman Ælfstan spits those words.

And with that confirmation sitting as heavily in my belly as badly cooked pork, we prepare for the night. I'm still tired from last night's watch duty, but when I'm woken to take the third watch, I find myself unaccustomedly refreshed, and take myself to Brute, who watches me with eyes seething with fury at being kept within the Wessex paddock. I run my hand along his nose, seeking the other animals who keep him company, my other hand never far from my seax.

King Æthelwulf made it clear many horses had been lost in the initial encounter with the enemy. I assume these animals are the replacements, and also the king's own force. In which case, I would expect the animals to be of a high calibre, and well trained to take the commands of their riders. Yet what I do see, in the gradually growing light of the spring day, is a host of animals, from pack animals to small-handed creatures, who'll be hardy, but not fast. Only a smattering of what I would think of as animals fit for a king and his warrior entourage are amongst them.

As my fellow warriors wake, I greet them, my expression far from happy, and it only turns more sour as a fresh great cloud of grey smoke rises into the air, bringing with it the stink of burning, and I swear I can hear the crackle of things being consumed by the flames.

The Viking raiders have drawn even closer to the encampment of the king of Wessex on his peak at Brent Knoll. If he was scouting the surrounding landscape yesterday, how can he have bloody missed them when I suspect they're less than half a day away? Admittedly there's a wide expanse of water below our feet to the south, but, as they have ships, and we don't, it's really not an impediment for them. Now I sense I'm surrounded by men who'd like to kill me, with even more coming to help them, should they fail.

17

A cry of dismay rumbles throughout the encampment as everyone wakes. Already, I'm moving towards the tent where Brute's saddle's been stored. I gather it into my hands, once my frantic actions find it, having bashed shoulders with my fellow warriors who intend to do the same, and I rush back to Brute. My beast stands placidly as I place his saddle in position. As I've been awake so long, he's already been fed his hay and crushed barley. He's even keener than I am to seek out where the smoke originates.

There are shouts from within the Wessex encampment, but the men of Mercia are all mounted and ready long before any of the Wessex warriors come to claim their horses. Ealdorman Ælfstan has us prepared, as the cloud grows wider and wider, pieces of ash dancing in the eddies of the air above our heads. The sullen and persistent threat of smoke, visible throughout our entire journey south, has become something much more menacing. It's as though the whole world south and west of us is aflame, but we don't ride out, not yet, because the Wessex force makes no move to join us.

'What are we bloody waiting for?' Oswy calls angrily.

'We're not to fight in place of the Wessex warriors,' Ealdorman Ælfstan reminds him, but his tone is gruff. I can tell he's as frustrated as we are. Aldhelm, the Wessex warrior from close to Malmesbury, is also prepared, as are the others with him. His face is twisted with fury, just like mine.

Eventually, King Æthelwulf marches towards us from within the defences of the hilltop site, dressed for battle but showing no inclination to hurry. He appraises us with a sneer, his warriors at his side.

'Terrified of a little smoke, are we?' he demands, lips twisted with disdain.

'My lord king. We're warriors. Much better to be prepared than caught with our arses out of our trews,' Ealdorman Ælfstan responds without heat, his gaze on those who rush after their king, frantically trying to secure those trews and boots. King Æthelwulf doesn't turn to look, but instead strides towards his horse, standing ready for its rider and with a groom having hold of the reins. The grooms and the warriors of Mercia are more prepared than the bloody king of Kent.

'My father, the king,' he adds, as though we don't already know that, 'has ordered we ride out and assess the damage. He commands you to join me.' I think the encampment should be being moved from its current position, but instead the initial dismay has drained away. Now the men not escorting King Æthelwulf seem more concerned with feeding their bellies than finding out what's happening, even as the smoke grows thicker.

'What will King Ecgberht be doing?' Ealdorman Ælfstan questions with an edge to his voice.

King Æthelwulf turns a furious gaze on him. 'Do not question my father's honour. He has many warriors to organise, and will be doing so.' I'm not alone in scouring the encampment from my vantage point in Brute's saddle, looking for said warriors. Certainly, the flood of Wessex men striding this way has lessened.

'My lord king.' Ealdorman Ælfstan inclines his head, but the words aren't an apology. They're far from one. They're cold and hang with intent. I notice three of Ealdorman Tidwulf's men share a knowing smirk. Luckily, King Æthelwulf doesn't see it. Instead, surrounded by fewer horsemen than Ealdorman Ælfstan currently commands, King Æthelwulf directs his horse around the encampment. As we circle the defences on the crest of the hilltop, I get a really good look at how many canvases there are, and what the men within them are doing. Many aren't even arming themselves, wearing only tunics and trews. They don't even move with their weapons belts fastened in place. From the king's tent, at the centre, however, I see a steady stream of warriors who are attired for battle entering and then leaving. There are a growing number of emblematic shields to assess as well. Perhaps, then, the size of the force is larger than I estimated, but just as quickly, I realise it's not. The section of the encircled ditch closest to where the smoke rises to the south and west is largely empty. King Ecgberht awaits more of his ealdormen joining him, or so the gaps imply.

I turn from evaluating the strength, or lack of it, of the Wessex king, to the area south of us. The bright daylight flounders in the thick smoke. I wince against the strange grey glare and wish I could see more, but it's impossible.

'Take ten riders north. See what you can find out, and then return here,' Ealdorman Ælfstan orders Wulfheard, hurrying to catch up with King Æthelwulf, who's streaked ahead, encouraging his horse to descend from the peak. Wulfheard opens his mouth to argue, but the ealdorman is already too far away.

I look from Wulfheard to Oswy, somehow unsurprised when I'm instructed to go with Oswy and Ealdorman Ælfstan. Cenred, Maneca, Kyre, and Goðeman join me, as do five of Ealdorman Tidwulf's men, while the Wessex warriors we fought not far from Malmesbury stay with us as well. I turn to shout to Wulfheard, but he's already turned away to fulfil Ealdorman Ælfstan's commands. Wulfheard's shoulders are tight. He doesn't like being separated from Ealdorman Ælfstan. Neither does the damn fool trust the rest of us with the task of protecting him.

As we slowly descend to ground level, we move through cloud, tinged with the stink of smoke. I cough more than once, and eventually pull my cloak hood so I can cover my mouth and not inhale the dry smell of smoke more than necessary. It almost helps.

We can see little, however. I'm sure, in the distance, I hear the shush of water hitting sand, although I can't see the sea, or even the river I know is nearby because I glimpsed it when we arrived. I confess, my eyes are every-where, determined not to be caught out by a random strike from one of King Æthelwulf's warriors. On we go. And then suddenly, Ealdorman Ælfstan calls a warning.

'Ware,' he cries. Brute obeys my instructions immediately, kicking up grass and mud as he digs his hooves into the ground to come to an imme-diate stop. I gasp, grateful for Ealdorman Ælfstan's position up ahead. I can't say King Æthelwulf's been paying anywhere near as much attention. I hear the cries of startled people emerging from the smoke, and grip my seax.

But, veering towards us, people walk as though built only of shadows, until they're close enough we can see smoke-filled, red-rimmed eyes, and the chalk-white faces of shock and uncertainty about what's happening. These aren't my enemy.

'Be careful,' I shout to someone who almost walks blindly into Brute. From beneath long, straggly hair, a thin face looks at me, lips compressed, eyes blazing with defeat.

'S... sorry,' the figure gasps. I can't tell if it's a man or a woman, even their tone deadened by the horror we ride through.

The smoky cloud spits forth more and more figures. Some tall, some short, some no more than children. I'm aware of the dry, hacking sound of those who've inhaled too much smoke. My heart thuds in my chest. I want to help these people.

'Come on,' Ealdorman Ælfstan calls gruffly. I only know it's him in front of me because I recognise the swishing tail and gait of his mount. 'Slower, but we must make progress.'

I encourage Brute, but not at any great speed, my fellow Mercians calling to those who walk towards us, ensuring they know we're there. It's horrifying. I reach for my water bottle, thinking to hand it to them, but then don't. Instead, I swig a small mouthful and return it to my saddlebag. I'll need water.

'Ahead and up the steep slope,' I encourage. 'King Ecgberht's there, with his warriors. They'll aid you.' I hope I speak the truth.

'A fat lot of help that will bloody do.' I hear the angry cry although I'm unsure who speaks, and wince. King Ecgberht should be doing more. It's one thing to summon his warriors, but I've not seen any of them engage with the enemy, while these poor people have evidently been set upon by the Viking raiders. Perhaps they lived in a coastal settlement.

As we move south, it grows warmer, uncomfortably warm. Now I do see King Æthelwulf again. He's brought his men to a halt. I realise why. In the near distance, there's a swathe of burning buildings and crops. The fields sway, and not with a mild breeze. Neither do they glow with gentle sunlight, but instead a fiery heart at their centre belches forth clouds of smoke. I hear the shush of sound below Brute's hooves, and witness the small creatures who live here, scarpering. Even the bloody rats. Brute neighs unhappily at the sound of scurrying claws. I bend forward and pat his long neck, offering muttered reassurances. I see his nostrils are dry. The smoke's doing him no good, and I've no more fabric to swirl around his face. I'm aghast he's scared of the rats, but my unease at what I'm seeing means I can forgive him that when he's otherwise so stoic.

'Bloody hell,' I gasp, Brute's reins slack in my hands.

'Bloody hell, indeed,' Cenred agrees. My eyes are itchy and too hot. I appreciate if we're not careful, the fire will be closing on us. For now, it's fields away but it is moving inexorably closer.

'We need to get out of here,' Oswy encourages Ealdorman Ælfstan, coughing at the end of those few words.

'We should retreat,' Ealdorman Ælfstan calls to King Æthelwulf, but there's no reply. I sense King Æthelwulf can't truly comprehend what he's seeing. He sits in the saddle, immobile, his shoulders slumped. 'My lord king,' Ealdorman Ælfstan implores, while the Mercians and I look back the way we've come. We need to be careful. We can't rush from here or we'll risk colliding with all the people we've just evaded.

I hear the cries of the wounded and terrified, and now my fingers tighten on my reins. Oswy rides towards me, shaking his head.

'Retreat,' he urges us. 'I'll wait for Ealdorman Ælfstan. Help those you can. Pick them up and place them on your horses, but be careful. I don't like this. If the wind changes direction, we'll be buggered.'

The crackle of flames is coming closer. I sense it in the sudden surge in temperature.

'My lord,' I call to Ealdorman Ælfstan, turning Brute. He turns his ash-grey face my way.

'I'm coming,' he promises, and is true to his word. He too encourages his already quite determined horse to turn back the way we've come. I listen for King Æthelwulf but don't hear the hooves of his horse or those of his men. The bloody fool. If they wait too long, they'll be nothing but ash and bone. I've no intention of allowing that to happen to myself and my fellow warriors.

It takes longer than I expect to encounter the first of those fleeing the fire. I thought they moved slowly, but perhaps sensing escape is close they hurry onwards, the slope building beneath their feet. Cenred's the first to scoop up two small children, held in the arms of a hurrying adult.

'I'll take the children,' he calls. 'Icel, take them,' he instructs me, indicating the taller figure. I rush to pull the hand of the person. I look into terrified, red-rimmed eyes, and can't tell if it's a man or a woman, even when I shuffle back in the saddle, and have them sitting before me, the reins to either side. I suspect, because they're not as tall as me, it might be a woman, but I can't be certain. Moving to join Cenred, I offer a smile to the two sets of frightened eyes.

'It's okay,' the dry voice reassures the children. It's filled with desolation. Then, from behind, I hear a thundering crackle, and a heated gust of wind.

'It's coming this way.' I lift my voice to shout to any who might hear it, from the scurrying rats to the hopping hares trying to dodge out of the way of people. From behind, Oswy's urging everyone to rush. Abruptly, two horses surge ahead of mine. Oswy and Maneca have people on their mounts. I shake my head, unsure how we missed them, but missed them we did. Ealdorman Ælfstan's just behind Oswy. He leads a horse or donkey, and also has a hazed figure in front of him in the saddle. Again, I can't determine the age of the person, or whether they're a man or a woman. There are more shrieks of terror echoing from behind us, I think, and I pause, listening.

'Don't stop,' Ealdorman Ælfstan informs me, voice hoarse. 'The flames are coming quicker than even Brute can gallop.' Swallowing my fear, I peer into the gloom, desperate to incite Brute to ride faster, but not wanting to risk him being wounded, or crashing into others also trying to escape.

It's as though we're descended into hell. All is chaos and fear. All is fire and heat. I'd welcome the brush of a cooling breeze. But I'm not to get it. Instead, the wind's hot.

I've not realised how far we've travelled away from the encampment. I keep peering forwards, hoping to see an end to the smoky cloud and the hilltop ahead, but it's impossible to see anything aside from grey haze.

Then, suddenly, we're in clear air, the smoky cloud behind me a diaphanous shape swelling and contracting as I gaze at it. It surges forward with a mind of its own, driven by the wind and the availability of growing crops to burn.

'Come on,' Ealdorman Ælfstan orders us with a croak in his voice, but I don't miss his lingering look behind us. King Æthelwulf isn't there. Where is the damn fool?

'Hurry,' I shout to those who've dropped to the ground, coughing, and pleased to be free from the smoke. 'It's moving this way,' I explain when they don't immediately obey me.

'Hurry,' the rest of the Mercians shout, the Wessex warriors we met near Malmesbury adding their voices to ours. Only now do the tired people who thought they'd travelled far enough away struggle to their feet and hurry after us. I give Brute his head, free from the smoke. He ambles to a canter, but no swifter. I don't push him. If he doesn't feel he can gallop, I won't order him to do so. But we move quickly enough that, within sight of the Wessex encampment on the peak, I pull Brute to a halt and help the person down. They turn, but Cenred's there with the two small children. The children join the adult, and with a murmured 'thank you' from the three, I turn back to aid more.

I get a good look at the cloud of smoke. Before, it was ash-grey and seemed static, now I detect the red glow at its heart and appreciate Ealdorman Ælfstan spoke the truth, it is moving forwards. I don't believe it'll reach the Wessex encampment, but only because a small stream runs through the landscape, and that, I hope, will ensure the flames have nothing else to consume. Brute falters below me. I grab his reins and clench my thighs so I won't fall, shaking my head, as three small mice scurry past. My horse really doesn't know what to be scared of.

Ealdorman Ælfstan's again at my side. We move back through the crowd of people running from the fire, scooping up those closest to the trailing edge of the smoke, but not entering it again. I still don't see King Æthelwulf, not in any of the three returning journeys I make, and fear grows leaden in my stomach. Where is King Ecgberht's son? Does he truly have no sense of self-preservation? The Wessex warriors from the encampment have stirred themselves to some action, descending from their peak. They hurry to help the survivors from the fire, but King Ecgberht's entirely absent until someone must inform the king his son is missing.

On my fourth return trip, I see King Ecgberht, mounted on his black horse, fully garbed as a warrior king, rushing through the crowd, with many warriors near to him.

'Where's King Æthelwulf?' he roars, time and time again, eyes peering angrily at us. No one answers because no one knows.

I look towards the cloud of smoke, sure it finally no longer moves forward, hoping the small stream I urged Brute to jump over has acted as a means of breaking the fire's ferocity. But there's no sign of the king's son.

I hear the thunder of hooves, and the cries of exhausted, ash-caked people trying to evade the heavy hooves of the warriors' horses. Then King Ecgberht's beside me. He eyes me with contempt, blocking the path of Brute. His words thrum with menace, and I shudder away from his rage, but I'm not sure he knows who I am with ash coating my face.

'Where's my son? Why have you abandoned the king of Kent?'

I open my mouth to reply, only to hear yet more horses, and thankfully, the voice of King Æthelwulf, demanding people move out of his way for he is 'the king of Kent'. I growl low in my throat, angry he's endangering people when he should have left so much earlier, but King Ecgberht doesn't seem to notice. He rushes to meet his son, no regard for the people unable to get out of the way of his horse. My lips curl and a snarl erupts from my mouth at the sound of breaking bones and the cut-off shriek of one of those trampled by the king.

I'm off my horse, running towards the injured person before I'm even aware of it, but all that greets me are the forever-staring eyes of a small child's body supine on the ground, with an ash-grey face. Only the firm grip of Ealdorman Ælfstan's hand on my arm ensures I don't strike the bloody king of Wessex's head from his neck there and then.

18

'What are you bloody doing?' King Ecgberht's voice is filled with rage as he sees me, hand reaching for my seax, although Ealdorman Ælfstan manages to prevent that by hanging on to me. Oswy's to the other side. The two men shelter me, as I glower into King Ecgberht's twisted face from atop his blowing mount.

'How could you?' I gasp.

'How could I bloody what?' he demands angrily. 'Get out of my way, Mercian.' His voice drips with contempt.

'You ran that child over, killed her when she was safe.'

'What child?' But King Ecgberht changes tack immediately. 'Why did you abandon my son?' I glimpse King Æthelwulf next to his father, his poor horse panting heavily, his rider staying stubbornly mounted, although I see the animal's struggling.

'Get off that bloody horse before it collapses and crushes your leg,' Oswy orders King Æthelwulf, saving me from having to state the obvious.

'Watch your tongue when you speak to me,' King Æthelwulf growls, only for the poor horse to stagger. Somehow, King Æthelwulf manages to spring free from the ailing animal, and stands aside as it folds down towards the ground, front legs failing beneath its chest.

King Ecgberht looks from the horse to his son, but if I think he's going to show any sense, he quickly disabuses me of that.

'You left my son with a horse in such a state. I'll have you tried for treason against the king's *mund*,' he roars. I endeavour to shake off those who hold me, but Ealdorman Ælfstan and Oswy are damn strong. I need to cough the smoke from my body.

'We did no such thing, my lord king,' Ealdorman Ælfstan speaks coolly. His words thrum while, at last, those who fled the fire are getting some help from the Wessex encampment above our heads. 'I ordered King Æthelwulf to flee with us. He didn't. Neither did his warriors. There was no reason why they didn't. Now, my lord king, I suggest you look to your people, rather than accusing us of crimes against your damn *mund*.'

'What?' King Ecgberht exacts, his face turning puce, which is quite a sight.

'Help your people, my lord king. And someone get this horse water or it'll die.' For a moment, no one moves. I slowly ease the tension in my body, realising King Ecgberht's oblivious to the life he's ended trying to reach his son. Instead, he beckons his son to him, and then dismounts, before pushing his son to take his place. King Æthelwulf kicks his struggling, collapsed horse on the ground and then does as his father commands. Cenred materialises, a bucket of water in each hand, which I have no idea how he's found. One he throws over the downed horse's back, and the other he holds before its head, hoping the smell will encourage the animal to drink.

'Slice its throat,' King Æthelwulf calls dismissively. 'It's no bloody use to anyone like that.' And with that, King Ecgberht moves back towards his hilltop encampment, walking beside his son, who rides, and without so much as a care for the people who've escaped from the fire. Or the unwell horse.

I shake my head, fury burning from me like the heart of the fire, but with enough awareness not to compound what's happened here by attacking the Wessex king. Instead, I bend to the lifeless form of the child, and place my hand over the still warm face to close those accusing eyes. I swirl my cloak from my shoulders, and place it over the child, scooping it into my arms and walking away, Brute watching me with calm eyes, the wounded horse finally drinking before staggering upright.

'Slit its throat, my arse.' I hear Cenred's angry words. 'And them allegedly so desperate for new mounts to replace the ones that perished at Carhampton.'

Aside from the distant cry of those within the hilltop encampment, and the soft words of encouragement from some of the Mercian warriors to people fallen on the ground, there's silence. I sense many watch me, but I walk, skirting the hill, Brute a presence at my side, Ealdorman Ælfstan and Oswy accompanying me. There's a nearby settlement, and I hope they'll have a priest.

As I go, more and more people join me, their faces etched with ash and tears, so eventually I appear at the burial site with many people besides me, eyes cast low, some weeping and wailing. There's much to be sorrowful for. Kyre's ridden on ahead, I realise, as a priest garbed in his robe and with the accoutrements of his profession to hand greets me at the burial ground just outside the settlement. The small church building is within the boundaries of the settlement, although the burial site is by the side of the road leading towards it.

The priest's a sharp-eyed man as he absorbs everything happening before him. I hear his soft prayers as I place the bundle at his feet. Already, six people lever earth from the ground to allow burial. The child feels so light, it's almost as though there's no weight to her. Now, as I stand back, I sense the loss from my arms, and a single tear drips down my ash-coated and bearded cheek.

'We'll see the child buried,' the priest speaks softly to me. I think he'll reach out and touch my arm, but he instead grips his rosary tighter. 'Others who've succumbed to the smoke and fire will also be buried here. Thank you.' Two women with bowed heads come forward to aid him in tending to the pathetic creature. I lower my head, absorbed with sorrow for the loss of this small life. But rage kindles within me. It's hot and fiery. For now, it's tempered and under control but I don't know how long that will last.

I turn to my fellow warriors, and nod towards them. Ealdorman Ælfstan offers me a sorrowful smile, and then tries to speak, only to cough violently.

'Come, men,' he calls to us when he can speak. 'We've witnessed all we need to see about the enemy and the Wessex response to it. It pains me to say this, but let's return to Mercia. And all here should know, King Wiglaf will welcome them if they prefer to leave their homes.' A murmur greets those words. I nod to show Ealdorman Ælfstan speaks the truth.

I can't deny his decision. We've seen all we needed to see. We've seen what horrors the Viking raiders are prepared to inflict on the people of Wessex. But more, we've seen how little regarded these people are by their own damn king.

* * *

I walk Brute back towards the hilltop encampment. I don't want to ride him. He'll be struggling as much as I am after inhaling so much smoke. A more gentle wind rustles my byrnie. I feel a shudder of chill, even though it's a hot breeze. It reminds me I've given my cloak away. Not that it matters. I'd sooner be a little cold now than cold forever, like the poor child.

The Mercians are as quiet as the Wessex warriors who seem to have attached themselves to us since we fought them not far from Malmesbury. I count them, but I'm sure someone's missing. More and more ash-stained people walk past us, many offering their thanks for aid, as they take themselves towards the settlement that will ensure the burial of the dead, as opposed to the hilltop peak of their king. No doubt, their welcome there will be warmer than from King Ecgberht's warriors in the encampment.

I don't know what to say. I decide it's better not to speak, and my fellow Mercians agree, so we're a sullen lot as we get closer to the paddock. I'm seeking out Wulfheard in the swell of people, aware the grey smoky cloud rises higher and higher into the air, but doesn't seem to be getting any nearer.

Suddenly, twelve mounted Wessex warriors appear before us. I look up from beside Brute, squinting at them, considering why they're before us.

'You Mercians. You stand accused of crimes against the person of King Ecgberht. Come with us quietly, and it'll go better for you,' the lead warrior announces defiantly from atop his horse. I don't miss they have no ash staining their faces or clothes. What have they been doing all morning? They've certainly not been aiding their fellow West Saxons. Only now do I realise the men ride with blades unsheathed. It's the most iron I've seen on a Wessex warrior since the fight with Aldhelm close to Mercia's border with Wessex.

'What?' Ealdorman Ælfstan barks, his voice remaining ash-clogged although his fury's easy to hear.

'You imperilled the king's son. You're to face justice for your actions, on the orders of King Ecgberht. Now, step away from the horses and come with us. The animals won't be hurt.'

'What?' Ealdorman Ælfstan demands once more. I run my hand along Brute's nose and step forwards.

'You only need me,' I call, aware of how I can ensure my fellow Mercians return to King Wiglaf to inform him of what's truly happening in Wessex. 'Let the other Mercians go.'

'Icel, no,' I hear both Oswy and Ealdorman Ælfstan complain, but a knowing smile blooms on the warrior's face. Evidently, King Ecgberht did recognise me after all, even through the ash coating my face.

'King Ecgberht said you'd be too honourable to allow others to face justice for your crimes. Now, come on, you Mercian whoreson.'

I tie Brute's reins high above his saddle, and fix Oswy with a glower. 'Tend to my horse,' I order him. He nods, his eyes never leaving my face.

'Icel, don't be such a bloody fool,' Ealdorman Ælfstan shouts, his eyes flashing with ire, now the Wessex warriors move to encircle me, their spears pointing at my allies, with more of the Wessex warriors reinforcing them. The Mercian force is entirely overwhelmed, what with Wulfheard and his half of my allies still missing. One of the enemy warriors moves towards me and yanks my blades from my weapons belt.

I face the ealdorman, determination on my face, rage on his.

'Return to Mercia. Tell King Wiglaf of everything that's happened here. It's better only one man face the wrath of the Wessex arsehole, not all of us.'

'No,' Ealdorman Ælfstan barks.

I feel a kick on my backside, and tumble forwards, just arresting my fall with my hands outstretched. I push myself upwards. A rope's looped around my waist as though I'm a damn cow being led to market.

'Take us all,' the ealdorman remonstrates, but the Wessex warrior who spoke is shaking his head.

'We have what we want. Now, be on your way before I change my mind, and order you all killed.' The spears again jut towards the Mercians, who are entirely outnumbered. It seems bizarre King Ecgberht has sent so many to threaten men I thought he wished to ally with. Perhaps, then, this was all a trap to bring me to justice for my actions against Wessex. It's been a very elaborate ploy, in that case.

The rope's pulled tight, and my hands are also bound. Ealdorman Ælfstan and Oswy continue to argue against the necessity, their voices rich with anger, but I'm yanked away from my fellow warriors, desperately hoping they don't try and start a fight, not when we're all exhausted from our encounter with the smoke. I hope they heed my words. After all, I am but one man of Mercia. If the Viking raiders continue to overwhelm Wessex then the shields of Mercia will be needed for far more important tasks than defending me.

I look up, fixing on the blue sky and soft clouds directly overhead, as opposed to the grey smoke, and walk where I'm directed, although my legs tremble beneath me. I know I'm doing the correct thing. I know I'm acting in the best interests of Mercia, but still, I'm fearful. The Wessex king wants me dead, I'm sure of it. Have I just willingly allowed him to ensure I meet my death?

I'm led to the side of the encampment from which I should be able to see the sea if there was less smoke in the air, the cries of my fellow Mercians finally dying away. I doubt they've given up on me easily. But, hopefully, they've realised now isn't the time to fight for me. They need to protect Mercia, and King Ecgberht evidently has no plans to counter the threat from the Viking raiders, despite King Æthelwulf's assertion to the contrary. I do spare a thought for Ealdorman Ælfstan having to explain to Wulfheard what's happened. That won't go well with either of them.

There's a tall oak tree with a wide trunk on the slanting slope. I'm not the first to be apprehended by the Wessex king.

I startle to see Aldhelm already there. He was the one missing when I assessed their numbers, I realise. I'd feared him lost in the smoke. Aldhelm's familiar forehead furrows as he sees me being brought towards the tree, but he doesn't speak. Quickly, my feet are bound by rope, which is then looped around the tree. I slump to the ground, thirsty but too stubborn to ask for water. With a kick from three of the Wessex bastards, they stride to where four others keep guard over the handful of apprehended men.

'What happened?' Aldhelm demands. I consider not replying, but realise he'll only keep asking questions if I don't.

'King Ecgberht rode his horse through a child and killed her. I told him as much, and in response, he accuses me of crimes against his bloody royal *mund*.'

'Bastard,' Aldhelm mutters, his tone implying what he thinks of his alleged king.

'What about you?' I query, while he reaches across and tries to hand me a small wooden beaker of stale water which I swig gratefully all the same. 'I thought you were with us?'

'No, last night I broke a few noses amongst the king's guards when they accused me of being a Mercian lover. No one liked that.'

'Wessex noses?' I ask, just to be sure.

'What other noses are there around here?' He shrugs, the ghost of a smile on his lips.

I don't reply, instead leaning as far back as I can with tied feet and hands. My breath is too fast, despite my attempts to calm myself. I feel as though I've fought twenty men, and killed them all. But I've not had that honour. Instead, the bloody king of Wessex has run down one of his own people and now thinks to berate me because his son's a foolish arse and didn't heed our orders. Everything's the wrong way round, and I've not even seen a bloody Viking raider yet.

'Get some rest,' Aldhelm mutters. 'They'll have you on some sort of duty all night.' I close my eyes, endeavouring to do as he says, but all I see is that child's dead face, and all I hear is the crack of broken bones and the thud of a falling body hitting the hard ground. I don't detect the sound of the Viking raiders, or the harness jangle of Wessex warriors going to protect their people. No. I hear them killing one of their own, and my heart's sickened and saddened, and just bloody angry and furious.

I knew King Ecgberht was a worm of a man and not the wyvern of Wessex he likes to be depicted as, but he's shown me how weak he is. How weak, uncaring and unfeeling. He doesn't protect the people of Wessex.

In this moment, I know King Ecgberht has no right to rule this kingdom. He doesn't deserve to be king, but the Viking raiders will be no better, either. What then is to happen to Wessex, and do I even bloody care when, surely, I'm about to die at the hands of the feeble Wessex king and his son? His need to seek vengeance against me has entirely blinded him to the threat of the true enemy. I hope his kingdom doesn't regret that. I hope Mercia doesn't even more fervently.

19

Somehow, I fall asleep and I'm kicked awake by more than one foot, my head lolled to one side, my neck aching and my tongue stuck to the roof of my mouth. I cough and peer blearily into the eyes of some Wessex turds.

'Get up, you snivelling piece of shit,' the one growls in a voice so deep it sets my teeth on edge. 'You've got some horse shit to shift and that's the most pleasant of the tasks set aside for you.'

'Water,' I request and the one kicks me again, but the other warrior, with a face of two halves, where he's evidently been sliced open at some stage and stitched back together oddly, reaches out and offers me a beaker. With my arms removed from where they were wrapped around the tree trunk, they flop uselessly to my sides, even though I want the water. I thought him kind, but now, as I grimace, opening and closing my hands, I realise he's as much of a cock as the others. As I endeavour to reach out, he pours the water over my dusty boots, laughing as though possessed, similar to a hysterical holy man, fleeing from the enemy with his robes around his knees. 'Bastard,' I huff, bending my knees to stand upright, and casting a surreptitious look around for Aldhelm. He's not there. Indeed, none of the apprehended men remain bound around the trees. The sky's turning to dusk and so, it appears, the prisoners are to be put to good use.

'Get a bloody move on,' the second man barks, as I cough and desperately try to alleviate the dryness of my throat, but there's no moisture in my mouth. I end up, hands pressed to my knees, desperately attempting to control my breathing.

'Give him the bloody water or we'll be the ones shovelling the shit,' the third man calls. Now a beaker appears below my head. This time, I snatch it eagerly and drink it slowly, not wanting to vomit it back up. I don't care it tastes stale and, no doubt, isn't from a fresh stream. These bastards, I appreciate, will take their particular breed of pleasure as they can. Arseholes. All of them. They're not arseholes because they're from Wessex. No, they're just arseholes, pure and simple.

'Better?' the deep voice demands.

'More,' I request instead, coughing again. This time, I'm handed the clay jug and pour it into my mouth with some care. Again, I don't want to vomit. I do need to force the dryness from my body.

'Right. No more. Get over there.'

I evade the next intended boot for my arse, not turning to look as I sense the man behind me falling to the ground, his balance lost. The two watching him shake their heads with disgust and I detect their scrutiny. I keep my face blank. They're not fine warriors. They probably never have been. But, I suspect, they've been lucky bastards in the past. They all carry one wound or another. The deep-voiced man limps as he walks ahead of me. What the man behind me has done to himself is beyond me, for now. But there'll be something. Men such as these are useful for the tasks no one else wants – like guarding the prisoners or moving the horse shit away.

I follow the two men, mindful I must take smaller steps than I'd like with my feet bound, and it's tough to do that while walking uphill. I'm almost relieved when they do take me to the paddock set aside for the horses. They could have done much worse. I'm not as happy when they hand me a wooden bucket, forcing me into the field, and once more bind my hands, so I have only enough leeway to hold the bucket with one hand, and bend to pick up the horse shit strewn all over the place with the other. My hands will stink. But then, I already stink of smoke, sweat and piss.

The three of them watch me keenly, as I bend and gather together the green rolls of horse manure. It smells, yes, but it could be worse. Much worse. They talk one to another, but never leave me alone, following me as I hobble and encouraging the horses to move aside when they crowd the way. Their conversation, as to be expected, is mundane. They don't speak of battle triumphs, or even what the enemy are doing, but of who drank the most ale last night, kicked the last prisoner the most times, and generally wasted their time doing nothing to aid the people of Wessex.

I grow accustomed to their talking, and allow the tediousness of my actions to soothe me. I'm not the only prisoner about this task. Others are more harshly treated. I hear the kicks of their captors and the shouts of anger, and know I'm doing the correct thing in getting on with it. I'm bound, but by fools. I could escape them easily, if I wanted to do so.

My thoughts are busy. Will the Wessex force attack the Viking raiders, or is this, as I suspect, a big game of bluff by the Wessex king? He's come here, to posture on his hilltop peak, but not to fight the enemy. I can't imagine he did all this just to trap me here, without my allies. And, after all, there are signs the Viking raiders are nearby. What will bloody Ecgberht do about them? Will he pay them off, as Edwin told me the Frankish kings have done?

'That's enough,' the deep-voiced man calls to me, when I've nearly reached the edge of the paddock. I've had to empty my bucket at least six times, trudging up and down to where the horse shit's being stored to the lower end of the steep-sided enclosure. The animals are restive at having so many strangers moving amongst them, but no one seems to consider what's best for them, not even the grooms, who must be sleeping while we work in the growing darkness. 'Now, something else for you,' he announces. They're all eating, chomping with their mouths open. I eye the bread they have enviously, and then my belly growls angrily. 'Here, this is for you,' and he thrusts it towards my shit-stained hands.

I take the bread eagerly, not giving them the pleasure of seeing any dismay at the state of it. I chew quickly. Making short work of the small piece of bread.

'Don't be thinking your friends will help you,' the one taunts. 'King Ecgberht told them they could have you back, when they return with five hundred Mercian warriors to support his attack on the enemy. We all know weak and feeble Mercia doesn't have that many warriors. So now, you labour at our instructions. You eat and piss when we say. Now, off to the latrine ditch. I've been told a new one needs digging.'

Digging I can do, even though I'm tired, aching and stink of shit. The words of these men ring in my ears.

With my feet hobbled, I more fall than walk, trying to keep myself upright with bound feet and hands over the uneven surface of the encampment. There was perhaps grass here before, but now the passage of too many feet has worn it away, revealing the soil beneath.

The smell of the latrine ditch is overwhelming, but we pass it without stopping, and then we come to a stop further around the side of the camp, to where, I realise, there's still a huge space where more Wessex warriors should be filling it.

'Here.' A shovel is thrust into my hand. I eye the terrain. It looks like it'll be difficult to even break through the crust of sun-baked soil on the top, but I set to anyway. I need the time to think about all I've been told, and to reconcile myself to the events of the day.

While King Ecgberht squanders what strength he does have, the Viking raiders, if I know them at all well after my encounters with them, won't be stopped. They'll come to finish the fight. King Ecgberht doesn't seem to realise that. He's an arse and a fool, and I'll not remain his prisoner for long. Even without a blade to hand, and with my feet and hands bound, I could overwhelm these three warriors, but not now. It's not yet time to do so.

Instead, I almost enjoy the physical exertion of digging through the hard, pebble-strewn soil, bringing the shovel up time and time again, to lay the dank earth to one side. They've not made it clear where they want the soil to go, so I pile it haphazardly. In the dark, men on the way to the latrine ditches will trip and maybe fall within it. That would make me smile.

Eventually, a bright moon appears in the sky, revealing how much I've done, and the three men, stifling yawns, take the shovel from my hands, and direct me back to where I'm once more secured to the wide tree trunk. I note Aldhelm, curled in sleep, and a few others as well. Then the silence of night overwhelms me. Even the cries of those enjoying too much ale or playing games of chance fade to nothing, as the encampment sleeps. I can't hear any sound from the nearby settlement either. My thoughts turn once more to the dead child, and my rage smoulders within me.

Every so often, a cloud of smoke wafts past, the smell coming first, the breeze driving it further and further north, although there's no sign of the fire advancing this way, no doubt because of the expanse of water below the hill. The Viking raiders have burnt a great deal of land and crops. They've terrified people into running away from the coastal location. They've killed at least four high-ranking Wessex noblemen and yet King Ecgberht's more concerned with me endangering his son and arguing with him for killing a child. King Ecgberht's truly blind to what's coming. I suspect even I don't appreciate the full extent of the savagery of the enemy. But I'm more aware of it than King Ecgberht. All I need to do, then, is wait for the enemy to attack the encampment, and in the confusion slip away, taking Aldhelm with me.

It sounds easy. It should be simple. But, of course, these things never are.

20

I'm once more kicked awake. I wrinkle my nose at the sour smell from my hands and body.

'Come on,' the deep-voiced warrior calls. 'The king wants you.' I blink grit from my eyes. I'm sure I've been asleep for only a short time, but it's daylight, or what can be construed as daylight, for it remains smoky. The haze won't lift from the ground despite the gentle breeze. No wonder my tongue still feels dry. I've been breathing in smoke for over a day now.

I'm unwrapped from the tree, and my hands are bound before me, with only a slight grimace for the green staining on them. I turn and catch the eye of Aldhelm, who watches me, perplexed. He offers me a slight shrug of his shoulders, and then winces, forgetting his arms are also secured.

'Come on,' I'm further urged.

'I need to piss,' I call.

'Get on with it then.'

'I need my hands,' I comment. 'Or at least one of them.'

'Make him piss his trews,' one of the others laughs. 'It's not like he could smell worse than he does.' But the deep-voiced man shakes his head, and releases my hands, pointing me towards a small bush. Eagerly, I release my stream into the soil, mindful of splashing myself, but managing to angle it so the arsehole who really doesn't like me has to jump back to avoid stinking of it.

I don't look up, despite his cry of outrage.

When I'm finished, my hands are once more tied, and I'm led through the encampment. Wessex warriors jeer at me from where they sit around campfires, cooking food and mending equipment. I shake my head. If this is anything to go by, then none of these alleged warriors are protecting Wessex. Instead, they're just biding their time, waiting for the enemy to attack them. These aren't the actions of a warrior king.

I'm once more kicked by the man with piss on his boots, and allow a tight smile to turn my lips upwards. I'm going to enjoy beating the crap out of him when I escape, I really am. Or, perhaps, he might be skewered by one of the Viking raiders. Such a death couldn't befall a nicer man.

I look upwards, perplexed despite the fact I've been told the king wishes to see me, to see I'm being led once more towards the king's canvas.

As we get closer, I see holy men rushing within, carrying parchments in their hands. They must, I presume, be the king's reckoners, men tasked with keeping the accounts of Wessex in good order. But I'm in for a surprise when I enter the canvas, and find not just King Ecgberht there, but others as well. My eyes narrow as I take in some of those, somehow entirely unsurprised to find Beornmod, the bishop of Rochester, amongst them all.

There's a chair set aside. I'm led to it, and have my feet bound to the wooden legs, while my hands remain tied before me. I really do smell, but I show no discomfort before King Ecgberht and his bastard son.

'Ah, Icel of Budworth, my lord,' Bishop Beornmod intones. 'King Ecgberht of Wessex lays charges at your feet for failing to protect the king's *mund*. We'll hear of these events, and then, a sentence will be passed on you. King Ecgberht is aware you endeavour to do everything as prescribed by law.'

Somehow, I keep the confusion from showing on my face. King Ecgberht smiles broadly from his seat, as does his son, King Æthelwulf, while Bishop Beornmod continues to speak. What the hell is this? The Viking raiders are burning Wessex crops and the king of Wessex intends to hold a bloody trial to find me guilty of meaning harm to his son?

'It's alleged you abandoned King Æthelwulf amongst the Viking raiders, yesterday, and also that last summer you threatened him by attacking him outside Canterbury. Further, it's also alleged you attacked and killed fine Wessex warriors on the road to Canterbury. And that's just the beginning of these allegations. Now,' and Bishop Beornmod turns to King Æthelwulf, 'my lord, you'll tell the court all you've seen and heard in relation to Lord Icel of Budworth.'

King Æthelwulf stands and walks forward, positioning himself on the only other spare chair, taking his time to settle his clothing and expression before starting to speak.

I don't truly listen to what he says. I'm astounded King Ecgberht hates me so much he's determined on holding a court of law now, when the Viking raiders must surely be close enough to the hill fort they'll attack him. I vaguely consider who'll speak on my behalf. As Brihthild was before me, I've no one who'll be my oath-helper. I'm a Mercian, in Wessex. My voice has no value.

These are the petty actions of a man who doesn't like being bested. I appreciate that. My successes against him must burn, even more than the threat of attack from the enemy. I've always thought King Ecgberht an arse-hole, now I have my proof, if more was needed. But, importantly, I realise I've already beaten him. No matter what happens here, I've prevailed against the bloody king of Wessex.

King Ecgberht doesn't mean to make this sham of a trial quick. King Æthelwulf talks at great length about my actions against him. Then more and more are called upon, men I don't even recognise, but who allege I've fought them, or killed their allies. They all speak with half an eye to the king, stumbling over their words, showing they've been told what to say. I'd shake my head at this affront to justice, but instead I breathe carefully, fixing the image of each warrior in my mind. There'll be a time, probably quite soon, when I'll have my revenge against them.

Bishop Beornmod questions them in tedious detail, constantly looking at me with a smug expression when they list my crimes against them. Occasionally, one or other reveals a wound. I don't believe I've fought these men. They'd not be alive had I done so. I've killed a great many Wessex warriors.

Eventually, Bishop Beornmod appears to run out of people to question, and he turns to look towards King Ecgberht expectantly, while I glower at him. King Ecgberht wears a self-satisfied smirk on his lips, and yet doesn't pronounce against me.

'We'll reconvene in the morning to determine on punishment. I suspect, however, that unlike the Mercians, we'll enact the ultimate penalty against those who damage the king's *mund*. Enjoy your last night, Icel, Lord Budworth.'

So spoken, he flicks his fingers towards me. I'm untied from the chair, and forced to walk away. But I don't. Instead, with my legs bound together so I can shuffle forwards, and with my hands before me, I turn to face King Ecgberht and his snivelling son. First, I glower at King Æthelwulf, pleased when he's the first to look away from my intense gaze. And then I fix on King Ecgberht. I hold his cold eyes, seeing in them not the ability to rule his kingdom well, but instead a self-satisfied belief this pretence of a court trial somehow betters what we did in Mercia when there was truly a crime to be accounted for. He believes this will right some sort of wrong.

'Take him away,' King Ecgberht commands once more, his tone accusatory. 'I'll see you tomorrow, Lord Budworth,' he taunts, but I shake my head, allow a smile to touch my cheeks, and half incline my head towards him.

'I doubt that,' I murmur, just quietly enough he can't hear me. His eyebrows furrow in confusion. He opens his lips to demand I repeat my words, but then a scowl forms on his face, and instead I'm manhandled away. I don't laugh, or chortle, or giggle, I hold myself firm, back upright, shoulders down, chin high. King Ecgberht has made a very serious mistake. A very serious mistake. Probably two of them. I doubt he realises it.

He will soon.

* * *

I'm returned to my prison, tied once more to the tree, and close my eyes. I need more sleep, but behind my shut eyes I'm considering what I must do to escape from here.

I can't rely on the Viking raiders attacking in the night, although that would make it much easier for me to flee. But I can rely on my lackwit guards to allow me more freedom than they should. They might even pity me for all must realise the king means to kill me tomorrow. King Ecgberht's such a spiteful arsehole. I see what he's thinking even before he does. The façade of my trial will allow him to claim everything was done as it should be, despite the lack of oath-helpers and the failure to allow me to speak and offer my own version of events. And that's forgetting, for the time being, that aside from King Æthelwulf, not one of those they had speak against me actually knew me, or had anything to say that was a true account of all they've seen and heard, as it should be.

Eventually, I sleep once more, but this time I'm woken, not by the guards, but by Aldhelm.

'Icel,' he whispers harshly. I peel my eyes open and look around me. We seem to be alone, darkness once more coating the land. I cough. I really need to drink more.

'What?' I ask him. He offers me what I suspect is a smile, although I can only tell from the glint of his teeth.

'They mean to kill you, and send your corpse back to King Wiglaf. They won't even allow Wiglaf the time to send the warriors King Ecgberht demands for your release.'

'I know that,' I mutter.

'Oh,' is his deflated response. 'What will you do?'

'Well, I plan not to bloody die, if that's what you mean,' I comment.

'Yes, yes, but how?'

'I'll escape.'

'How?' he further questions.

This, of course, is the problem. How will I flee? I'm bound. I've no weapons. I've not been fed much in the last day. I certainly need more water in my body to be able to fight the enemy and run from this place without collapsing in a heap, unable to defend myself.

'Wait and see,' I caution him, not prepared to say anything. I don't suspect Aldhelm, but it's suspicious we've been left alone, in the darkness. I can't imagine the three guards have the wits to realise I might mean to escape, but there's someone behind their actions. Perhaps, then, they might know me well enough to suspect me.

Aldhelm chuckles darkly. 'Take me with you,' he suddenly pleads. I grunt in reply. I'll need his aid, I imagine. But I'll also need a good opportunity. I suspect I can't wait until tomorrow, when they take me back before King Ecgberht. Admittedly, I'd like nothing more than to wait until then, grab a blade from someone and kill King Ecgberht and his son before everyone, but that's too much of a risk, I'm convinced of it.

Instead, I'll have to bide my time for something else to offer the opportunity.

Glancing through the rustling leaves above my head, I eye the sky. It's a cloudy night. There's no moon to illuminate the landscape, and once more dirty grey smoke-filled clouds occasionally obscure my vision as well. The smell of smoke seems, if anything, to have intensified as I try and work some moisture into my mouth. My tongue feels like a fish salted to last throughout the dark time of the year. I distract myself with thoughts of the enemy. Are the Viking raiders coming closer? Why wouldn't they? They've already overwhelmed the Wessex force once. Why not do so again? I would, if I had the number of warriors they appear to have. They've already caused chaos, not that King Ecgberht appears to appreciate that.

The encampment falls ever more silent, the occasional farts of the horses and cattle filling the air. I also hear the occasional call of one sentry to another. They don't sound that concerned, despite everything I've seen, and let alone what they've been told. But then, men who've never encountered the Viking raiders are arrogant bastards who believe they'll be easily overwhelmed. Having met the enemy, more than once, I know that's far from the case. A little more respect from the Wessex warriors would do them no harm. I doubt it will happen, however.

In the distance, a sudden cry has my eyes blinking open where I've succumbed to sleep. I cough and wish I'd not woken. I almost choke, my tongue so firmly wedged to the roof of my mouth. I really do need some fluid. And then I have my wish. A light sprinkle of rain on my face, falling through the leaves, immediately intensifies. I tip my head back, mouth open, and will more of the heavy rain to fall into my mouth. I'd like enough to at least stop my tongue feeling so huge in my mouth.

I swallow, the taste like the sweetest honey, and then swallow more and more. So eager to drink, I pull at my bindings, unheeding of the fact it wrenches my shoulders uncomfortably backwards, my arms spread to either side of me around the wide tree trunk. And that's when I feel it. For a moment, I don't recognise what it is, too intent on drinking. Aldhelm's also woken from his sleep, and while he was going to complain about being drenched, his words have fallen silent, as he mirrors my actions in catching the rainfall on his tongue.

I swallow and swallow, allowing my face to feel the heaviness of the rain on it, the sweaty dust covering me, slipping from my face. I could laugh with delight, but I don't, because I'm sure my ties are slipping. Unsure what to concentrate on, I endeavour to do both, drink the rainwater, and also work my arms loose from their bindings. I also kick my feet out ahead, to where the water drums on the ground, hoping it will loosen those bindings as well.

The rain's so heavy, I hear the horses and cattle complaining loudly, and the odd cry of someone who's clearly fallen asleep outside and been woken by the deluge.

I kick my feet. It's too dark to see, and the sentry fires are little more than sullen glows in the dankness, but somehow Aldhelm realises what I'm doing. I hear him also working at his leg ties, trying to rub one leg over another, and in that way release his feet.

I pull and tug on my arm bindings. One of the ropes is looser than the other, and almost too quickly, that for a moment I suspect this has been done on purpose, I slip my left hand free with a shudder of pain, the feeling returning to my fingers so forcefully in a buzz of pins and needles I bite back my cry.

For all I pull at the other arm, I'm still firmly held, despite the rope becoming loose with the weight of the rain. I bring my feet up to my arse, and turn towards the right hand. Of course, I'm better with my right hand than the left, but turning, I manage to get my hand on the knot, straining with my legs to cross one arm over my body. The rain drums so loudly, I can't hear anything else. I don't even think to consider I might be being watched. Wherever the guards are, they're not here. This is my opportunity. Angrily, I work at the remaining knot, but it's stubborn. Pushing my feet entirely beneath my arse, I bring my teeth to work on it. It tastes disgusting. My only just sated mouth doesn't enjoy the coarseness of the hempen rope, or the knowledge I've no idea what the rope's been used for in the past. But I must escape.

It's painful, my neck straining, my thighs burning. I'm contorted like a spider stuck on its back, one of its legs missing so it can't right itself. And then the knot gives. It's a small movement, almost miniscule, but it gives me the length of rope I need to work my left hand into it. My right hand comes free and, ignoring the lack of feeling in it, I reach for the bindings on my legs and then slither free from the ropes around my belly. I pause, for a moment, but I can't hear anything above the drumming of the rain aside from the angry lows of the cattle. They've nowhere to shelter from the deluge.

I catch sight of white eyes and hurry to Aldhelm's side, wincing as I do so. My legs are stiff from sitting in such a position for so long. I stagger and plunge my hands into the mud forming beneath the tree but I don't care. I wipe my already filthy hands on my filthy trews. I won't leave him here. After all, if it comes to a fight, I might need his help. It's always better to have two warriors to face the enemy than to do it myself. He can watch my back while I slaughter my foes.

'Come on.' I fumble the knots. He's got his feet free, but not yet his hands. His rope has become tighter, not looser, and as my blood thrums in my head I fear it's all taking too long. But I don't consider leaving him here. When the guards wake, and find me gone, they'll blame him if I do, with his bindings half undone. 'Come on,' I growl angrily. He's pulling on the rope. 'Slacken it,' I complain, and he does so. Like me, he's desperate to escape.

Abruptly, the rope on his right hand comes free and his left is then much easier to release. He wiggles free from the snake-like binding across his chest, and staggers upright. I grab him before he falls forward. He gasps fetid breath into my face.

'Now what?' he gasps. He feels weaker than I do, but then he's been a captive for longer than I have.

'We escape,' I state.

'But how?'

'This way,' I encourage, determined to move north, away from the encampment, and down the slope.

'On foot?' he growls. I consider his words for the briefest moment.

'Yes, on foot. We can't steal a horse. The grooms would hear us. We need to leave. Now.' I think he's going to argue with me, especially when I realise he's limping heavily from some wound I've not realised he's gained, but he nods.

'Come on.' He leads on, back through the collection of trees. It's so dark beneath them, I walk into a sharp branch, which forces me to place my hands in front of me. The dark rain clouds are a boon for us, but it makes it almost impossible to move quickly. I kick a tree root and wince at the stab of pain, and in that moment lose sight of Aldhelm.

From behind, I hear nothing above the drum of the rain and the sound of leaves shaking with the weight of the water. From ahead, I see nothing but impenetrable blackness.

'Aldhelm,' I whisper, but of course, he can't hear me above the sound of the heavy rain. I won't risk shouting. Someone will come to check on the captives, and then they'll start to chase us down. I'm sure of it. No one will want to explain to King Ecgberht they've lost the man he wanted to execute come the daylight.

I press on, down the hillside. I don't know this area. I don't find Aldhelm. I don't hear him calling for me. Instead, arms ahead of my face so I don't skewer myself on a branch, I press on, hoping I'm moving north and not in a circle, back towards the encampment. It's impossible to see anything but the strain in my thighs assures me I move downhill.

Abruptly, I step clear from the trees. I only know because I sense the space before me, and also the wind intensifies, driving rain into my face. I scrunch my eyes shut from the pain of it hitting my face.

'Now bloody what?' I mutter. I glance behind, but it's so black I can't even sense where the Wessex encampment might be on the hilltop. Wherever Aldhelm is, he's long gone.

With nothing for it, I move forward, straining to listen for the sound of moving water in a river, or even from the sea. I don't want to find myself on a perilous ledge.

The wind presses against me, trying to make me turn my back on it and perhaps find shelter for the rest of the storm, but I keep going. My breath is hot. I open my mouth to catch more rain and wish I could shut my eyes, but I must keep them open, even though I can see little.

It feels as though I've woken from a dream and don't know where I am. I have to force myself onwards. I kick a stone, and it rattles ahead. I wince at the stab of pain in my left big toe. I bend low, run my hands over the ground, but this is no road. Instead, it could be a field, or perhaps a trackway used by the cattle. It's certainly not anything that gives me any idea as to where I am. I wish I could remember our journey here, but I can't.

I move onwards, but moments later something slithery touches my face. I gasp in fear, arms protecting my face. I can't tell what it is. It could be clothing. I narrow my eyes, trying to make sense of what I might be able to see in the darkness. Is that a building? I sniff, but the heavy rain has scoured all smell apart from the freshness of a heavy storm. I walk towards it, winning free from whatever touched me. Could it be some clothing left out to wash in the rain? Hands before me once more, I shuffle slowly forward. If anyone could see me, they'd wonder what I'm doing, but of course, no one would be out in such a heavy storm, in the darkest part of the night, by choice.

I reach out, thinking there's a building there, but there's nothing. My hands sweep only rain aside so I press on, hoping I still direct my steps north.

I strain to hear anything, animal or person, but it's impossible. The drum of the rain is all around me. I keep shuffling, but when nothing else stops me, I begin to move more quickly. I've no idea how far I've come since escaping, but it won't be far enough. If I keep going all night, perhaps I'll find somewhere to shelter during the daytime and then I can press on under cover of darkness tomorrow.

I consider, if I'd decided to steal a horse, if my progress would be quicker, but I don't believe so. Horses can't see in the dark either, as far as I know. I banish the thought. I'm sodden. Everything I'm wearing is stuck to my skin, making it difficult for me to move with any great speed. My trews adhere to my thighs. I suspect they creak every time I move, but I can't hear it. My back's drenched. My hair dangles down my face so I have to keep moving it away, although I do lick the moisture from it when I realise the water's pooling there, and it's easier to catch than merely opening my mouth wide.

I feel the ground start to fall away once more, the strain in my thighs telling me I'm going steeply downhill. I consider where I am, but it's a useless thought. I don't know Wessex. I certainly don't know where I am. I strain to hear running water. I don't want to fall into a stream, or worse, something much deeper. The ground beneath my feet grows increasingly steep. I feel my feet slipping with the rain flooding down the hillside, along with me. But I press on. I'm sure I'm making good time. I take small steps, not wanting to risk slipping. But my boots are growing wetter and wetter, and then it happens. My right foot goes from beneath me, and I flounder, trying to fall backwards and not forwards as my leg shoots out ahead of me. I land on my arse, rattling my head, feeling the pulse of pain from where my hands rest on pebbles or something that digs into my hands.

'Bollocks,' I explode, wincing and trying not to cry at the sudden agony.

I rest there momentarily, aware water now pools into my trews and my arse is drenched, but I need to shake the pain from my hands, and ensure no stones are embedded in them. I feel the right with the left, and the left with the right, grimacing at the sharp discomfort. But there are no stones there now. I'm sure I bleed, however. I lift my left hand to my nose and sniff it, and then lick it. I'm convinced there's blood, but perhaps not much. It could be that I've grazed my skin, and nothing else.

Pushing upwards with my hands, I feel the strain in my thighs, and sense the land before me falling away even more. I suspect I should stop until it grows light, but I can't take the chance. Instead, I lean back on my thighs, taking the strain there, and resume walking downhill. My knees hurt, my thighs as well, but that doesn't stop me. I carry on, and eventually sense the path I walk even out. I stand tall once more. I still can't see anything. I look up, assessing the sky, but the clouds entirely cover the moon and stars. Not a single piece of light shows.

I step onwards. The night's my friend, and my enemy. I wrinkle my nose, scenting the air, but it tells me nothing aside from the smell of smoke has finally dissipated. I walk with my hands outstretched before me, but there just feels like a void. Nothing gets in my way. Even the path I'm following appears reasonably flat. I kick no stones and feel no stones beneath my feet. I wish I knew where I was.

And then my right foot slips in something, the sharp crack and accompanying smell assuring me I've stepped in a days-old cow pat. I grimace. But press on. I don't sense any large animals nearby, but I suspect I might be in a field used for pasture. Continuing to walk with my hands before me, I anticipate meeting a fence or hedgerow; instead, I kick something else, the sound loud and echoing. I reach out with my hands, and they rest on a low piece of stone. I feel raindrops rebounding from its surface. This then is a drinking trough for the animals. I pause, briefly, but decide I'd rather drink this water than continue trying to catch the rain. Plunging my hands into the water, I drink deeply, cupping them together, and only then reach them in and give them a quick slosh of water, before continuing on my way. Hand outstretched, I do encounter a hedgerow, the edges of the spring growth prickling my already wounded hands. But I need to do so to find the way out of the field. How I've entered it, I don't know, but I'm certainly enclosed and I don't want to be.

I mutter to myself, unhappy at where I am, and then my hand encounters nothing but air. I reach with my other hand, trying to decide if a gate is in front of me, or something else. I wipe the water from my face once more, and then lean forward. Whatever this is, it does appear to lead out of the field. Without more thought, I lift one leg over the edge, and then the other. But I don't immediately jump clear. Holding there, I release one hand and reach out with it once more. I'm sure there's something there. But there isn't. The dark and the heavy storm are playing havoc with my senses. I pull myself off the stone wall and turn around. The advantage of the rain blowing into my face is I can determine when I'm facing the wrong way. I turn, and then, happy I must be facing towards the north, set off again.

I can't hear any cattle. Wherever they are, they're not here. I press on, mindful the ground beneath my feet has altered once more. Now I can see buildings before me. I'm convinced of it. I step towards one of the shapes, only to rear backwards as my head hits a wooden strut.

'Bollocks,' I huff, blood pooling into my beard from where I've walked into a supporting beam. I wince, and clench my drenched arse to stop from crying out. I allow myself to breathe in and out at least five times before I continue on my way. And that's when it happens.

Out of nowhere, I feel something hit me, clean in the face, the wide metal shape assuring me it's not a sword or blade, as I plunge to the ground, trying to stop my head from hitting the ground, even as greater darkness closes in around me.

21

I wake up and moan, trying to lift my hand to rub it over my throbbing nose, but it doesn't move when I command it. I peel open my eyes and then groan. I'm attached to the tree where I was held captive. The daylight's bright, and the three Wessex captors are grinning and kicking me.

'Gave us a bit of a fright there, you arsehole,' the one growls. 'But a good Wessex woman attacked you with her bloody shovel, and so now you're here with us once more. You made it all of half a day's walk from here. You really must try harder next time. Oh, wait. There won't be a next time.'

I groan again, wishing my entire body didn't pulse as it does. I feel like crap. My nose throbs. My hands pulse. And my head. Well, the less said about that, the better. Right now, I feel it might be preferable to accept the executioner's rope around my neck.

I glare at the three men, but the sunlight's too bright, and instead my eyes close, unable to tolerate the intensity.

'Come on. It's nearly time to see the king.'

I force myself to open my eyes and look around, trying to make sense of what time it is. The encampment's busy with another day's task. It smells damp but also hot. The rain of last night's quickly rising in the air. It can't be that late, but it must be late enough these arseholes have managed to find me and bring me back here. I must have been on the back of a horse, but I have no memory of it.

'Water,' I mutter through throbbing lips.

'Not wasting it on you,' one of the other bastards taunts. 'You'll be dead soon enough.'

Unceremoniously, I'm hauled upright by the three, who all stink, but evidently not as bad as I do, for the one drops my arm and steps away, so I flounder and almost take down the other two as I hit the ground with a jolt felt through my teeth.

'Stop titting about,' the one calls to the other, and now the man steps closer again, but his eyes are crossed and he wafts his hand in front of his nose to ensure I know how much I smell. I can't say he's much less fruity.

I'm dragged through the camp because my legs aren't heeding my commands. My thighs ache as though I've dragged twelve dead bodies to the graveside. I lift my head, and see the king's tent coming ever closer.

'Tell him he won't want him inside,' the one calls to the other. 'He'll stink the place up.' I'm aware the camp's still. The smell of smoke has dissipated with the heavy rain. I don't believe that means the Viking raiders have gone anywhere, but the Wessex warriors are lethargic, seemingly content to do little but watch me being led towards their king. If I were the Viking raiders, I'd be preparing my attack right now, catching these arrogant arseholes out, determining the best way to dash up the hillside. Yes, it's steep, but with no one seeming to care about why they're here, I doubt they'll be spotted.

As the one man bows low and gains entry to the king's tent, I wait outside, with the other two. I spare a thought for Aldhelm. I hope he managed to get further than I did last night. I expect, if we'd stayed together, I'd be in the same situation now. And he'd be at my side.

'Fancy being undone by a goodwife and her shovel,' the one chuckles to the other.

'Shut up,' the third whispers harshly. 'We don't want them to know we lost him during the bloody night.'

'Ah,' the one acknowledges, sudden comprehension on his scarred face. 'You might be right there,' he agrees. The king's warriors watch this without seeming to see it. They stand rigid before the king's tent, and from within I hear King Ecgberht's voice but not the words.

I peer upwards, drinking in the view overhead, the white clouds, the blue of the sky stretching ever onwards. I've messed this up. I can't say I've anyone to blame but myself, but it boils me King Ecgberht has so much control over me, at this moment. The Mercian trial against Brihthild and the former queen of Mercia has evidently frustrated the hell out of him. His petty revenge is just that. Yet I'll be the one to lose my life because of it.

I consider my uncle, Wynflæd, young Cuthred and my fellow warriors. I even think of Lady Ælflæd. I'd hoped to see her at Kingsholm, but I didn't. I'd have liked to spend time with her, perhaps in the easy camaraderie we once shared when we were so much younger, and all we cared about was keeping a horse alive.

Even King Wiglaf's going to be pissed by King Ecgberht's actions. And Oswy, Wulfheard and Ealdorman Ælfstan? They'll seek vengeance for what King Ecgberht means to do here today. I hope they kill him, I really do. Admittedly, I'm but one man. Maybe they won't risk it. But I doubt that. I know my fellow warriors. When they hear of my death, for no doubt the weasel intends to send my corpse back to Mercia for maximum impact, they'll vow to kill in return. In such a way, King Ecgberht will hope to weaken Mercia. I pray he's not successful.

'Ah, here we are.' I turn and meet the eyes of King Æthelwulf. He wears court finery and not warrior's garb. It's as though they have no concept the enemy are out there, just out of sight, despite the very obvious cloud of smoke, admittedly much dampened by last night's storm. They play this as though it's a game, and I know it's not. 'Soon be over.' King Æthelwulf smirks, and then dips into his father's tent. I hear more conversation, and the thrum of people preparing themselves, but I allow my mind to wander, considering Wine, Brute and Bicwide. Who, I realise, will hold Budworth when I'm dead? I've made no arrangements. I should have done. But I'm young, and thought I'd live forever, not die here, at the king of Wessex's pleasure. What a damn fool I've been.

I allow myself to wallow in misery. How has this gone so wrong? We came to seek out the king of Wessex when he approached King Wiglaf for assistance. Did he always plan to execute me, or is he taking advantage of my presence here?

Belatedly, I realise King Ecgberht has stepped from his tent, King Æthelwulf at his side, and bloody Bishop Beornmod. I'm adding him to the list of bastards I'll hunt down and kill after this, should I somehow live through it.

'Dear me. A rough night.' King Ecgberht smiles as he sweeps me from head to toe. I consider telling him about my night-time excursion, but telling tales won't stop what's about to happen. 'I believe we have a sentence to pass on you, for imperilling the king's *mund*. It will be your death,' King Ecgberht postures, his son nodding eagerly along. I spit aside a wad of blood from my mouth in their general direction and the pair both shudder away. I grin at them, enjoying the sensation of pissing them off.

'I'm sure you're aware, my lord kings, passing the incorrect sentence on a man will imperil your soul with the Lord God.' I mutter this, just to enjoy the shudder of fear on both their faces. They mean to take their spiteful vengeance against me for thwarting their plot against Mercia, but they'll do so knowing one day they'll burn in hell.

'Bring the rope,' King Æthelwulf calls roughly, although I don't miss the blanching of his face, or the shudder of unease from his father. 'Take him to the oak tree and suspend him from the tallest branch. Witness it, and then have his body sent north, with a guard of four. King Wiglaf will know we killed the traitor.'

Shaking my head to be forced back towards the tree, I hold King Ecgberht's eyes for a moment longer. 'Not even the old gods will approve of this,' I speak firmly, minded of Wynflæd's insights into what makes King Ecgberht the man he is. A swift glance from Bishop Beornmod assures me he's ignorant of King Ecgberht's devotion to charms and talismans. 'I'll hear you scream in hell,' I mutter, allowing myself to be led away. 'And your screams,' I roar over my shoulder, 'will be much, much louder than mine. For I'm innocent of your fabricated crimes, and all here know it, as will my Lord God.'

'Shut him up,' King Æthelwulf bellows, but the three men have nothing to do that with, other than their hands, and none of them feel like risking it. Instead, I get a boot on my arse, and stagger forward. I consider if Bishop Beornmod will come to say the last rites for me, or if they'll continue with their pettiness and allow me to die unshriven. And that's exactly what they intend to do.

I'm returned to the tree beneath which I've been held captive for so long.

But, if I'm worried this is going to be over quickly, I needn't. None of the three men can fling the rope over the tallest tree branch. I doubt they could throw it over a horse stood patiently before them. I sink to the ground, holding my head beneath my bent knees, my thoughts scattering all over the place. I've heard a man will see his life flash before his eyes as he dies. I didn't expect it to be now. I'd attempt to run, by while the three guards are ineffectual, many of the bored Wessex warriors crowd the space behind me, offering their advice and generally looking forward to watching a Mercian dangle from the rope.

I close my ears and don't listen to them, focusing instead on what I've accomplished in my short life, and the people I've loved throughout it. I consider my mother, Lady Cynewise and my uncle. It seems I'll be meeting them much sooner than I expected. That's not entirely reassuring.

Eventually, I'm pulled onto my feet, and an effort is made to place the noose around my neck. I kick out a little bit, and generally try to avoid it, but I'm never going to be able to overpower the three men, especially now two of the king's warriors have been sent to ensure the task's completed.

I sense the rough hempen rope around my neck, and stare back at the hateful eyes watching me from the growing crowd. Do I hate the Wessex warriors as much as they do me? In that moment, I don't know. I liked Aldhelm. I've even met a few others I quite liked. Admittedly, not many of them. Not that it matters now.

I feel the pressure on my neck building, and endeavour to gasp more air into my body, as though that will help me. My hands have been bound behind me, my ankles have once more been tied together as well. When they lift me, I'll have nothing to stop me from being hanged by the neck. There are no friendly faces in the crowd. There's no one who'll come to aid me. My allies are far from here.

I feel the tug, and the vibration in the hempen rope as six men pull it tight, lifting me clear from the ground. I point my toes, trying to retain my hold on it for a few moments longer, looking at the sky in the distance, and not at the baying pack of Wessex warriors who hunger for my blood, although it won't be gained in a shield wall or on the slaughter field. I decide I do hate them. Craven, all of them. All of them.

The binding around my neck grows tighter, and tighter. My feet lift clear, I try to gasp, my mouth opening and closing like a fish, but no air gets within. I'm suspended by my neck. Again, those I've loved in my life cycle before my eyes. My uncle. Wynflæd, Cuthred, Wulfheard, Oswy, Cenred, Ealdorman Ælfstan. Lady Cynehild, who told me the truth of my birth although I'd rather never have known. Even my father. And then I sense a presence there with me, even as I'm gasping, gasping, flailing and trying to kick out, fighting my bound hands which won't come loose. I sense my grasp on this life growing thinner. No air in my body. My head pounding. The darkness closes in. I can't even hear the sound of the enemy shouting and calling to one another. I don't feel the piss that drips from my trews.

I relax. There's no point fighting, not any more. Not that I could, even if I wanted to.

And then, I hear it, as though from a great, great distance. A roar. A bellow. A shriek and then more shrieks.

The tension in the rope abruptly slackens. I hit the ground, my feet failing me so I land on my knees, the impact jolting me so fiercely I breathe in even though I never thought I would again.

I blink my eyes open, and see the Wessex warriors surging away. That's when I hear the unmistakable tongue and voices of the Viking raiders.

I shudder and gasp, watching the world from my vantage point, slumped to my side now, feet rushing past, and the thunder of horses.

I realise I'm saved. If only I can escape the Viking raiders who've come to savage the king of Wessex's hilltop encampment.

He will pay for his crimes against me. Perhaps, after all, there is some truth in the thought that the enemy of my enemy is my ally.

22

Feet rush past. And more than one lifeless corpse faces me. I shudder, unsure how such a complete reversal has been possible in the short a space of time it's taken to nearly hang me. Were the Wessex warriors truly so concerned with witnessing the death of a Mercian warrior they abandoned all their sentry posts? It seems impossible and yet there's no other explanation.

I try to force myself upright, to get free from the overwhelming Viking raider force attacking the Wessex warriors, but my body's unresponsive. I still need to flood it with air, and bring my heartbeat back to a normal level. And, of course, I remain bound at feet and hands.

Another corpse thuds down in front of me, blood from a severed throat landing in my open mouth. I choke down my cough, uneasy with the scrutiny of one of the bastard enemy, breathing heavily, war axe to hand. I sense his interest, but he must assume I'm dead, and no doubt the rope around my throat assures him of that. Having yanked the seax from the lifeless hand of the man he's killed, he rushes onwards. I hear shouts and cries, shrieks and prayers, but I remain where I am. I'm hoping the chaos will pass.

I'm becoming aware the enemy have attacked uphill from the east, and not the south or west. They must have come inland and then determined to assault the Wessex force that way. I think of the settlement where the girl was buried. I pray they've not suffered. At the same time, I hope the enemy will move through the encampment and allow me time to escape.

I'm not to have my wish. Confident for the time being the foemen are gone, I manoeuvre myself upright and shuffle towards one of the dead men, moving like a slug, forcing my legs out and then digging my heels into the mud from last night's rain to get closer. The sightless eyes are unnerving, but it's the abandoned seax in his hand I want. I run the rope binding my ankles over the blade, lifting my lower body and feeling it in my belly, and, thankfully, the rope fibres part surprisingly quickly. Then, I turn swiftly, having the use of my knees now, and lower my hands towards where I hope the seax is. I wince as I misplace it and feel the burn of a fresh cut, but then my hands are free too. I reach up, yank the rope from around my neck, mindful I'm going to be marked for some time by the cord that was embedded there, and grab the corpse once more. With no thought for him, I pull the byrnie free with much effort, sweat and general complaining. Then, I force it over my head with a suppressed cry of agony. No part of my body doesn't hurt. I manage to get one arm inside the material, and struggle with the other, the noxious smell of the dead man's sweat assuring me I don't smell that bad, despite all I've endured in recent days.

Finally, the byrnie's in place. It's a bit loose, but better loose than too tight, or so I assure myself. Next, I take his weapons belt, a momentary pause for the loss of my fine eagle-headed blade, stolen by the Wessex bastards no doubt, and then I'm crouching beneath the trees, eyes peering all around me.

The fighting's fierce although it's moved away from my location. The Wessex warriors have belatedly managed to form a thick shield wall to prevent the Viking raiders getting closer to the king, or at least the king's tent. I suspect he's still there. Certainly, the bloody Wessex banner flies over the tent, depicting the Wessex wyvern as though it'll appear in the air and overwhelm the enemy. Damn arse. That should never have given away his position.

It feels all wrong, however. It's as though the Wessex force is stopping the Viking raiders from reaching the coast, when surely that's what they want them to do. If they fight them for this strip of high Wessex land, the enemy will be within Wessex proper, while the Wessex warriors hold the coastline. They'll be trapped between the ships and the enemy. I consider what I should do. I want to get far from here. I don't care about the Wessex force, and yet, as much as I hate the Wessex bastards, I really, truly despise the Viking raiders. They wounded Lord Coenwulf and tried to take away his dignity. They kept him from his wife before her death in childbirth. They were cruel. I hate cruelty.

I stand, still unsure of what I'm going to do, but then the decision is taken from me. From behind, there's a thunder of hooves. I look up to see a Wessex warrior rushing towards his king. I don't know who the man is, but he's adorned as though a lord, complete with shimmering byrnie and helm. Even on the back of a horse, he looks tall. And certainly, more able than King Ecgberht and his son.

'To me,' the man bellows. I find my feet obeying, despite my intentions to run north. 'To me. We'll press them and they'll part for us,' the voice asserts confidently. He's followed by many, many warriors on foot, puffing their way up the incline of the hill. There are more, I suspect, than currently fight to protect the king. I really wish I knew who the lord was, even as I scoop to collect a dead man's shield from his lifeless hands, and hurry to join his warriors. Behind him, there are another six men on horseback, the animals caparisoned as though some ancient warriors I've heard the scop praise. I wish I knew who they were, for I've never seen horses bedecked as they are, or men who seem to be merely shapes beneath so much iron and leather.

'Form a shield wall,' the first voice bellows. The ground's sodden from the heavy rainfall and I slip, wincing at a sharp pain in my groin from having my legs spread so wide, but quickly I'm upright once more. I really don't wish to catch the attention of the seven mounted warriors. I'm sure they'll know me for a Mercian, and certainly a traitor, for my neck's too visible even with the stolen byrnie. At the next body I pass, I again bend and force a helm from the dead man's head. It's a well-made item, and it fits my head well, although I refuse to take the linen cap, soaked as it is with the man's blood from his neck wound.

'Hurry,' a rider behind me calls. I do that, turning to see if he specifically means me or if another has caught his attention. Reassured it's just a general request to get on with protecting the king of Wessex, I join some of the other warriors, standing ready to move against the exposed back of the Viking raiders. The intention is to crush the enemy between the might of the two Wessex forces. I see now there are mounted warriors to the other side of the shield wall. The men must mean to coordinate the attack, having perhaps crested the slope from the other side. I'm impressed by the decision when it's been made in the heat of the moment.

'Shield wall,' we're ordered. I don't look at the two Wessex warriors to either side of me. I do snap my shield into place between theirs, feeling the strain in my arms, and down into my legs. My crotch is pulsing with pain, and my breathing remains ragged. My intention might appear to be that of a warrior about to aid his allies, but as soon as I can, I'll run from this place. Even now, I realise I'm not far from the end of the shield wall. Behind me, the horses are breathing heavily, the warriors on horseback lifting their voices to direct the attack.

'Advance,' is the next command. I pick up my feet and do so, heeding the dead beneath me and the slick mud from last night's rain, the impact of it worsened by the press of so many feet in this direction. The work is slick and dirty, as dirty as I already am.

With a bellow of sound, the shield wall smacks into the back of the Viking raiders, and I hear their aggrieved shouts and cries. Whatever they've been doing, their intention has been on beating back the Wessex force and reaching the king's tent, and not on what was happening behind them. They've erred in that. I hope.

'Attack.'

My shield's up against the back of a Viking raider, his hair long and straggling down his back, talisman's clacking in it. We're pressed so tight to him, he can barely turn to battle me. Instead, with a wild strike from his seax, he lands a lucky and not at all well-aimed strike onto my helm. I blink the dripping sweat from my eyes, wishing I'd been able to drink before finding myself here. I'm even drier than a salted fish now. The blow, while a lucky one, slows my responses. My shield arm drops a little. I sense the warrior to my left growling angrily. I don't reply. I can't give away I'm Mercian by speaking.

Instead, I grit my teeth, feeling the ache in my jaw from holding them so tightly together, and lash out with my seax. I score a line along his neck, his hair severing beneath the blade, and a thin line of blood erupting. My enemy roars, and the man next to him turns to face him, perhaps only know realising he's under attack from behind as well as in front. The man to my left hits out with his war axe, right through the iron of his helm, and eyes stare at me without seeing while a shimmer of maroon slides down his neck.

His ally lifts his voice to gabble to those beside him. Abruptly, the shield wall buckles as many Viking raider warriors turn towards us, faces etched in fury, where they're visible. The sound of their harsh voices echoes up and down the line. I press my shoulder into my shield.

The first kill by the Wessex warrior was a good one, but he's angered the rest of the bastards now.

They fight fiercely. I don't know what to protect and what to allow to be hit. I'm already so bruised and battered, what does it matter if more injuries are added to it? But they also have sharpened blades and edges, and they glimmer with madder-red in the daylight. I can't grit my teeth any harder, but I tense my body, from my arse to my shoulders, and jab with my seax. The strike goes wild, and there's another crash on my helm. I blink repeatedly to clear my vision, and in the intervening time another blow lands on my helm. I shake my head, the helm wobbling from side to side without the use of the linen cap beneath it. It slips and now I can only see out of my right eye, which is entirely shut. I can't risk moving my hands to right it. I reach out with the seax, stabbing again, but encountering nothing but air. The man to my right fights fiercely. I hear him breathing heavily, but whether he's having any more success than me, I'm unsure.

The enemy force their way against us. My hold on my shield slips. I redouble my grip, force my shoulder back into it, hoping my footing remains firm. Again, I stab with my seax, aiming for anything I can hit through the gap in my shield and the warrior to my right. There are shouts and cries. The air's filled with the sound of shrieked prayers, of boys crying for their mothers, of men demanding the bastards just die. But the fight isn't going our way. I detect it in the shudder of shield, and the judder of blade, and in the very obvious fact I've yet to draw blood. Every time I strike out, I get nothing but air, or the sharp tingle of meeting more iron but never blood.

A war axe swings dangerously overhead. I move my head to avoid it, and somehow end up even more in its trajectory. The strike does push my helm back into position so I can see out of both eyes once more.

A seax slices across my exposed right shoulder. It doesn't cut skin but the wool stuffing of the byrnie erupts from the confines of the material. I hear what I suspect are joyous cries as, somewhere, the Viking raiders taste success. The shield wall holds, but we're moving backwards now, down into the ditch surrounding the Wessex encampment. Now the Viking raiders are above us and, if I thought they'd hit me repeatedly on the head before, now the blows are heavier and better aimed. They can see what they want to hit. It's not the same for us.

The man to my right goes down in a shriek. I turn to pull him back up but he's already dead, a seax blade in his open mouth, blood pooling down its edges. I sense him being dragged away and the warrior behind him taking his place. But the shield he was holding falls low, and a war axe comes for my right knee. I stab down, trying to deflect the blow, and I do, but it takes much of my strength.

The new warrior's finally in position, both shields raised once more, but now they're against the enemies' legs, and not their chests. Our shields are low against their bodies. Theirs are still in place. I take the offered chance and stab into the thigh of the man I face. I'd like to reach the point there where he'd breathe his last, blood flowing from his body too quickly to stop, but my attack's ineffectual. I crash against his thigh but not even a score of blood shows in my blade's wake.

I feel myself growing weaker while the enemy grow stronger. The man to my left collapses. I turn and catch sight of a war axe embedded in his helm. He's not alone. The Wessex shield wall shudders and collapses on itself. The shouts of the mounted warriors do nothing to stop it. There are too few men to adequately replace all those lost. I've no one to my left, although the warrior to my right continues to fight as though possessed by some inner spirit assuring him of victory when I can only taste failure.

The Viking raiders use the gap to my left to step around me. I turn, whipping the shield with me, ignoring the grunt of frustration from the Wessex man beside me. I face three Viking raiders, all sheeted in the blood of the Wessex warriors, one with red-rimmed teeth, one with blood splattered teeth and another with a nose streaming with blood from beneath his helm.

They wear byrnies, helms, and have small, round shields before them, and all of them carry war axes in their hands.

The one looks to the other, and then advances on me. I meet his attack with my seax, wishing there were warriors with spears to thrust between the legs of the bastards. But, whatever's happening in the original shield wall, the Wessex warriors are making no progress against the enemy.

I look around. The warriors on horseback continue to encourage the Wessex warriors to fight, but they've moved aside, as though acknowledging this part of the shield wall will falter. Instead, they shout at the men who are now to my right.

I meet the attack with my shield, wishing the bastard wasn't so strong. I'm weak. I've not been fed properly for days. I need water. He doesn't care about that.

My shield counters the attack. I advance with my seax extended, determined to blood the bastard. He offers me a grin, and now swings the war axe again, and this time one of his allies joins him, the one with the bloodied nose. They shout to one another. The words are indecipherable but the smirks on their faces assure me they're enjoying this. They don't fear me, even though I overtop them. Their confidence almost robs me of my final pieces of strength and conviction I'll survive this day and return to Mercia.

But I'm not about to bloody die twice in one day.

23

I time my attack carefully, taking a moment to calm my racing heart and consider how I can beat the two warriors. Can I use their confidence against them? I doubt it. But perhaps there's something else.

I wait for the original man to advance, war axe swinging almost lazily in his arm. I thrust my shield towards it, and skip into the other enemy. He's not expecting it, it's clear from the way his war axe isn't ready to attack or his shield prepared to defend. I jab at his neck with my seax, and this time I raise more than a score on his skin, although not by much. But, close to him, and with the other man held off, I follow up the seax slice and thrust my elbow into his throat. His eyes widen in shock, his weapon forgotten about as his hands go up to his neck as though having them there will make it possible for him to breathe.

He thuds to his knees. I jab down into his shoulder, blood welling quickly. The third man's beginning to realise what I've done. Almost in slow motion he spurs himself towards me, but he'll be too late to rescue his friend. I stab into the other shoulder and the flailing man, unable to catch a decent breath, falls to the ground. I lower my shield and, with the other war axe on its backward swing, bunch my fist and aim for the other bastard's throat. His shield swings wildly to protect him. I graze it with my fist but also manage to land some of the strength against his neck.

But he's still breathing and now the other Viking raider is close enough to threaten me with his war axe. Still, I've managed to kill one of them. I retreat behind my shield, head low, while both of them swing ineffectually at me. I shuffle forward, an idea forming in my mind. When I can, I bend low and grab the war axe discarded by the dead man. It feels strange in my hand. The handle's wooden, worn smooth with use, and the weight of the axe head threatens to pull my arm forward.

I grip it carefully, no more than a few heartbeats to consider how best to use it. And then, I drop my shield, and with the seax in one hand, the war axe in the other, I swing both wildly, distracting the enemy. They step back instinctively. I slash the war axe across the one shield, and then quickly hook it and pull it down, stabbing through the open mouth of the man with the bloody nose with my seax. He startles, and dies, just like that.

The final man takes one look at me, and a sweeping gaze at his two allies, and runs back towards the rest of his warriors, through the advancing Viking raider shield wall, because here the Wessex warriors are all dead. No one thinks to come towards them because the fighting's swinging alarmingly towards the south. I bend and rest my hands on my thighs, taking the time to fill my body with good air.

Only then do I turn back and survey the fighting.

The Viking raiders are winning. There's no denying it. Soon, they'll have killed the reinforcements as well as those close to the king of Wessex. I survey the Wessex encampment, somehow unsurprised to find the Wessex wyvern banner gone. I don't believe the Viking raiders have it. I suspect the Wessex king has gone, abandoning his warriors to their deaths.

I spare a thought for the poor bastards. It's one thing to hate the Wessex warriors. It's another to be faced with their white, staring faces, and to know they died when their king was too craven to fight with them. King Ecgberht might have more decades behind him than in front, but he should still fight to the death with his warriors. That's his duty. As a warrior king. Only, as I'm discovering, his long reign has more to do with the fact he's not a warrior king.

But I need to protect myself, and not think about the Wessex warriors.

Pulling the war axe free from the dead man, I heft its weight, and hook it onto my stolen weapons belt, preferring to hold my seax and shield. I look once more, but no one's peering this way. No one at all. Now's my chance to escape. I take it.

I scurry towards the tree where I was kept captive, my feet slipping more than once on the slick mud and bloodstained slaughter field, and then hear a rushing of horses' hooves behind me. Hurriedly, I crouch beside the wide oak tree, determined not to be seen. What I see makes me growl low in my throat. I knew King Ecgberht was gutless. This I should have expected, and yet it fills me with anger towards the arsehole.

There are no more than ten horses, and atop one of them sits King Ecgberht, adorned as though a warrior, but nothing that shiny has been anywhere near the shield wall.

King Ecgberht, and I'm sure his son is with him, rush from the battle-field, using the section of their own collapsed shield wall to escape the intensity of the Viking raider attack still veering towards the south.

I remember King Wiglaf once fled the might of King Ecgberht. That made him weak. That made him hated. He's done everything in his power since to protect Mercia, even setting aside his wife to do so, but King Ecgberht? He has no honour. No compunction. He abandons his warriors to be slaughtered, like cattle come blood-month, and now he rushes towards the east. To safety.

How I hate the bastard.

But I don't have time to relish seeing him be all I've known him to be. I need to flee.

With the shrieks of the dying and wounded in my ears, I turn and run the way I tried to escape last night. I must be careful, but quick, I'm absorbed by the comfort of the trees that are nearby on the north-facing slope. It's here I lost Aldhelm. I hope he lives.

Wincing, aware I hurt all over even if the thing plaguing me the most at the moment is the bloody cut on my finger from trying to free myself from my bindings, I quickly remove the helm, and rub the sweat from my face, and then wedge it back into place. I carry shield, seax and the war axe of the dead men. But my entire body thrums. If I'm forced to fight again, I don't know how I'll manage.

I also need to drink. Desperately.

Remembering how long I was lost beneath the trees the other night, I'm astonished to step free from them only a few moments later. Turning back the way I've come, I still see the remnants of the Wessex encampment on the peak. Ahead, a trackway stretches northwards, snaking down the steep hillside. I hurry to follow it. In no time, I'm convinced the Viking raiders will move to find survivors. They're lethal. They'll want no one to outlive their attack. That King Ecgberht and his son escaped eastwards, I hope will have them turning that way once more.

My feet are fleet beneath me. Quickly, I'm covered by a thick hedgerow which will mask me for the time being from any casual look this way. A little later, I find a small stream and bend to cup my hands and drink eagerly. My belly growls with hunger, but I only have water.

I see no one, not even those who must live here, for there are dwellings lining the trackway. Wiser than their own king, they've already abandoned the place. I risk dashing into one house, but while the furniture remains, there's no readily accessible food. I do take an abandoned beaker though, cupping it in my hand. When next I find a stream, I'll be able to drink more easily.

Time and time again, I argue with myself about not looking behind me, but I can't help it. I don't feel safe. Not at all. I sense I'm being followed, no, I sense I'm being hunted, and the sensation makes me scratch my sweat-streaked neck repeatedly.

I run on until I stagger to a halt, at the point where the flatter landscape veers alarmingly down. Here is where I fell. I understand why in the daylight. I also see I'd not have managed to escape this way, so while the hillside feels similar, I must have encountered it in a different place. There's a deep river at the bottom. I scan right and left but don't see a bridge to aid me, or even the means by which I escaped further than this last night. I pause, unhappy to be thwarted now, but I continue down anyway. That way, I'll be hidden from any who think to look for survivors from the battle.

Once more, I lose my footing, my aching body unable to perform as I need it to, so I end up sliding down much of the hillside on my arse, using my feet to stop me.

At the bottom, I stop and look upwards, and then lie flat to the ground. Voices drift to me, and they're not speaking West Saxon or Mercian. I close my eyes, wishing such would make all of my body disappear, but of course, that's not the case.

I wait, barely breathing, for the sound of others crabbing down the pebbly incline, but it doesn't come. Eventually, the voices drift away. But still I wait. They might just have fallen silent and I can't risk looking again to see if they're there. Instead, I delay, allowing my body to grow cold from so much effort, and only then do I stand, and only then to shuffle to an area a little more protected. I duck below the rocky roof of the cave-like structure. There's a small trickle of water. I use the beaker to gather as much into it as possible. It's gritty but I drink it all the same.

I don't know how far advanced the day is. I feel as though I've done enough for three days in just one. I'm tired, hungry, dirty, bloodied and bruised. And I'm still a long way from home. I might have evaded my death at the hands of the Wessex king, but now I fear the Viking raiders are my true enemy.

Unbidden, my eyes close, and my breath stills, and it's only when I cough myself awake some unknown amount of time later, I realise I've been asleep. The day's tinged in greyness, the night almost upon me. I'd feel a whole lot better if I were on the other side of the river.

I strain to hear voices, or footsteps, or anything at all, and that's when my eyes narrow. I sit forward, forgetting in my haste about the stone roof above my head, grateful I still have my helm on, as I hit myself on the rock.

There's someone on the other side of the river, I'm sure of it. I lean forwards, trying to make out the shape in the growing gloom. I open my mouth. Shut it again. Squint, and then move from the shelter of the cave-like structure.

'Aldhelm?' I mutter to myself. And now he forms before me, eyes seemingly fixed on me, his arms making hurry-up motions. I realise it is Aldhelm, and he knows how I can cross the river.

On shaking legs, I force myself upwards. He walks to the side of where I'm standing on the other side of the river, and I mirror his movements. The water appears to be deep and there's no bridge to aid me. Across from me, I see him pointing down, into the water. I feel my forehead furrow, and look down, but stand, shaking my head. I can't swim it. I'm too tired for that, and the current's strong. I fear I'll be swept away with the weight of the byrnie I wear.

Still he nods, and I shake my head. I sense his sigh from where I am, and then he lowers himself down the riverbank. I want to shout at him not to risk it, but can't chance being heard. The enemy might still be hunting for me. But then my words die on my lips, for Aldhelm isn't submerged in the water. Indeed, he's standing, the water barely above knee height.

I lower myself to look, reaching out with my arm, and squint. It's not clear enough to see, the water churned and murky with mud, but I do think there's something down there. Or perhaps I hope there is. Carefully, I lower one foot into the water, and gasp at the coldness. I wince, but my foot quickly rests on something. I shake my head, astounded. I don't know how Aldhelm knows about this, but as I place my other foot beside the first, I hold my arms out to either side for balance, and then quest forward with my foot. Almost immediately, I encounter nothing but an empty space, and my balance falters with the water's flow. But I lean forward, shifting my weight, and then my foot hits something else.

I'm astounded. There are stepping stones, hidden beneath the water. More confidently, but carefully, I shuffle forward, and then stand on another stone or rock, the surface worn smooth by the passage of water. I'm grateful Aldhelm knew about these.

I continue my way across the river, one of the stones much further away than the others so I have to reach out and touch it with only the tips of my toes. For a moment, I hover, hideously aware I wear my heavy byrnie and hold my weapons. I should have removed my byrnie. But then I'm moving onwards, and in almost no time I'm near enough Aldhelm can call to me.

'Hurry,' he urges, and I do as he says. I catch him looking upwards, and fear the enemy are there, but urge myself to be careful while hurrying. If I rush, I might miss one of the stones and tumble into the water.

Aldhelm's back on the riverbank, and he offers me his arm to help me pull clear of the water.

'How did you know?' I gasp, but he doesn't answer.

'Quickly. They can't discover the crossing or we'll never know any peace,' he mutters, and I hasten to follow him. On this side of the river, there are thick trees growing, and quickly we disappear beneath them, and only then does he pause, and look back the way we've come. It's almost impossible to see the other side of the riverbank, but I hear the voices of the enemy easily enough as they shout to one another.

'My thanks,' I gasp, shuddering with the cold working its way up my legs.

'How did you survive?' he asks at the same time, but we don't have time to discuss this. Not now. 'Come on,' he encourages. 'There's an abandoned building at the top of the hill. I have a small fire and some food. We'll warm you up and then continue on our way. We can talk then.'

Appreciating his wisdom, I follow him. My legs ache immediately, the way up the hill as difficult as the way down. My cut hand smarts and now my neck's pulsing as well. I've slept, and that's given my injuries time to make themselves felt. It's not much fun. By the time I'm at the top of the hillside, feeling safe because thick oak trees cover our path, I'm gasping with thirst once more and shuddering with hunger.

'This way.' Aldhelm presses on, and although it's a relief to be on relatively flat land, it's still a good distance away. When we make it within the small stone building, with a roof made of thatch, I sink to the ground. It's been swept clear of detritus and a small fire set within a circle of stones.

'Were you waiting for me?' I gasp, bending to remove my boots and socks, and then shrugging from my damp trews. My legs are a welter of bruises, and bright pink from the cold water.

He takes my trews and hangs them on a hook protruding from the wall. He shakes his head.

'No. I waited here to see what would happen. I heard the commotion of the enemy and came looking for anyone who might have survived. I only caught sight of you by chance.'

'Then you have my thanks,' I murmur. He's busy building the fire with sticks I didn't even see him gathering as we walked up the hillside, and then hands me a container of water. It's not a beaker, which I realise I've left behind in my haste, as well as my shield, but instead a large wooden bowl. How he's found it, I don't know. Quickly, he also offers me a chunk of cooked but cold meat and I devour it, not caring when the juices drip down my chin.

'What happened?' he asks, when I've finished chewing, and so I explain it to him. He shakes his head, disgusted with the attempts to kill me. He's astounded when I tell him how I survived, but then, with the news that King Ecgberht has fled, his face turns thunderous. 'He's a spineless bastard,' he mutters. I nod. I'm not going to argue with him.

'What now?' I question, when I finally feel warmth on my legs.

'You need to rest. Your neck looks awful,' he comments, 'and your hand might be infected.' I look at it then. The flesh remains white with cold, but the cut from the seax blade isn't knitting together as it should.

'Bollocks,' I huff. 'I need to clean it and pack it with honey.'

'I don't have honey,' he offers, with a wry smile, indicating our surroundings. They're far from well maintained and well provided for.

'I didn't expect you to.' I return the smirk, and then wince, and rub my hand over my face. I've more cuts there.

'It's a long way back to Mercia, on foot,' he cautions.

'I could use heat to seal it,' I mutter. 'It wouldn't take long, but it would bloody hurt,' I growl, thinking of my eagle scar and all the other hurts I've endured since becoming a warrior of Mercia.

'But it would ensure you keep your finger.'

'It would, yes. I'll clean it and then you can hold a blade against it.' I work quickly, making use of some of the water and part of my tunic to clean the filth from it, wincing at the foul aroma and yellow pus I force from it. With a growl, I hold my hand towards Aldhelm. He has his seax in the heat of the fire, and now presses it against my skin.

I grit my teeth, determined not to shriek, but sweat beads my face and the aroma of sizzling flesh fills my nostrils. Still, I hold my hand steady, not prepared to go through this more than once.

When I'm happy, I move my hand aside, and gaze at the livid, pulsing skin. I grimace, and then cough aside the stink, but that merely reminds me of my raw throat from being more than half strangled, and then I cough again. I feel wretched, and I'm still not safe.

'Get some sleep,' Aldhelm informs me. 'We'll move out when it's dark. I've seen few people since coming here, but it would be best for us not to be seen by anyone else. I know the river divides us from the south, but it only goes so far inland, and the enemy might know of this and come this way anyway.'

Gratefully, I lie down, and immediately my eyes close, and I'm asleep. But my dreams are dark and twisted, and I wake, gasping for breath, the memory of my almost-death too vivid.

It's darker now, and Aldhelm watches me from behind the fire. His eyes are dull with fatigue.

'Well, you're awake now. We may as well go. I know the way, I think. We're still far from where I live, but I've a good memory for roads and trackways.'

I blink sleep from my eyes, and reach to pull my trews, socks and boots back on. They're far from dry but better than sodden from the river crossing.

'How many days?' I question, forgetting about my hand, and wincing as I run my clothing over it. It pulses like a bastard.

'On foot, at least four. But, at night, it'll be harder. And I believe I've heard the enemy nearby. I dampened the fire in case any came to see why they could smell smoke.'

I grimace. 'What weapons do you have?'

'Not many. A seax, but no byrnie. I didn't stop to take one, as you did.'

'I have a helm and a war axe as well as the byrnie and seax. I left my shield behind. It's not much.' I wince as I stand.

'But you're a good warrior,' he asserts.

'I am, yes. But these aren't my usual weapons.' He looks distinctly unhappy, but then, so am I.

'Well, we'll see what happens,' he murmurs, and directs me from the hovel we've sheltered within. Immediately, the cool of the night closes over me, but at least it's not bloody raining. And there's a bright moon overhead to guide our steps. Still, I'd sooner have Brute with me. Which reminds me.

'Did you see the Mercians when you escaped?'

'No. I've seen no one aside from you and a few locals. I've heard horses but not seen them.'

Aldhelm's steps are firm as he leads me onwards. I realise I've no reason to trust him, other than he's helped me, he hates King Ecgberht and I did already quite like him. I should perhaps be more wary, but I'm too exhausted to consider it. If he intended to kill me, or hand me over to the enemy, I feel he would have done so already.

'This way,' he directs, and I follow him willingly. It's a long way to Mercia, but I will return to my homeland. I vow it. I've been half killed by the Wessex warriors, and set upon by the lethal bastards who are the Viking raiders, but I'll not die here, far from home. I simply won't allow it.

24

I think we make good time on our first night. Certainly, we're not seen by anyone, even as we hurry past settlements, where dogs bark and cattle low unhappily from their pastures.

We don't consider stealing anything along the way. I think, if there were any horses to be found, I'd be tempted, but while I see oxen in the darkness, dull eyes watching us, we see nothing even resembling a horse or donkey. My feet pulse and my legs hurt, but I don't complain, even when exhaustion has me moving forward without truly being able to see what I'm doing.

As the grey light of dawn once more tints the horizon, Aldhelm beckons me beneath a huge, spreading oak tree, far enough away from the path we're following as to be off the regular route, and hopefully, in that way, avoiding prying eyes.

'We sleep,' he instructs me. 'I'm too tired to keep watch, and you're too exhausted, so sleep with your weapons to hand.' The words are far from comforting, but I sink to the ground eagerly, and turn to sleep, blades just in reach. I have to hope I don't skewer myself on the edges in my sleep.

A sound wakes me, sometime later. The space we're in is flooded with light. I turn, grab my stolen seax and look for Aldhelm, but wherever he is, he's not here.

Carefully, listening to voices nearby, the actual words too indistinct to decipher, I sit up and then move my feet beneath my arse, to balance on the balls of my feet, wincing at the noise of last winter's leaves crunching beneath me. I have to hope the voices are far enough away they won't hear me.

I glance around, yawning widely at such an awakening, but I can see little aside from dazzling sunlight through the gaps between the leaves and branches. I'm torn. Should I look for Aldhelm, or move away? The conversation's certainly getting closer, and my heart stills, because the words aren't West Saxon or Mercian. The Viking raiders then have found their way over the river, or perhaps they returned to their ships and have come further north. Why they'd be seeking me, I don't know. Perhaps they aren't. It's more likely they're just scouting for some other poor bastard to rob and kill.

I turn my head from side to side, trying to determine where they are, but it's not possible beneath the tree. Sound seems to bounce all over the place, one moment close by and the other much further away. There's either a substantial force, or more than one group of the enemy.

I reach for my stolen war axe, and heft it into my left hand, and then slowly stand upright, or as upright as I can get beneath the lower branches. Carefully, wishing my injured hand didn't pulse uncomfortably, I move backwards, one slow step over another. I emerge from beneath this particular tree, and risk looking around me. There are more trees, but not many of them. I see bright daylight overhead. But the enemy voices remain close. Mindful of trying not to hit the branches and rustle the leaves, I forge a path through them, seeking the end of the treeline and, I hope, somewhere better to hide.

I wish I knew the location better, but I don't. So I move carefully, quickly, only turning to face the way I'm going when I draw closer to the edge of the treeline. Still, I don't step clear from it. For all I know, there might be more enemies to that side of the small collection of trees.

The view greeting me isn't reassuring. Far from it. Below, there's a trackway, but there are mounted warriors moving on it. I've no idea of their identity but suspect, because of their clothing, they're Viking raiders. I'm surprised to find them on horseback. Where have they managed to get horses from, unless these are the Wessex ones they've stolen? I move backwards, without looking, and suppress a shriek as a hand closes around my mouth.

'Shh,' a voice menaces me. 'Shh.' Delayed, I bunch my fist to fight my enemy but the hand's immediately dropped. I whirl and see Aldhelm, his eyes wide with fear and worry, while I unclench my fist. 'We're bloody surrounded,' he whispers. 'Viking raiders to the east and to the west and they're moving north.'

'Bollocks,' I huff, moving back to hide beneath the same branch Aldhelm's using. 'What do we do?'

'I don't know,' is his less than reassuring reply. 'If we're not seen, we can still creep northwards.'

'But we'll have to evade them all the way,' I murmur. Neither of us wishes to speak too loudly. We're on a small rise. Our voices could carry lower.

'We will, yes. But we can't stay here, either. We've no food.' As though to prove the point, Aldhelm's belly rumbles loudly, and mine echoes in sympathy, the sound horrifyingly loud. 'We can't go south again. The enemy are moving this way, or at least some of them are. And they are the enemy, and not Wessex warriors, although you, my friend, perhaps fear the Wessex warriors as much.'

'Bollocks,' I repeat, hunching my shoulders to try and drive the discomfort of sleeping on the ground from them. 'We should wait until darkness, and move on again. They'll rest at night. Won't they?'

'Perhaps, but it's risky to sleep now.'

I shake my head. 'I didn't say we'd sleep. We shouldn't move, though. How many of them are there?'

'Too many to count. They're mounted, as well, so can move quickly than we can on foot.'

'Perhaps we should steal some horses,' I murmur. 'Then we could ride more swiftly than they can.'

Aldhelm doesn't immediately dismiss the idea. I wish I'd kept my mouth shut.

'That would be very risky,' he murmurs, eventually. 'But, perhaps it would be a good idea. We could even release the horses. Then they couldn't follow us. I imagine they're Wessex horses, anyway. The enemy shouldn't have them.'

'I'm not sure I meant it,' I immediately reject.

'You might not have done,' he replies. 'But it's a good idea, nonetheless. So, we'll wait here, elude them, and then tonight, we'll find their camp and steal their horses.' Aldhelm's eyes sparkle as he speaks. I don't share his enthusiasm.

'Better to just avoid them and press on during the night, while they sleep, surely?'

'It was your idea,' he counters. 'And, if we don't take horses, we'll only face the same problem tomorrow. We can travel at night, but they'll still capture us during the day.'

I grimace. I can't deny his logic, and then I hear a flood of conversation nearby and hold my finger to his lips. He nods in understanding. We stay silent and still. I wince to hear the barked language of the enemy, and then silence falls, quickly flooded by the sound of someone taking a long piss. The sound has me wishing I'd had time to empty my bladder too. Eventually, after what feels like half a day but is much less time than that, the noise of water hitting the ground stops and voices move once more through the trees.

I'm sure they're coming closer to us, but I dare not move to check. I meet Aldhelm's eyes, and they reflect my terror. I don't risk breathing too deeply. I lick my dry lips, desperate to piss and find something to drink, but aware I'm surrounded by the voices of our foemen.

If they discover us, we won't better them. If they find us, we're as good as dead. I shudder at the remembrance of the noose tightening around my neck. Perhaps it would have been preferable to die there, than here, now, on the edge of a bastard Viking raider blade.

But the voices move off. I expel my held breath.

'Bollocks, that was close,' I mutter. Aldhelm nods, words seemingly beyond him. The voices drift towards the north, and finally, unable to put it off any longer, I move aside and release my stream into the woodland, bending my knees low so as to reduce the sound of the impact. My legs shake at the strain in them, and by the time I've finished, I'm biting my lip to stop myself standing upright to stop them giving way.

I turn back to Aldhelm. He's moved back towards the treeline. I join him. We can see the horses and riders but they're not looking back this way.

'Should we stay here for the rest of the day?' I suggest. He grimaces.

'I don't see we can do anything else. If we're seen in the daylight, they'll come for us, and we won't be able to overwhelm so many. There are at least twenty mounted riders on this road. I don't know how many on the track-way, but certainly many more than two.'

'If we wait, they'll attack any settlement they come upon.'

'They will, yes,' Aldhelm unwillingly confirms. 'But what can two of us do against so many?'

I don't reply. There's no need. We'd be useless against such numbers, and if we died fighting them, we'd not be able to join a more concerted attack against the enemy, which I wish to do as soon as I have my Mercians to battle beside.

'Then we wait. We'll continue as soon as it's grey enough they might mistake us for shadows.'

'Agreed,' Aldhelm confirms, but neither of us are happy about it.

Beneath the trees, there's no source of water, and so I spend much of the rest of the day desperate to drink, but unprepared to risk finding water. We don't hear more mounted warriors, but we can detect voices. There are Viking raiders following the initial riders on foot. That makes our inten-tions for the night more difficult. Still, we can't stay here.

Eventually, I step free from the treeline, and assess the lessening light.

'We can go,' I murmur to Aldhelm. 'We need something to drink.'

'Come on then.'

We descend from the hilltop, following the better road to enable us to move more quickly. In no time, we come upon a small stream, and it's clear the enemy have been here because there's a lot of hoof prints in the mud beside it. And horse shit. I walk along the stream a little and then bend to cup as much water as possible and drink it swiftly. I drink until I can't fit any more within, and only then rejoin Aldhelm, who's not drunk as much as me, or who has better hands for cupping water. I'm not sure which but he's assessing the way forward, hands on his hips.

'I suspect the two forces have joined up,' he mutters. 'All those warriors on horseback and the foot warriors as well.'

'So, should we go back to the other trackway?' I question, looking along the well-defined roadway ahead.

'We'd be slower if we did. It depends whether we intend to steal horses or not.'

I don't reply immediately, my thoughts whirling. Would it be better to move more slowly, or more rapidly? Are the enemy heading for Mercia or simply seeking any Wessex warriors who escaped the slaughter field? Do I need to return to inform King Wiglaf so he can reinforce the border between the two kingdoms? I bite my lips, unsure what the best solution is. Only then, there's no more time for thought.

They come at us from out of the gloom, no more than six mounted warriors from the south. We've no time to hide, and neither of us can reply as a gabble of Norse words floods the air.

'Bollocks,' I exhale, wishing for a cloud to cover the bright glow from the moon. What was helpful moments ago is now far from that. 'We'll have to fight them,' I whisper to Aldhelm. We've not fought together before, only against one another. But Aldhelm has another idea.

'No, pull a rider to the ground, and steal a horse. We can rush from here then. We've no chance against six mounted warriors.'

I assess his words, and realise he's right. 'Fine. We'll do that. Which way do we go when we have horses? They'll follow us.'

'They will, yes,' he confirms, preparing himself for the onslaught from the warriors who are still a few moments away. So far, I don't believe they've thought to grab weapons. They must still think we're their allies. The gloom of the coming night shrouds us. For now. 'We follow the stream inland. At some point, we'll veer off it.'

I'm not convinced by his decision, but there's no more time to think.

The lead warrior, finally realising we're not his allies, encourages his horse towards us, war axe in hand, a cry of fury billowing from his open mouth, although what he means to do with his war axe I'm unsure. Perhaps he believes we'll simply allow him to gallop at us and have our faces smashed in with his heavy blows. If he does, he's a damn arse, and no better than a bastard Wessex warrior.

Another belatedly joins him, and both hasten towards us.

'Take the one in front,' Aldhelm instructs me. I grimace. The horse is moving really fast, the war axe lifted high. To pull him from the horse, I'll need to allow him very close. I stand, watching the horse approach, mindful I might need to dive aside if I mistime my attack.

Closer and closer they come, the rider stretching towards me with his war axe. That's when I launch myself at him, arms outstretched, no blade in hand, relying on my body weight to drag him from the horse. Only my hands miss entirely, and instead I impact the horse's backside, the animal shrieking in pain, as I thud to the ground, winded, and the animal rushes past me.

Immediately, I realise I'm in trouble. I can't see Aldhelm, but the other four horses are coming towards me. If I try and scurry aside from the horses' approach, I'm likely to have a hoof in my face or belly. Instinctively, I pull my legs to my chest and wrap my arms around them, head close to my chest, reawakening every hurt in my body at the unusual position. A thud on my back assures me my ploy has only been partially successful. As the clatter of hooves passes over me, and then the sound of water splashing reaches my ears, I uncurl my tight body, blowing through my cheeks. The men are trying to turn their horses, and the first man, whose horse I managed to miss, is struggling to get the injured animal under control in the distance.

I grimace, and meet the gaze of Aldhelm, where he's managed to steal a horse from one of the warriors who now lies in the stream. The man's bleeding heavily, his eyes closed in pain, the water turning pink beneath him.

'What the hell was that?' Aldhelm complains angrily. I grimace again, stepping forward, wincing as I do so. I might have been hit on the back, but my leg also hurts.

'Go,' I urge Aldhelm, but he shakes his head, eyeing up the four warriors who are trying to come back at us.

'Get the grey stallion,' he urges me. 'I'll distract the other bastards.'

A stab of pain has me arching my back, but I nod.

'Now,' Aldhelm insists, and encourages his stolen horse into the pack of four beasts. Three of the riders eye him with fierce resolve, weapons to hand, but the horses are having none of it. The final horse, the grey stallion, is panting heavily. He could be bleeding, but right now I focus on his rider. The man is some indeterminate age, between very young and somewhat old, but it's the unease on his face making me believe I could overwhelm him more easily than the others.

Almost hopping forward because of the pain in my leg, I rush the horse. While the three other riders shout unintelligible words to one another, all trying to overwhelm Aldhelm, who's showing himself to be a good rider, I dash to the remaining single warrior. This time, I time my attack better, and get my hands on the rider's leg. He shrieks, lifting his left arm as though to punch me, but I beat him to it. My fist's furled tightly, and despite the ache in my back, and the wobble of my leg, I hit him with everything I can. My fist crunches into his chin, and his eyes lose focus. Immediately, I pull him to the ground, and thrust myself into the grey stallion's saddle. I grimace at the heat in the leather, and then turn to Aldhelm.

He's embroiled in a proper fight with the three remaining riders, the horse I originally tried to steal remaining far away, its shrill neighs having me wishing I'd been more careful with it.

'Come on,' I urge Aldhelm. His eyes sweep over me, and a look of satisfaction touches his face. But he's not finished yet. His grip on one of the men allows him to strike into his throat with his other elbow. As the man coughs and gags, Aldhelm offers the horse a sharp slap to the rump and the animal clatters into the other two horses. 'Come on,' I urge again, directing the horse to follow the narrow stream inland. We should perhaps ensure the foemen are all dead before we try to escape, but there are too many of them. We've been bloody lucky so far.

Not, of course, that the stream's easy for the horses to move along quickly with their hooves. I feel the splash of water on my boots, and grimace at the smell of blood assuring me the one opponent's bleeding his last into the river, but I try to focus on escape. The moon remains bright overhead. We can see a long way. I look ahead, and not behind.

The horse is far from the tallest I've ever ridden, but it's confident, and doesn't seem disturbed by the change of rider, or the rocky surface we're crossing.

From behind, I hear the enemy shouting, but they don't come any closer. Perhaps they've decided trying to kill two men isn't worth their time. Or they know something we don't. I hope it's the former and not the latter.

'Well, that went bloody well,' Aldhelm eventually comments. We've been silent for a while, listening to the swirl of the water and the clatter of hooves over stones.

'Not my finest moment,' I confess, once more arcing my back. I'm going to add a hoof print to all the other marks on my body after this trip to Wessex.

'No, it wasn't,' Aldhelm allows himself to chuckle, relaxing now we have horses to help us. 'Not much further, and we'll move onto another road, I think. If I know where I am, that is. Then we can travel more rapidly. Where do you think they're going? Do they mean to attack Mercia?'

'Who knows?' I grimace as the horse finally missteps and I fall forwards over the beast's neck. He rights himself quickly enough, and so do I. 'If they're not encountering any opposition, then yes. Mercia will be where they're aiming.' The thought is far from reassuring. But at least here, and with a horse beneath me, we stand the chance of evading the enemy – if we come across them, that is.

'Why did they go inland in the first place?' Aldhelm muses, but I've no answer to that.

'More importantly, why isn't the king of bloody Wessex trying to protect his kingdom?'

Aldhelm makes no reply. There's no justification for what King Ecgberht's done. He knows how lethal the enemy are, and yet he thought to force Mercia to fight on his behalf, even though he had enough warriors to combat them himself, if he'd not been so focused on holding me accountable for imperilling his son. If he follows the law, then he must now convict himself of the same offence against his own *mund*, bloody arse.

The night drags. Aldhelm eventually directs his horse away from the stream, and we do seem to be on some sort of road, or trackway. It stretches northwards, although for a brief moment Aldhelm pauses and eyes the way south, only to shake his head.

'No, we go north,' he mutters to himself, because I've not even argued we should go south. But of course, that's when we realise we're no longer alone.

25

The voices are rough, and distinctly West Saxon in tone. I share a worried look with Aldhelm.

'Bollocks,' he huffs. There are mounted warriors coming this way. Their words reach us. They're not moving stealthily. I've no idea where I am, or where to go. 'This way,' Aldhelm urges me. He encourages his horse onwards, northwards. 'We have to outrun them,' he whispers to me. I know he's correct. If we're caught by the Wessex warriors, I'll have a noose around my neck once more before I can lift my seax to defend myself. This is turning into a truly terrible few days.

We don't move quietly, but swiftly. The horse I ride is no match for Brute, or even Bicwide, but it keeps a good pace with Aldhelm's beast. Which is good. I strain to hear over the sound of my too-fast heartbeat but then realise I'm not doing any good, tensing my already aching back as though I'll be struck at any moment. I need to focus on escaping and evading the damn bastards, and not on worrying when they'll strike.

The landscape around us dips and lifts. I can't scent the sea, so we've come inland a substantial way. In the distance, I detect the hint of light on the horizon and yawn widely. I've not slept properly for what feels like days. Exhaustion drags at me. More than once, I sense myself falling forwards in sleep, despite the speed of my horse and the threat of attack from behind.

'We'll have to stop soon,' I call to Aldhelm. He doesn't respond. I flick a glance towards him, but his face is turned away from me. 'Aldhelm.' I say his name a little louder.

'I heard you,' he growls. 'We can't stop yet.'

'The horses are slowing,' I argue.

'I know that. They're still behind us. Damn fools are on the wrong trackway to find the Viking raiders.' I consider if they know that. Are they purposefully seeking the enemy where they know they won't be? I wouldn't be surprised. Everything I've learned about the Wessex warriors and their commanders assures me they only like an easy fight. The Viking raiders don't fall into that category. Not at all.

Neither do the Mercians. Not any more.

'It's getting too light,' I call a short time later. 'They'll see us.'

'I know. I know.' Aldhelm's tone is aggrieved.

'So, we should stop.'

'Yes, yes. But not yet.' I turn then, unease forcing me to do so. I think to see the shimmer of iron and blades chasing us down, but although I sense the enemy are there, I can't see them in the dark gloom of dawn now the moon has set and the sun has yet to fully emerge from behind the horizon.

I grip the reins tightly, and then my horse stumbles. This time, the animal goes down on one leg. I spring from the saddle as best I can, not wanting to go down with the animal if it rolls. I can't have a crushed leg to go with everything else.

'Bollocks,' I growl, jarring my teeth and reminding myself of the pulsing pain in my back, neck and hand. Ahead, Aldhelm slows, as the horse rights itself, and walks forward gingerly before putting all its weight on its front leg again.

'This way,' Aldhelm calls to me. I've no idea where he thinks we are, but his voice does sound more confident. I follow him, leading the limping animal, hoping there's somewhere we can hide from the enemy. Away from the trackway, because it's not one of the more formal roads, depicted in stone that the giants once threaded through the land, the landscape's quickly overwhelmed by summer growths, the grasses tall and tickling my nose. Aldhelm forges a path through them. They almost overtop the horses and me. Once more, I hope he knows where he's going. Surely, the enemy will realise someone's left the trackway when they see the passage through the tall grasses.

Sweat drips down my spine now I'm not riding, and every step jolts my back so I'm forced to grit my teeth and press on. Just as I'm about to demand to know when we're going to stop, Aldhelm does just that. I feel my forehead furrow. I've no idea where we are, or what this place is.

'Come on, inside,' he urges me.

'Inside?' I grumble. 'It doesn't have an inside, does it?'

'You'd be surprised,' he assures me. Ahead is something that looks like an earth bank. It could be a natural formation, but I suspect it's not. And I have my answer as we pass through some sort of stone entranceway and are plunged into darkness. There's a damp smell within, pervasive and unpleasant, but it's only damp and not the smell of the dead.

'What is this place?' I question. Aldhelm's busy removing the harness from his horse, and allowing the animal to rest with its back against the mud and stone-built walls within.

'This, my friend, was once a burial chamber. Now we can rest here, and no one will find us.'

I shudder at the thought of what happened here in the past, but Aldhelm seems entirely unconcerned.

'Come on. Get some sleep. We're still a bloody long way from Mercia and now we have the Viking raiders and the bastard Wessex warriors looking for you. We'll need all our wits about us if we're to make it home without being discovered.'

His words are as reassuring as half-cooked bread to a starving belly. But I do as he says, slumping to the ground, where the horse I stole already lies, and rest against the side of its body. I run my hand over the animal's face, meeting the intelligent eyes, and then I must sleep, for when I'm next aware of what's going on, I feel refreshed, and also not refreshed, but Aldhelm's urging me to wake up, his expression twisted with fury.

'Bloody hell,' he growls. 'It seems everyone is after us.'

I don't know what he means, but then realise there are once more voices, reaching us from outside.

'Bollocks,' I explode softly, standing with a grimace, and hurrying to add the saddle and reins to the horse.

We've not finished trying to escape. Far from it.

'Who is it?' I question him. Aldhelm shakes his head from where he stands close to the exit.

'I don't know, but we're not going to wait to find out.'

I need to piss and drink, and no doubt the horses do too, but there's no time. There never seems to be any time.

'Couldn't they be locals?' I urge him. 'Can't we explain who we are?'

But he's already denying the suggestion. 'No, Icel, we can't. Whoever they are, we need to get away. If the Wessex warriors come here and ask them who they've seen, they'll tell them. If it's the Viking raiders, they'll find a way to tell them as well. No. Come on. I think we can move to the far side of the mound, and escape before they get any closer.'

'How do you know where they're coming from?'

'Less questions, and more action, my young friend,' Aldhelm urges me, and without allowing me time to argue with him, he strides outside, leading the horse. I hurry to follow him. I feel as though all I've done since I found him is follow where he leads. For a traitorous moment, I consider if he is my friend, and then dismiss it. I've no one else to help me. I've no idea where Ealdorman Ælfstan and the rest of the Mercians are, but they had to leave me behind, because I made them, and now I'm doing the best I can.

Outside, the daylight's bright. I blink as I follow Aldhelm around the side of the structure. I can't truly see anything. The long grasses block my view both ways. There's a thin track pressed through the grasses, but I doubt the feet of these people made it. It's more likely an animal track.

Dampness presses into my clothing. I wish there was more of it so I could sate my thirst. The voices Aldhelm heard appear to come from very close. They're West Saxon, I'm sure of it, but whether they're warriors or not, I've no way of knowing.

Ahead, Aldhelm once more disappears amongst the long grasses. I hurry to follow him. If I lose him now, I'll have no idea where I am, or how to get home. I see the horse's tail and use that to guide me. Aldhelm must be guiding the animal. I consider when we can mount up and gallop from here. My back's aching badly. I sense the bruise must cover most of it. I was lucky it was only that bad. I know people can die from a hoof to the body. While I'm grateful not to be dead, I wish I'd managed to evade the bloody kick too.

We move swiftly, and my trews and boots are swiftly drenched with dew. Overhead, the sun's out but it doesn't feel warm enough to have dried the dew from the grasses. I consider how long I slept for. Perhaps not as long as I might have hoped.

The voices fluctuate, at times far away, and at others I turn, expecting them to be following me. There's never anyone there other than my fears stalking us.

'We can ride now.' Aldhelm appears before me, already mounted. I hurry to follow him, wincing at the pain from my assorted wounds. We remain surrounded by tall grasses. I look around when I'm in the saddle. I can't see where we slept. I can see a vast expanse of grasses, gently tipping in the breeze.

'Where are we?' I hiss.

'Away from the people. Now we need to move more swiftly. I know the horses are tired. I'm bloody tired too, but we shouldn't see people if we follow this track.'

'This is a track?' I question, astounded. I can't see it depicted in the grasses.

'Yes, a very old one. Few use it these days, but once upon a time, this was one of the main routeways, or so I've been told by those who know these things. It leads towards the stone circle.'

'Stone circle?' I question, but our conversation's at an end. He encourages the horse onwards. I follow him. I keep looking all around me, seeking people, animals and dwellings, but the landscape's particularly empty. I can't imagine the place is deserted, but the grasses are very tall and the route Aldhelm follows is so poorly depicted, I suspect he's making most of this up. I admire his confidence.

Finally, we find a stream, and all of us drink deeply, and I get time to piss and rub water over my sweaty face. Aldhelm eyes me.

'You look terrible,' he offers, smirking. 'Half strangled, and the other half of you badly beaten.' And then he pauses, assessing me in a way he's not done before. 'And yet, I suspect this is quite normal for you?'

'Well, not normal, but it happens a lot more bloody often than I'd like it to.'

'I'd heard of you, Icel, before we met. King Ecgberht hates you. King Wiglaf highly esteems you and so his son hates you. And, it's said, you've no fear of meddling in any fight between Wessex, Mercia or the Viking raiders. It's a pity you were too young to fight the warriors from the kingdom of the

East Angles. You might have ensured the king of Mercia lived.' For a moment, I consider if Aldhelm suspects who I am. Certainly, he appraises me keenly.

'But I was too young. And one man can't stop everything. Not even me,' I chuckle, but it turns into a cough that makes my back ache. About now, I'd welcome seeing Cuthred and his pack of supplies from Wynflæd, but of course, he's far from here. Safe, I hope, at Tamworth with Lady Ælflæd and the children. I wish I was there.

'Indeed,' Aldhelm muses. 'I knew those kings, Beornwulf and Ludica. They were little better than King Ecgberht. Overly confident and with little regard for the damage they'd cause with their actions.'

'King Wiglaf isn't like that, not now,' I murmur, uncomfortable with where the conversation's going, and eager to use my coughing fit to cover any telltale giveaway I might give.

'Then, I think I might need to take myself to Mercia, and stay there. I'd sooner fight beside men who know how to battle, and for kings who know how to reward their followers.'

'When we get back to Mercia, I can speak to Ealdorman Ælfstan, or Lord Coenwulf,' I suggest.

'But first, we must get to Mercia.'

'Where are we?' I question.

Aldhelm offers me a pensive expression. 'Not far from where Mercia and Wessex first clashed, at the battle of Ellendun, over a decade ago. Everything's been crap since then,' he offers conversationally.

'So, you know the way home?'

'I think I do. I've only been this way twice, once on the way to the battle, and once on the way home.'

'We need food for the horses, and for us.'

'I know that,' he grumbles. 'But I can't pull it from up my arse, so quit your moaning, and let's get moving.'

I turn to my horse. I detect a plaintive look in its eyes I also feel. At least the animal isn't limping. Whatever caused it to falter was a momentary thing.

'I know, my friend, I know,' I murmur, mounting once more. I still can't quite reconcile where we are with the lack of people. I'd expect to see people fleeing the enemy, but the landscape seems devoid of anything, aside from grasses swaying in the wind. The sound of voices has long since faded, and with it, my exhaustion has returned. It's not yet midday, and already I want to sleep.

The pathway we follow eventually opens up, and at least I do see a settlement ahead. Smoke drifts into the sky from within the dwellings. I turn to Aldhelm. He has his eyes narrowed, and seems to be on his guard.

'Let me do the talking,' he commands. I don't argue with him. We're not yet in Mercia. These people might see me as an enemy.

The people who come to see us are interested and wary, but not scared.

'Greetings,' Aldhelm calls. 'Do you have bread and oats for hungry travellers?'

'We can if you can pay,' a gruff voice responds, and a man wearing a leather apron forges a path through the small crowd. It's evident he's the blacksmith with such huge arms. The livid burn on his right cheek helps identify him as well.

'I can, yes, my good man.' Aldhelm shows a collection of coins in his hand, and I consider where they've come from. Perhaps the saddle, or a body he stole them from.

'Then, yes, we have bread and oats.'

At that, Aldhelm dismounts, and beckons for me to do the same. 'Tell me, good man. Any news of the Viking raider attack here?'

The blacksmith blanches at the comment. 'Not here, no. Why, where are they?'

'Far from here, at the coast,' Aldhelm reassures, as we're brought two big chunks of bread and cheese by a woman who eyes us coolly. I take it from her, with a murmured thank you, more an opening of my mouth than actual sound. I suspect I shouldn't reveal I'm Mercian.

'We've heard nothing of that, or seen the bastards either,' the blade-smith reassures the worried murmurs of the people of the settlement. 'No Wessex warriors either,' he continues. I find that knowledge almost more reassuring.

A young man brings a bucket of oats for the horses, and the animals eat hungrily, the sound of their crunching drowning out the murmurs of worry from the people of the settlement.

'Tell me, are we far from Malmesbury?' Aldhelm continues.

'A day, no more than that,' the blacksmith comments. 'We trade there, often. The monks are generous.'

'They are indeed,' Aldhelm agrees between mouthfuls.

'You look like you've been in the wars,' the bladesmith adds, lifting his chin to indicate our attire.

'Yes. We've been set upon by the enemy. Now we're seeking our fellow Wessex warriors.'

'Well, you won't find them here. More likely to find Mercians than Wessex warriors. The king of Wessex little concerns himself with events here. It was better when we were ruled by Mercian lords and their king.'

The words surprise me, but of course, these people have little say in who governs them. They're farmers and craftspeople.

'I agree with you.' Aldhelm cracks a smile. 'Perhaps we should ask the Mercian king to fight for us.'

'I hear he's not that much of a warrior, either,' one of the other men comments, his face lined by the sun, as he holds a hoe in his one hand. These people, I suspect, have few visitors and are eager to learn of what's happening beyond the confines of their village.

'I hear he's better than King Ecgberht.' Aldhelm chuckles.

I keep quiet and eat. This intrigues me, but for all the conversation between the two men is calm enough, I suspect a tension thrums through it. Does Aldhelm know these men after all? Are these people hiding Viking raiders, or Wessex warriors in their main hall? Something doesn't feel right. I wish I knew what it was.

'Tell me,' Aldhelm continues. 'If we follow this track, will we reach Malmesbury?'

'No, not that one.' Aldhelm's pointed northwards. 'That one will lead to Mercia. Malmesbury's to the west of here.'

'Then you have my thanks. I'd have gone the wrong way.' Aldhelm inclines his head towards the bladesmith. 'We'll be going now. Good day,' Aldhelm calls, mounting quickly. I follow, wishing we could allow the horses more time to rest, but Aldhelm's good humour has evaporated.

'What's the matter?' I question when we've left the settlement, although I keep looking over my shoulder to ensure we're not being followed.

'They lied,' Aldhelm confirms angrily. 'They lied. They mean to send us the wrong way. For what reason, I don't know, but I can suspect well enough.'

'You believe the Viking raiders have been here?'

'Them, or the Wessex warriors. Someone's got to those people before us,' he grumbles, face reflecting his fury. 'And now we have a conundrum.' I'm not sure I like where his thoughts have taken him.

'Conundrum?'

'Yes, do we head into whatever enemy is nearby or do we simply rush for Mercia?'

I breathe deeply. I know all the arguments I could make here. How we're alone. How we're just two men. How we can't do anything against a vast force, of either Wessex or Mercian warriors. How we should return to Mercia and inform King Wiglaf of what's happening. But equally, I'm no craven. I don't fear to battle the enemy. I haven't for many summers now. I might not want to do so, but equally, I'm a warrior of Mercia, and it's my responsibility to protect her.

'Lead on towards the enemy,' I inform him. He flashes me a relieved smile. Even now, after everything we've been through, Aldhelm doesn't understand my resolve towards keeping Mercia safe.

He'll learn. Probably much sooner than he wants to do so.

26

We follow the track they told us to take to reach Mercia, although Aldhelm knows it will take us to Malmesbury. There was never going to be an argument from me about that. We might be close enough to Mercia I swear I can smell it in the wind, but there are too many enemies who threaten my kingdom.

If it's not with their words and underhand actions, it's with their swords, seaxes, shields, spears and warriors who mean to kill all who stand in their way. Bastards, all of them.

And it doesn't take us long to find them. I'm sure I might be starting to get a grasp of the landscape around me. I soon have my answer when we stand on a rocky outcropping and look towards Malmesbury Abbey. Even if the blacksmith hadn't lied to us, we'd have been able to hear the sound of warriors from a long way off and we'd have turned this way anyway.

We can't see the coast from here. We are, however, greeted by a vast force of the enemy. From here, I can't tell who they are, but I don't think it's a great surprise to think they're the Viking raiders.

King Ecgberht of Wessex, craven that he is, has allowed the enemy to sweep from Carhampton, deep into Wessex and now they almost threaten Mercia.

'Bollocks,' I expel softly, my horse tired beneath me, head hanging low.

I'd like to dismount and give him time to rest, but I need to reach the opposing force.

In the gentle breeze, I see the familiar banner of Mercia from atop the pinnacle of Malmesbury. King Wiglaf is far from the weak man he once was. King Ecgberht won't defend his kingdom so King Wiglaf will.

'Mercians?' Aldhelm confirms. I nod.

'We need to reach them,' I comment. Whether there's been fighting during the day or not, I'm unsure, but as dusk settles over the landscape, whatever fighting there was, if there was some, has stopped. The Mercians hold the higher ground, where the abbey nests. The Viking raiders are moving to surround them to the west. I wish them luck with that.

'Hum,' Aldhelm muses, squinting keenly at the sight before us.

'The Viking raiders have made a great deal of effort to get so far inland,' I murmur.

'A day or two, no more than that, if they've brought their ships and not ridden. I suspect some have ridden all the way from the Wessex encampment.'

'But how do we reach the Mercians?'

Aldhelm's again slow to respond, and then when he turns to face me, I almost fear he'll say it's impossible. But, I should know better. This is his home. He knows the trackways well.

'Follow me. The coming night will cover our movements. We'll be with the Mercians before first light. Whether we'll be fit to fight beside the Mercians is another matter entirely.'

The words aren't the most reassuring, but as a harsh shriek from an eagle flying overheard floods my hearing, I know I'll do so. I might be on my knees, eyes closed in sleep, but I would still fight the bastards. They'll not get any closer to Mercia.

* * *

Not that the going's easy. The horses are as tired as we are, and there's little light by which to see as darkness falls.

'It would be a kindness to leave them,' I eventually admit. With my own exhaustion and my aching back, I don't feel like walking but the horses will injure themselves if we force them onwards.

'We'll find a handy-looking field to leave them in. One with water,' Aldhelm admits too willingly. Without the horses, it'll be difficult to evade capture should we be seen. Grudgingly, I admit the horses are making a great deal of noise with their staggering steps.

Still, it takes a while to find somewhere we can abandon them. The settlements nearby are deserted. No doubt, they've sought shelter with the monks, or skipped further north into Mercia. Close to one abandoned settlement, we allow the horses into an enclosed area. There's a water trough and also some forsaken hay nets. Whoever lived here, and I hear Aldhelm mutter a name I assume belongs to the people, has left in a hurry. I enter the dwelling, and rest my hand close to the hearth fire. There's the tiniest feeling of warmth from it. I make my way to where they might store bread or cured meat, and my hand encloses on a leg of pork, roasted over the fire, but abandoned in the rush. I sniff it, and take a small bite, before returning to Aldhelm, and sharing with him.

The two horses have had their saddles and harnesses removed and now stand, drinking and eating slowly. I sense their exhaustion.

'I found this,' I call to Aldhelm, who sniffs it too, and bites delicately.

'It tastes good. They must have overlooked it in the hurry to leave here.'

With a final parting rub over my horse's long nose, I follow Aldhelm. His steps are sure, despite the lack of light. I consider whether we should take a brand with us, but bite back that comment. Aldhelm would have suggested it if he thought we needed one.

Instead, we eat the food in silence. I feel exposed. I've spent more than enough time hiding beneath trees and in deep woodland, but here there isn't woodland. Instead, I sense the expanse stretches out all around us. There'll be nowhere to run if we're discovered by the enemy.

Aldhelm's footsteps never falter. Every time I feel too fatigued to continue, I consider my allies. It's imperative we reach them. I've seen what the Viking raiders can do. We must prevent them from doing the same within Mercia.

'Not far now,' Aldhelm eventually mutters. His voice shows the strain of his tiredness. 'We made good time. We should get some sleep before making the final part of the journey. If we don't, we'll be put to use too tired to be helpful.'

Although I want to argue with him, I admit he's correct.

We hunker down with a stone wall at our backs. It seems out of place here. I can't see it belongs to anything. As so many other monuments I've seen of late, I suspect this was built by those long-ago giants.

Between one breath and the next, I fall asleep, and wake to gentle warmth on my face and the sound of Aldhelm having the longest piss I've ever heard.

I hurry to my feet and release my stream into the long grasses as well. All the time, I'm peering around me, trying to make sense of where we are. I look up and catch sight of the abbey building in the near distance.

'Come on,' Aldhelm urges me. 'If they're going to fight, they'll be at it soon.'

'And you'll be fighting on behalf of Mercia?' I question. I realise I've not thought to ask this.

'I'll be fighting for my people, and my landholdings, yes. If that means standing shoulder to shoulder with the Mercians, then I'll do so.'

The closer we get to the hill ahead, the more alert I become. From what we saw yesterday, the enemy were moving to encircle the location. Whether that's been achieved or not, I don't know. We no longer stride onwards, but look around us. The path's old and evidently well used by the locals. Aldhelm seems to know where all the twists and turns are, and more than once he beckons for me to stop walking until he's happy there are no enemy nearby.

'Come on,' he urges me. I feel my forehead furrow as he once more appears to know how to cross a deep river without the use of a bridge. This time, there aren't stepping stones beneath the water, but instead ropes tangled high in a nearby tree. He pulls a long rope down with a grin. 'If it's good enough for the children,' he coos, taking a run up and not giving himself time to think about whether it's a good idea or not. He swings low over the water, his arse almost touching it, and just about lands on the other side with only a slight moment of worry he'll end up in the water, which he prevents by sitting down.

He stands, and thrusts the rope back towards me. I rush to catch it, missing the first time, but on his second swing I grab it.

Unhappily, I pull on the flimsy material. I've had about enough of bloody rope of late. But the branch it's attached to feels firm, only a faint rustle of leaves reaching my ears.

'A run-up's needed,' Aldhelm hisses towards me.

Grimacing, wishing once more my body didn't ache so bloody much, I step back as far as the rope will allow, and hurry to run towards the gurgling water, much deeper than I'd like it to be. At the last moment, I lift my feet and close my eyes tightly, as I surge over the water. It's as close as I've ever come to flying. I confess, it feels pleasant enough until I sense the momentum faltering. But Aldhelm's there, and he grabs me before I swing back over the water.

'Let go,' he urges me, and quickly I'm standing, astounded such a tactic has worked so well. Aldhelm pulls on the rope, but it won't come loose. Instead, he reaches as far up as he can, and severs it with his seax. It's not the best way of preventing others from following us on to the far side of the river, but it's all we can do for now. 'Come on,' he once more urges me, and together we surge up the steep plateau the settlement sits upon. It's tough going, but with the growing daylight, we do reach the top quickly, although out of breath. Now I understand why the Viking raiders are in such a position. It's as though they're hemmed in by two rivers encircling Malmesbury. Perhaps, then, they've travelled with horses and on foot and not with their ships.

'Who goes there?' an angry voice calls to us.

I wipe the sweat from my eyes and look up to see the eyes of one of Commander Eahric's men.

'Icel?' he gasps, recognising me immediately. 'We heard you were captured, and probably dead by now.'

'No. Not that easy to kill me,' I call, sagging with relief, but indicating my throat at the same time.

He winces, and turns to call to another.

In no time at all, we're surrounded by Mercians, and Ealdorman Ælfstan strides through the collection of warriors, his expression difficult to read. When he comes even closer, enfolding me in his arms, and is quickly followed by the rest of my fellow warriors, including Oswy, who I suspect has a tear in his eye, I appreciate they truly thought me dead.

'Alright, enough of this crap,' Wulfheard's gruff voice calls. 'We've still got a bloody battle to fight.' But as I stride to his side, even he offers me a cuff on my shoulder, which has me wincing. As always, he shows no sympathy and offers no apology. Then the abbot appears, and with an assessing glance between me and Aldhelm, inclines his head towards him.

'My lord. It's good to see you. Your men are here, ready and waiting to serve.'

'Lord?' I startle.

'Yes, Lord Aldhelm,' the abbot confirms, a gleam in his eyes for not alerting us to that the last time we met. 'Now he's returned, I'm confident, with the aid of the Mercians, the enemy will be driven away.'

I turn to Aldhelm, my mouth an 'O' of surprise. He laughs.

'Two can play that game, Lord Budworth, they really can.'

27

King Wiglaf watches me approach him. He has an unfathomable expression on his face but he grins when I'm before him.

'I see King Ecgberht tried to take his revenge?' He indicates my neck with a finger and a wince.

'He did, my lord king, yes.' I incline my head respectfully, grimacing with the movement.

'Bloody arsehole,' the king explodes, and then grins even more widely when he sees Lord Aldhelm, as I must now call him. 'You can't keep an old dog down, my friend.' The two embrace. I confess, I thought my miraculous survival would please the king more. Evidently not. 'Now, how do we beat the bastards and show the king of Wessex and his pestilent son how warfare is conducted?'

I don't expect to be asked this when I've just arrived, and swallow, unsure of what to say. However, it's Lord Aldhelm who's actually being questioned by the king.

'The enemy will struggle to fight uphill, as you found yesterday. And they're also restricted as to how they can approach you. So, I suggest warriors to either side of this triangle shape they're wedged between, to stop them escaping via the river, and a force to assault them from the above. I take it you've been gathering stones and other missiles to rain down on them?'

'Yes, we have,' King Wiglaf confirms, nodding. I consider how these two know one another but now isn't the time for such reflection. I also wonder why Aldhelm didn't introduce himself when he travelled to Kingsholm. Perhaps he didn't want to, or perhaps he and King Wiglaf did speak and I was unaware of it.

'The trick will be to get them to retreat and then we descend from the promontory and hound them back to the coast. If we don't kill 'em all first.'

'I'd thought the same,' King Wiglaf confirms. I survey those with him. King Wiglaf has brought much of the might of Mercia to drive back the enemy. I see Ealdorman Muca and Tidwulf, if not bloody Sigered. No doubt, he hides away in Tamworth, determined not to risk himself in the coming battle.

'Are you convinced they'll try and reach us here?'

'Yes. They're crazed fools who believe themselves invincible.'

So spoken, Wulfheard leads me away from the king. I'm taken to where there's good food to eat, and even better, the welcome sight of Brute. I walk towards him, forgetting about any need to eat, and Oswy's tasked with bringing me a bowl of pottage which he places into my hand with a smile, while Brute looks surprised to see me. I'm surprised to see him as well.

'They said you were dead. Brute and I were having none of it,' Oswy offers conversationally. 'We came upon the king's forces two days ago. He'd already decided Mercia needed protecting. Tell me, how did you escape?'

'Ironically, I have the Viking raiders to thank for that. I was more than half dead when they attacked the Wessex encampment. I had to pretend to be a West Saxon in the shield wall and escaped when they were overwhelmed.'

'You've had quite the adventure, haven't you?' he muses, as I eat eagerly. Lord Aldhelm's remained with King Wiglaf.

'How do they know one another? The king and Aldhelm.'

'No idea. But they certainly do. The abbot thinks highly of Lord Aldhelm as well. Now, come on, eat up and I'll sort out your equipment for you. Not your byrnie, of course, the bastards took that, but we do have your seax. That byrnie you wear is far too big and you can't fight in it.'

'But I have fought,' I reject.

'Not well, if that bruise on your chin is anything to go by, and the slice around your neck, and whatever else you've done to yourself. Anyway, we have much of your equipment still, alongside your horse. I assume we'll be sent to drive the enemy from Malmesbury when they finally turn tail. Better to be ready, my young friend.'

With a final caress for Brute's flank, I follow Oswy, wishing I felt young, but I don't. Perhaps, I consider, I should refuse to take part in the coming fight. But no. I've survived so far. I'm sure I'll manage another half-day, or however long it is, fighting the Viking raiders. I've always known I hate them. In the last week, I've had the feeling confirmed, on multiple occasions.

Ealdorman Ælfstan's warriors have been given a dwelling to rest within – well, actually a stable or animal barn – and it's there Oswy takes me. He's full of conversation about who's injured with what, and I allow his words to pass me by. I need to know everything, but equally I'm pleased to have time to breathe without fear of being attacked, by either Viking raiders or Wessex warriors. Admittedly, we do still need to defeat the enemy, but with my fellow warriors that's entirely possible. I find a grin on my tight cheeks, only banished when Oswy forces me to remove my stolen byrnie, and he growls at the hoof imprint on my back. A monk's summoned, and a salve is spread over my entire back, as well as my burnt hand, raw neck and a thousand other hurts, and only then am I allowed to dress once more.

I welcome the feeling of the new byrnie, and my weapons belt, even if I can hear Oswy and Wulfheard muttering about my fitness to join the fight. Not that they have much say in it.

The Viking raiders, prevented from taking Malmesbury yesterday, are eager to try again. Fully armed, but not expecting to be called upon yet, we make our way to the peak where Mercians are preparing to attack the enemy who think to swarm up the steep hillside.

'They'll never make it,' Oswy asserts. I realise he's correct.

'They're going to give it a bloody good go, though,' Wulfheard states. And he also proves to be right.

From below us, we all hear the sound of men being called forward. They don't even appear to notice the slope, or to consider how they'll be undone by it. Not even when the first stones rain down on them do they stop. Not even when their allies are bloodied by carefully thrown spears and the few arrows available to the king do the enemy even consider giving up on a bad idea.

It sounds as though thousands of foemen seek to overwhelm us. On top of the summit, there's little sound but the commands of Eahric and others of the ealdormen as they encourage the men to continue their defence. As the pile of prepared stones, barrels, buckets and anything else that can be rolled down the hill gradually lowers, I start to worry. The enemy show no signs of retreating. They're fiery and determined.

'It won't be long now,' Wulfheard astounds me by stating confidently. 'We should prepare the horses. We can't race them down the slope from here. We need to take the gentler path, the one the enemy don't know about.'

'I don't know about it either,' I complain, but follow my fellow warriors eagerly enough. King Wiglaf's also instructed a similar number of his mounted warriors to join us under the command of Ealdorman Ælfstan. I find them with the horses, already preparing.

'Come on. We don't want to miss it,' the one shouts to Wulfheard. I can't help thinking they're not anxious enough about the enemy. Having fought them, repeatedly, I know they don't battle as we might expect our fellow Saxons to do so. That's what makes them so successful.

'Icel, don't look so worried,' Wulfheard calls, and still I'm apprehensive. Only as we make our way down a sloping path the monks lead us to do I understand why my fellow warriors are unconcerned.

The route we take is behind the slope the enemy fight up. It's a tricky path to follow. We don't ride, but lead the horses. I feel the strain in my knees and thighs, reminded of the hills I've descended in recent days. The hillside's densely covered in trees and weeds, making it appear as though it's entirely insurmountable. As such, although a force of Mercians is already in place to stop the foemen sneaking behind us, they can't be seen by the enemy. Only when we emerge between the twisted hedgerows of vicious thorns will the Viking raiders realise they've been deceived.

'How will we get the horses through?' I question.

'We've dug it out,' Oswy crows. 'Or rather, some other poor bastards have been forced to do so. We just move it out the way, go through, and then these lot will cover it once more.'

I shake my head, surprised by how much thought's gone into this.

'The king's been planning this for a while?'

'Not the king, Lord Aldhelm. Malmesbury's in his possession. And he always means to protect it. Now, get ready. As Wulfheard said, it won't be long.'

Carefully, I mount, checking to ensure I have my weapons and shield to hand. I'm not as convinced as the others this will be easy, but it'll be preferable to having no horse and no blades with which to fight. And no allies at my back.

Abruptly, I'm aware the roar of the enemy has changed tenor. Before, they were filled with determined shouts. Now, I sense a modification in the cries. I might not understand the words they call one to another, but I recognise panic and fear when I hear it. I glance upwards, but it's too steep to determine what's happening up there. The Viking raiders have certainly attempted something no Saxon warrior would consider doing. There's never any gain to fighting directly up a hill.

'Stop daydreaming,' Wulfheard shouts to me. I turn, meet his eye, and offer Brute a reassuring stroke along the top of his right front leg.

'Come on, boy. Let's show these Viking raiders what it means to fight a real enemy, and not the weak king of Wessex and his son.'

With that, the hedgerow ahead is moved by brave men, prepared to absorb the many thorn strikes, and Brute follows the other horses into a quickly growing wedge of land, close to the riverside. On the other side of the river is Mercia proper. Here, we're in a landscape that's been fought over by the Mercian and Wessex kingships for many, many years. The Mercians mean to show it should still be Mercian. I allow a smile to touch my lips, and then lift my arse from Brute's saddle, the better to let him follow his fellow horses.

The Viking raiders will face our wrath. I'll enjoy killing as many of the bastards as possible with the shields of Mercia at my side.

I really bloody will.

28

The ground's ragged, perhaps often flooded, with tufts of grasses in places I don't expect. It reminds me of when we fought outside Canterbury. Brute absorbs it with his long legs and sure footing. A sudden shriek assures me the Viking raiders, already endeavouring to regroup, or retreat, have seen us emerge from a location they thought impassable.

From the far side, I detect other mounted Mercian warriors seeking to stop the Viking raiders escaping. I allow myself to think the outrageous suggestion might be successful against the bastards.

Shouts of angry Norse words already ripple through the air. The Viking raiders, somehow convinced they had only one way of taking the settlement of Malmesbury from those defending its peak, have discovered there were other means of reaching the summit which would have saved them the lives of many men, crushed beneath stones and anything else that could be flung from the plateau.

The function of the mounted riders is to stop the enemy escaping to the water, and if that can't be done, then to ensure they travel west, towards the sea, and not further into Mercia, or admittedly, Wessex. Closer to the River Avon which encircles Malmesbury, I appreciate our foemen have ships they could scurry away in. Already those to the rear of the attack, able to see better than those in the thick of it, are turning towards the ships. They sense their defeat. Now we must make it a reality.

'Stop them,' Ealdorman Ælfstan roars. While I'd like nothing more than to direct Brute towards the heart of the brutal fighting, I know that's not my task. Instead, I take my horse towards where the Viking raiders are attempting to flee.

I see no more than five ships to my right, or rather, to the north. If the rumours were correct, and thirty-five ships attacked Carhampton and Wessex, they've not risked bringing as many along the Avon. There are even fewer to the southern side of the wedge in which the enemy are currently trapped.

There's a startled cry from ahead. I swoop down from Brute's saddle with the war axe I stole from a dead Viking raider, and a resounding bang thrums through the air, knocking the enemy to the ground. Admittedly, I wince at the giant sweeping blow, my back pulsing with the action.

I don't stop to skewer him and ensure he's dead, because I'd need to dismount; instead, I encourage Brute onwards to where Ealdorman Ælfstan already prevents three men from bolting onto the waiting ship. It's riding low in the water although there's no one on it. Yet. We need to keep it that way.

Wulfheard quickly joins Ealdorman Ælfstan, while Brute and I move to block entry to the next ship. I remain mounted. The small vessel's longer than Brute, by at least three times, but I hope to stop the enemy jumping onto it, because it's moored nose on to the muddy embankment, the sound of gurgling water only distant because of the angry and terrified shouts and cries of our opponents. I don't know where the longer ships are, but it makes sense that only the smaller craft have risked the journey inland.

Another enemy warrior races towards me, moving so fast I fear he'll fall because his legs pump so quickly beneath him. His headlong dash aids me. At the last moment, he loses his momentum, and stumbles forward, one foot hitting an uneven tuft of grass. I swing the war axe towards him, missing his head entirely because I mistime the stroke, but thumping into his chest instead.

With a shriek, I'm forced backwards, managing to remove my feet from the stirrups, so I fall without breaking any part of my body. I land on my back, winded, but other than that, not badly injured, aside from reawakening all of my old hurts. Instinctively, I reach to touch my head, somehow surprised to find it still attached to my neck. I sense Brute turning to face me, and then his long black and white nose peers down, his consternation mirroring mine.

'Sorry,' I huff, rocking myself upright as soon as I can, wincing as I do so, taking deep breaths to combat the agony shooting along my spine. I gather my lost war axe with one hand, having first fisted it a few times to drive the pins and needles from it. I look down at the figure lying there, knocked onto his back by the force of my war axe blow. He's not much older than me, a thick blond beard and moustache covering his face, his eyes fluttering where he seeks consciousness. I grimace, but stab into his chest with my returned seax, stilling his beating heart. I don't feel pity for him, but I appreciate it's a waste of a life to die, here, without earning any battle glory for himself.

Oswy's joined me. He remains mounted, turning his horse to face the enemy.

'You all right there, Icel?' he calls, voice filled with a mixture of amusement and concern.

'Not bad,' I pant. I decide to stay beside Brute rather than worry about dismounting to finish off the warriors Oswy will knock to the ground. I lift Brute's reins above his saddle so he won't trip if forced to run, or is startled by something else.

The enemy are fully in retreat now. The force from the summit are slowly starting to descend. The foemen are trapped between them and the Mercian horses flanking the wedge-shaped piece of land between the curve of the River Avon. I realise some are already forgetting about the ships, running to the west instead of to the ships. I wish them luck with that. The journey, I've been told, is at least a day on horseback. We will, when this is over, have to hunt them down.

Three men rush towards me, round shields held before them, fury evident in the set of their visible jaws below their helms, and their cries to one another.

Oswy glances at me, perhaps trying to decide whether he should dismount, but he doesn't. From such a height, he'll be able to clatter his seax onto their helms. I stand with shield and war axe, ready to strike them, Brute behind me.

The first man comes up short. I see his two fellow warriors continue. I detect a smirk on his thin lips at such a trick, but my attention turns to the other two.

They have shields and war axes, but I can't say the war axes look sharp, and the shields aren't in the best condition either. Perhaps they've not cleaned them since attacking Carhampton, or King Ecgberht's encampment. Or maybe they're men who thought to make a name for themselves and earn better equipment from their leaders. They might not be warriors at all.

I move to intercept one of them, growling low in my throat. Words pour from his open mouth, but I don't understand them. The only thing I comprehend is the need to fight to the death. His, not mine.

With Brute staying behind me so he blocks easy passage to the waiting ship, I swing the war axe wide, too aware of the ache in my back by doing so, closing quickly on the man who directly faces me. I'm aware Oswy's engaged the final man who thought to allow his alleged allies to absorb the force of my attack. Craven, or perhaps intelligent. I don't know. He'll be dead soon enough.

My blow lands on the shield of the first man. The crack of iron on wood is loud, but it doesn't stop him. I feel his hot breath on my face, as his forward momentum forces me back, one step, and then two. He was running fast. I manage to dig my feet into the tufty grass. Now we're standing closely together, two wooden shields with iron bosses separating us, but not much else. He has a war axe, and he strikes, trying to swing it so it impacts my back. Perhaps he's seen my discomfort, or perhaps his war axe handle is simply so long, it's the natural length of his strike. I swivel to avoid the blow, wishing once more I wasn't so badly bruised.

His ally stands behind him, panting, chest heaving, eyes wild as he assesses whether to aid his friend or take a chance on reaching the ship. The bastard decides to abandon him. It gives me the opening I need. I step clear, quickly, and turn into the second man with my war axe, so focused on reaching the ship, he doesn't even defend himself. My blade impales him high on the shoulder, wedging there, his eyes flickering in pain.

'Bollocks,' I huff, hanging on the war axe but unable to work it free.

He screams in agony, hands also trying to pull the blade free. But his ally comes behind me, his war axe swinging wildly. I have my shield in one hand, but I'm turned the wrong way, shield protecting me from the screaming, bleeding man who for the moment doesn't think to attack me, while his friend can hit against my side and back.

Abruptly, the wounded man remembers his blade. His face twists and blood quickly floods from the wound. Despite the agony he must be in, he tries to stab me under my war axe arm, although it does nothing to aid me in releasing the war axe.

Angry at myself, breath harsh in my ears, back pulsing, neck throbbing, I step back, and quickly reach for my seax. I'm more skilled with this blade, anyway. I was merely enjoying playing the enemy at their game.

I jab out, once towards the man with the war axe embedded in him and blazing eyes, and once toward the foeman who thinks to best me by taking advantage of my distraction. I strike neither of them, but give myself some room to manoeuvre and consider my next moves.

My eyes flash between both men. I wish they didn't look so bloody confident. Even the wounded one licks his lips and growls at me. I should have mounted and allowed Brute to bring his hooves to bear on them. I know how bloody painful such a blow can be. Now I don't have that option. Oswy's no help. He's engaged with the other foeman, and there are more and more of the enemy coming towards us, desperate to reach their ships. This is the first time they've been bested by their enemy. Their fear's palpable, and it's every man for himself as some knock others over and don't stop to aid them to their feet.

I jab once more towards the unwounded man, giving myself time to consider what to do. The two enemy call one to another. I wish I knew what they were bloody saying. I might need to learn their tongue. It would aid me in such situations.

I size them up. By rights, it should be the unwounded man that strikes me, but I sense this isn't what's about to happen. I thrust my shield up moments before the injured man staggers towards me. I punch my shield out, aiming for and hitting the handle of the embedded war axe. He howls like a vixen, what remaining colour there was draining from his face. He resembles a day-old corpse. I continue to press against him, even when he steps back, desperate to get away from the pain of my shield forcing the war axe even deeper into his body.

Fury covers the elements of his ally's face I can see. He stomps towards me, breathing ragged. He might know he's going to die here, but he's not going down without a bloody good fight. I plunge my seax towards him, the sound audible as it sweeps through the gentle breeze. He jerks backwards, my blade going for his suddenly exposed throat. I press my advantage against the already bleeding man. Oswy's finally overwhelmed his enemy because he swings his sword, neatly impaling the already wounded man with a blade down his back. I turn immediately to battle the remaining foeman, moving with quick jabs of my seax, my shield before me to protect from his blows with the war axe. He steps backwards, unaware there are others there now too. Cenred hits him on the head with the hilt of his seax and, eyes losing focus, I jab into his neck, where his shield has fallen low.

I bend, as he drops to the ground, panting heavily, grateful my allies have aided me. But that's only the first of the enemy to come against us. We still stand between them and their ship.

I cast a sweeping glance around my fellow Mercians. The ships are protected against the Viking raiders reaching them. It's made some of the fools frantic. I hear men flailing in the water, desperately trying to reach their ships from further away than they should. More than one of them sinks below the deeper water, and never surfaces again.

I lick my dry lips, and turn to Brute. My fellow warriors remain mounted. I decide to do the same, and rush to mount up with all the grace of a three-legged rat with the pulsing pain throbbing through my body.

Sweat beads my face. My lips are dry. My tongue sticks to the roof of my throat. Ironic when behind me there's a river I could drink, although perhaps not now, with the death cries of bastards who thought to evade us.

I bring Brute between Oswy and Cenred's horse, and the animals, surprisingly, don't object to being so close together. Viking raiders see us blocking the path, and those ahead come to a stop, only to be knocked over by those following on behind, not looking at those ahead but only on where they're going.

A cacophony of iron and wood resounds through the air, as well as the outraged cries of those at the bottom of the pile of fleeing foemen being crushed to death. Those even further behind merely clamber over backs and arses, eyes fixated on their promise of safety provided they can reach the ships.

These enemy, I note, have better equipment. These must be the true warriors of their oath-sworn lord, or however it works amongst the Norse, who know how to fight and do it well. Those we've faced already were perhaps similar to when the king calls upon the fyrd. Their equipment wasn't the best, although they no doubt hoped to receive better when they'd overwhelmed us.

The men wear blood on their faces and byrnies as though by design. I hate them already. They've been killing good Mercians, and the abbot's warriors. Admittedly, if they've killed some of the Wessex warriors, I won't hold that against them.

I growl low in my throat and Brute, sensing the unhappiness thrumming through my body, rears, although I don't order him to do so. His front hooves kick out, one, two, and I realise he hungers for their death as much as I do.

'Ware,' Oswy rumbles. I don't need his caution, as Brute lands once more on all four legs. He moves beneath me, forwards and back. For a wild moment, I consider what he intends to do. But then Brute settles, body taut, awaiting my commands.

The foemen come towards us, some helping others keep upright, but mostly on their feet and with blades and weapons to hand. The majority have long hair, visible beneath their helms, bedecked in anything from blackened iron to some sort of shimmering imprint on the metal covering their foreheads. Their shields are black and red circles, and in their hands they carry swords, shields, spears as well as war axes. One even carries the longest war axe haft I've ever seen, two-handed, without the protection of a shield.

'Watch the big bastard,' Oswy urges. I can hardly take my eyes from him as he attempts to slide down the side of Cenred to reach the ship.

'Ware the big bastard.' I repeat the caution. Cenred's horse moves one step back and one step forward. I think that would be the best plan. I don't say it aloud though. No doubt Cenred already knows he can't risk his horse having its legs knocked from beneath it.

I eye the warrior with a long sword. He walks arrogantly, chin defiant, showing me his throat. I think he might be their oath-sworn lord. I wish I had a spear I could slide through their shield wall. But I don't. For a long moment, what happens next hangs in the air, uncertain. The enemy assess us, just as much as we assess them. The moment's broken when Cenred's horse bunches its back legs, and soars over the bastard with the two-headed axe. I hear the horse's legs impact him with a wet thud, but there's no time to watch. The action has unleashed us.

Brute rears. His hooves hit the shield of one of the men, forced forwards by the confident bastard with the sword. While the shield absorbs the blows, the man crashes to the ground. Brute walks over him arrogantly, his front hooves remaining on the shield, the man crushed beneath it. I hear his cries of terror, quickly stifled, and keep my gaze on the warrior who sends the man to his death.

Beside me, Oswy's fighting, I sense it rather than see it. There's no space to either side. Brute advances again, his back legs on the shield of the dying man. Now three men shared terrified glances towards their leader. They don't wish to be the next to die, here, crushed by the weight of a horse.

I feel my lips twist in disgust, as the leader considers who it'll be. I don't allow him to think about it. He's as gutless as King Ecgberht of Wessex. And I've had enough of men who send others to die in their wake, and then take the spoils of victory.

I grip Brute's sides tightly, a slight movement, but one he obeys all the same. Now, like Cenred's horse, he bunches his back legs and we hasten forward, crashing into the three men awaiting the orders of their leader. The first falls, the second tumbles beneath him, dragged down by the falling weight of the first man, as though two trees too close together when the woodspeople come to coppice. The third skips backwards, only to crash into the leader of these men. He has his arms before him, and pushes the man away, back into Brute's advance. I lean from my saddle, and swipe a blow across his throat where he seems to bounce from Brute's side. I witness a shiver of blood on my horse and pray the bastard hasn't wounded him too badly.

Then I face the weak bastard.

He glances from side to side. Whatever he sees there isn't reassuring. I don't look. I trust my fellow warriors. They'll scythe through these bastards. I need to kill the leader.

His eyes peer behind me, as though he can make the river and his ship come closer. But I'm in front of him. Brute blocks his path.

And then he astounds me. Quickly, before I can understand what he's doing, he drops his shield, and crouches to the ground in a clatter of iron and leather. I bend low, to skewer him, but he's out of reach of my seax, as he risks escaping through Brute's legs. Brute hates it. He turns, and I hear a thud of something, but I can't see what's happening, and then the man's through Brute's legs and standing once more, while Brute's still halfway turned.

A roar of outrage leaves my mouth as I hurry to dismount, kicking my stirrups aside, ignoring the aches in my body, and rushing towards the bastard. He has his back to me, and he's no more than three steps away from hitting the riverbank. I lower my head, and crash into him, so we both fall to the ground, hitting the muddy embankment with a resounding thud that once more has me wishing my back didn't hurt. I'm on my front, lying over him. He's on his front, but his hands are already clawing at the mud, great fistfuls of it being sent behind him, landing with too much accuracy on my face, as I reach for my seax, lost from my hand in the crash of our meeting.

He twists beneath me. I'm reminded of my first fight in the woodlands with my uncle, when the bastards tried to kill me, and I had nothing but a rock with which to kill them. I try to get my knees up beneath me, and plunge them against the enemy's back, but he's a feisty git. Not even the cloying mud threatening to choke off his air is stopping him. The stink of the river mud is foul so close to it.

He makes it to his knees and bucks me clear. I land on my knees, wincing at the thud, grateful the mud provides some protection and I've not settled on stones. But he's still not on his feet. I reach out, and hook his right leg with my right arm. He kicks out. I taste more mud, but at least still have all of my teeth. I yank again, aiming for his left leg as well, but he slips it out of reach, while I sit back on my knees, and continue to pull his right leg.

With my left, I fumble for my seax, but it's out of easy reach. The next thing I know, more mud hits my face, and I close my eyes, unbidden, to prevent it impacting my vision. In that moment, a fist hits my helm. Instinctively, I release my hold on his foot, hands encountering another hilt instead. I surge upwards, and once more stretch for him with my empty hand. This time, while he struggles for balance on the muddy riverbank, I hook his weapons belt with my hand, and put all of my weight into the movement, hoping to knock him to the mud once more, while my other hand endeavours to get the weapon I've grabbed the right way round.

He turns to face me, eyes wild with flashing fury, words dripping from his mouth I don't understand, but can imagine well enough. I punch up with my left fist, but wince when I hit his byrnie-covered shoulder, jerked into my path at the last moment, and not his chin, which would have seen him bite his lip.

He pivots quickly and punches me in the face. I feel it as a crash against my left cheek, knocking my head to one side. But I have his war axe the correct way round now, and I swing it at him. It crashes into the unprotected space where I've pulled his weapons belt low enough it's bunched around his byrnie, pulling it free from where it was held in place. He staggers again, going down on his right knee. I surge onto my feet, crashing his own blade into his back, unaware if I cough aside sundered skin and flesh or mud, and not caring which it is as my frenzied attack intensifies.

His shrieks flood the air. I sense him trying to pull my legs from beneath me, but I hold firm, allowing the mud to suck my boots beneath it to provide stability. Slowly, his frantic attempts to escape still. And yet I can't stop my attack. I hate the bastards. All of them. This man was craven with his allies, and a bastard against the Saxon people of Wessex.

Repeatedly, the war axe buries itself deep into his back, even when he's entirely still and blood pools on the muddy riverbank, and only then do I stop, and suck in much-needed air, swivelling because I'm aware I'm under scrutiny, and I can't move my booted feet yet. Brute watches me, his eyes wise with understanding. That's when I stand upright, force my boots free from the deep mud with an unpleasant squelch and slurping sound and really get a look at what's happening around me.

The enemy are in full retreat towards the top of the triangle wedge, but they still outnumber us. Yanking the war axe free from my dead enemy's back, I look to the ship I've been protecting, still there, although no one's yet managed to board it. Eagerly, I crash my blade into its wooden hull, stepping into the water up to the height of my boots, using it as a means of cleaning them at the same time. My strikes are more well placed this time, low down, where the water flows above the planks of interwoven wood, and pieces of wood fly into the air. While my back screams in agony, I don't stop until I hear the slurp of water breaching the ship. Then, I don't return to Brute, but stamp to the next ship. While the enemy try to reach them, attacking my fellow Mercians, I'll make it impossible for them to flee in them, should they manage to get close enough.

I glance at the fighting, seeing Oswy and Cenred hard at work, Wulf-heard and Ealdorman Ælfstan labouring together to prevent three warriors reaching the ship. Maneca and Kyre are ahead of me, doing the same. The pair fight back to back, swirling in a circle so the enemy never know where to expect a blow. Their horses watch on from the riverbank. Again, I use the war axe to forge a hole in the ship, being more careful this time, timing my blows better because exhaustion is dragging on my shoulders and aching back.

Panting heavily, I turn to face the fighting as soon as water once more breaches this ship. I'm unsure how I can continue battling, but know I need to do so. The conflict's far from won. I gasp for air, and stagger towards Brute, who's been following my path, but staying out of the way of the flying wood. His hooves are filthy, I notice. It'll take me half a day to scrub the mud from his shins.

Pulling myself laboriously onto his back, I realise one of the ships has managed to make it onto the river proper, wallowing in the deepening flood. I assess the situation, but there was never really going to be any doubt about my next actions.

With a gentle click of my tongue, and pressure from my knees, Brute steps forward, into the water, and together we move towards the ship, frantic eyes from five men watching our approach. Their evident fear emboldens me. I suspect I'm pushing Brute too far. But their terror rein-forces my belief we can succeed.

With speed that surprises me, Brute canters towards the ship, or at least moves as quickly as he can against the pressure of the water.

With another click of encouragement from my tongue, Brute does what Brute does best. The next thing I know, we're standing in the hull, Brute's weight forcing the ship even lower, water threatening to slip over the sides. My blade's out and attacking as I slide from his side, wishing I could leap but unable to do so. I'm grateful the ship's wide enough to allow me to move. I shuffle towards them, absorbing the motion of the ship in my screaming knees, as they argue loudly over who'll face me first.

'Come on, you bastards,' I roar, and go to work.

Brute lowers himself into the water. I'm not on his back as he does so. The movement's ungainly, but the water isn't that deep and the ship wallows with five dead men staining the bilge water. And a few hoof-made holes as well. He waits for me patiently, perhaps sensing my abject exhaustion. I force myself to mount him from the side of the ship, the water flowing below his knees. At least he'll have clean shins now. He strikes out, walking confidently, not concerned by the force of the water, while I lick sweat and blood from my lips having killed those five foemen. I can't say they had good deaths. My lips taste disgusting. Only as we near the riverbank do I look up to meet the disbelieving gazes of Oswy and Cenred.

'Bloody hell,' Oswy explodes, shaking his head, helm sheeted madder-red, which drips freely down his shoulders as he does so.

'It had to be done.' I shrug, becoming aware more and more of Ealdorman Ælfstan's men watch me, including the ealdorman himself. I'm unsure what I see reflected on his assessing gaze. It might be respect. Equally, it might be quiet fury for endangering my horse, and myself, in such a way.

Purposefully, I avoid looking at Uor. I don't wish him to be devising some new scop song to laud me with. I did what had to be done. I'd do it again.

Behind them, the slaughter field glistens white and grey, sunset-red and marbled blue. The dead are many.

'Is it over?' I call, astounded by how weak I sound. If Brute wasn't carrying me, I fear I might fall, and succumb to the water, so exhausted some might think me dead, although I'm not.

Ealdorman Ælfstan twists from surveying me to looking where the enemy remain.

'I suspect so, yes,' he comments blandly. I can never tell whether Ealdorman Ælfstan hungers to fight and kill. I suspect he does, but that he must mask it with the veneer of the court. 'You'll do no more,' he instructs, and by that I assume he means the others will follow him as they hunt down those still retreating. 'For the rest of you, come on. We can't have the other bastards taking their share of the battle booty.'

Only then Ealdorman Ælfstan pauses, and looks at me once more, grimacing.

'One of you needs to stay with him.' Groans greet the instruction, but another shouts to say they'll perform the task. I meet the equally bloodied and bruised face of Aldhelm, my fellow survivor from the Wessex encampment at Brent Knoll.

'My lord.' He inclines his head to Ealdorman Ælfstan, and even Wulfheard bites back his denial. Lord Aldhelm's a fierce and lethal warrior, as I am.

'Very well, and my thanks.' Ealdorman Ælfstan inclines his head towards him. 'The rest of you, hurry up. Look, King Wiglaf allows his warriors to walk the slaughter field.'

A shriek from overhead and I glance up, wincing at the action which excites the rope burn around my throat. It's no raven there, come to feast on the dead, but instead, an eagle. I find it reassuring. The eagle is Mercia's emblem. Oftentimes, an eagle has shown itself to me in times of dire need. However, this time its cry is triumphant. I feel a broad grin on my cheeks, which I instantly regret, as they rub against my helm, and the motion cracks the sweat encased there. No doubt, some mud has also found its way beneath the cheek guards.

'Bring me back something good.' I lift my voice to call to my fellow warriors. They encourage the horses to pick a path over the dead and dying, no doubt keen to reach the point of the wedge shape through which those who walked or rode here endeavour to escape. Momentarily, Wulfheard pauses, assessing me once more. He puffs through his cheeks, shaking his head. I'm sure I hear the words 'half-cracked bastard' leave his lips. I'd say the same to him, if I could summon the energy to do so.

Aldhelm, I realise, has also encouraged those warriors who owe him their oath to chase the enemy. I recognise the men I first faced not far from here, when they were Wessex warriors preventing us from returning to Mercia, and therefore our enemy. It pleases me to see them hale and well. How times have changed. I hate the Viking raiders. I despise the Wessex warriors who declaim themselves King Ecgberht's warriors. Aldhelm and his men aren't like them.

'That went better than I expected,' Aldhelm comments lightly. He's rubbing his horse's right shoulder. I consider if the animal's wounded or if, like me, he's just taking pleasure in the simple delight of being with his horse, the enemy all dead, or fled. His blade shimmers wetly where it rests on his thighs.

'I'll be pleased to see the back of the bastards,' I agree. I glance towards the peak above my head. From here, it's much easier to see Mercia's emblem flying in the wind. Malmesbury thinks itself part of Mercia, not Wessex, but that's an argument for another day, and another king. King Ecgberht isn't here. Where he is, I don't know, and I don't care. Certainly, I'll not be stepping foot in Wessex proper again during his lifetime. And perhaps, not during that of his son's, either. While the Viking raiders have proven themselves to be merciless bastards, the Wessex king, and his household warriors, have shown themselves to be weak and poorly led. They have no honour. And they let a personal need for vengeance cloud their judgement. They should have thought of defeating the enemy before they sought revenge against me.

'Admittedly, they do fight well, though,' Aldhelm surprises me by saying, his voice warm with respect. 'Much better than the Wessex arse-holes.' I grin again. How quickly he's decided to no longer count himself amongst that number.

I indicate the dead with a jut of my chin. 'Shall we?' I suggest.

He shakes his head. 'I'm too bloody exhausted to even consider pilfering them,' he exhales, and now I laugh.

'I feel the same. Is there someone to perform the task for us?' I question.

'In all honesty, Lord Icel of Budworth, I don't wish to have anything these lot had. Mere trinkets, mostly made of tin or copper, if I'm not mistaken. I think we should go back to the abbey. Find ourselves a bed, and finally get some sleep.'

Abruptly, I yawn, widely, and I close my eyes, allowing the sun to warm my eyelids, and the shadow of the eagle to temporarily darken them. Then I open them.

'I couldn't agree more, Lord Aldhelm of Malmesbury?' I ask, for I don't know the answer.

'Oh, nothing quite that grand, my friend.' And together, we allow our horses to pick a path back towards the secret passage we used to walk down to reach this location. As I go, I survey the dead. We've triumphed here, against the Viking raiders, and that feels good. But the Viking raiders are lethal, as I know them to be, and the majority of the Wessex force has suffered at their hands. It's the warriors of Mercia, with the aid of Aldhelm and his men, who've triumphed. What this means for the future I don't know. Will the Viking raiders understand they've been bested by the warriors from a different kingdom or will they assume we're the same as the Wessex warriors? If they realise we aren't the same, will they continue to attack Wessex but leave Mercia alone? I truly don't know. But, what I do know is King Ecgberht and his bastard son still live. They'll not stop seeking their vengeance against me. I wish them luck with that. What they should be doing is countering the threat of the real enemy, but weak men will not realise that. They'll be blinded by what they perceive is the true menace. Mercia, and King Wiglaf, must defend itself better than ever before. We must ensure the Viking raiders never step foot within Mercia again.

I go to open my mouth, to ask Aldhelm what he thinks, but the thunder of hooves has me reaching for my bloodied seax, my muddled thoughts believing the Wessex bastards have come to end my life when I'm exhausted and weak. I only relax when I see King Wiglaf and Commander Eahric riding towards us. Commander Eahric's gore-splattered; King Wiglaf also shows some signs of having been amongst the bloody end of the battle.

'Icel, Aldhelm, well done,' King Wiglaf calls. He eyes me, searching my face for something, just as Ealdorman Ælfstan did. I don't know if he finds it. Then he grins broadly, and lifts a hand to indicate the field of harvested flesh. 'Mercia can overwhelm all, be they the Viking raider bastards, or the Wessex fools,' he shouts, voice rich with delight, and with that, he follows the other horses towards the fleeing enemy.

As he goes, I speak softly, not intending for anyone else to hear. 'Long may that continue, my lord king. Long may that continue.'

But I know, with a sickening pit in my belly, that this is merely the third of many such encounters. The Viking raiders will not stop. Not until Mercia reaps them like wheat during the harvest. And it will be Mercia and her shields that perform the task, not the Wessex fools. It will be Mercia who prevails against the Viking raiders. And against Wessex. Mercia's shields will be triumphant.

* * *

MORE FROM MJ PORTER

Another book from MJ Porter, *Lords of Iron*, is available to order now here: https://mybook.to/LordsOfIronBackAd

HISTORICAL NOTES

I have followed Hoskins' identification for the location of Croft Hill in Leicestershire (Mercia) as the place where the religious synod of 836 took place. Aside from the survival of Charter S190 (more below) we have no other reference to this synod. The article by Hoskins is freely accessible and can be downloaded. (George Hoskins, W. [1950]. Croft Hill. *Transactions of the Leicestershire Archaeological and Historical Society 26*. Vol 26, Leicestershire Archaeological and Historical Society. pp. 83-92. https://doi.org/10.5284/1107792). I confess, I realised once the book was written that Hanbury and Croft were two different places. Apologies for merging them together.

The exact bishoprics for Husa and Cunda, as named in Charter S190, are unknown, although every other bishop on the charter has been identified. It's been suggested they were from the kingdom of the East Angles. Although this has been dismissed by historians, I've used it as it ensures each kingdom is represented at the Croft synod, aside from the Northumbrians.

Charter S190 survives in four manuscripts, not all of them complete. It's deemed to be contemporary, or at least a contemporary record of what happened, although with some later additions by historians who've studied the period in great detail and are truly experts. You can find details on the online resources PASE (just type PASE in your browser) and the Electronic Sawyer, and I've accessed the translation by Dorothy Whitelock in *English*

Historical Documents Volume 1, which I was lucky enough to grab a copy of during lockdown, and which I use all the time. It's the first-edition version, and I am aware a second edition is the usual one that's cited. King Wiglaf's son, Wigmund, doesn't witness this charter.

The *Anglo-Saxon Chronicle* (A) for 833 corrected to 836 states (on p. 62):

> Here King Egbert fought against 35 ship-loads at Carhampton; and great slaughter was made there, and the Danish had possession of the place of slaughter. And Hereferth and Wigthegn, two bishops, passed away; and Dudda and Osmod, two ealdormen, passed away.

A is believed to be the oldest version of the *ASC* although not the 'original' version. I won't bore you with the details again, but do check out my website www.mjporterauthor.blog for more information. Other versions of this entry show the number of ships as XXV, which I think is twenty-five. (I went to a school that had a VI in the title, and it took me years not to write IV by mistake). This section of the *ASC* only mentions Wessex, highlighting its preoccupation with the West Saxon kingdom, where it was conceived of in the 890s. We don't hear anything of assaults on Mercia throughout this period, but it's believed attacks by the Viking raiders had been causing difficulties since the initial *ASC* reference to the one on Lindisfarne in 793. Although, the 793 reference is the first mention in the *ASC*, it's believed there were earlier attacks within the British Isles which haven't been recorded. The identification for these comes from archaeological excavations, and for Mercia, records in the charter evidence which appear to identify attacks on religious establishments. The first official account of an assault on Mercia is from 842, when London was attacked, according to the A version of the *ASC*.

Was Cornwall part of Wessex at this time, or not? I find Cornwall very confusing. We have records of King Athelstan forging an alliance with them in the 920s, as he did with the Welsh at Hereford, and at Eamont with the rest of the coalition (see the *Brunanburh* series) and this casts doubt on whether Cornwall should be included in 'Wessex' at an earlier date. I've shied away from Cornwall in the past (aside from in my earlier *Pagan Warrior* trilogy when it was certainly a kingdom in its own right) because of this. But Carhampton, unless I'm very much mistaken, is in Somerset, not

Cornwall, and I do feel more confident in saying that did form part of Wessex. Cornwall has very strong traditions of its own and has been much studied by historians, and not just because of its very association with the Arthurian legend. And speaking of which, yes, I did send Icel to the fictional home of the Eorlingas I created for *Men of Iron*. Why not? I love threading these little consistencies through my Mercian tales. I hope you enjoy them as well.

This brings me to Malmesbury. I visited Malmesbury as part of their Athelstan 1100 celebrations in September 2024. Malmesbury is associated with King Athelstan, as he's believed to be buried there, although no one knows quite 'where'. The reasoning for this is that King Athelstan, with his alleged Mercian upbringing, preferred to be buried as near to Mercia as possible, alongside his cousins, who perished at the battle of Brunanburh. However, Malmesbury's location on the Mercian/Wessex border fascinated me, and I realised I could add it to this narrative of 836. The location was associated with the earlier Mercian royal family, and had only recently fallen back under West Saxon domination after the battle of Ellendun in 825 (precise location still unknown). As with events in Kent at this time, it's all a little bit shaky, and details are lacking. However, the border region to the west of Britain between Wessex and Mercia is complex because there's no fixed boundary, such as the River Thames, to truly define it. I've made much of Malmesbury's high location, mainly because there's a delightful account of a monk who lived there (in later centuries) who thought he could fly with the aid of wings. Do check out the story of Eilmer of Malmesbury. I couldn't, however, find the correct name for the abbot of Malmesbury at this time, but I'm not alone in this. It seems there is a lack of information.

Brent Knoll hill fort was chosen as a location for this story after I'd written the first draft and had a bit of a panic because my editor is from that part of the country. There are many hill-fort and hilltop sites in Somerset, many more than I thought, although that doesn't mean they were all in use at the same time, or were even used for defence and protection as is so commonly thought. You can find details for Brent Knoll on the Atlas of Hill-forts of Britain and Ireland website, which includes a lovely lidar image. My understanding is that it's not been excavated but has potentially been damaged by later quarrying. I also understand, thanks to a YouTube video, that it stands very prominent in a largely flat location, and it is very steep before reaching the peak, which is somewhat flatter.

I did write the fire scene when the terrible fires were being reported in the US. As a child, I was evacuated from a forest fire while on holiday near Bend, Oregon. It was an incredibly surreal experience. I vividly recall being driven through the landscape after it had been declared safe to do so, as well as the kindness of those who provided sanctuary to pesky holidaymakers. Thank you.

Thank you for reading the latest *Eagle of Mercia Chronicles* novel. Icel will return. Soon.

ACKNOWLEDGEMENTS

I wrote much of the first draft of this book in January 2025. My father died in March 2025 when I should have been working on structural edits. Never a fan of structural edits, it was challenging, and I would like to thank my editor, Caroline, for trusting me to get on with it, as well as Ross, who always has the delight of working through my manuscript once I've added new elements, and who then has to make sure everything makes sense – no doubt a particular challenge on this occasion.

Also thanks to my proofreader, Shirley, my audio narrator, Sean, and to the whole team at Boldwood Books. It's an honour to have you championing my books.

I would also like to thank my author buddies for checking in on me and for making sure I was doing okay, I'm looking at you Elizabeth R Andersen and Kelly Evans *smiley face*.

Now also seems like the right time to thank all the author friends I met at HNS2024, in Dartington, alongside my dad, for what would prove to be his last 'work trip', and who enthusiastically spoke to him about antique maps and writing, and made his trip thoroughly enjoyable. Special mention to Matthew Harffy and Steven A McKay, who I sat next to at the dinner and who managed to keep the conversation almost genteel, while my father spoke with author S. G. Maclean to the side of us. I know he thoroughly enjoyed himself, and it was a pleasure to see him so enthusiastically welcomed, even if he was a bit confused that everyone knew me as MJ and not by my first name. Thank you from the bottom of my heart for making the occasion so memorable.

ABOUT THE AUTHOR

MJ Porter is the author of many historical novels set predominantly in Seventh to Eleventh-Century England, and in Viking Age Denmark. Raised in the shadow of a building that was believed to house the bones of long-dead Kings of Mercia, meant that the author's writing destiny was set.

Sign up to MJ Porter's mailing list here for news, competitions and updates on future books.

Visit MJ's website: www.mjporterauthor.com

Follow MJ on social media:

 x.com/coloursofunison
instagram.com/m_j_porter
bookbub.com/authors/mj-porter

ALSO BY MJ PORTER

The Eagle of Mercia Chronicles

Son of Mercia

Wolf of Mercia

Warrior of Mercia

Eagle of Mercia

Protector of Mercia

Enemies of Mercia

Betrayal of Mercia

Shield of Mercia

The Brunanburh Series

King of Kings

Kings of War

Clash of Kings

Kings of Conflict

The Dark Age Chronicles

Men of Iron

Warriors of Iron

Lords of Iron

WARRIOR CHRONICLES

WELCOME TO THE CLAN ⚔

THE HOME OF
BESTSELLING HISTORICAL
ADVENTURE FICTION!

WARNING:
MAY CONTAIN VIKINGS!

SIGN UP TO OUR
NEWSLETTER

BIT.LY/WARRIORCHRONICLES

Boldwood

Boldwood Books is an award-winning fiction publishing company seeking out the best stories from around the world.

Find out more at www.boldwoodbooks.com

Join our reader community for brilliant books, competitions and offers!

Follow us
@BoldwoodBooks
@TheBoldBookClub

Sign up to our weekly deals newsletter

https://bit.ly/BoldwoodBNewsletter

www.ingramcontent.com/pod-product-compliance
Lightning Source LLC
Chambersburg PA
CBHW011759010726
47497CB00012B/3207